**He raised her hand and pressed a kiss to it, his thumb brushing against her fingers as he drew back.**

*That* touch was more than comforting. It made the hairs on the back of her neck stand and her heart skip a beat before working double time. For a moment, she forgot how to breathe. She swayed toward him, inhaling the clean sweet scent of citrus, her head spinning.

For the barest second, his grip on her hand strengthened, as though he, too, had experienced something unexpected, and then he pulled away.

"No." She raised a hand to his cheek, and he stopped still. His lips were so perfect, so pink, so soft. She stroked them, and he inhaled swiftly. Even through the silk of her gloves, she could feel his warmth. Unsure of what she'd see, she looked up, meeting his gaze. His green eyes swam with the desire she knew he could see in hers. He didn't soften, though. He sat as rigid and as beautiful as marble.

She leaned forward and the breath that proved he was living mingled with hers. Slowly, tentatively, she raised her lips to his...

D0376635

## Praise for Samara Parish and the Rebels with a Cause series

"Readers will be eager for more."
  —*Publishers Weekly* on *How to Deceive a Duke*

"Dazzling."          —*Booklist* on *How to Deceive a Duke*

"Historical romance fans will be happy to find another strong-willed, science-minded heroine and the duke who loves her, and they'll look forward to the next story in the series."   —*Library Journal* on *How to Deceive a Duke*

"A sparkling new voice in historical romance delivers a satisfying story of love on the edges of the beau monde."
  —*Kirkus Reviews* on *How to Deceive a Duke*

"In this dazzling debut, Parish gives historical romance readers everything they could ever desire in a novel...[A]n extraordinary romance that succeeds on every level."
  —*Booklist* on
  *How to Survive a Scandal*, starred review

"With the perfect combination of drama, sensuality, and emotion, this refreshing story is sure to make a splash."
  —*Publishers Weekly* on
  *How to Survive a Scandal*, starred review

"Amelia and Benedict are an appealing pair, and watching them become their better selves—the heartbeat of all satisfying romances—is delicious and thoroughly gratifying."
                    —*BookPage* on *How to Survive a Scandal*

"A breath of fresh air in historical romance."
                    —Anna Campbell, award-winning author,
                        on *How to Survive a Scandal*

## ALSO BY SAMARA PARISH

*How to Survive a Scandal*

*How to Deceive a Duke*

# How to Win a Wallflower

## SAMARA PARISH

**FOREVER**

NEW YORK  BOSTON

This book is a work of fiction. Names, characters, places, and incidents are the product of the author's imagination or are used fictitiously. Any resemblance to actual events, locales, or persons, living or dead, is coincidental.

Copyright © 2022 by Samara Thorn

Cover design by Daniela Medina
Cover art by Sophia Sidoti
Cover photographs © Brenda Ross Photography
Cover copyright © 2022 by Hachette Book Group, Inc.

Hachette Book Group supports the right to free expression and the value of copyright. The purpose of copyright is to encourage writers and artists to produce the creative works that enrich our culture.

The scanning, uploading, and distribution of this book without permission is a theft of the author's intellectual property. If you would like permission to use material from the book (other than for review purposes), please contact permissions@hbgusa.com. Thank you for your support of the author's rights.

Forever
Hachette Book Group
1290 Avenue of the Americas, New York, NY 10104
read-forever.com
twitter.com/readforeverpub

First Edition: December 2022

Forever is an imprint of Grand Central Publishing. The Forever name and logo are trademarks of Hachette Book Group, Inc.

The publisher is not responsible for websites (or their content) that are not owned by the publisher.

The Hachette Speakers Bureau provides a wide range of authors for speaking events. To find out more, go to www.hachettespeakersbureau.com or call (866) 376-6591.

ISBN: 9781538704509 (mass market), 9781538704493 (ebook)

Printed in the United States of America

OPM

10  9  8  7  6  5  4  3  2  1

**ATTENTION CORPORATIONS AND ORGANIZATIONS:**

Most Hachette Book Group books are available at quantity discounts with bulk purchase for educational, business, or sales promotional use. For information, please call or write:

*Special Markets Department, Hachette Book Group*
*1290 Avenue of the Americas, New York, NY 10104*
*Telephone: 1-800-222-6747 Fax: 1-800-477-5925*

*For my husband and the peace that I find
in your company and your quiet.*

*For my grandmother,
who taught me the love of books.*

# Acknowledgments ─────

I would not want to be on this journey without the incredibly talented, kind, generous writers who have been with me through every plot twist on the way. Lauren Harbor, Justine Lewis, and Bethany Bennett have all saved this story in some way at some point, and I will always be grateful. I should also add my sister in here, who dropped everything to be an emergency reader and whose unvarnished honesty, paired with uplifting enthusiasm, was so critical in my not infuriating all of Romancelandia.

Thank you to my agent, Rebecca Strauss, for all her support and guidance through this process. I look forward to our trans-Pacific Zoom chats so much. I come off them feeling like there's nothing I can't do.

I have the best team in the world on my side at Forever. My editor Madeleine always knows exactly the right question to ask to help get the story past its hurdles. There is so much that a new writer like me has to learn, and I'm lucky to have her there to teach me. The Forever marketing team, Dana and Estelle, are the queens of cool. I love what they're doing and am excited to be part of it. Thank you to the production team, copy editor, cover designers, sales team, and every other person who touched this book in some way.

Thank you to Susan, Terry, and Becca at the Better-Faster Academy, whose coaching has been invaluable, both in helping me understand my process but also my characters. For anyone who knows CliftonStrengths—Charlotte is high Woo and Communication. John is high Relator and Intellection. Those conflicting personality traits are the very heart of this novel.

As always, I want to thank my family and my friends. I can only do what I do because I have a husband who supports me, who will pick up the slack when I'm on a deadline, and who will brainstorm with me when I need it.

I *don't* thank the other members of our little family, though. Topher, Rhaegal, Booth, and Whiskey, I love them but they are complete menaces—walking across my keyboard, chewing my notebooks, pawing me in the face when they need attention. And the constant need to go in and out and in and out! If it weren't for them, this book would have been finished earlier and in a much calmer fashion.

Writing and puppies—it is a disaster combination.

### *Content Notes*

Content notes for my novels are available at samaraparish.com/content-notes. Please be advised that these may contain spoilers.

# How to Win a Wallflower

# Chapter 1

W ell, this is a damned mess."

John winced as Edward, Duke of Wildeforde, dropped the stack of papers he'd been reviewing onto the duke's orderly desk.

It *was* a damned mess. Every aspect of Walter's passing had been a nightmare—from his drunken plunge over the edge of the king's pleasure barge into the filthy Thames to the discovery of his cast-aside account books that showed that he, Viscount Harrow, had run the estates into the ground.

"I'm glad to have you home, finally," Wilde continued. "But I'm sorry it's under these circumstances."

John didn't share his friend's sentiment. He was *not* glad to be home. Had his brother not died, leaving John with the title and estates, he'd have been perfectly happy in his tiny shack on the edge of the American wilderness. He would never have returned into the jaws of London society if he'd been given a choice.

He ran his hand through his hair, tugging at the ends of it. The extent of his brother's folly became more and more apparent each day. "I can't understand it. They kept lending him money. What p-p-possessed them?" John winced at the stumble of his words. Thinking of Walter made his chest tighten and tongue trip over itself so that he once again felt like a scrawny, stuttering outcast about to be ridiculed.

Wilde showed no sign that he noticed John's faltering. "Your brother hid his situation well. There was not a whisper of money troubles amongst our circle."

"Of course not." John shouldn't be surprised. Walter had always been the charming brother. He'd used his good looks and silver tongue to maneuver every situation to his benefit. No doubt each person he owed money to assumed they were the only person to whom he was in debt, and that it was a one-off—a loan made in an exceptional circumstance that was no fault of Walter's at all.

The accounts were clear. Walter had lived as though he were flush, yet he'd not spent a cent on anything he should have.

For the past three months, John had been traveling from one estate to another, fulfilling his blasted duties. He beheld the same sight over and over: farmers' cottages in terrible states of disrepair, fields unsown, wages unpaid, and the viscount's houses stripped of artwork, furniture, and silver tea sets. The books presented to him by haggard estate managers were in equally poor condition, so full of red ink they resembled a slaughterhouse.

Walter had completely bankrupted the Harrow estates and then died, leaving John to manage the fallout.

"Can any of the estates be sold?" Wilde asked.

"No." Damn the bloody entail. If he could sell even one of them, he'd be able to prop up the rest for long enough to find a solution. Now every move, every breath, took him one step closer to his own bankruptcy.

"And the money you had personally, before your brother's death, the income from your steam trains and Fi's matches?"

John looked at the ceiling as if there were an answer somewhere behind the chandelier sconces. "If I sink every cent I have into it, there's enough money to fix the worst of the problems—patch leaks in the tenants' roofs, purchase enough seed that we could sow next season, pay back wages to the staff. But there's not enough money to support everyone who relies on Walter—me—until the next harvest. And there's not enough blunt to satisfy all the debts he racked up in town. They are considerable."

The thought of hardworking tailors and other folk having to absorb a loss to their business because of his brother's irresponsible decadence made John's stomach roil.

"I can loan you money." Edward opened his top drawer as if to satisfy the issue then and there. "It won't be enough to put everything to rights, but it will pay off his debts here in London and tide you over for a few months."

John shook his head. He didn't want Wilde's handout. It might ease the pressure in the short-term, but it wouldn't solve the real problem. It would only put strain on their friendship when, in six months, he would still have no way of paying off the debt.

"I'd rather not."

Wilde frowned but nodded and closed his drawer before leaning back in his chair, clasping his hands behind his head. "There is one surefire way to raise the blunt you need. And to raise it quickly."

John straightened. He would accept any solution that didn't include borrowing more money.

"Marry an heiress."

His split second of hope sputtered like an engine out of steam. "That's not an option." He tried to keep the frustration from his tone. It wasn't Wilde's fault John was in this mess. He was just trying to offer a helpful suggestion. But the thought of being forced onto the marriage mart was nauseating.

Finding a wife would require wooing one—throwing himself headfirst into a whirlwind of balls and dinners and long walks through Hyde Park with women who would, no doubt, be whispering behind his back, mocking his stutter and his awkward small talk, and wishing he was his handsome and charming brother.

Even if John survived the process, he couldn't bear the thought of having to share a life, a house, and a bed with another person. He preferred his solitude and always would.

His friend raised an eyebrow. "You're a viscount now. From an ancient and well-respected line. The cits and Americans will line up for the chance to make their daughters Lady Harrow. A decent number of the *ton* too, at least until they discover how deep in the hole you are."

"I c-can't." His heart raced at the thought of it. "I've only returned to England to settle Walter's affairs and ensure responsible stewards are in place. Once I'm out of this mess, I'll be on the next ship back to Boston."

No, marriage was not in the cards. He would need another way to raise the blunt.

Wilde didn't press the issue. Instead, he crossed to the liquor cabinet and retrieved two cut-crystal glasses. "Stay for a late dinner. Fi is desperate to see you again, and it will be one less meal you have to pay for."

John snorted as he accepted a glass of brandy, grateful for lighthearted teasing. Wilde had been finding ways to drag John out of his head since they were in boarding school. "You don't have anywhere to be?" Surely a duke had social commitments lined up.

Wilde retook his seat, shrugging as he did so. "The Bradenstocks' ball. He and I had planned to discuss a proposed survey of new farming technology and how it could help the economy, but Charlotte will be there. She'll remind him of its value."

Across town, as the night was wearing on, Charlotte sat on a stool behind potted palms in the ladies' room at the Bradenstocks' ball, easing her feet from the too-small shoes she'd squeezed them into. Grace had warned her not to wear them. The lady's maid had predicted this situation exactly, but the shoes were pretty. The trimming matched her gown perfectly, and so she'd ignored Grace's eye roll and worn them anyway. And then had suffered through three excruciating dances, because a Wildeforde kept her commitments and a lady wouldn't abandon her dance partner.

Besides, Edward needed help to push his agenda forward, and the right word in the right ear during a country dance could have a greater impact on wider society than most would think.

She pressed gingerly on her heel. The skin bubbled. At this rate, the blister would be rubbed raw before the night was out, which was problematic because she had plenty more dances to go and conversations to have.

She could plead a headache and go home, but that would be its own form of discomfort. Her eldest brother and sister-in-law both worked long hours. When they had free time, they cleaved to each other. In the past, she'd sought William's company, but he'd been gone for almost four years. The younger Stirling brother's letters had been few and far between since he left to fight the war in Burma.

Which left Wildeforde House feeling a little lonely. And *anything* was preferable to loneliness, so she would dance until her feet could hold her no more, regardless of the blister.

There was a soft *snick* as the door opened, and she quickly dropped her skirts back over her knees, ready to stand and announce her presence. And then she heard it, the snide, nasal voice of her sworn enemy. *Luella.*

"This entire night is dreadfully dull. I'm ready to peck out my own eyes for some entertainment."

"Don't do that, Lulu. That's such a pretty dress and Madame Genevieve would be livid to see it bloodied."

Charlotte didn't need to see Luella to picture the syrupy smile her nemesis would be doling out to her minion. The hairs on the back of Charlotte's neck rose and she couldn't help but grit her teeth.

"Why thank you, Annie. Lord knows it cost my father a pretty penny."

Charlotte could believe that. Every season that went by, Lord Heywood invested considerably more money into ensuring his daughter was the finest dressed young lady of the *ton*. As if that could make up for Luella's personality. But you could wrap a viper in pearls and it would still try to eat you.

"I know it's early, but have we made a decision about this year's debutantes?" came the voice of one of Luella's hangers-on.

As stealthily as she could, Charlotte pressed one of the palm leaves aside so she could get a better look at the gaggle of girls. Luella, Lady Anne Ridley, and Miss Howard. The two younger girls looked at Luella with what bordered on adoration. Luella only looked at herself in the mirror, touching at her perfect coiffure.

"They're all insipid," Luella said. "When was the last time a debutante took London by storm?"

"Lady Elizabeth Feversham, last year," Miss Howard said.

Luella shook her head. "No. She was pretty and had a decent sense of style. But her dowry was paltry, and she only garnered three proposals."

Charlotte was fairly certain Lady Elizabeth only garnered three proposals because the men of London were observant enough to see she was madly in love with Lord Hillington, to whom she became engaged a scant two weeks into the season. Luella's dismissal sounded an awful lot like jealousy.

"Miss Stansgate. Two years ago? She turned down six proposals before she accepted Lord Pearson."

Luella wrinkled her nose. "Her eyes were set too close together. How seven men saw past that, I will never understand."

Yes, the jealousy was strong in Luella's voice. Charlotte was surprised the others couldn't hear it.

"Lady Charlotte Stirling. The Duke of Wildeforde's sister. Four years ago."

Luella's eyes narrowed and her lips thinned. She grunted in response, and Charlotte took petty pleasure in being a lemon on Luella's tongue. Before she could say anything, though, Lady Anne piped up. "Truly? *Lady Charlotte?*"

The disbelief in the young girl's tone rubbed like sandpaper. Was it so unbelievable that she had burst onto the London scene like a firework?

Luella's eyes turned to flinty stone as she ignored the conversation. Miss Howard, never the first to sense an undercurrent, turned to her friend to respond. "Oh yes. She had twenty proposals in her first season. No one has had that many in almost two decades."

A crease formed between Lady Anne's brows. "And yet she remains unmarried. Was there some sort of scandal?"

"No." In the mirror's reflection, Luella grabbed hold of Lady Anne's gaze like a snake choking a puppy. "The rest of society simply realized what I had from the start. Lady Charlotte is an insufferable, sanctimonious do-gooder. Her constant charity-pushing is grating. Her perfect manners and perfect dress and perfect conversation make her perfectly uninteresting. She should have accepted a proposal when she had the chance, before she'd bored everyone. I'd be surprised if she landed a baron now."

*Oooh. That woman.* No one could get Charlotte's temper

up like Luella. She shoved her foot back into the dratted shoes and stood. The potted palms that had concealed her rustled and three heads swept in her direction.

Two faces fell in horror when they saw who stood there. The third, Luella's, simply smiled, and Charlotte had the distinct impression that Luella had known she was sitting there all along.

She took a deep breath, ready to fling insults back in their direction, because she would not let this woman best her. But as she opened her mouth, the words died on her lips. Because a Wildeforde did not engage in conflict publicly. Even if it was with the worst woman in London. A Wildeforde was measured and thoughtful, because one never knew when Edward would need her influence, and so her behavior had to be above reproach.

She snapped her mouth shut and Luella snorted, aware she'd won yet another battle.

Charlotte squared her shoulders and walked straight past them through the door. But it did not close quickly enough to avoid the words that floated through it.

"Do you see? I told you. Completely uninteresting."

*Chapter 2* ──────────────

I am not uninteresting." Charlotte sat at the dresser while Grace made quick work of the pins holding up her hair.

Her lady's maid's expression was completely sincere as she responded. "No, my lady."

"And I am not *sanctimonious*."

"Not at all."

"And I am not a *do-gooder*." Ugh. The word conjured up images of pious spinsters. Of bland women with nothing else to do but convince other people to support their cause. Which was not her at all. She had plenty of things in her life besides her projects.

"I mean, obviously I *do good*. I am a duke's sister, after all. It's my job to help the needy. I'm supposed to put the weight of the Wildeforde name behind worthy causes. But since when is that a bad thing? It's something that should be aspired to."

At that, Grace raised her eyebrows. "Your efforts mean a lot to many people, my lady. Don't let some unkind words stop you from making a difference."

The assurance mollified her somewhat. She *was* making a difference. More of a difference than any other young woman of the *ton*—except, perhaps, for Fiona. But no lady could compete with Charlotte's sister-in-law when it came to impacting society. No lady had Fiona's unique education or her experience as a businesswoman.

Instead, young ladies were supposed to turn their hands to social causes, rather than scientific. Charlotte had managed to increase the standing of several female playwrights through her patronage. She had launched a program to help destitute women find a life in service, started an animal rehoming organization for farm animals that had outlived their usefulness, and she had taken an active interest in the welfare of orphans.

She was helpful. She solved problems. She was who people turned to when they needed assistance. *Drat Luella.*

"I am *not* uninteresting. Luella is a spiteful cow, excuse my horrendous language, who resents me because I foiled her plot to trap my brother into marriage. That's why she spreads such unkind rumors."

It was infuriating. Charlotte worked so hard. She said yes to every committee she was asked to join; she was at every social event worth noting, and she still found time to lend her presence to those newer to society—the ones who needed a duke's sister to make their ball a success. Her dance card was full night after night because the more bashful gentlemen of the *ton* knew she'd not embarrass them with a rejection.

She was beloved, even if she'd yet to find true love. Her future as a grande dame was set.

And then there was Luella. Equally sought after for no good reason.

"She is just awful, Grace. And how dare she criticize me for not yet finding a husband? She's been out two years longer than I have and she remains unwed."

Finishing the last of Charlotte's braids and securing it with a ribbon, Grace caught her mistress's gaze in the mirror's reflection. "She may well be jealous, my lady. She had no proposals after that first one, and she is only human, not actually bovine."

Charlotte only just held back a growl. She didn't want logical and empathetic responses. She wanted somebody to agree that, yes, Luella was the devil. Certainly, her maid was right, but that knowledge gave Charlotte no satisfaction.

"This is not how it works, Grace. You are supposed to support me in all of my endeavors. Even my petty, myopic, self-indulgent ones."

Grace laughed, and despite the clear affection in her tone, Charlotte still felt her companion pull away another fraction. Four years ago, Grace would have loyally agreed and helped to plot Luella's demise, but since getting married last year to Swinton, Edward's driver, the friendship had changed, almost as though Charlotte was being outgrown.

Grace hadn't spent the night in Charlotte's room since her wedding and Charlotte no longer felt she could share all of her secrets without sensing an undertone of you-will-understand-when-you're-married in the responses.

It was not unlike the undertone that had worked its way into her closest friendships when one after another got engaged, then married, and were now even bearing children.

"Perhaps you should seek your sister if you wish for partial advice."

"Perhaps I shall," Charlotte said, trying not to let her disappointment show. She would seek Fiona. There was no one more used to cruel things being said about her than a Scottish female chemist, common born, who'd worked in a factory and had worn men's clothing before marrying a duke and being subjected to all sorts of slander.

No one ever said Fiona was uninteresting, though. Odd, perhaps. Scandalous. An upstart—all insults that Fiona barely registered. She was who she was, and she made no apologies for it.

It was admirable. And if Charlotte was a little jealous that her new sister had changed the world, impressed half of society without bending backward for it, and found the love of her life, well, that jealousy was to be expected, surely.

Grace held out a dressing gown for Charlotte to step into. "Will you need me again, my lady?"

"No. Thank you. Please ask a footman to bring some hot milk to the study." She tied her dressing gown with a knot and stepped into the slippers on the floor by the bed.

Fiona and Edward would be having a nightcap in their shared office. After Luella's attempt to force Edward into marriage, there was no chance either of them would mirror Grace's tolerance of Luella's behavior.

Halfway down the corridor, her slippers began to chafe against the blisters. She kicked them off and picked them up, letting them hang from her fingers. It might raise an eyebrow with the footmen on duty, but both Ned and Fi had seen her in worse states of undress than this.

As she got closer to the study, she could hear Fiona's laugh through the open door. Smiling to herself, she picked up her pace. David, the footman standing by the doorway, started forward, his eyes wide as he saw her in her night-clothes, barefooted with her hair in braids. He moved to block her entrance.

"Oh, David. It's *fine*," she said, rolling her eyes and step-ping around him. "It's not as though we have visit—" She stopped still, both her words and her feet, because they did have a guest. Seated in the armchair opposite Fiona was John Barnesworth, relaxed and smiling.

John, who had been the subject of all her childhood dreams.

John, whose name she'd scrawled over and over in her diaries.

John, who had never returned to London once he'd left for Oxford.

John, who had left for Boston years ago and she thought she'd never see again.

John, who was Lord Harrow now.

He was every bit as lovely as he had been when she last saw him. His longish chestnut hair, much in need of a trim, flopped into his eyes in a roguish manner. It was streaked with gold from the American sun. His skin was a shade darker than she remembered, and his emerald eyes stood out in contrast.

Emerald eyes that looked up as she entered, flaring in surprise. He stood quickly and bowed fluidly. She had always admired that about him—the gentleness and grace with which he moved. Her brothers were both overly tall, with a bulkiness that drove their seamstress to despair. John was all long, slender lines and graceful movement. He was the embodiment of a perfect gentleman.

As he moved, an urge to reach out to him almost overwhelmed her. As his gaze traveled her person, her *dressing gown*, and landed on her bare feet, she hugged herself instead, her slippers knocking against her side.

She had fantasized about seeing John again so many times, and in all of those fantasies, she'd been in a ballroom, surrounded by other men, dressed in her finest clothing. His eyes were drawn to her, and he would have a moment of double take as he realized the beautiful young woman in front of him was the grown-up version of the gangly girl he'd barely noticed.

She did *not* imagine him seeing her with her hair in braids and wearing nightclothes, as though she was unchanged from the child she'd been when he last visited.

"What are you doing here?" She regretted the words the moment she said them. It was bad enough that she was dressed as she was. Now she'd let her embarrassment make her churlish.

He raised an eyebrow as he straightened. "Leaving." He gathered his jacket from the back of the chaise longue and slung it over his elbow. From the small table, he picked up a notebook, tucking it under his arm. He nodded to Edward and Fiona, the latter of whom rolled her eyes. "Get gone then, if ye dunnae want to stay. We'll talk more of this tomorrow."

As he passed Charlotte, he gave her a smile that was really more of a grimace, and left without a backward glance.

"Well," she said, mortified. "That was rude." Of course, he'd simply answered her rudeness in kind. She had no one but herself to blame if he didn't bother with a basic greeting after all these years.

"Don't mind John," Edward said. "He wasn't expecting to see a half-dressed girl appear wielding a pair of slippers."

"I'm not *wielding* anything. My feet hur—" She narrowed her eyes as her brother chuckled. "Oh, you are bothersome," she said, annoyed that he'd once again gotten a rise out of her. "What is he doing here?"

"John? He has returned to England." Edward didn't take his eyes off her as he swirled the brandy in his glass, an infuriating knowingness in his stare.

She knew exactly what he was doing, what he expected her response to be, yet she couldn't put on the disaffected expression she wanted to.

"Clearly," she ground out. Of course, John had returned to England. She'd been expecting his arrival for months. One couldn't ignore a summons from the crown, and when one became a newly minted viscount, that was as good as a summons. "What is he doing *here*? At midnight? While I'm in my nightclothes?"

Edward cocked his head. "I don't think any of us could have anticipated you being home this early, let alone ready for bed."

Charlotte rubbed her forehead. "You're being deliberately obtuse, brother."

Edward sighed and rubbed the crease between his brows. "Given he's Fiona's business partner and my friend, he joined us for dinner. His cook has been…indisposed. But Char—"

"Well, it would have been nice to have been invited." She knew Edward was about to scold her, and she interrupted before he could. "In my own home. After all the dinner parties I've thrown on your behalf, you can't even invite me to this one."

"Char…" There was a faint note of warning in his tone. They had argued about John before. Edward had a ridiculous notion that she and John would not be a good match, which might have been true when John was a second son who never ventured out into society, but he was the viscount now. And in London. He would have to be out in society. John would be a perfectly acceptable match.

"The *least* you could do is inform me that we're having guests for dinner, given that it will throw my entire meal plan off for the week."

"He is not for you and you are not for him," Edward said bluntly, ignoring her comment.

Charlotte's face heated. "You're being quite presumptuous to think that he's even on my mind." But of course, he had been. The moment she'd heard of the previous Lord Harrow's passing, the possibility of John returning had wormed its way into her brain.

Her silly little heart had leapt and the equally silly voice in her head had whispered that he was who she was waiting for. He was why she'd never accepted a proposal, even when she'd decided she would. He was why the word *no* had snuck out of her mouth every time, unbidden. She'd never have admitted it to herself when he was gone from England and unlikely to return, but now that he was home, she couldn't hide from the fact of it.

And Edward suspected the truth. She was sure that he

did. She would not give him the opportunity to wrest it out of her, though. "Good night, brother," she said before their conversation became a spat that the duke would inevitably win. "I'm going up."

~

John's cheeks burned the entire walk home. It wasn't a long walk—Harrow House was on the other side of the Mayfair block. The two homes even shared a garden wall—and by the time he strode up the front stairs, his embarrassment had not abated.

His behavior had been unacceptable. It had been unacceptable for a viscount, who would be expected to manage basic conversation, and unacceptable for a gentleman, who would be expected to treat his friend's younger sister with at least a modicum of cordiality.

But John hadn't been prepared to talk with anyone other than Wilde and Fi tonight. Socializing with strangers consumed an enormous amount of energy, and untangling his brother's financial knots had left him with little to spare. The sight of Charlotte, grown now into a woman, had felt— *big*. Consequential. He couldn't accurately describe it.

It was as though the very sight of her burned through every molecule in him and hearing her voice would burn through the remnants of that, leaving him changed in a way he wasn't prepared for.

Perhaps, if the conversation had started out more benignly—a "Good evening. How do you do?"—he might have mustered up a few lines before excusing himself.

*What are you doing here?*

Lady Charlotte's terse inquiry had been a sharp reminder that he was unlikely to find an easy welcome in this society. Not from people who adored Walter, who mourned his passing and likely resented John's presence. Not from people expecting a lord and getting a poor facsimile instead. And apparently not from someone who, had he thought about it, might have been predisposed to give him a chance, given his close relationship with her family.

Had Charlotte crossed his mind at all in the past few years, he would have hoped that during their first encounter in almost a decade she'd have been a little less...frosty. As it was, the appearance of Edward's sister had come as a complete surprise. More surprising was the realization that the child who'd hung in the peripheries during his youth was a child no longer.

No, Charlotte was all grown up. Tall, willowy, with a jaw as stubborn as her brother's, a complexion that had flushed pink as she'd seen him, and penetrating deep blue eyes that had, for a brief moment, stolen all breath from him.

Had she crossed his mind at all in the years since he'd seen her, he'd have anticipated that she'd be a beauty. It was logic. She shared the striking Wildeforde features.

She hadn't crossed his mind, though. In his head, Charlotte had remained a spindly young girl in braids, a pinafore, and pantaloons. Perhaps it was that dissonance that had thrown him off. Rarely was his brain so out of step with reality.

He pulled a large key from his coat pocket. Yesterday, upon returning to Harrow House for the first time in a decade, he'd been forced to let go the people who worked there. It had been regrettable. He didn't like to put anyone out of work, but he couldn't pay the wages for more than a skeleton staff. He would make do with a butler, a housekeeper, and a cook. That was still three more servants than he was used to. Three people with whom he shared his space.

Given he'd been opening his own front door since he left for Oxford, he'd discharged Mosely from that duty, along with most other duties as recompense for the half pay. The butler could attend the door for visitors, but John needed no such assistance.

Besides, the fewer people forced to live his odd hours, the better.

He unhooked a lamp from beside the front door and lit it using the sole burning wall sconce. With his financial situation the way it was, there was no budget for leaving rooms and hallways lit when he wasn't home.

He made his way to the study, smiling to himself as a loud, snuffling snore broke the silence. Newton, the Scottish deerhound whose long body stretched the entire length of the chaise longue, had his head propped up on the arm of it. He opened one eye as John placed a lamp in the corner of the desk, and his tail waved slowly, before his eyes closed again and the snoring resumed.

There was just enough light from the lamp for John to read. To distract himself from his misstep with Charlotte. The new edition of *German Review of Physics* sat on his desk between his correspondence with a biologist from Paris and the latest business reports from the engineering firm he shared with Fiona and their business partner, Benedict Asterly.

The firm was on track to deliver its next shipment of steam engines by the end of the year. There would be a lump sum payment on delivery, but that was too far away to be of any use to John's current situation. They had discussed the idea of expanding the firm's production capabilities, but that would require an upfront injection of cash—an investment he was no longer in a position to make.

*Damn.* He pushed away from his desk and stood at the tall windows that looked out into the darkness of the garden. As he rested his arm against the glass and his head on his arm, the trappings of a London town house almost disappeared. He could pretend for a moment that he was back in a small, one-room house on the outskirts of Boston.

~

She couldn't help it. Charlotte had gone back to her rooms in a huff and had been about to climb into bed when she'd noticed a flare of light from the darkness outside her window. Habits formed a decade ago kicked in. She quickly padded to the window.

Her bedroom, on the topmost floor of Wildeforde House, directly overlooked Viscount Harrow's backyard. Nothing of interest had occurred in that garden for years—not since John had left for Oxford. Walter, the last viscount, and his father before him had occasionally taken a stroll along the manicured paths, but neither had caught Charlotte's attention. The thirteenth Viscount Harrow had been old and mean, and the fourteenth Viscount Harrow had been all too aware of his own good looks and supposed charm. London had fallen at Harrow's feet and the women of her acquaintance had fluttered and fawned at his attention, but he'd always given Charlotte the shivers.

The *fifteenth* Viscount Harrow, well, he'd had her attention from the moment she'd first set eyes on him. He'd been the most beautiful young man she'd ever seen. He'd been sitting beneath the large oak, leaning back against the trunk, a book in his hands and a pencil tucked behind his ear. Over the days that followed, he'd alternated between sketching and sleeping, his chestnut hair flopping into his face. Every now and then, he would run his hand through it, tugging at the ends as though something in his mind needed evicting. It never took long before his locks stood out at wild angles and smudges of charcoal stained his face and his perfectly cut, perfectly fashionable clothing.

The notebook was quickly replaced by another, and then another, each covered with cloth of a different color. Lady Harrow must have been spending a fortune on supplies.

Finally, after a week, the tableau changed. Edward joined John in the Harrows' back garden and from then on, the two had been almost inseparable. But if Charlotte had thought that her brother's newfound friendship would lead to her meeting their neighbor, those hopes were quickly dashed. Edward had always been quick to shoo her away.

So, in the past decade, her relationship with John had not progressed beyond more than the *very* occasional and brief salutation.

She had watched as John had become taller, had filled out across the shoulders, had grown fashionable side beards and started pulling his hair back into a gentlemanly queue.

She'd listened as Edward had talked of the fun the two boys had at school together. Then one summer, John hadn't returned from Oxford as he usually did, and she'd not seen him until tonight, when the first words out of her mouth had been... brusque. How could she blame him for leaving abruptly when she had spoken so churlishly?

The gardens now were pitch black. The light that had flared a moment ago came from a room on the ground floor. She couldn't see into it, but, as though fate were intervening, John came into view, leaning against the windowpane, staring out into the darkness.

His expression was bleak, and her fingers twitched, wanting to smooth away his frown.

"Notice me," she whispered. It had been all she'd wanted as a young girl, and it had never happened. "Notice me." And just like that, he raised his eyes in her direction.

"Drat!" She spun to the side, her back flattening against the wall by the window, her heart thundering. "Drat it all." How humiliating to be caught mooning over him like some child. She snuffed the candle and prayed that he hadn't seen her.

"Stupid, stupid, stupid," she said as she fumbled her way back to her bed, stubbing her toe in a painful reminder that this was real life, not a fantasy, and that she'd had enough of John noticing her in her nightwear, thank you very much.

*Chapter 3* ⸺

$R$eally, Josie. I hardly think that level of detail is necessary." Charlotte's tone was more abrupt than usual, but a night of fitful sleep would do that, and her dearest friends would forgive her.

Indeed, Lady Josefine Augustus Pembroke responded by sticking out her tongue and then retrieving a spool of gold thread from her basket.

"They are orphans, not actresses," Charlotte continued. "Where do you expect them to wear something like that?"

Josie shrugged and licked the end of the thread. "It's pretty. Don't orphans deserve something pretty?"

Charlotte rolled her eyes. "I'm not saying they shouldn't like what they're wearing; I'm simply saying that you could sew five dresses in the time it's taken you to embroider that one."

Unfazed by Charlotte's logic, Josie took the hem of the

dress in hand and added accents to the elaborate edging she'd been working on this past fortnight. "Well," she said. "I would prefer one pretty dress to five plain ones."

There was no arguing with her. Josefine was as impractical a person as Charlotte had ever met. Thankfully, her lack of common sense was offset by the sweetest of natures. Charlotte turned to the third in their party, Lady Henrietta Hastings, for support. Hen deliberately kept her eyes trained on her own work, staying well out of the spat.

Charlotte finished casting off the blue knit jumper she had been working on since last Tuesday. She'd become quite good at knitting these past months. It wasn't a craft she'd bothered to learn when she was younger—embroidery was more appropriate for a woman of her station—but when she'd heard that the Hollyhock Orphanage was in dire need of clothing to dress the young girls in their care, she'd quickly formed a circle to meet the need. With the weather as it was, a knitted jersey would be far more practical than a sewn pinafore.

Henrietta wrinkled her nose, a frown forming between her brows as she studied the project in her lap. "Have you decided how you are going to approach Mr. Drumwithel this time?" she asked, without looking up.

*The Reverend. Insufferable man.* Charlotte had never met a more arrogant, condescending man, and her brother was a duke. She entertained the most arrogant lords in London on a daily basis. "I'm going to refuse to hand over any of these clothes until he lets me through those orphanage doors," she said as she wove the loose end of the yarn through the hem.

"Perhaps Mr. Drumwithel is correct. Perhaps it's not an appropriate place for a lady to be," Josefine said.

"And perhaps we should be the ones to determine what is and is not an appropriate place for us to be," Charlotte said. "The Reverend is more than willing to take the money we raise and the clothes we make, but he has yet to demonstrate any evidence that these clothes are even making it onto the backs of his wards. Why, for all we know, he is selling these for a profit and those children could be wearing rags."

Hen held up the jersey she'd been working on, lopsided with dropped stitches and one arm significantly longer than the other. "You think he's selling these for profit?"

Josie snorted, and Charlotte, had she not been trying to prove a point, would have done the same. "Well, not yours, obviously," Charlotte said. "But Josefine's could fetch a pretty penny. One more reason you should focus on quantity, not quality," she said to her friend. "So Drumwithel isn't tempted to sell them."

Josie stuck out her tongue once more and continued on with her tiny, tiny stitches.

"Has anyone heard anything about a certain viscount?" Henrietta asked before the bickering could start in earnest. "This morning's papers say that he was seen arriving in London two days ago."

Charlotte turned her attention back to the perfectly knitted jersey resting on her knees, but not before she saw both friends train their eyes on her. Neither of them spoke, and after a long, frustrating minute, Charlotte balled the knitting in her hands and stared back.

"Fine. I saw him last night. He joined Edward for dinner."

"And?" Josie asked.

"And I don't want to talk about it." As she lay there trying to sleep, it had played on her mind how ridiculous she must have looked swathed in her voluminous nightgown. Not even one of her *nice* nightgowns, but the six-years-out-of-fashion but oh-so-comfortable nightgown that was now slightly too short to be appropriate. Good grief, she hadn't even been wearing her slippers. *He saw my toes.*

She sank down in her chair, wishing the floor would open up and swallow her.

"You *don't* want to talk about it? You, who talked of nothing else when you realized he would return to England?" Hen raised her eyebrows in disbelief.

"Not to mention all those years prior," Josie added. "We discussed him so often as children that he's mentioned a hundred times in *my* journals."

"One moment…" Henrietta's brow creased. "How did you see him at dinner? You were with Peter and me for dinner last night and then we were at Francesca's ball."

"Quite," Charlotte bit out.

"He was still there when you returned?"

"He was."

"Well, that was lucky," Josie said. "You looked splendid last night. Truly Madame Genevieve outdid herself with that blue silk."

"She did." It would be a snowy day in hell before she told her friends the truth.

"So why are you so snippy?" Josie asked, her brows drawn together in concern. "You saw John, your lost love, for the first time in what? Ten years? I thought you'd be ecstatic."

Charlotte swallowed hard and did her best to appear unaffected. "It didn't go as I thought it would."

Her two friends shared an apprehensive look. "No?" Hen asked.

"He was...curt. And rather dismissive. Perhaps I was mistaken in my earlier assessment of him. Perhaps he wasn't the gentleman I thought he was." Even as she said the words, she knew them to be false. She'd as good as told him he wasn't welcome with her shocked demand to know why he was there, and like a gentleman, he'd left. Drat.

Her friends' looks of apprehension deepened, and then Josie, who could always be counted on for support, said, "Well, how foolish of him. He'll find it a hard thing, moving in our circles after his brother's death, and he wouldn't have had a better ally than you."

"True," Hen added. "And if you deign to grace him with your assistance settling in, he had better show his appreciation of such fortune with better manners."

Josie cocked her head, her lips pursed in thought. "Of course, if you were to help him, that would be the kind thing to do."

Hen nodded in response. "Very true. Quite the charitable thing."

Charlotte could see what they were about. Josie and Hen thought that if they appealed to her kindness, she would be bound to offer John her help, and then who knew what might happen next?

And they had a point. Offering to help pave his way into society would be a good excuse to see him. A good excuse to spend time together. His close friendship with Edward and Fiona made it almost expected that she would offer her assistance, didn't it?

⁓

John was drifting in and out of somewhat peculiar dreams about toes—pink, soft, and slender. There was a touch, a caress, and the feet flexed; the soles arched; the toes curled. Through the fog of sleep, he could feel the throb of his cock.

A sharp knock at the door woke him.

"Damn. *What?*" From the floor beside the bed, Newton raised his head and barked, echoing John's frustration. Mosely had been told not to wake John in the mornings. His best ideas came at night, and this morning he'd still been working on his projects as the chambermaids rose.

His bedroom door opened a crack, just wide enough for the butler's profile to show.

"Lord Heywood and his daughter, Lady Luella Tarlington, to see you, my lord."

"I'm not at home." That was one of the few benefits of London society. It was perfectly acceptable to lie about one's presence and refuse to see people. If he were in Boston, he would have had to open the front door himself and then pretending to be absent wouldn't have been an option.

"They have a solicitor with them, my lord. They plan to wait until you are 'at home' regardless of how long that might be. Although they hinted that it should not, in fact, be long."

*Blast.* John groaned. Walter's ever-growing list of

creditors was proving more and more troublesome. This was not the first time a lord had shown up at his door demanding money. Nor was it the first time he'd been approached by a solicitor. But it was the first time he'd had to face the lord and lawyer at the same time.

He threw the blankets off. "I'll been down shortly. Show them to the study."

His mood did not improve in the time it took to throw on clothes, find his spectacles, and hastily tie a cravat. He tempered it, though, as he walked down the corridor to the study. It wasn't Heywood's fault John's brother had run up debts. The man had a right to call them in. What continued to amaze John was the fact that every creditor thought they were the only individual to whom Walter owed money. His brother's charade had been remarkably effective.

The butler opened the study door as John approached, Newton padding quietly beside him. John took a deep breath, held it for a count of five to keep his frustration at bay, and exhaled before he entered. "My lord," he said as he bowed.

As he rose, he noted a woman by the window and re-called that Mosely had mentioned a daughter. Though why Heywood would bring his daughter to a meeting about what were, presumably, gambling debts, John couldn't fathom.

She turned, an eyebrow raised, and stared at him, her gaze traveling from the tips of his toes to the still-tangled knots of hair he was suddenly conscious of. He could feel his anxiety building. He didn't want to be the center of anyone's attention. He didn't want such scrutiny. Especially not from one of the *haute ton*. He already knew how they viewed him.

Beside him, Newton growled, his body stiff, his hackles raised. John put a comforting hand on the deerhound's neck.

Lady Luella regarded Newton with a condescending look before locking eyes with John and delivering a tiny, dismissive *hmph*. Then she returned to staring out the window.

John's gut twisted at the brush-off. Newton's growl deepened, and the deerhound took a step forward, placing himself between John and the intruders.

"Is that dog safe?" one man asked.

"Quite," John responded, but he did cross the room and open the door to the garden. Reluctantly, Newton exited, but not before stretching up to put his paws on John's shoulders. Standing on his hind legs, Newton was bigger than most men. Every "guest" in the room shrank back.

John closed the doors and took a seat at his desk, in front of which the two men sat. Lord Heywood was grey-haired with the look of a man who knew plenty of decadence and little work. His cravat, stuck with a diamond the size of a robin's egg, was tied in an intricate knot beneath his double chin. His violet velvet coat stretched taut across his paunch.

The lawyer, by contrast, was lean in the way a fox was, and had the same predatory air to him. "Lord Harrow, I take it you know why we're here?"

John nodded.

"Then I'm surprised you haven't seen fit to address the issue earlier," he said.

From the window, Lady Luella muttered, "Indeed."

John drew a deep breath and exhaled slowly, trying to fool his body into relaxing. He wanted nothing more than to tell the condescending lawyer he was one of a hundred creditors so far, and that he could bloody well get in line. But until John had found his feet in London, he'd keep that information to himself.

"With respect, seeing to my brother's obligations has been a time-consuming experience." More than they could know.

"Regardless," Lord Heywood said, "you've been in England for months. You should have made the time to visit your fiancée."

John's stomach dropped, and his jaw dropped with it. *What the devil?*

"P-p-pardon?" He flushed as he stumbled and cut short the rest of his question. *What blasted fiancée?*

He looked at Lady Luella, just as she turned to face him once more. Objectively speaking, she was beautiful. Her hair was a pale shade of blond. Her face was perfectly symmetrical. Her lips were full with a lusciousness that was echoed in the lines of her figure. But despite this, his blood ran cold at the sight of her. It was her eyes. They were hard and mean and had the same look to them he'd seen many times over in his life—always before a cruel insult was thrown his way.

Marriage to this woman would be a miserable thing.

Her father and the solicitor exchanged glances. The solicitor leaned forward. "Your brother entered into an engagement contract with Lord Heywood a year ago, the day before his...incident."

The day before Walter died. The same day Walter had cleared out what little funds remained in the estate accounts. "My brother is dead." John had inherited Walter's debts, but surely not his fiancée as well.

"The contract your brother signed didn't specify *which* Viscount Harrow was to marry Lady Luella. Just that the Viscount Harrow would."

*Damnation.* John removed the glasses from his face, cleaning a nonexistent smudge from the lens, buying time to gather his thoughts. Walter could not have made John's life any more difficult had he planned it. "You have a copy of this contract?" he asked eventually, hoping there was an escape within it.

Lord Heywood's face reddened. "Are you calling me a liar?"

The lawyer shook his head at his employer and reached into his satchel for a sheaf of papers, sliding them across the desk.

John scanned them quickly. It was a contract, and, from his experience, it appeared legally binding. At the bottom of the second page was a signature—unmistakably Walter's.

He didn't need to scan it a second time. That was the thing about a perfect memory. It only took one quick glance for the image to be burned permanently into John's brain, a memory ready to be retrieved at a moment's notice.

The pertinent lines remained clear, even as he closed his eyes and sighed. The contract didn't specify Walter's name. It didn't specify the fourteenth Viscount Harrow. It simply said that Lady Luella Tarlington would marry Viscount Harrow.

He'd have his solicitor look for loopholes, but he wasn't confident the man would find any. Another line from the contract stood out: Lady Luella's dowry—eighty thousand pounds.

It was an enormous sum. Combined with what John

already had in his bank account, it would see the estates free from debt, the fields sown, the cottages repaired, and the houses staffed.

When Wilde had suggested marriage as a solution to John's problems, John had balked at the thought of having to woo a wife. But here one was presented to him, with no need to search her out, and her dowry was more than he needed.

It was an amount that was almost unreasonable, which gave him pause. "Why so much?" he asked.

Lord Heywood's lips thinned. "It's a generous offer. Much more than you deserve."

"Is she defective?" As soon as the words were spoken, he knew they were the wrong ones.

"Defective?" Luella's voice cut through the air like metal wheels braking against a metal track. "Like you? P-p-poor st-st-stuttering id-diot. Yes, I've heard all about your deficiencies."

John froze. His tongue locked up against the back of his teeth. The sound of the solicitor *tut-tut*ting felt like gunshots ripping through silence.

"Luella, shut up," Heywood said, scowling. He turned back to John. "She's not a virgin, and half the *ton* knows it, though no one has come right out and said it. Her tongue has run off every suitor that might have overlooked that point, except Harrow. The real Harrow, that is. That boy found something to like in her."

That "something" was undoubtably the chit's dowry, but her vicious nature had likely appealed to Walter as well. Like attracted like, after all. John looked at Luella. Her gloved hands gripped together so forcefully she was probably losing circulation. He could tell from the slight depression beneath her tightly pressed lips that she was biting the inside of them. Her expression was stone.

"I'll think on it." It was all he could say. He needed her dowry, but God, marriage to her…

The stare she gave him could have slaughtered a fully grown American buffalo. "Let's be clear. It's bad enough that I'm forced to marry Walter's lesser brother, who is neither as handsome nor as witty. I won't have people thinking that you aren't ecstatic at your good fortune."

His good fucking fortune, indeed. Damn Walter.

"You'll call on me tomorrow morning," she continued. "You'll make it clear that you're determined to earn my affections." With a final sniff, she swished her skirts and stalked out of the room.

John turned to the two men still sitting in front of him. The lawyer's eyes were wide, as though he himself could not quite believe her comments. Lord Heywood bore a look of half anger, half resignation. "The day my daughter becomes your problem, I'm going to open a bottle of the king's scotch. I'll see you soon, Harrow."

He stood and followed his daughter out of the room. The lawyer nudged the contract on John's desk before he followed.

John wanted to toss the papers in the fire. He wanted to call Newton, head to the docks, and board the first ship back to America. He wanted to crawl into a dark corner and hide.

But he couldn't. Because when he agreed to return to England to take up the mantle of the viscount, he agreed to take responsibility for the welfare of all those who relied on him. That didn't mean he couldn't return to Boston. In fact, he planned to return as soon as humanly possible. He simply couldn't do it until he'd sorted out the crisis Walter had left and installed some responsible, trustworthy stewards to run the place in his absence.

Perhaps sorting out the crisis meant marriage to a woman like Luella. But could he leave a wife as easily as he planned to leave his estates? Even one as awful as her? The dowry could be his salvation. It could see him home before the end of the year. But even though she was as caustic as stomach acid, abandoning her didn't sit well. He didn't think he could do it, which meant taking her to Boston with him.

If she was this wretched in London, just imagine what she'd be like when forced to endure the comparative savagery of America.

John stood and pushed the door open for Newton to enter. Then, he crossed to the lounge at the other end of the room, untying his cravat as he went. Perhaps if he closed his eyes now, he'd manage a few hours' sleep.

He had just settled in when a shriek of outrage split the air. "You cannot possibly be considering marrying that witch."

*Chapter 4* ————————

Charlotte was incandescent with rage. How dare Luella speak to him in such a manner? How dare she try to manipulate yet another man into marriage after her failed attempt with Edward?

Charlotte stood peeking out from behind the open door that hid her as Luella stormed out, the skirts of her dress swirling like the violent maelstrom she was. Hot on her heels were Lord Heywood—a self-important jackass who Charlotte avoided—and a plain man in working trousers.

She waited until all three had turned the corner at the end of the corridor before she emerged.

"Grace, wait here," she hissed, taking the heavy ceramic Dutch oven from her lady's maid's hands. With a deep breath, she entered John's study. He was lying on the chaise longue, head resting on one arm, feet crossed casually on the other.

If she weren't so angry, she might have paused. She might have stopped to revel in the way his long eyelashes rested against his tanned skin and how one hand lay on his chest—his long and beautiful fingers curled.

But she was too angry to experience anything more than a moment of appreciation. "You cannot possibly be considering marrying that witch."

John started. His eyes flew open, and he sat quickly, his head whipping toward her. "Lady Charlotte?" he asked, reaching for his spectacles. "What are you doing here?"

She couldn't tell him the truth, that she was simply here to see him. That his presence last night had reignited the fascination that had lain dormant for years. That she was here to work out whether to give that old feeling breath or if she should smother it and shove it into the deep, dark recesses of her mind.

"I brought you luncheon."

He raised his eyebrows.

"Edward joked that last night you visited for a free meal. I'm certain he was exaggerating, but just in case there was a kernel of truth to his remarks, I thought I'd bring dinner. No charge." She gave him a bright smile and crossed the room to put the dish on the table that sat between the lounge and two armchairs.

"It's Oxford pudding," she said, to fill the silence. "Your favorite." She cursed inwardly. On the rare occasion John had joined them for dinner all those years ago, he had wolfed it down, and once made an offhand comment about his mother not serving it as often as he'd like. But no normal person who didn't have an out-of-control tendre would remember such a thing. Her ears burned hot with embarrassment.

"I mean it," she said in an effort to distract him from her unbidden admission. "You cannot marry that woman. She is an evil, hideous, conniving witch who very nearly trapped Edward into marriage. She was in cahoots with my *mother*, for goodness' sakes."

John flinched at the mention of the Dowager Duchess of Wildeforde. Charlotte had never understood why he had spent so many hours at Wildeforde House when her mother barely acknowledged his presence and, when forced to, was acerbic at best.

At least she hadn't understood until Edward had told her that as bad as their mother was, John's father was worse.

John sighed. "It's complicated." He took off his spectacles and cleaned the glass with the end of his loosened cravat. As he dropped it, the gentle curve of his throat was exposed.

She swallowed, trying to ignore the hot flush that swept over her. She would not be distracted by a patch of skin. "And you think it's beyond my reasoning capabilities?" she asked. "It's too complicated for a feather-headed little girl to understand?"

He quickly straightened, two lines forming between his brows. "I don't think you're feather-headed."

It was absurd, the flutter those words set off within her. It wasn't even a proper compliment. *I don't think you're feather-headed* was only one step up from *You're not objectionable*.

She tented her fingers in front of her, resting the peak against her lips, giving him a look that she hoped said, *I'm a serious adult*.

"Try me then," she said.

John sighed. "Your brother wasn't exaggerating when

he said I couldn't afford dinner. The Harrow estates are in more trouble than you could know, and Luella's dowry is...generous."

That the previous viscount had racked up debts without it becoming common knowledge was not a complete surprise. Many a person lost their head when Lord Harrow gave them that dimple-cheeked grin. The question was exactly how much debt he had gotten into. "Her dowry is how generous?"

John's eyes widened. She couldn't blame him. It was entirely inappropriate for a woman to be discussing money with a man in such a manner. But she also couldn't help herself. The thought of John—her childhood infatuation, the boy she'd pined over for years—marrying her sworn enemy was so dreadful it made her stomach churn and overrode all sense of propriety.

She pursed her lips and refused to add to her comment. It was Edward's favorite technique to make people talk, even if they didn't want to, and she had made herself a master of it.

"Eighty thousand pounds," he said, once he'd realized she would not abandon the question.

Her heart and jaw both dropped. "Eighty thousand pounds?" she whispered. That was an obscene amount of money. The only women with dowries that large were uncouth Americans whose only hope of moving up in the world was to buy their way into a society that didn't want them.

Charlotte's dowry was respectable. She'd insisted Edward tell her what it was before she debuted, and it sat at the neat and not insignificant sum of fifty thousand pounds. "Do you need so much to pay it off?" she asked.

"At least."

*Eighty thousand pounds of debt.* The previous viscount had always been perfectly kitted out and a generous host, but Eighty. Thousand. Pounds. "That's an absurd amount. Surely the previous Lord Harrow could not have spent such a sum?"

"It appears so," John said bitterly. "If it wasn't spent, then it was siphoned off and I do not know where it is now."

Charlotte sagged against the back of her chair.

"And there's no way to obtain such an amount other than marriage? There's no piece of land that could be sold?" That was how gentlemen tended to manage such misfortune.

He rubbed at the rim of his glasses. "All of it entailed."

Charlotte ran a finger across her lips as she considered the situation. She could not allow this travesty to happen. Quite beside the fact that Charlotte felt green with envy at the thought of John married to anyone other than her, John was a good man. Luella was a cruel viper who would tear him to shreds with her vicious tongue.

This abhorrent union could not happen.

"Lady Luella is not the solution. I don't know what is, but I will help you find it."

# Chapter 5 ――――――――

Raise my dowry." It was the first, most logical solution she could think of.

Edward's eyebrows shot up. Even Simmons, who was the best of London butlers and rarely expressed any kind of emotion, cocked his head as he turned from the front door to help Edward from his greatcoat.

"Should we discuss this elsewhere?" Edward asked, handing the butler his hat and gloves and glancing around the foyer. Two footmen stood nearby whose eyes were trained on their slippers, but who weren't, in fact, as part of the wallpaper as they'd like to appear.

Charlotte had been waiting on the stairs most of the day for her brother to arrive home, sitting on the landing, swirling patterns in the thick pile of the rug. She didn't want to wait any longer, not even as long as it took to walk to Edward's study.

"Don't you think it's time, Ned?" she asked as she trailed after him down the corridor. "This is my fourth season and I remain unmarried."

Edward didn't answer until they'd reached the study and the door had firmly shut. He turned to her, his arms crossed, with the expression he normally reserved for disagreements with their brother or when casual negotiations with an ambassador over port turned hard.

"Your dowry is incredibly generous. Your lack of a husband is not due to a lack of money."

From the desk by the window, Fiona cleared her throat, drawing attention to her presence. She tucked a tooth-worn pencil into her braid and gathered her papers. "Should I leave?"

Edward nodded curtly, but Charlotte held up her hands. "No. Stay." John had been Fiona's mentor. He'd been the one to teach her chemistry and physics after he'd caught her reading his scientific treatise rather than sweeping the floor as she'd been hired to do. Fiona owed John her entire career. If the subject came up, she would definitely side with Charlotte on the matter.

"It is a generous dowry, brother, and I'm appreciative. But it's clearly not enough. I've had but two suitors this season, and neither were the caliber of men to make my insides flutter." Her insides hadn't truly fluttered in years. There had been the occasional flip when a particularly handsome man had said something flirtatious. But the heart-racing, breathless, butterflies-rioting-inside-her feeling that characterized her interactions with John had disappeared when he had.

She'd thought they'd disappeared for good until she'd seen him again last night.

Edward rubbed the spot between his eyebrows. "What sum do you think will attract a gentleman that fifty thousand would not?"

"Eighty thousand pounds."

Edward dropped his hand, his eyes wide. He stared at her as though she'd grown two heads.

He was going to say no outright. She was certain of it. He had that cautious expression he used when he was looking for a way to deny a request without beginning an argument. She'd seen it during the dinner she'd arranged with the German ambassador the month before, and he was giving it to her now.

Fiona used her husband's momentary silence to interject. "That's a very specific number, Char," Fi said, crossing to her husband and pushing him not-so-gently toward the armchairs by the fireplace. "What need do ye have of *eighty* thousand pounds?"

*Drat.* She'd wanted to avoid this particular part of the conversation. She'd hoped to first convince Edward to increase her marriage settlement and then speak to John before sharing the plan with her siblings. When dealing with the duke, one needed all of one's ducks lined up neatly.

But it was clear Ned was not about to agree to the increase without a more specific explanation.

She took the seat opposite the two of them, spread her skirts out neatly, and then folded her hands in her lap. Edward's fingers drummed on the chair's arm.

"John is being forced to marry Lady Luella Tarlington because her eighty-thousand-pound dowry would solve his financial predicament. *Luella.*" She added the last for emphasis.

Edward's expression shifted. It was as grim as the gathering clouds outside. The drumming stopped and his fingertips pressed into the leather. "No."

It was the answer she'd expected, so she remained calm. It was merely the first point of negotiation. "Why not? You can afford it. You're one of the richest men in England."

Edward closed his eyes for a long moment before he opened them and caught her gaze in his weary one. "Charlotte, be reasonable. It's not about the money."

Drat. Money was easy to haggle. "Then what? John is your friend. I would think that you'd want to help him secure his estates and stay free from the fangs of that woman. Fi, tell him."

Fiona shook her head softly and the hope Charlotte had been holding on to slipped. *How could she?* After everything John had done for her, how could Fiona turn her back on him?

Putting aside the steep disappointment, Charlotte turned her attention back to the man who held her future in his hands. "Well then? What reason could you have not to support one of your oldest friends?"

Edward's face twisted at her criticism. "I will support him in every way I can," he said through gritted teeth. "But that does not include allowing him to marry my little sister in order to save his own hide. Money be damned, it is not a union that I will stand for."

Charlotte couldn't remember the last time her brother had raised his voice at her. She never gave him cause to.

Her eyes burned hot, but she refused to cry in front of him. She drew on the anger that roiled in her belly. "Why would you do this? After you wrecked everything by sending

William away, you swore you'd not repeat your mistakes. You promised not to dictate my choices. You allowed me to turn down every proposal, even though I knew you wanted me to find a husband. Why are you so insistent on having your way now that I'm finally doing as you wish? And in a manner that would help everyone?"

He shifted in his seat, settling in for a long fight. "You want a reason other than your request to near double your dowry?"

"*Yes.* I know you, brother. You don't make decisions based on money. You make decisions because you think they are right. So, what is your true objection to my marrying John? Tell me. Because from my point of view, it makes perfect sense. I must marry and so must he. It would be a convenient match."

"Because it would break you, Char. Because you have loved him your entire life and his marrying you for your money would break you."

Embarrassment engulfed her. They had argued about John before, but never had Edward so blatantly spoken of Charlotte's infatuation. For him to use it against her now was cruel.

Besides, it was an irrelevant argument. Just because there was no love between her and John now didn't mean they wouldn't find it ever. She would be his wife. Over time, love could grow.

She turned to Fiona for support once more, pleading silently.

Fiona responded with a sigh. "I'm sorry, Char. But I agree with yer brother. It's nae wise. 'Tis not a match that could work."

She clenched her skirts in her fists, not caring about the deep creases she was creating—just needing some physical release for frustration. "How can you know that? How can either of you possibly know that?" Their presumption was infuriating.

"Because you're not a good fit, Char," Edward snapped. "You're too different. You love people. You need to be around them. You haven't been home a single night this month. John would hide away from the entire world if he could. He only returned to London because his brother died and I have no expectation of him staying. One of you would be miserable in that union, and I will not chance that it be you."

Fiona leaned toward Charlotte, putting a restraining hand on her husband's arm. "I thought you want to marry for love, Char," she said gently. "Wasn't that why you turned down all those proposals? Why would you accept a marriage of convenience now?"

She had been looking for love. She'd turned down so many exceptional matches because she'd been searching for someone who ignited that spark, that giddiness, those rioting butterflies. But they had never come. Season after season she searched, and season after season she was left wanting. The only person she'd ever been drawn to was John. He might not love her, but at least she knew he would treat her well. He and Edward wouldn't be such close friends if John were a cad.

"I didn't think love would be so hard to find," she admitted. "Now that it's clear that a grand romance isn't in the cards for me, why shouldn't I marry if I could achieve something worthwhile doing so? At least we know that we all *like* him. He's been a kind and loyal friend to you both."

Fiona reached over and put a hand on Charlotte's knee. For a second, Charlotte thought that perhaps the argument had been won. But then Edward spoke.

"No. It is my greatest wish to see you happy. Marriage to him won't deliver that. If John is foolish enough to propose, I will not give my permission."

John was asleep once again. Once again, he was dreaming, this time of pink lips that were in constant movement— thoughtfully pursed, quirked in amusement, thinned with skepticism. They smiled at him, shyly. Teeth caught the lower lip. He couldn't wrest his eyes from them. Couldn't stop his body from reacting to their fullness, to how soft and kissable they were. He slid his hand through long, black tresses.

*Knock, knock.* Newton barked.

"Blast it, Mosely."

The door opened slightly. Through the crack, the butler called, "Lady Charlotte Stirling to see you, my lord."

Lady Charlotte. With midnight black hair and full, pink lips. His memory was too perfect not to know exactly who he'd been dreaming about. *What the devil is she doing here?*

John pulled on stockings and breeches and jammed his feet into slippers. He shrugged into the shirt he'd left hanging on the back of a chair and quickly put on a waistcoat and jacket. He tied his cravat as he walked down the hallway, Newton padding after him.

As he reached the foot of the stairs, he paused. None of the drawing rooms were in a state to receive visitors. John had opened as few rooms as he could get away with when he came home. Surely Mosely hadn't admitted her into John's private rooms again.

The butler caught John's hesitation. "She's waiting out front, my lord."

"Thank you, Mosely." He nodded. Taking a fortifying breath, John stepped outside. The grey clouds that had formed yesterday still obscured the sun, but given the way Charlotte beamed at him, it was a good thing. Much more brilliance, and he'd be blinded. "Why are you standing out here?" *Damn. Should have started with a greeting.*

She tipped her face toward him. Her eyes crinkled at the corners as though she hadn't noticed his appalling manners. As she caught him in her gaze, his heart kicked hard, almost as if it were struggling against him. Her tongue flicked across her lips so quickly, a normal person might miss it. But that image was now burned into his brain along with every other memory of her, and instinctively he knew where his dreams would take him tomorrow.

"Good afternoon, my lord," she said, oblivious to the direction of his thoughts. "It would be inappropriate for a single woman to visit a man's bachelor lodgings."

This whole blasted scene was inappropriate. Wilde was his best friend. Charlotte was Wilde's sister. These heady thoughts were a betrayal.

Newton, who had trailed John to the front step, barked and jumped up, his front paws landing on Charlotte's shoulders. She faltered only for a second, eyes blinking at the dog whose snout was suddenly only inches from her own. Then she grinned, and gave both ears a good scratch, seeming not to care about the dog hair that was covering her kid gloves.

"Down, Newton," he barked, heat creeping up his neck. Newton never behaved this poorly.

The dog sat, his tail wagging briskly in the dust of a stoop that hadn't been swept in God knew how long, looking up at Charlotte adoringly.

Trying to ignore the way his companion's immediate acceptance of Charlotte made John's insides tighten, he focused on his uninvited guest. "You visited yesterday. Was it not inappropriate then?" It would be best for all involved if Lady Charlotte came over less.

If she thought him a grouch, she didn't give a hint of it. "Yesterday I brought food with me. In my experience, society will overlook a lot of questionable behavior if you sweeten the experience with a good meal."

"And today?" Surely her standing alone on his doorstep, in full view of those who were walking down the street, was also questionable.

"Today, we're to promenade."

John could not think of a less appealing way to spend the afternoon. The thought of getting dressed up and strolling through the *ton*, leaving himself wide open to any pointed arrows they shot his way, made him shudder. "Lady Charlotte—"

"Call me Charlotte." Again, she hit him with that bright smile, so dazzling he almost forgot what he was about to say.

"Charlotte, this isn't a good time."

A small crease formed between her brows. "Why not? What were you doing?"

"Sleeping." And enjoying every minute. Especially the dreams he was having of raven hair and pink lips and skin so soft it begged for his touch. No one in their right mind gave up dreaming for the odious task of walking through Hyde Park.

The small snort she gave dislodged a brick in the wall that he was desperately trying to erect between them. "Goodness. Well done," she said. "I would sleep until mid-afternoon every day if my commitments allowed it. How heavenly that must be."

"Quite." And he would still be sleeping if she hadn't invited herself over.

"But you're awake now, and we can take Newton for a walk."

Newton barked. His tail swished side to side with excited vigor, his jaw lolling open, his lips pulled back in a wide doggy smile.

*Blast.* John sighed, unable to refrain from rolling his eyes. "Now there is no choice. You uttered the 'W' word."

John hadn't been to Hyde Park in well over a decade. He had driven past it a few times in recent days as he traversed London paying calls on all the tradesmen to whom he owed money, but each time he'd been so focused on the tasks before him that he hadn't paid attention to the *ton*'s favorite playground.

He and Charlotte were gaining the attention of the flocks of women who strolled the path and picnicked on the lawn. They would look in his direction and snap open their fans, bending their heads to whisper behind the decorated rice paper.

Nausea swirled in his stomach. He tried to relax, but his muscles remained clenched tight and his jaw clamped shut.

Charlotte looked perfectly comfortable under such a microscope. She acknowledged the strangers with a quick wave or greeting but never allowed them to engage her in lengthy conversation, deftly rebuffing all questions directed at him in a manner that left no one offended.

Despite her apparent willingness to be at his side, she would pull subtly on his arm each time a new person caught her attention, as though she would flutter from one person to the next were he not there weighing her down.

He would leave her to her socializing, if he could. If walking off mid-promenade weren't exceptionally rude. If Newton wouldn't consider a walk cut short the grandest of betrayals.

Yet, regardless of his discomfort at the onslaught of people, the touch of her hand on his forearm felt like a mainstay. When the gossip around them threatened to overwhelm him, he focused his attention on that point, where the warmth of her fingers through her gloves held him steady.

"I have a solution for our problem," she said once they had reached a relatively deserted section of the park.

Warning bells rang. "*Our* problem?" It had been a mistake to reveal so much to her yesterday. But there was something about her that teased words from him when he'd normally stay quiet. Despite the lack of logic or reason, his instincts were to trust this woman whom she barely knew.

His body swayed toward her, unbidden, without permission or input from his mind.

"Yes," she said. "*Our* problem. I love Edward. His dilemmas are mine. You're Edward's oldest friend, so your dilemmas obviously concern him, which means your problems are ours, which is lucky for you because I am *very* good at problem-solving."

She was so like her brother. She shared the same Wildeforde arrogance. The same Wildeforde loyalty. The former was a characteristic not uncommon among the *ton*. The latter was a trait he was unused to, given its utter absence within his own family.

But Wilde had been a steadfast friend for decades, always by John's side in the face of cruel taunts and unlikely challenges. That his sister was equally faithful should not have been unexpected.

Luckily, Charlotte barreled on with no need for him to put his thoughts into suitable words.

"You're going to speak with Lord Campbell about potential mining opportunities on your estates. He was completely destitute this time two years ago, with three daughters unwed and a wife with a penchant for collecting Ming dynasty china. Then, he found a coal seam under his property and now he's so brimming with cash, his butler must beat away fortune hunters with a sharpened broom handle."

There was such satisfaction in her tone that the part of him that hated to disappoint people was tempted to congratulate her for the suggestion, however unfeasible it was. The other part of him wanted her to stay well out of his business. "There are no coal seams near any of my properties," he said curtly.

Her brow furrowed. "How do you know?"

"Coal is predominantly found in the north, where peat bogs are more abundant. My estates are further south."

"Oh." She colored slightly, pursed her lips, and for a moment her eyes flicked toward her shoes as though he'd embarrassed her. Before he could apologize, she raised her gaze, squared her shoulders, and turned to him. "I hear that investments in companies such as the Dutch East India Company, or other such imports, can be quite lucrative. My friend's husband purchased a stake in the company a few years back. They seem rather flush, to be honest. I've rarely seen her wear the same thing twice, though I can't agree with such waste."

The Dutch East India Company, and ventures similar, were not avenues he would explore. The scientific community was a wide, closely knit network of philosophers that spanned the globe, which was how John knew exactly the damage such companies were wreaking on the countries they traded from. There wasn't a single capital city in Europe, Asia, or the Americas where John did not have some associate, and the stories they conveyed alongside their scientific discoveries horrified him.

But such stories were not fit for ladies' ears, so he offered a different excuse. "There are few short-term investments that could deliver the funds I need within the necessary timeframe. Most investments need a full year or more to mature and I don't have that." He had hoped to be back in Boston by September.

Lady Charlotte narrowed her eyes, tapping her finger against the shaft of her parasol. "There must be another way. Something more palatable than marriage to Lady Luella. Have you nothing left to sell?"

His temper darkened even further, until it matched the increasingly gloomy skies above. "Trust me, anything Walter could sell before he passed, he sold. There is not a single piece of artwork on the walls. The silver is gone. Even some curtains have been taken by his tailor in lieu of payment. The only thing of value I have is the engineering firm, and selling that is not an option."

He'd spent his adult years building that company. It was literally the product of his sweat, blisters, and endless nights grappling with challenge after challenge. The firm was his life, and those connected to it—Asterly and Amelia, Wilde and Fiona, Oliver the foreman—were his true family, the only people in this world who could be counted on. Selling his shares would be selling his soul.

Besides, he needed the biannual dividend it paid to keep the fires lit in the many homes he was now responsible for. And, when one of the ideas currently knocking around his brain fully formed, he would need that partnership in order to bring it to fruition. He needed Fiona as a sounding board and Benedict to help turn a theoretical concept into a physical product. No, he could not sell the firm.

"There wasn't a single thing left on the walls?"

John shook his head. "Even his wardrobe was bare."

Charlotte's brows furrowed. "That's odd. Walter was superbly dressed to the end. I saw him the night before he died, you know. I remember thinking the opal buttons on his jacket clashed awfully with the gems in his cufflinks. It was far too ostentatious to be fashionable, even with our set. A family could live for a year off that outfit alone."

Walter's extravagance was not a surprise, but now that Charlotte mentioned it, the lack of clothing in the home when John arrived was odd. His mind began its usual leap-frogging of thoughts when Charlotte sighed deeply and his attention caught on the slight *whoosh* of her breath and the way her shoulder relaxed against his arm and the slowing of his own heart rate as though his nervous system was somehow intrinsically linked to hers.

She continued to nod toward the groups that were looking her way, but her parasol twirled in her fingers in a way he imagined her mind was circling over his predicament.

Now would be the moment to head off any further interference, to reestablish a distance between them. Yet the words refused to come.

"This really is a pickl—" The parasol lurched to a stop as her fingers clenched the curved ebony handle. Her lips thinned the way her brother's did when he was confronted by something distasteful.

John searched their surroundings, looking for the source of Charlotte's discomfort.

*Damn.* There, making a slow but deliberate journey toward him, was Lady Luella Tarlington, flanked by two young women whose expressions weren't nearly as artful. Where Luella looked as calm as a balmy summer day, her sentinels looked like vicious guard dogs.

Beside him, Newton's ears went flat, a low growl reverberating through both him and John.

John gave him a reassuring pat on his flank and the growling stopped, but Newton's teeth remained bared. The set of Charlotte's jaw suggested that beneath her saccharine smile, her teeth were likewise clenched.

"Well, well, well," Luella said. "What a surprise to see you, my lord. When you didn't pay a call this morning as I was expecting you to, I assumed you were on your death-bed. What other reason could you have for not following through on your commitment?"

He'd made no such promise to the chit and was tempted to say so, but a public dismissal would draw attention. Not to mention it would probably destroy the only salvation open to him at the moment, as much as he was loath to accept marriage as a solution to his predicament.

So he forced a smile. "Lady Luella. You look beautiful. That color becomes you." God, he hated the artifice of this society. He couldn't wait to get away from it all.

Her eyes narrowed and John was certain he was about to experience a tongue-lashing. But the blows never landed.

Instead, Charlotte's fingers tightened almost impercepti-bly on the sleeve of his coat. "Lulu," she said. "Tell me you haven't fallen so low as to demand a man's presence in your drawing room? Wouldn't that be rather desperate?"

Luella's eyes narrowed. "Desperate? Like saying yes to every do-gooder cause, joining every committee, and championing every misfortunate wallflower that enters so-ciety because that's the only way you can get anyone to like you?"

Charlotte went rigid, her fingers digging into his arm fully now. A quick look down showed the blood draining from her face. Her throat bobbed. The quick-witted come-back he expected never materialized.

"Was there something you wanted?" he asked, when he realized how deeply the insult had affected Charlotte. Luella's smug expression was vile. There was nothing John hated more than a bully, and he'd spent far too many years as a target not to see Luella for exactly who she was.

The shrew dragged her eyes from Charlotte's stricken expression and turned her attention to John. "Lady Mortlake is having a gathering tomorrow night. There will be an invitation waiting for you when you return home. I look forward to seeing you there."

A gathering. Where he was going to have to talk with other members of the *ton*. Where he was going to have to practice niceties he didn't feel. It was on the tip of his tongue to tell her where to take Lady Mortlake's invitation, but until he found another solution to his financial woes, he couldn't set fire to this particular bridge. He swallowed hard. "I'll b-be there."

The scorn on Luella's face as he stumbled over his words caused heat to creep up his neck. The two sentries she had with her twittered.

"It's a shame that you're not invited," Luella said to Charlotte, throwing one last triumphant look in her rival's direction as she left.

"Well," Charlotte said, plastering a clearly false smile on her face. "That was unpleasant. One more example why we need a way out of this situation."

⁓

Charlotte was still fuming at Luella's comments when John dropped her off at the front of Wildeforde House. Luella was simply the *worst*. How dare she insinuate Charlotte was unlikable? And in front of John! Charlotte's ears burned just thinking about the insult—which was patently untrue.

She was beloved. She worked very hard to be so. Supporting causes was charitable. Joining committees was responsible. Making wallflowers comfortable in a ballroom was kind. Only a monster like Luella would suggest that any of these were bad things.

"I'm fine, Grace," she said in response to her maid's concerned look. "Go about your errands. It's only two blocks to Lady Pembroke's home. I'll be perfectly fine without an escort. Her maid can accompany us to Bond Street."

"If you're sure, my lady."

Charlotte was sure. She needed to walk off her embarrassment. There was no good reason that Luella's comments should have frozen Charlotte's tongue as they had. Luella had said plenty of awful things in the past and Charlotte had had a retort for each of them. But Luella's snipes had never hit so personally before.

John, to his credit, had been perfectly kind. Once Luella had departed, he'd made no mention of the comments and had instead described a recent report on the long-term effects of the eruption of Mount Tambora. She'd had no idea the particularly chilly year of 1816 was due to a volcanic eruption, nor that debris could hang in the air for such a long time. The yellow skies that she'd thought uncommonly pretty, but that she hadn't questioned the provenance of, were, in fact, the result of sunlight interacting with gases in the atmosphere.

His storytelling had almost distracted her from her anger. Almost. Until he'd taken her hand and told her, "I like that you champion wallflowers."

And then she was reminded once more of how Luella had thoroughly bested her, and how frustrated she was, and how she needed to be better prepared for their next encounter.

She'd been marching quickly toward Josie's home on the corner of Berkeley Square for no more than thirty seconds, rehearsing future comebacks to such insults, when a young man with a shock of curly orange hair that clashed vividly with his bright red soldier's uniform appeared from nowhere. He clamped a hand onto her wrist and dragged her toward a waiting hackney cab.

"What the devil do you think you're doing?" She swung her reticule, taking satisfaction in the solid thud as it hit her assailant up the side of the neck. There was a roll of pennies inside; William had taught her that safety trick long ago.

"Ouch. Blast. I'm *sorry*." The boy tried to raise both arms to protect his head, wincing as he did so. That was when she noticed the sling holding one wrist against his uniform.

"You *are* Lady Charlotte Stirling, sister of Captain Stirling?"

Charlotte's hand clenched around the strings of her reticule, ready to swing once more. Only the mention of her brother gave her pause. William had been in the army for almost four years—ever since Edward had thrown him out of the house and cut him off for his irresponsible behavior. She'd received only sporadic letters from him since. "Who's asking?"

The boy's free hand tugged at the frayed edge of his sling as he looked around before leaning close to her and whispering, "I have a message from the captain. He asks that you come to him immediately."

Her heart plummeted. It was a ruse, surely. A cruel one, given how desperately she wanted to see her brother again.

If William was home, the army would have sent official word to Edward. William would have returned to Wildeforde House, or at least to his bachelor's residence, and sent for her through a proper footman, not a grimy lad in a uniform so worn and filthy it was almost unrecognizable.

"My brother is fighting in Burma. Now leave me at once and be glad I don't report you for accosting a lady in the streets."

"Sorry 'bout that," the boy muttered. "Captain said you weren't an uptight one." He dug into his jacket pocket and then held out his palm. In it was a ring she knew well—one that bore the Wildeforde crest. It was a masculine version of the ring that currently sat snug on her right hand. It bore a small sapphire.

She snatched it from the boy's hand. "Where did you get this?" she asked as her fingers closed over it, pressing the metal into her palm.

"I told you—your brother. Please. He needs you."

It would be beyond foolish to go anywhere with this man. He was a complete stranger and clearly not a gentleman. She should call for help. But the thought of William in trouble pulled at her. He was the person she loved most in this world, and she'd always been there for him when he needed her.

"If Will has truly returned, then why haven't my brother and I been informed? If he's hurt, then surely his superiors would have informed the duke."

The boy shrugged, but he was not practiced in artifice well enough to conceal the fact that he was hiding something. "I don't know why. I just know he needs you, and there is no time to argue." There was a strained tremor to his voice. His fingers were twisting the knot of his bandage and he watched her with such desperate intensity that she was inclined to believe him.

It was possible. Her brothers had fallen out badly before William joined the army. Will had sworn that he'd never speak to Edward again. It did not beggar belief that he would return to England and not send word through proper channels.

"Where is he?" she asked. "Take me to him now."

*Chapter 6* ─────────────

The hackney cab drove for almost thirty minutes before it hit a series of potholes, almost pitching Charlotte forward into the lap of the soldier—Private Thomas James—before it pulled to a stop in some unknown part of London. She alighted from the carriage and was immediately accosted by the smell of rotting refuse and urine. The footpath wasn't paved. Instead, long wooden boards sat atop the mud. The grey clouds overhead had begun to release their encumbrance, the odd fat raindrop plonking onto the makeshift footpath.

The buildings were narrow and black with soot, as though they'd never been washed. Children ran with dogs across the street, mindless of the muck getting between their bare toes. Behind her, a bucketful of water splashed onto the verge.

"This way, my lady." Private James took off toward one of the grimy buildings, not checking to see if she followed.

As she stood on the doorstep, her heart thundered, and she found herself wishing that she had something more substantial than a roll of pennies that she might use as a weapon. She was tempted to run, but the gold ring with its Wildeforde crest was warm in her hand. If William was truly in danger, she needed to help him.

They climbed up a set of dark, narrow stairs. The young soldier pushed open a door on the right of the landing without bothering to knock. Charlotte hesitated in the doorway. The room was cramped and gloomy. There was one window, but the layers of grime hindered the light from getting through.

There was a table, two chairs, and a bed around which several men stood. On the edge of the mattress was a doctor's satchel.

"Captain Stirling's sister is here," Private James said as he quickly made his way to where the others stood. One man stepped backward and she could see a figure lying beneath a white sheet.

*William.*

She rushed to him, pushing aside another bedraggled soldier and leaning in close. "Brother."

She put her hands on his cheeks and kissed his forehead. His skin was hot beneath her lips.

"Will," she whispered, her throat tightening painfully.

His eyes opened. They were cloudy and dazed, but they sharpened a fraction when he saw her. "Charlie." His voice rasped, barely making a sound as he called her name. He ran his tongue over his lips, which were dry and cracked and an unhealthy shade of white.

"Water," she demanded, keeping her sentences short to

avoid her anger spilling over. The doctor pushed a glass into her hand. "Sit up, sweetheart." She stroked her brother's hair. Private James leaned over the other side of the bed, slipping a hand behind William's back. Next to her, the other soldier did as well. Together, they levered William into a sitting position.

She held the glass in front of his lips and tipped it slowly. He drank greedily and then coughed, slumping against the headboard.

Charlotte rounded on the physician. "He's parched. Why haven't you been forcing him to drink?"

The physician wiped his spectacles with a handkerchief. "He's barely been conscious since I arrived, my lady."

Hot tears stung her eyes. It was untenable that William, brother to a duke, had been allowed to suffer in such a manner. "How long has he been like this?"

Private James spoke, taking a small step back from her as he did. "He was injured two months ago, but the wounds were healing well until last fortnight. The fever started off the coast of Portugal."

"We should have stayed on the ship," the unknown officer hissed. "We should never have ventured ashore."

"How was the captain to know he'd fall in the muck?"

"His injured leg might have been a clue."

"Enough," she said. "Show me the injuries." She steeled herself before looking down at William, who struggled to keep his eyes open. The boy pulled back the sheet, exposing William's arm, chest, and thighs. A wide bandage, stained from seeping blood, wrapped around Will's midsection; another wrapped around his right thigh and yet another around his right forearm.

Charlotte had never seen anything like it. The worst injury she'd seen was William's sprained ankle and scraped hands that time he fell from a tree trying to break into Edward's study.

*Ned.* He needed to be here.

"Fetch my brother. The duke needs to know that Will is home, that he's hurt."

Before anyone could act on her instruction, Will grabbed her hand with a ferocity she was surprised he could muster in his current state. "No," he croaked. "You cannot tell him."

"Will, you cannot be serious." She reached into her reticule for a handkerchief and wiped the sweat from his brow. His dark curls glistened with moisture. "He will want to see you."

Will's fingers gripped hard enough for her to wince. "I do not want to see him. I hate him, Charlie. I will never forgive him for what he's done to me."

For the millionth time, Charlotte cursed Edward's idiocy. He'd been out of his mind with fear the night that Fiona had been arrested for treason, but it was no excuse for disowning his brother and packing him off to the army. Will might never forgive the duke, and if that was the case, it would be what Edward deserved.

It left her in somewhat of a quandary, though. Despite his action, Edward loved his brother. *He* would never forgive *her* if her silence prevented him from apologizing to William before he died.

A lump formed in her throat. Will couldn't die.

She turned to the doctor. "What's his prognosis?" she asked, trying to keep her tone measured.

The doctor pushed his spectacles up his nose. "Captain Stirling will survive his wounds, although he may never walk normally. My primary concern is the fever. It has taken hold of his body. Bloodletting may work, but there are no guarantees."

"And if he were to die of this fever? How long would that…" She swallowed. "…take?"

"A day. Perhaps two."

She drew in a ragged breath as she turned her attention back to Will, who'd succumbed to unconsciousness once again. His whole body flinched, over and over. Perhaps his fever dreams had taken him back to the fighting.

She raised his damp, cold fingers to her lips and pressed a kiss to them, trying to bring his mind away from whatever was causing him such a fitful rest and back to her.

She would give him the night to improve. If the fever hadn't broken by morning, she'd send for Edward.

Private James used his one good arm to drag a stool across the room for her to sit on, running his fingers through his carrot-colored curls as she sat at her brother's side, where she could hold his hand yet still reach to stroke his hair.

"You've missed a lot, brother," she murmured. "So much has happened since you left." His fitful shudders eased at the sound of her voice, and she breathed a sigh of relief. She looked up at the soldiers in the room. "Fetch some notepaper. I'll need to send word to my maid to make my excuses if I'm going to be here all night."

Facing her brother and stroking his hair, she launched into a summary of all the titillating things that had happened over the past four seasons, keeping up a stream of conversation that dipped and paused like music—a melodious lullaby for a grown man who had always loved a scandal.

As dawn broke, so did his fever. His breathing softened, and for the first time that night, his eyelids stopped their frantic flickering.

# Chapter 7 ──────────

John was as late to Lady Mortlake's gathering as he could reasonably be. If he had timed it correctly, all the pre-dinner pleasantries would be over and he would only need to force himself through a meal and one drink before he could make an excuse to leave.

At least, he hoped that was all he'd need to do. He did not know what Luella meant when she'd said he would have to act as though their engagement was mutually desired. It was a statement that couldn't be further from the truth. John didn't want to marry anyone, but especially not her. Their life together would be miserable.

As the butler announced him, John quickly scanned the room, making note of who was talking to whom and each facial expression as they looked his way. Most of the attendees regarded him as though he were a specimen under glass, ready to dissect. It was to be expected. Walter was a man who never missed a party. The *ton* knew him well. John had avoided society for the better part of a decade and the *ton* knew him not at all. No doubt there would be intense curiosity about the man who'd replaced the beloved fourteenth Viscount Harrow.

His hostess, Lady Mortlake, scowled as she came to greet him. "You're late."

"Pardon, my lady," he said carefully. "Unexpected traffic."

The countess *humph*ed and returned to the guest she'd been talking to. With little enthusiasm, John searched for Luella. Better to get the unpleasantries over with.

Instead of the caustic maybe-fiancée, John found Charlotte. She'd just been laughing; he could see it in the way her blue eyes crinkled. As she turned to him, her gaze brightened and the corner of his mouth twitched in total defiance of how the rest of him was feeling. She was not supposed to be here, and yet he was absurdly pleased that she'd come.

She wove her way through the gawking crowd until she was standing before him, looking up at him with eyes full of joyful anticipation. Although, now that she was close up, he could see the slight shadows beneath them. "Lord Harrow."

The way she said his name, as though it were code for something else entirely, sent shivers through him.

"You look tired. Are you well?"

She arched a brow. "You are genuinely terrible at small talk, aren't you?"

Blast. Even though her tone was friendly, his stomach twisted at his misstep. He hated the surface-level conversation of these events, but even he knew better than to begin a conversation with an insult. Especially toward a woman he was coming to like. "I meant no offense."

She pursed her lips. "Luckily for you, I am incredibly difficult to offend. And I am well, thank you. Simply a trying afternoon followed by a sleepless night. Nothing a warm milk and some rest won't solve. *You* look exceedingly well tonight." She gestured to his wine-colored dress jacket.

Charlotte might admire it, but the close crop of the jacket across his shoulders and stiffness of the embroidery at his collar merely amplified his discomfort. He suspected his smile was more of a grimace. "I didn't want to risk Lady Luella's wrath. Who knows what parts of me might go missing if I appeared in less than my best?" He hadn't resigned himself to the need to marry her, but neither was he ready to sever that one chance to save the estates.

Charlotte snorted quietly, a surprisingly undignified sound coming from the refined woman in front of him. "You don't need to concern yourself with Lady Cruella tonight. I hear she was lured to the McGoughlin ball when word got out that the rarely seen Viscount Harrow would be in attendance. Which may or may not be an entirely falsified rumor given you are, in fact, here."

The quick twitch of her shoulders and her cunning smile left him with no doubt that she had strategically placed said rumor.

"Does that mean I can leave?" God, if he could get out of a forced conversation with lords of the *ton* that would be a perfect outcome for the evening.

Charlotte cocked her head, her lips pressed together

disapprovingly. "Of course not. Goodness, John, were you raised by monsters?"

He had been born to a man with hard fists and a shrew with a vicious tongue. So, yes; he had been raised by monsters. He wasn't about to share that, though.

"I see you obtained an invitation." As he said the words, he realized how pleased he was that she'd done so. The night felt less onerous with her there.

"Well, when Lady Mortlake heard that Edward and Fiona had other plans and that I would be all alone in an empty house, she insisted I join you all this evening."

"How convenient. I take it you ran into her by accident."

She smiled. "Of course. Though I must admit, it's not my preferred set to associate with. There is a reason Luella enjoys this company."

Just when he thought he was enjoying himself, the dinner bell rang. The sound sent unease coursing through him. He didn't know who he should escort into the dining room— he hadn't been out in society for almost a decade, and even back then his interactions with the *ton* had been limited— but he did know they were likely to be disappointed that their dinner partner for the evening was the reticent lesser viscount.

"Lady Burberry," Charlotte said, when she noticed his predicament. She pointed to a woman who looked to be in her eighties and was standing by the door, waiting for him, her fan tapping at her side. Yes. Lady Burberry looked unimpressed.

An older gentleman approached, acknowledging John with a subtle nod and offering his arm to Charlotte. With a regretful smile, she untwined her hand from John and tucked it into the crook of the man's elbow. They didn't get two steps toward the dining room before she stumbled.

John lurched forward, grabbing her free arm before she could fall to the floor and take the grey-haired lord with her.

"My apologies, Lord Walderstone," she said. She pressed her hand to her chest, as if overcome with embarrassment. "I seem to have twisted my ankle." She leaned heavily against John, and he debated the merits of carrying her to a chair.

"I don't want to keep you from dinner, my lord," she continued. "I hear Lady Mortlake is serving trout for the first course and I know that it's your favorite. Lord Harrow will wait with me, if you don't mind escorting Lady Burberry."

Lord Walderstone looked more than pleased to escape. John would have done the same if he could, given how the entire party stared over their shoulders at them as they went in. God, there was nothing he hated more than attention of these people.

Before John knew it, the room was empty save for Charlotte, himself, and a footman who had appeared with ice and a chair.

"Are you in much pain?" he asked as he knelt before her and placed the wrapped ice on her ankle, unable to help himself from noting its delicate curve and the soft sheen of the silk that covered it.

Charlotte brushed her skirts. "Of course not, silly." This time, her mischievous smile sent his stomach flip-flopping. "It is not even a twinge, but this way, we are sure to be seated next to each other."

"Oh." Her machinations became apparent. God forbid

she ever turn them toward him. He stood and held his hand out to her, shivering slightly at the press of her fingers in his. "You are terrifying."

~

As terrifying as Charlotte's subterfuge had been, it was nothing compared to dinner. Despite Walter having supposedly died owing money to at least half of the guests in attendance, they had naught but praise for him. He'd been a proper lord, born and bred for the title. Unlike the current viscount. More than a few of the guests made snide comments about John's life in trade.

*"A true gentleman would never."*

*"I mean, what could possibly persuade a person to work? Shudder."*

*"There are some pages of the newspaper on which a gentleman should never appear. The business section is one of them."*

Forget that his engineering firm was the only chance these people had of being repaid. For an aristocratic gentleman to concern himself with business was beyond the pale. One could only imagine what they'd say if they knew he frequently rolled up his shirtsleeves and assisted in the factory he'd been overseeing.

Charlotte did her best to dull the blows. She could turn a conversation with a witty quip or an innocent-seeming question, and the bullies would find another topic, but John couldn't avoid conversation entirely. He kept his contributions short and the comment "I couldn't say. I've not been in England" close at hand.

Of course, not taking part in the conversation meant that his attention kept drifting back to the woman next to him. It was a problem, the way his chest contracted erratically as she smiled at him, as though the sight of her bypassed the normal function of his brain and went straight for his nervous system. She was his best friend's sister. Definitely out of bounds. Attraction to her would lead nowhere.

Logic didn't overcome his body's painful awareness of her, however. By the time dinner was over, his foul mood was fouler.

"We have two options," Charlotte said brightly as he escorted her into the drawing room, completely oblivious to the impact her fingers had settling on his arm. Blast, she was inconvenient. "The ladies have suggested a game of charades," she continued.

Any unwanted energy that still thrummed through his body at her touch was quickly quashed. "You must be kidding." Standing before a crowd of strangers trying to communicate some trite phrase through mime was perhaps the most ridiculous "game" that he could think of.

More than that, shouting out words under pressure would lead to his tongue tripping over itself in the most humiliating way. He was not about to open himself to the ridicule that would follow. "Is departure the other option?" The ghastly dinner was over, Luella wasn't there, and there seemed little point in remaining where he clearly didn't belong.

She *tut-tut*ted. "No, John. Your other option is whist. Lord Mortlake is a curmudgeon who refuses to play any kind of parlor game, and he's looking for another pair."

John's body loosened a fraction. Whist was harmless

enough. One could play it in complete silence, and that was the next best thing to leaving. It was a game that required no effort from him. That was the thing with a perfect memory—playing cards was as easy as breathing. He could keep track of every card that had been played and calculate what was likely to be played next.

"Whist it is then."

Before he could stop her, Charlotte reached for his hand, expecting him to escort her as a gentleman would. Her fingers enclosed his, and he stifled a groan at the need that pulsed through him. Damn.

He let her guide him toward the table by the window looking out over the drive. The rain that had been threatening to spill for days had started at last. As raindrops passed the outdoor lamps, they created ripples in the puddle of light below.

"It's pretty, isn't it?" Charlotte said, her gaze following his. "Sometimes I'll have Swinton stop at the top of Grosvenor Street on the way home so I can watch the light change on the pavement as people pass. There's nothing quite as lovely as the city at night."

Her expression was all rapture and innocence as she put a hand on his arm, her fingers fairly burning through the fabric of his jacket. "Here come Lord and Lady Mortlake. We need to crush them." And her expression was no longer innocent at all.

~

John and Charlotte quickly proved an unstoppable pair. Charlotte's countenance was almost entirely inscrutable.

But he quickly picked up on the slight changes in mannerisms that communicated the strength of her hand. The brief downcast of her eyes told him she didn't have the cards needed to win the trick. A finger over the top edge of her card said she was poised to deliver a killing blow.

The quick flick of her tongue over her lips? He couldn't match that to the cards she played. It was almost as though it formed a different conversation entirely, one that caused his cock to twitch as his stomach had earlier.

She made the game that he thought would take no effort at all considerably taxing. Keeping track of the cards was more difficult than it should have been when he kept forgetting to actually look at the hands played because his eyes were constantly drawn to his partner.

Nevertheless, within thirty minutes, the two of them had Lord and Lady Mortlake pinned down, and his lordship knew it. His expression became increasingly dour as the game continued, but he played long after a sensible man would have thrown in the towel, all because of Charlotte.

When Mortlake made a backhanded comment about the fifty quid Walter owed on his death, a muscle ticked along Charlotte's jaw before she launched into a witty stream of conversation that fairly dazzled their hostess. The two women giggled and gossiped, and every time Lord Mortlake went to end the match, Charlotte teased him lightly in a way that might have seemed innocent and flirtatious to others. To John, it was clear she knew how much money they were winning and had no intention of letting her target go. She was out to take their hosts for everything.

It was terrifying how she managed her opponents—the way she beguiled them, blinding them to their own situation.

If she ever turned those charms against him, he would be absolutely lost.

As the last trick was taken, Charlotte gathered the tokens and added them to the small hoard she had accumulated by her elbow. "Another hand?" she asked innocently.

Winning this hand had brought their night's takings to exactly what Walter—John—owed. It was clear Charlotte wanted to keep playing, but John had enough problems without making new enemies. "It's time to call it a night," he said.

Mortlake rose from the table the moment the words were out of John's mouth. Lady Mortlake huffed. "This was *so* diverting," she said, despite her obvious disappointment that the game was over. "We must do it again sometime. Soon." She patted her husband's arm.

"Perhaps." Mortlake scowled at John. "Give me a minute. I'll meet you in the hall."

It was an implicit invitation to leave, and John was more than happy to accept. He'd stayed far longer than he'd intended already.

"Yes." Charlotte stood and tugged at her gloves, smoothing the wrinkles to mask the fact that they'd just been involved in a massacre. "I must also be going. I'm so sorry that we didn't have the opportunity to visit the ghost in your receiving room. I shall pay a call tomorrow and we will see if we can entice it to show itself."

In the hall, John held Charlotte's coat. As she slipped a hand through, she was suddenly within the circumference of his arms. The scent of her, an English summer garden, infiltrated his awareness, causing the back of his throat to tighten and the hairs on his neck to rise.

She was so close; he'd just have to tilt his head the slightest bit and his face would be buried in her midnight curls. He swallowed. Hard. Thank God she faced away from him.

She turned, and with only inches between them, a heat, an energy, pulsed. He clasped his hands behind his back because the alternative was to rest them on her hips or sink them into her hair.

"Thank you, my lord." Her cheeks flushed prettily as she ducked her head and looked up at him through long lashes.

His throat closed completely, and his heart raced because this was exactly the situation he always tried to avoid—one where his chest and throat and tongue all seized and if he was forced to utter even a single sentence, his stutter would humiliate him completely.

She brushed a stray hair behind her ear. His gaze followed the movement, his lips yearning to trace it.

"Harrow." Lord Mortlake's voice was the ice water he needed. He stepped away from Charlotte and the hold that she had on his insides released.

Mortlake held out a folded piece of paper. John took it and flicked it open. There it was—a promissory note for fifty quid in Walter's hand, signed several months before his death.

"Thank you," John muttered. One debt down, only a hundred more to go.

# Chapter 8 ————————

The difficulty with John's brain was not just that he remembered everything—he could see every word he'd ever read and every expression on a person's face—but that his mind continued to make connections between all the different pieces of information. Possibilities erupted like popping corn.

Today the endless ideas that plagued him were a discordant mix of Edward's sister, potential applications of theoretical concepts in the recently published *Chemistry of Europe*, and Edward's sister.

His habit was to fill his notebooks with these thoughts and ideas, annotations and lines, connections and questions. Each page would be rife with references to other pages in different notebooks. Only the act of purging his thoughts on paper ever brought him the quiet he craved.

But thoughts of Charlotte—her name, her likeness, the

memory of her naked toes peeking out from beneath her nightgown—didn't quiet no matter how many pages he filled. His journals, the existence of which could be subpoenaed in any court case relating to the intellectual ownership of his inventions, were becoming less the documentation of his engineering and more like a smutty novel.

There were kernels of genuine worth in there, though. To focus his mind on the development of ideas that might bring in a much-needed additional income stream, he tossed his latest journal on the floor by his desk, shrugged on his coat, and pulled his gloves from the pockets of it. He would see Fiona. Half of his ideas were about her matches as it was. If he was talking business, surely thoughts of Lady Charlotte could not intrude.

He glanced through the glass doors toward Wildeforde House. There was a door in the wall separating their two gardens that hadn't been used in over a decade. Perhaps he'd remind Wilde of it. It would be quicker than constantly traversing the block.

The walk was brisk and invigorating, but he hesitated when he reached Wildeforde House. From the street, the residence seemed alive with activity. All the outside lamps were lit, creating a wide, sweeping, welcoming arc of light along the drive. A footman was brushing down the stairs, and as Simmons opened the door to ask the lad a question, John could see maids crossing behind him, arms full.

He should go. He would have to tame his thoughts on his own. He'd almost turned back, but his feet, illogical and unbidden, propelled him forward.

Simmons had the door open. "His lordship or her ladyship?" he asked as he took John's coat.

"Fi, if she's available." If they were about to entertain, she'd be inundated with tasks.

Instead of leading John to Fiona and Wilde's study, Simmons took him left, to a drawing room that overlooked the front garden. It was as unFiona-like a room as he could imagine. The wallpaper was pretty shades of yellow and pink, and a long bench that spanned the length of the room was laden with vases and intricate flower arrangements. Still-life watercolors hung on the walls and both chaise longues were adorned with tiny blush cushions edged with lace.

This was Charlotte's room. The details all spoke to her nature: her love of pretty things, her attention to comfort, her kindness. He inhaled and caught the same scent of a summer garden that he'd smelled last night. It set off an unwelcome fluttering within him.

It had been a mistake to come here. Sitting on her chaise longue, enveloped in her smell, was hardly going to make him think of her less. But if he was honest with himself, perhaps this was exactly why he'd hurried to visit—his body could not continue resistance after a day of thinking about her.

"John." Fiona's voice yanked him from his musings. He looked up to see her standing in the doorway, her head cocked.

"You're wearing a gown." The only time John had seen her in women's clothing was years ago. She'd had a single dress she wore to church on a Sunday. Tonight, she was clad in green silk, in a dress with flowing skirts and sleeves that would absolutely catch alight in a lab or snag on their half-assembled steam engines.

Fiona rolled her eyes and crossed to the chair in front of

him, collapsing onto it casually, in a stark juxtaposition to the finery she wore. "Aye, the French ambassador is coming to dinner, along with half the House of Lords. So I'm wearing a dress."

She looked...different. Gone was the earthy, raw, common-born engineer he knew. Instead, she looked every bit a duchess.

Their lives had irrevocably changed. The farmer's daughter and the second son now a duchess and a viscount. Neither was where they should be—in a factory covered in a layer of coal dust, working with the sound of a blacksmith's hammer to accompany them and the occasional trumpet of a steam train.

She didn't look unhappy, though, in this new life. In fact, despite the gown and the elaborate hairstyle that the old Fiona would have groaned over, Fi looked whole. Joyous.

"I should go," he said. "You're clearly busy."

She waved a hand. "Stay. I'm nae as busy as ye'd think. Charlotte has it in hand. I just need to show up and be agreeable. What brought ye here?"

"I have an idea, a way to cut the amount of material needed for the match heads by two-thirds."

Fiona's eyes widened, and she leaned forward. "Tell me. But tell me over dinner."

⌒

It was the second night in a row that John had dined with his peers. Unlike the sharp edges of the previous night's conversations, where he'd found himself deflecting pointed comments about his work and cutting remarks about how wonderful Walter had been and how John must surely be concerned at being the lesser viscount, tonight the conversation ran gently. Dare he say *pleasantly*?

The guest list had clearly been curated for a purpose— in among the lords were ambassadors from several European countries with which the government was trying to negotiate treaties. Every Wildeforde had their role. Edward and Fiona talked political and social influence with the men in attendance. Charlotte's politicking was more subtle; she worked on the women in attendance. Her conversation was more indirect, but there was no doubt that over breakfast the following morning her true value would be felt.

In stark contrast to the company at his earlier foray into society, those in attendance did not have the same derogatory attitude toward industry. They worshipped Fiona, constantly asking about her latest project and what she thought of this innovation or that recent development.

Once the attendees twigged that Lord Harrow was *the* John Barnesworth, the man whose safety improvements to Hedley's steam engine had accelerated the adoption of rail travel, curious questions were lobbed in his direction. It was talk he was comfortable with and he barely tripped over his tongue at all. Before he knew it, dinner had become drinks in the drawing room—the men choosing to stay with the women.

John hung at the edge of the room, propping up the wall while the rest of the assembly found places to sit and listen to Charlotte as she sang and played the piano. The pages of sheet music were turned by the eager son of the Spanish ambassador. There was a look of adoration on the boy's face as he gazed down at her. John couldn't blame the lad. Her voice resonated with the collective sighs of her audience, creating an energy that quickened his breath and heightened his senses.

He didn't know how it was possible, but when she smiled, the entire room fell away, as though whoever she was smiling at was the only person who existed. When that smile reached him, his heart pounded.

So focused was he on the woman in front of him, he didn't notice her brother join him until Wilde was leaning against the wall facing him, arms crossed.

"She's exceptional, isn't she?"

John nodded. "Indeed. The young Señor Di Osma seems entirely besotted." He was *not* jealous of the boy, even if he had a flash of yearning to be the one turning her pages.

"She looks happy, don't you think?"

"She does." John didn't think he'd ever experienced the joy that was in her expression. The lightness of it, its carefree aspect, was completely foreign to him.

"She's in her element, hosting events like this," her brother continued. "Char needs people the way most men need air. It sustains her. It drives her. If she were ever to be removed from society, she would likely wither away. Do you understand?" Edward's expression turned hard. There was nothing in it that reflected their decades of friendship.

John felt a red-hot wash of shame engulf him as understanding struck. Wilde was warning him off Charlotte.

Of course he was. Wilde knew him for who he truly was, every flawed molecule of him. No one understood John like he did, and if his oldest friend thought him an unsuitable match for his sister, then clearly he was. It stung, but it wasn't a surprise; it just reinforced what he already knew.

Ladies like Charlotte belonged with real lords who could navigate society's turbulent waters, not sink beneath them. She belonged with someone who was attuned to the social whirl, who could play host to her hostess rather than skulking at the edges like a blasted wallflower.

She was sunshine, and he was a dull winter's day. She was joy and life and laughter, and that vivaciousness was foreign to him.

She loved people and he could barely manage basic conversation without insulting someone or stumbling over his words and clamming up. Even if the thought of her had followed him about all day, they were clearly not a concept that would work in practicality.

She needed someone else. She needed a man more like Walter.

His stomach turned at the thought. She needed a man like Walter, but kind. Regardless, that man was not John.

He met his friend's stony stare. "It's understood. It's not a thought I'd ever entertained."

Wilde nodded, glimpsing no sign of John's lie. "Good, because I fear she is not so rational about the matter. She's always gotten too damn close to her projects. To save you, she may well sacrifice herself."

Like a young lady to a netherworld monster.

Charlotte finished playing and gave her hand to Di Osma, allowing him to help her stand. The boy's chest puffed forward as they stood in front of the assembly, Charlotte dipping into a curtsey.

When she stepped away from the piano, she was joined by half of the guests. Her laughter drifted across the room. She truly was in her element surrounded by the highest of *haute ton* and acting as a general in her brother's political battles.

This life was as far from John's one-bedroom cottage in the wilderness as it was possible to get, and ultimately, that was where he wanted to be.

And Charlotte would wither away there.

⁓

As the evening wound down and Charlotte no longer needed to flit from person to person to ensure her guests were happy and engaged, she was able to give more of her attention to John, who was currently sitting with Fi and the French ambassador.

He stood as she joined them, offering his seat.

"No, it's fine," she said. "I'll have to get up in a moment, anyway." Lady Brostward would soon leave, and as Edward's hostess, Charlotte would need to pay her regards.

John nodded but didn't smile or look her in the eye as he did so. A thread of unease wove through her. They'd been friends last night. Now he acted as though she were barely an acquaintance.

*Just his friend's younger sister.*

Charlotte perched herself on the arm of Fiona's chair. The conversation, which had paused the moment she arrived, leapt back into life. Charlotte could understand none of it. Something about ignition temperatures.

Fiona bit the tip of her thumbnail before shaking her head and then wagging her fingers at John. "No, I agree. I think if we were to replace the antimony sulfide with white phosphorus the flame would be steadier."

John sat for a moment, his body language mirroring
Fi's. He tapped his fingers against his lips as he considered
Fiona's words. "On its own, it's not combustible," he said
eventually. "But if the striking surface contained elements
of red phosphorus in addition to glass?"

The French ambassador, who almost always ended his
visits to Wildeforde House in deep conversation with Charlotte's sister-in-law, nodded his agreement. "That might
work. There was a paper in *Philosophical Transactions* that
suggested something similar."

John clicked his fingers. "Yes! Fi, you have all that's
needed, don't you? We could start trials tomorrow."

The more they went on, the more Charlotte's discomfort
grew. She knew she was not the most intelligent woman.
But generally, she could understand the thrust of a conversation, could follow along with it, or she at least had enough
information to pretend to follow.

She couldn't even pretend right now. The entire conversation went completely over her head.

"Fi, you're a genius," John said, raising his glass
toward her.

Fi waved him off. "Nae. I simply had an excellent teacher."

Charlotte's discomfort morphed into full-blown jealousy.
Fiona was so at ease in this kind of conversation. She was
the most intelligent woman Charlotte had ever met, and
while Charlotte adored her sister and was so grateful that
Edward had found love with a kind and thoughtful woman,
tonight's conversation was a reminder of all the ways in
which Charlotte was lesser.

She was the daughter of a duke, cousin to the king, and
had had more proposals than she could count on her fingers,

and yet she would never be able to discuss what made the universe work. She'd spent her entire life doing exactly as society expected of her—she'd had governesses and finishing schools and endless hours of practicing what she ought—and still she'd somehow found herself uneducated. Her head was full of people and gossip. Try as she might, she would never change the world as her sister had.

John glanced at her briefly and then looked away. He must think Charlotte a complete idiot, given how little she contributed to the conversation. She had been awfully stupid to think a woman like her could ever be loved by a man as intelligent as him. He needed a wife like Fiona, someone who could converse on the subjects that interested him.

The discomfort became too much. Fi, John, and the French ambassador were so deeply engaged in conversation they didn't even notice when she stood. Rather than interrupt them, she quietly made her way to the door where Lady Brostward was preparing to leave. Edward was already there.

She gave the grande dame's fingers a squeeze and kissed her quickly on the cheek, pushing aside all her feelings to once again play the part of the perfect hostess.

The rest of the guests took that as a sign and one by one they left, until eventually, it was just four of them. Edward and Fiona sat together on the chaise longue, swirling patterns on each other's limbs with their fingertips. It was clear the night was over and that her brother and his wife wanted to go upstairs.

"Shall I walk you out, my lord?" she asked John.

Edward gave them a sharp look which, judging by the

way John's features drew in tight, had subtext she could only guess at.

Nevertheless, John rose and offered his arm. They walked in awkward silence to the front door, where Simmons handed John his coat and gloves. As he dressed, Charlotte couldn't help feeling incredibly foolish. She'd had a child's tendre for John for so many years, but tonight showed that if they weren't talking about his predicament, they had very little to say to each other. They had so little in common.

Simmons finally handed John his hat.

"I hope you had a lovely evening," she said.

"It was very agreeable, thank you." Again, he barely looked at her. Was that where this friendship had ended up? Last night they had been a perfect pair, playing in total synchronicity, and tonight he could barely spare five words for her.

"Will I see you tomorrow, then?" She cursed the hope in those words. She shouldn't want to see him again. That way lay heartache, clearly. But her desire to see him prevented her from keeping her mouth closed. "We could walk Newton again. We could think of new ways to extricate you from your abominable engagement."

John sighed and finally looked her directly in the eyes. "Lady Charlotte, I cannot marry you."

"Oh." Her heart dropped. If only the floor would do the same and swallow her whole. She fought back humiliated tears. Had her foolish infatuation been so obvious?

She pulled together enough of her shattered pieces to at least appear whole, because a Wildforde never showed weakness. "Thank you, Lord Harrow." Because really, what else was one to say when a proposal you never even made got rejected? All the suitors she'd turned down had managed a brief if ill-felt show of thanks for her time.

John ran a hand through his hair. The way he tugged the ends of it caused strands to escape from their queue, standing out at all angles. "I don't plan on remaining in England. As soon as I can free myself from my brother's debts, I will hire stewards whom I trust to oversee the title and its affairs and I will return to America."

"Oh." The evening was getting better and better. He was leaving. That hadn't been a possibility she'd considered, and her shattered pieces fractured further.

"Well, good night then." She thought she saw regret in his expression, but that was likely just the blur of tears. She smiled tightly and then turned on her heel, hastening back to the drawing room, trying not to let the footmen she passed see how broken she was.

She'd been foolish to hold on to hope. Edward had refused his blessing for a match; it had become clear she and John had nothing in common; and he needed a bride with a larger dowry than she could give. Still, there was some small part of her that had thought it could all work out.

She hadn't realized that once he'd settled his affairs, she would never see him again.

In her room, Grace had already lit the lamps and closed the curtains. Charlotte should leave them like that, despite the temptation to go to them and pull them aside just slightly. Just enough to see whether he was in his study.

No. Closed was better. She didn't want to see him ever again. She didn't think that she could handle the embarrassment.

Grace helped her change from her dress to her nightgown,

unpinned her hair and brushed out her curls, working in silence. That was one of her most valuable traits—she was whatever company Charlotte needed. She was a gossip when Charlotte had news to share, and a fortress of silence when Charlotte needed company but not conversation.

The long, rhythmic strokes of the brush were comforting. When Grace finished braiding Charlotte's hair and tied it with a ribbon, Charlotte almost asked her to stay the night as she used to.

But Grace had her own life now, outside of tending to Charlotte. She had Swinton, who no doubt expected Grace to join him in their room.

Charlotte climbed beneath the covers and the lady's maid snuffed the lamp, leaving Charlotte truly alone.

She lay in bed for the better part of an hour, resisting the temptation to go to the window. Eventually, it was too much. She kicked off the bedclothes and padded her way to the window, only opening the curtains a crack—just enough to see if John was there.

He was leaning against the glass door, his head resting against his arm, his arm resting against the window. From this distance, she couldn't see the nuances of his expression, but she could see his hand clenched by his side.

He was in an impossible situation—trapped through no fault of his own. Faced with a choice between seeing his people suffer and shackling himself to Luella.

He was a good man. He would choose the happiness of his tenants over his own feelings, which meant that unless Charlotte could find another way out, he would marry Luella, and Charlotte's archnemesis would have the one thing Charlotte had ever coveted.

*Chapter 9* ———————

Charlotte's heartbeat thrummed as the carriage drove the whole two minutes around the block from Wildeforde House to John's residence. After his comments the night before, who knew what her reception would be? Did not wanting to marry her also mean not wanting to remain friends? Charlotte was friends with many people she didn't want to marry.

Would he turn down her help in fear of her throwing herself at him matrimonially? She'd lain awake the night before, carefully putting aside her hurt and humiliation and bricking it in, like a dead body she didn't want found.

The reality was, John needed her help; she cared about him, and who *was* she if she wasn't helping those she cared about?

Luella's comments two days ago still burned in her memory. *That's the only way you can get anyone to like you.*

It *wasn't*. Plenty of people liked her, and not because she was always giving of herself. People liked her because she was nice. Maybe too nice sometimes, but it was better to be too nice than not nice enough. The reason she was helping John was definitely *not* in a desperate attempt to win his approval. She was helping John because it was the right thing to do and a Wildeforde always did the right thing.

Besides, there were no circumstances in which she'd concede a battle with Luella so easily.

When the carriage pulled to a stop and the footman opened the door and flipped down the step, she peeked her head out to see who might be around. Yes, it was ridiculous to take a carriage around the block, but given she'd chosen not to have Grace accompany her, it was best to go unseen.

Satisfied that there was no one around to start gossip, she alighted, burdened with a large ceramic dish, and marched up to John's front door.

Much to her chagrin, John's butler did not have the door open by the time she hit the top steps. She rested the dish on one hip and rapped the brass knocker. While she waited for the door to open, she kept an eye out on the street, hoping that no one would see the Duke of Wildeforde's sister entering Viscount Harrow's residence sans chaperone again.

Finally, the door opened. "I'm here to see Lord Harrow," she said, giving Mosely her most winsome smile.

"He's not receiving visitors, my lady."

*Drat.* "Well, let me in and we can discuss it inside." Every second she spent on the doorstep was an added risk to her reputation.

Frustratingly, the butler remained firmly planted. In fact,

he put a hand on the door as if he was about to shut it in her face.

"I brought leftovers," she blurted out. "Far more than the viscount can eat before it goes sour. I'm not sure what he'll do with it all."

Mosely pursed his lips before stepping aside.

She quickly crossed the threshold and ventured inside far enough that she was out of view of the street. She handed the butler the ceramic dish. Mrs. Price had made double portions of last night's dinner at Charlotte's request, specifically so that John and his household would be subsisting on more than bread and cheese.

Thankfully, the cook hadn't batted an eye at the petition. Charlotte had made many similar ones over the years.

"His lordship can't still be asleep, honestly?" It was near to four in the afternoon. There was sleeping in, and then there was *sleeping in*.

"I'm uncertain that his lordship ever went to bed, my lady." There was a hint of disapproval in Mosely's tone.

Charlotte brushed a curl from her face. "Is he in his study?"

"Yes, my lady. But again, he isn't receiving visitors."

"I'm not a visitor. I'm practically family." At least, John and Edward were practically family, and she was Edward's sister, so by extension...

She strode through the corridors, her nerves racing ahead of her. A sane woman would hide from the man who so thoroughly rejected her. She would cross to the other side of the street whenever they came into close proximity, so they would never need to deal with the awkwardness.

The thought was tempting, but in the early hours of the

morning, when she should have been sleeping but couldn't, her mind had conjured another solution. One that should have been obvious two nights ago. One that would help ensure that Luella never got her talons into him.

Charlotte and John would gamble their way out of debt.

Given his mind and her conversation skills, only a handful of members of the *ton* could truly challenge them. The rest were easy pickings. And luckily, society was obsessed with cards. Every dinner party and every ball had a room tucked away where lords and ladies sat in their finery, gossiping as fortunes changed hands.

She and John could take some of that fortune. The solution was so fine that it bulldozed past her embarrassment.

The study she entered looked nothing like the room it had been when she'd visited mere days ago. What had been a relatively tidy state of affairs the morning Luella had voiced her wretched demands now looked like a pig's wallow. Books and letters and periodicals were strewn all across the room. Scrappy bits of paper were pinned to the wall, ruining the finish.

And in among mountains of notebooks were almost a half dozen—contraptions. That was the only word she could think of to describe the collection of things in front of her— jars wrapped in foil, sharp blades attached to rods. Metal bars circled by copper. She could not make heads or tails of what they were or what they should be used for.

Sitting cross-legged on the floor, his back leaning against the glass door that led to the garden, head lolling to the side, was John, his eyes closed. In sleep, the frown lines that had been ever present had vanished. He looked softer, less serious. At some point, he'd removed his cravat, unbuttoned his waistcoat, and the ties of his shirt neck had come loose. The wiry strands of hair that covered his chest were the same chestnut brown as the hair that currently flopped at all angles over his face.

This was the most intimate experience she'd had with a man. Never had she seen one in such a state of dishabille. At least not one who wasn't a sibling. A warmth pooled in her belly. The temptation to reach for her fan was almost overwhelming. She shook out her fingers, dragging her gaze from the bare patch of skin at his chest.

Mosely had said John hadn't gone to bed that night. Perhaps he should have. He was going to wake with the most crooked of necks. It was unhealthy to fall asleep at such angles. He clearly needed rest, but should she leave him there or should she wake him and send him to lie down somewhere that was less likely to leave him with body aches when he woke?

He cracked one eye open, and she jumped, hand to her throat in surprise.

"Lady Charlotte? What are you doing here?"

She could appreciate his confusion. After last night's conversation, he no doubt expected her to be anywhere other than his study without an invitation. "Forgive the intrusion, but I have an idea." She simply needed a moment to recollect her thoughts following the . . . distraction of his person.

John snorted. "At least one of us has an idea. I've been searching for one all night and yet it eludes me."

Charlotte gestured to the surrounding chaos. "Is that what this is? The search for an idea?"

"It's the search for an escape." He scrubbed his hands over his face. "It's in these papers. I just can't find it."

Of course he couldn't. No one could find anything in this mess. He was worse than Fiona. "Perhaps it would be easier to find if the place was more organized."

He grunted. "Perhaps."

Good grief. He was even more taciturn than usual. She hadn't thought it possible.

"And what are these?" she asked, gesturing to the spools of wire and metal boxes that had taken over the chaise longue.

"That's the beginning of what could be a revolutionary communication device."

Charlotte didn't know how much needed revolutionizing, unless it was a way to keep a quill ever sharp. "That box looks nothing like a pen."

Despite his exhaustion, John's expression brightened. "It won't be if I can get it working. I'm going to call it the telegraph. Messages sent from a distance."

"Aren't all messages sent from a distance? At least written ones."

John furrowed his brow. "True. But these will be delivered by electric signals sent through wires connecting houses, even miles away. Almost instantaneous communication."

"Instantaneous communication." As she said the words the impact of his idea was clear. No more stained gloves or fingertips, no more sand that inevitably found its way where it wasn't wanted. No more waiting for footmen to come back and forth. She could talk with Hen and Josie whenever she wanted. "Well, that sounds *divine*. Goodness, that will net you a fortune. You'll be hailed a hero. Every household in England will want one."

He cocked his head. "Will they, though? It sounds rather horrific to me. Who wants to be contactable all the time?"

Of course he would think that. She had never met someone who recoiled from conversation as he did. "Why are you working on it if you don't like the idea?"

John paused. "I enjoyed my life in America. I enjoyed the solitude I found there, but there were times I would have liked to have spoken with my friends. Waiting three months to exchange letters was hard."

She could imagine. It was torturous every time the season ended and society went back to its country estates. Charlotte would write and receive a dozen letters a day, but it didn't compare to the immediacy of in-person interactions in London. Living in a whole other country would be unbearable.

"I don't think I could do it. I couldn't imagine being that far from my family." She brushed off her skirts as though she could brush off the melancholy of the thought. "Is this how you will save your estates? Your telegraph?"

Perhaps he didn't need her help at all. That was deflating.

John took off his spectacles and rubbed the bridge of his nose. "*If* I can find a way to generate and store electricity. *If* I can find a way to have the electrical signals converted to something visual. *If* you're correct and this proves something that people will spend money on. That's a lot of ifs and a long time before those questions are answered."

"So not a guaranteed solution, then?"

"Not quite."

"What about this one?" She walked over to his desk and picked up another contraption.

"I'm looking for a way to filter sewage."

"Sewage?"

"Human waste," he said. "Excrement," he added when she didn't respond.

Charlotte dropped the device, sniffing her fingers hesitantly, relieved when all she could smell was rose-scented silk. "Charming." She crossed to stand in front of him. His head still rested on the glass. One arm was casually thrown over a device with a series of sharp blades that looked like a torture machine. "And what is that one?"

He sighed. "Wouldn't it be nice to cut lawns with exact precision and little effort? Even with the sharpest scythe, there is variation in length of the grass purely because of the arc of the swing, and the amount of labor involved is considerable. This could bring hours back to a gardener's day—if I can make it work."

She had never really considered *how* lawns were cut. All she knew was that the greater the size of the estate, the more likely it was that there were goats.

"So you're creating all of these things at once? How do you hold it all in your head?" Creating a single one of them seemed more complex than she could imagine.

He chuckled, but there was nothing amused to his tone. In fact, it seemed rather grim. "It's not something I have any control of. Trust me; I'd give almost anything to be able to forget."

Given he'd still made no attempt to stand, she sank cross-legged in front of him, shifting aside a hunk of metal and a spool of wire so that she could spread her skirts neatly.

"How does it work? Your memory?" She'd heard Fi mention it before, that he never forgot a thing. It couldn't be possible that he remembered *everything*, though.

John gave a wan smile. "I simply need to see something and the image of it is burned into my brain. Anything that I want to recall, I retrieve in the same way one searches through the stacks of a library. Once I've found where the image should be, it springs to the front of my mind. I can see it as perfectly as if it were in front of me."

It sounded remarkable. And completely unbelievable.

"What was I wearing the first time we met?" Not that she could prove him wrong. Even she didn't know the answer to that.

He gave her a smile. "It was in your brother's room. Wilde and I were doing very secret boy stuff and you burst in. You were perhaps ten years old? Eleven? Your hair was lopsided, as though your maid had been half-drunk, and you were wearing a yellow pinafore with green leaves printed across it and lace on the hem."

She remembered that pinafore. It had been one of her favorites. Her hair had been lopsided because she'd put it up herself. She'd been too young to have a lady's maid and Edward had braided her hair every morning and every night. When she'd heard that the boy from across the garden had come to visit, she'd begged a housemaid for some hairpins and clips, and fashioned it into an up-do herself. She'd thought it was pretty. She'd have been mortified to learn how amateurish it had truly been.

"The next time we met?" she asked.

John closed his eyes, as though he were rifling through his thoughts. "You were no longer in a pinafore and pantaloons. You were wearing a proper dress that came down to your ankles and had sprigs of holly all over—it must've been around Christmas time."

Charlotte's throat tightened at the way he recalled her so vividly. She had memorized everything about him—what meals he ate fastest, the way he took off his spectacles whenever her mother was in the room, how he always gave William an apologetic shrug when Edward shooed his younger brother away.

It made her giddy to hear that he remembered the details about her as clearly.

"And the last time we met?" Her voice barely made it through the viselike squeeze her heart had on her throat.

His eyes flew open. "Last night?" He searched her face and then sighed. "You were the most beautiful thing I had ever seen and your expression when we said good night was the worst. That is an image I wish I could somehow forget."

What on earth was she supposed to say to that? It was so at odds with his sentiments the night before. Dash it, this man made no sense. She pointed to the mass of wire that lay next to her. "Tell me more about this one," she said. "What does it do?"

"It makes electricity."

"Electricity? It makes light?"

He shook his head. "Not quite. Electricity can *make* light, but it is not light. Some of it cannot be seen at all. There is an idea about this that is bouncing around in my brain, but I cannot grasp it. I know the seed of it is within a book, but I cannot remember which one."

She looked at him skeptically. "Is that not what your brilliant memory should do?"

John scrubbed at his eyes again. "Yes, but I haven't slept in forty-eight hours, so my memory is proving fallible."

Charlotte looked at the mountains of books strewn around the room. It would take a year to search every page of them. "If you found this missing clue, it would, what? Tell you what to do next?"

John picked up his spectacles from where they lay beside him and cleaned them with the edge of his rumpled shirt. "I don't know what the clue is going to tell me. There's just a tiny voice in my mind telling me there is a piece of information I need. It was on page sixty-four. The margins were wide, and it was about a third of the way down the page, but for the life of me, I can't remember the title."

Charlotte cocked her head. "Can you remember what the cover looks like?"

His jaw dropped open. "It was blue." His voice was more animated than it had been since she walked in.

"Dark or light?"

"Light blue, which meant it was an issue of *Philosophical Transactions* or an issue of *Advancements in Physics*. Charlotte, you're a genius." He climbed to his feet and offered her his hand. As his fingers enclosed hers, she felt a frisson of energy shoot through her.

"Help me find the article," he said as he started searching through the haphazard piles of journals and books. Every third or fourth journal he pulled out of the stack and tossed into the sky-colored pile on the floor.

"Here," he said, handing her one. "Page sixty-four. We are looking for the word *kinetic*."

They both spent several minutes in silence sorting through the stacks until John looked up. "You came with an idea," he said, as though he was only just now hearing her words.

"Yes, but it's not nearly as interesting as any of yours."

She would never have an idea as important as his. He was like Fiona. He was going to change the world. He already had. The steam engine he'd designed was far less likely to decapitate its operators than previous iterations. The newspapers said it had saved many, many lives.

"It was a way to get out of the engagement, though," he said. "Some other way to come up with the blunt." He looked at her with all the hope of a wallflower wanting to dance.

"If you won't marry your way out of debt—"

"I won't."

"And it will take too long for you to find a way out with your new devices—"

"It will."

"Then there is only one solution. We earn your way out. Every ball has a gambling room. We make a list of who you owe money to, find out which parties they'll be at, and we play until we win."

*Chapter 10* ————————

The hack dropped Charlotte on the street outside the building housing William's apartment. Now that she didn't have urgency overriding her senses as she did with her last visit, she was very much aware of the street and how out of place she must look. Her caramel-colored silk pelisse, which had felt suitably plain when she dressed, now seemed rather ostentatious with its clean white lace on the hem and matching white gloves. She had paid little attention to her footwear when she'd put her slippers on, but against the muddy wooden boards that ran alongside the road, the jeweled clips looked decidedly unsuitable.

There was a tug at her sleeve, and she looked down to see a street urchin with a dirty face and wide eyes looking up at her. The girl must have been no older than eight, and her arms poked like bare winter branches out from a torn and ragged dress.

"'Scuse me, ma'am. Do you have a coin?"

Charlotte reached a hand into her pocket to draw out her purse. Before she could extricate it, five other children appeared, grubby fingers outstretched.

She had little money on hand—the stores she frequented extended lines of credit to her family—but at the bottom of her reticule was a roll of pennies and two wrapped peppermints. She distributed the pennies and apologized to those who missed out, giving them a sweet instead. It was clearly not an inferior alternative. The peppermints were quickly unwrapped and popped into grinning mouths. The children who received the coins looked on with jealous expressions.

"I'll be back tomorrow," she promised. "I'll bring more sweets with me then."

The children scampered and Charlotte once again faced her brother's building, fortifying herself with a deep breath and brushing down her skirts, trying not to notice the marks made by dirty little hands.

Private Thomas James opened William's door. His uniform was crumpled, his red coat unbuttoned, and the white cotton of his sling had greyed. He bowed awkwardly and stepped aside.

Charlotte gave him a tight smile and crossed the room to where her brother lay sleeping, putting a hand on his forehead. His fever might have broken several days ago, but until the festering wound on his leg healed, she would be hypervigilant against its return.

"The sawbones was here this morning," Thomas said, sidling up next to her. "He said the captain is making good progress."

"That's good news." She dropped a quick kiss on William's forehead and then turned to the boy who had been acting as nurse. The shadows under his eyes had deepened since she'd last been there. His curls had become tangled knots, and he had a hand lying unconsciously on his belly, like his stomach needed a good filling. "You look as though you haven't slept in a week," she said.

He smiled wanly. "You'd think that after three years on the battlefield, I would have mastered the art of falling asleep anywhere. Not the case, unfortunately. The floor makes for an uncomfortable mattress. Especially with this." He nodded toward his injured arm.

It was only then that Charlotte noticed the ball of clothes lumped in the corner.

"You're sleeping here."

The boy nodded. "Just until the captain is well enough to take care of himself. Then I'll report to my superiors. I should've reported days ago—no doubt I'll be reprimanded—but I couldn't leave him."

Charlotte wiped aside the hair that had been plastered to William's sweaty forehead. "How was he hurt?" She hadn't asked before. Previously, she'd been focused on the present rather than the past. But with Will out of the woods, she needed to know what he'd been through, even if she wasn't sure she could stomach it.

The boy shifted from foot to foot. "There was a blast. The captain heard it and instead of retreating, he ran toward it. There were still men left in the area that he wanted to see clear. It was the second explosion that caught him." Thomas trailed off, his eyes clouded, his face pinched as though he were reliving the battle.

Charlotte put a hand on his arm, seeking to bring him gently to the present, to safety.

He shook his head at her touch, and his eyes focused. "There was so much blood."

Charlotte's veins ran cold.

"We used our rifle slings as a tourniquet and wrapped his chest with Private Gray's shirt to keep him alive until we made it to the field hospital." Charlotte wasn't sure he noticed the way his fingers dug into William's bedsheets.

This boy and his compatriots had saved her brother's life. It was a debt she'd never be able to repay. They would stay in her heart forever.

"Thank you," she said, the words barely escaping her tightened throat. She placed her hand on his cold one and gave it a gentle, hopefully grounding squeeze.

"The captain would've done the same for any of us. Most officers were content to stand safely at the back and watch other men fight. The captain wasn't like that. He was side by side in the thick of it, every time."

Charlotte swallowed hard at the image his words brought to mind—of her sweet, funny, mischievous brother facing gunfire and death. It was a world away from the London scene he'd been accustomed to.

"What will you do now? Once Will heals and comes home?"

"I'm not sure, m'lady. I'm too injured to continue soldiering." He gestured to the sling around his arm. "They'll discharge me the moment I report in. And I'm not good for much else. The doc says I won't be able to lift or carry again, which rules out most jobs. I can't read, so I can't go into a clerical position. There's the Chelsea pension the army gives, but it's a pittance. Certainly not a livable wage."

"Can your family not support you?"

He quirked his lips. "There is no family, m'lady. That's why I enlisted, for the promise of three meals a day and a roof over one's head. Napoleon was dead. Who knew they would find another war to fight? Especially one so far away in a place so hellishly hot."

The young private's story snagged around the branches of her heart. She couldn't imagine a life without family. Hers might be ofttimes dysfunctional—her brothers rarely got along and her mother was a cruel-hearted harpy. Her cousin, the king, had more scandals to his name than the rest of the family combined—but despite all the Shakespearean drama, she had blood.

She didn't want to consider what it would mean to be alone in this world. "Can the army not find you work? Surely they have a responsibility to do so."

"The army does not care what happens to you once you're discharged, m'lady." The young boy swallowed, his Adam's apple bobbing up and down. "If you're too injured to work, and you're too proud to beg, there are few other options."

Charlotte looked at the boy in front of her—a young lad who had fought for his country and saved her brother's life, a boy who could be no older than her—and imagined him sitting in a gutter, hat in hand, begging for food.

Rage writhed through her at the injustice of it. This would've been William's fate if Will weren't the brother of a duke. Regardless of the feud between her siblings, Edward would never have let William go hungry and homeless.

"I am sorry that you're in this position," she said to the boy. "Give me a few days. Let me see what I can arrange." Perhaps there was a position for him at one of Edward's estates. Simmons wasn't in the habit of hiring disabled help, but Thomas had saved William's life and for that the stuffy head of the household staff would find a place for him.

She only wished she could find places for all of them. She'd never thought about what happened to men when they returned from war—not even in the days after Will's enlistment. Logically, she knew they couldn't all come home whole, but she'd assumed that those who hadn't would be looked after.

Instead, Thomas was standing here tending to her brother despite the anxiety he was feeling at his future prospects, knowing there was little support to come. "The Wildeforde family owes you a great debt, Private James. We will not let you be cast aside."

The boy ducked his head, but for a brief second, she saw a flash of hope in his eyes.

"What did you say, Charlie, to make Private James blush?"

Charlotte whirled to face her brother, sagging against the mattress with relief as she saw his eyes were clear, if somewhat pinched at the edges.

She and Thomas helped him to sit upright, and she took a glass of water from the bedside and held it to his lips. Will drank heavily, quickly finishing the glass and asking for another. That was a good sign. That was a very good sign.

"What do you need?" she asked him as she took the empty glass.

"Food," he grunted. "And brandy."

Charlotte reached into her reticule and pulled out the banknote that she'd stuffed in there that morning. She handed it to Thomas. "Here," she said. "Take this to somewhere nearby that sells a decent meal. And for goodness' sake, make sure you get enough for you both."

He grasped it and raced out of the room. "He's a nice boy," she said as the door snicked closed.

"They were all nice boys." Will's tone was leaden, burdened with a pain she didn't know how to ease, his expression bleak. Not once, in all their years together, had she seen such a look on his face. They'd been as thick as thieves when they were younger—relying only on each other in the face of their bitter mother and Edward's school term absences.

She had been there the day Will returned early from boarding school to confess he'd been expelled. She'd snuck into his rooms when their mother had whipped him for one of his pranks. She'd held his hand after that last terrible fight with Edward. Through it all, William's fire had been momentarily dampened, but it hadn't been quenched. This William, whose expression held no life in it, wasn't someone she recognized.

"You're certain that I can't fetch Ned or Fi? They would love to see you. They've both missed you terribly."

William jerked away from her. "Don't interfere, Charlie. I will be the one to deal with Edward, to make him understand exactly what he did. This is not your problem to fix. You're a damn busybody."

She recoiled at the anger in his words. He'd never spoken to her like that. Not once. Even when she'd been a frustrating, annoying little brat who had followed him everywhere, even to bed when her nursemaid had the night off.

His outburst stung, but all injured animals lashed out. As she turned away, not wanting him to see how his words had impacted her, her gaze fell to the table pushed up against the wall. To the half-empty brandy bottle on it. The doctor had given strict instructions not to mix alcohol with the painkillers he'd prescribed. Clearly, those instructions were being ignored.

Dash it, Will. He'd always had a drink in his hand before the war, but she'd thought he'd have had more sense than to drink now. Injury or not, he was about to hear exactly what she thought of his stupidity.

But when she turned around, brandy bottle in hand, he was staring up at the ceiling, tears in his eyes, hands twisted in the sheets.

"Will?"

He turned to her, a tear dripping from his cheek to the pillow. "Did he dispose of my things when he threw me out?"

She put the brandy back on the table and crossed to him, squeezing his hand in hers. "No. Ned did everything he could to bring you home. The general...he was militant in his adherence to your commission contract. But your things are as they were before you left. Rest easy, brother."

Will gripped her hand painfully. "Mr. Bighead?"

"Is safe on the foot of my bed." Charlotte had no memory of their father, but Will did. The patchwork doll had been the last gift the previous Lord Wildeforde had given his son.

She dropped a kiss on Will's forehead. "I'll fetch him for you. I'll be back shortly. I love you, brother."

He didn't respond and as she closed the door to his apartment, a tear spilled down her cheek. He was hurting, and she had no idea what to do. How could she, a woman who had faced little hardship, soothe away the wounds of war when she had no true understanding of what he'd faced? And she never would, not unless she could convince him to talk to her.

"M'lady?"

She brushed the tear away and faced the woman who was approaching. She was an older woman in a clean, serviceable gown, who sported a no-nonsense expression.

"Yes? Can I help you?"

"Ye ken the captain?"

"He's my brother. You are?"

The woman's hands bunched her skirts. "I manage the building. I'm sorry, m'lady, but yer brother cannae stay. The other tenants cannae handle the screaming."

Charlotte swallowed. "The screaming?"

"Every night. I feel for the lad, I do. But I have a business to run and I cannae charge full rent from tenants that cannae get a wink of sleep at night."

Charlotte's knees weakened. How much must he have suffered to be plagued with constant night terrors? He needed to be home, within the safe embrace of his family, however much he thought otherwise. "I simply need a little more time," she said. "Just a few more days to convince him to return."

The landlady was about to say no, Charlotte could tell, so she cast a hand into her reticule, looking for something to stave off the eviction. There was a handful of pins and that was all. She reached for the broach she would normally wear, but she'd hadn't put it on before she left. Her eyes fell to the jeweled clasps on her shoes.

"Here," she said, desperately. She crouched down and yanked the clips from the leather. They were amethysts, surely enough to earn a little grace. "What compensation do you need for him to stay the rest of the week? I'll pay the neighbors' rent if I must."

The woman gave her a figure, and Charlotte agreed without hesitation. She had pin money. If she couldn't convince William to come home by the end of the week, then there were plenty of trinkets like her shoe clips she could sell.

She pressed the clips into the woman's hands. "I just need a little more time to fix everything. But I will. You'll see."

John stood at the entrance to the Mottram ballroom, trying hard to force a smile and appear as though he were happy to be attending his first ball in over a decade.

Trying hard not to dwell on what had happened at the last ball he attended, where he'd finally gathered the courage to ask his crush to dance and had been fool enough not to realize she'd only accepted in order to make a mockery of him. As she'd walked off the dance floor, leaving him alone as the first strains started, he'd wanted the floor to swallow him. All the nearby dancers looked at him askance. From within the watching crowd, he'd heard his brother's sneering voice. "P-p-poor B-b-barnesworth."

That was the last time he'd joined the *ton* when it gathered in large numbers. Was it any wonder that his stomach was in knots now?

Charlotte brushed her skirts just before they stepped into the ballroom doorway, and then she turned and brushed John's lapel before snatching her hand back, her ears flushing red.

"I...Sorry...I'm not sure why I just did that."

John knew exactly why. She saw a problem and she fixed it, without conscious thought half the time. It should annoy him. Instead, it was bizarrely endearing.

She handed the butler their invitations, and no sooner had their names echoed through the room than a cacophony broke out. All heads turned in their direction, desperate to lay eyes on the newly minted viscount who had been estranged from society for so long.

His skin crawled, as though the caustic stares sent in his direction reacted with his skin. He pushed back the hair that flopped into his eyes, glad his left hand could hide in his pocket because he couldn't stop the anxious *tap, tap, tap* of his fingers. "We're here for as short a time as possible," he muttered.

"Of course." Her tone was guileless, but the question was whether they shared a similar understanding of "as possible."

A wave of guests swelled in their direction, mostly young girls being prodded by their mothers. At their crest was their hostess, Lady Mottram, who greeted them with a glowing smile. "Lady Charlotte, how lovely to see you again."

Charlotte clasped hands with her. "Lady Mottram, such a stunning display, as usual." She gestured to the intricate flower displays that ringed the room, each housed in a Chinese porcelain vase. Just one of those vases would pay six months' wages for John's London staff.

He took Lady Mottram's hand and bowed over it, letting the training his mother had forced on him all those years ago rise to the fore.

Lady Mottram fluttered her lashes with all the enthusiasm of a debutante. "My lord, what an honor to have you attend. I do hope you'll tell me all about where you've been these past few years. Perhaps during a waltz? There are two."

John stiffened. "I don't dance." The words came out far more terse than he intended, and Lady Mottram's smile became pinched at the edges.

Charlotte stepped on his toes. "What Lord Harrow means to say is that it's been a long time since he's attended a ball and he needs to get his bearings before he risks the dance floor. He wouldn't want to cause a collision."

Lady Mottram seemed a little mollified, and Charlotte leaned forward, positioning herself between him and their hostess—a human shield deflecting further comments away from him. "I have heard that Dame Edna Evensbury will join us this evening," she said. "What a delight her singing is. However did you manage such a coup?"

Lady Mottram preened. "Such secrets are best kept close to the chest, dear girl. But I do hope you'll enjoy the performance. Excuse me." Their hostess moved to greet the guests that had entered behind them.

"You don't dance," Charlotte muttered as they threaded their way deeper into the room. "Goodness, John. Could you have said that any louder? Now that's all the guests are talking about." She gestured to the ripple of fans as raised eyebrows turned in his direction and the women in attendance whispered to each other.

"I am not hopping around like an insect under glass for

any woman. It's best they know now, so I won't be forced to disappoint them later."

Charlotte snorted. "You really don't understand women, do you? You could not have delivered a more direct challenge had you slapped them with your glove."

Indeed, on closer inspection, the women in attendance were looking at him as though he were prey to be captured.

"We're here to play cards, Charlotte. There's nothing else in the equation."

Charlotte rolled her eyes. "We can't very well walk into the gaming room, win every trick, and walk back out again. Our scheme would be far too obvious."

"Which means?" he asked with a sinking feeling.

"Which means it's time for you to meet some more of your peers."

⁓

He couldn't breathe. Whenever he and Charlotte remained in one position for more than a few minutes, the circle of people talking, talking, talking at them tightened.

Young women, nudged by their mamas, hovered at the peripheries until Charlotte invited them to join the conversation and then he'd been bombarded with questions about the weather (unseasonably wet), how he was enjoying the party (just barely), and what he thought of the latest dress fashion (it all looked the same to him).

Once the circle reached a critical point of women, young men joined the fray. He knew a handful of them by name—they'd been a few years beneath him at school. The men were...scornful. They barely acknowledged John and were quick to interrupt when the women directed questions his way.

Perhaps they thought it would annoy him. They clearly didn't realize that they could have all the attention if that's what they wanted.

Charlotte's charm was in full force. She did not discriminate with her affections. She flirted with every man and woman who stood before them. The effect that she had on the gathered party was visible—young women stilled their fidgeting hands and spoke with more confidence; young men puffed up their chests. They all leaned toward her without noticing and looked to her for approval when they spoke.

She glowed.

John found it hard to comprehend. Surely, she could not *like* all these people as much as she appeared to. Surely, she was bestowing sunshine on them all because she was too kind to shine on a few and not others. Surely, she found this constant attention at least a little exhausting.

Viscount Lionell wandered over to their group. The relaxed confidence of the women fled as they flicked their eyes toward their skirts, their necklines, and their gloves. John could understand their sudden self-consciousness. Even he could appreciate Lionell's good looks. The viscount had golden-blond hair pulled back in a perfect queue, his cravat tied in the kind of intricate knot an expert valet would spend an hour on, and sky-blue eyes that focused on Charlotte the moment he joined the group.

Lionell had looks, a title that had been his for more than five minutes, an estate that was known to be in very good health, and a reputation for being everywhere. This was a man who would be Charlotte's perfect partner.

"My lady," he said, bending over her hand and leaving a kiss that lingered long enough that John felt the urge to thump him.

Charlotte tugged her fingers from his and grasped her fan with both hands. "Lord Lionell. It's a pleasure to see you again."

"You are as beautiful as always. There isn't a woman in the room that could hold a candle to you."

The ladies around John felt the blow. Their energy shifted, and their eyes darted away from the couple in front of them.

Charlotte laughed lightly, an affect that would sound amused to most people, but John saw the sharpening of her gaze, like a blade against a whetstone. He wouldn't change places with Lord Lionell for the entire eighty thousand pounds needed to drag him out of trouble.

Charlotte batted Lionell's shoulder with her fan, the sharp *crack* out of step with her playful smile. "How abominably rude. I trust you've met my friends, Miss Ashby, Miss Portsmith..." she rattled off names as she gestured to their companions.

The girls ducked their heads as though trying to avoid Lionell's attention. It was only then that John realized Charlotte's affections so far that evening had been spent on the outcasts—Americans and misses and shy young ladies who didn't fit current beauty standards. These women weren't fidgeting because they felt some sort of desire for Lionell. They feared him.

As an outcast himself, their pain resonated. His first instinct was to take each of them by the hand and guide them away gently, but that would only make them larger targets later.

Lionell flicked the barest glance at their companions. "Your association with them is quite to your credit, Lady Charlotte. Your charitable endeavors are second to none. My mother speaks of your good work often."

Miss Ashby paled. Miss Portsmith's hand went to her chest as though Lionell's remarks were physical.

Charlotte drew in a deep breath and for a moment, John wasn't sure what he was about to witness; the way she shifted slightly, as though to put herself between the girls and their bully, the way she drew herself taller, shoulders straightening, chest rising, made him wonder if Charlotte was about to break her fan or her fist against the vicious viscount.

John would step in, of course, after she'd landed one good blow.

To his surprise, her smile only widened. "It is not charity, Lord Lionell, although I can understand how you'd be confused given your lack of experience with the matter. My companions are liked for their personality rather than a title. One day, perhaps, you'll develop one and then you'll see what I mean."

The insult was delivered so smoothly, as though she were commenting on the weather, but it was not lost on anyone. Miss Ashby couldn't suppress a smile, and even the way she brought her fan to her face couldn't disguise her mirth when the corners of her eyes clearly crinkled.

Lionell obviously noticed, because a muscle ticked along his jaw and the tips of his ears turned bright red. "There are only two aspects to a title-hunting American's personality: vulgarity and boorishness."

The amusement fled from Miss Ashby's expression. In

that brief second before she trained her gaze on the floor, John saw her eyes fill with tears.

Charlotte's anger was palpable. Her fingers tightened around her fan, and he couldn't help calculating what force would be required for her to draw blood with it.

He stepped forward, standing side by side with Charlotte, as her lieutenant or sidekick or whatever she needed in the moment.

"Miss Ashby," he said, without dropping his gaze from the cruel viscount. "Would you grant me the honor of this dance?"

# Chapter 11 ⸻————

He was a bit of a hero, Charlotte decided, watching as John spun Miss Ashby around the dance floor. She'd been able to cut Viscount Lionell down to size, but she would never have been able to achieve what John had.

When the reclusive Viscount Harrow, whose rare presence in society only made him more intriguing, announced that no woman could inspire him to dance and then asked a girl to waltz, he was effectively singling her out as remarkable.

He'd rescued her from Lionell's taunts and, in the process, made her worthy of attention from London's most highly admired. Charlotte felt fine about that. *Absolutely fine.*

It was a kind and courageous and admirable thing that he'd done to put himself in a situation where he was awfully uncomfortable simply to help a stranger. And it was for that reason that the fizzy, bubbly feelings she'd always had for him were settling into something more tangible. She'd always thought him kind, but to see that kindness and selflessness in action only made her admire him more.

But of course, it had to be a dratted waltz he was dancing with Miss Ashby. She was not jealous. Not jealous at all. So what if his shoulders were broad and his arms promised strength and they encircled another woman?

So what if his bearing was perfectly tall and proud? So what if his legs were long and lean and his skin-tight pantaloons molded to thighs and calves that needed no padding and those same legs pressed against another woman's skirts?

"Excuse me," she said to the girls around her who were also standing, mouths agape, watching the most beautiful man in the room dance with their friend.

She went to the retiring room for a moment of peace to gather all the threads of her emotions and wrap them back up, but she was only there for seconds when the door swung open, cracking against the wall with a bang. The attendants flinched and stood at attention.

Charlotte turned slowly, fixing an unfazed aspect to her expression, suspecting who it was before she even laid eyes on them.

"What are you up to?" Luella hissed at Charlotte.

Ever mindful of who was watching, Charlotte smiled sweetly. "Lady Luella, how lovely to see you again."

The smile Luella returned was as fake as her own had been. She threaded her arm through Charlotte's and towed her toward a corner where they couldn't be overheard.

"I repeat, what are you doing?"

"I'm dancing and talking and trying to relieve myself, which you are interrupting."

Luella's eyes narrowed. "With Lord Harrow. What are you doing with the viscount?"

"Nothing," Charlotte snapped. "We have not even danced together."

"And yet all the talk is of how the reclusive viscount is spending his time with a certain duke's sister. He is *my* fiancé. There is a contract."

Frustration boiled up inside her. "A contract that he didn't sign. That he had no part in. That he doesn't *want*." Luella truly was the devil.

"If that's the case, then why hasn't he cried off? Why hasn't he come to see my father or sent word to our solicitor to say that he will not honor Walter's commitment?" Luella's voice wavered at the fourteenth Viscount Harrow's name.

*Walter.* Luella had been on a first name basis with him. It had been more than an arranged match then. A courtship, maybe? Regardless, it didn't excuse Luella's attempts to trap John now.

"Perhaps the temptation of your dowry is proving difficult for Lord Harrow to break from. That was the purpose of your father offering such an obscene amount, was it not? To encourage men to overlook their distaste for you?"

They were cruel and hurtful words, and Charlotte regretted them the moment they were out of her mouth. Whatever enmity there was between the two of them, she had never before said something so bitter. Not to anyone. Not to a person's face, anyway. A Wildeforde was better than that.

Charlotte went to apologize, but Luella's expression was so full of hatred that she recoiled.

"You are jealous," Luella spat. "Walter loved me, and now his brother will marry me and you'll still be the duke's little sister on the shelf."

A wash of shame crept over her. Luella was right. Charlotte *was* jealous. Luella could solve John's problems in a way that Charlotte couldn't. If John's creditors got impatient, there was still a very good chance that Luella would end up married to the man whom Charlotte cared for.

She hadn't known that Walter and Luella had loved each other, but had she been aware, she would have been sick with envy that her nemesis had found love first.

She couldn't bring herself to deliver a retort, though. Her insult had been an unkindness borne of ill-feeling, and she deserved the insult she received in return. Both of them lost this battle.

"Good night" was the only thing she trusted herself to say before returning to the party.

An hour later, she'd barely said two words to John. He'd danced three times with other women, and every time he and she stood together and the strains of a new song started, another lord would ask Charlotte to dance. And a Wildeforde did not turn down a dance if she was free.

John would sometimes follow, sometimes not. Either way, he ensured the wallflowers were the subject of envy. Not that he was enjoying the attention. He seemed coiled tight, as though ready to flee at the slightest provocation.

His head kept turning toward the gaming room, where they'd yet to make an appearance.

Charlotte tried to keep her attention where it should be—on her dance partner, Lord Mallen—but her gaze kept returning to John, whose audience was billowing in size as the night wore on and more people arrived.

Lord Mallen kept up his usual stream of conversation and it was a good thing Charlotte could talk under water if she needed to because she, hopefully, carried the conversation forward without him being at all aware that her focus was elsewhere.

John couldn't be comfortable. He was a man of few words, and the crowd he was surrounded by would demand more than a few from him. He slipped a hand into his pocket and Charlotte could imagine the *tap, tap, tap* of his hidden fingers.

She circled her dance partner, ducking beneath the arms of the couple next to her.

John pushed his spectacles up his nose.

She circled again, holding Lord Mallen's hand high as a couple ducked beneath.

John crossed his arms.

She circled again.

John was gone.

As Lord Mallen escorted her down the middle of the line, she scanned the crowd. She only had to follow the ripple of turning heads to find him. Some of the younger women ducked behind their fans, hiding their blushes. Older women—married, widowed, spinsters—did not even bother to hide their ogling. The elusive viscount, more handsome than they'd expected and just as intriguing.

He escaped the ballroom through the door that led to the main house. Was he leaving? What had been said? They still had a job to do.

Despite the urge she had to follow him immediately, she kept on dancing. There were only a few refrains left, not worth the gossip that would ensue if she left the floor midway through. So she smiled and laughed and looked for all the world as though she weren't deeply concerned. When the music ended, she didn't wait for Lord Mallen to escort her.

"Excuse me, my lord. I have a pressing matter to attend to." She wove in and out of the crowd, avoiding those who would want to engage her in conversation, smiling apologetically as she navigated her way around groups.

Once she reached the foyer, there were two paths he might have taken. The first led outside to where the carriages were, but she didn't think that he would have left before they'd visited the gaming rooms.

The other path led down the hall. There were sitting rooms in that direction and an orangery. He might have gone into any of them.

The first three were locked; clearly their hosts did not want to risk the scandal of inappropriate liaisons. The door to the orangery was not. As she pushed it open, the sweet scent of citrus hit her.

Lamps were lit along the paved path that ran the perimeter of the room. Another path meandered through the potted garden. She took it, knowing a bench seat sat in the middle of the sanctuary. As she turned a corner around an old and large bergamot, she saw him there, lying on the bench, his legs hooked over one end, his head propped up against the other. He was staring up through the glass ceiling to the sky beyond, where the moon, hidden by heavy clouds, cast a silver glow to their edges.

He was beautiful like this. The tension that had infused his expression since they'd arrived at the ball had vanished. "You look thoughtful," she said.

He lurched upward at the sound of her voice. "Charlotte," he said, his shoulders relaxing as he realized who had intruded on his space. He stood immediately. "This is not the most effective of hiding places, then."

"Not one I would rely on, no. Are you well?" That he had come in here to hide suggested he was not. She clasped her hands firmly together to keep from brushing back the lock of hair that had flopped into his eyes.

"I'm well. I simply needed a moment to breathe." He gestured to the bench, and she sat at one end, spreading her skirts so that they folded in neat waves.

"I needed a break from all the...fawning," he said as he sat, leaning with his back against the side of the bench so that he faced her.

"Much to the chagrin of the ladies. You seem most popular." She hoped her jealousy hadn't escaped into her tone.

John grimaced. "Popularity is not my preference. I'd much rather we go straight to the gaming room. Small talk is exhausting." He took off his spectacles and pulled a handkerchief from his pocket.

It was interesting, this idea that people exhausted him, though it explained his absence from society. "I find the opposite true," she said. "Nothing energizes me like a crowd. When the season ends, I count down the days until it begins again."

He cocked an eyebrow. "You don't find the conversation vapid and superficial?"

She cocked her head. "No."

His lips pressed thin and he tapped them with his fingers, a sign that he was mulling things over. "How often can you talk about the weather before you feel as though you're a parrot?"

She rolled her eyes. "I rarely talk about the weather, at least not with friends, and I'm friends with almost everyone."

John shook his head. "It's not possible. You cannot have that many friends."

What a bizarre statement. "Why not?"

"Because friends are those who you can trust completely, who are there for you, regardless of time or distance, who truly know every aspect of you."

Charlotte had never thought to define friendship, but if she had, it would have been a somewhat looser definition. "How many friends do you have?" she asked.

"Five."

"*Five?*" He said the number with such immediate conviction. Charlotte couldn't count the number of friends she had if she were given a day to do it. "But you have people you work with every day. Surely, they're friends?"

John shook his head. "We're friend*ly*. I like them well enough, but no; they aren't friends."

His reasoning was so foreign. If you spent time together and you were friendly, wouldn't that automatically constitute a friendship?

"Goodness, then what am I?" she asked. "One of your

special five?" She regretted the words as soon as she spoke them. It was difficult enough to be told he did not want to marry her. Her heart couldn't take being told he didn't even consider her a friend. She held her breath, waiting for the answer.

He cocked his head, his soft lips pursed in thought. "No."

"Oh." All breath escaped her, and she sagged under the heavy disappointment. "Well, that's flattering, that I'm not even a friend." She tried to keep the hurt from her voice but had little success. They should just go to the gaming room and get this night over with.

He straightened, a hand reaching out and landing in the space between them, just inches from her leg, nudging the edge of propriety. "You are not a friend. You're something I cannot classify."

His words electrified the space between them, as though they were a promise, implied but not made, that changed the order of things. She could classify him well enough—he was an unrequited infatuation. An impossible tendre. A man who would likely break her heart with a mallet that she, herself, put into his hands. "Well, I'm not sure that's better," she said, shifting uncomfortably. "You make me sound awfully like a strange bug."

He smiled. "You are a little strange to me. Your entire world is, with its constant flitting about. Why can't you be alone?"

No one had ever asked that of her before. Everyone knew she was a social butterfly who could be found at almost every ball, who danced with every man who asked, and who was rarely at home. It was part of what people admired about her. John was the first person to speak of it as though it were a flaw, or something unusual that had to be explained.

The truth was, being alone made her jittery. Her eyes would keep flicking toward the door, wishing that any-one would enter. She rarely allowed solitude to happen. On the occasional morning that she had no plans, she'd seek her brother or sister, or have Grace attend to her in the sitting room. The murmur of conversation would quiet her nerves.

"You know my mother," she said. John nodded. He'd been on the receiving end of the dowager's sharp tongue on more than one occasion. "Well, after my father's death, she developed exceedingly high expectations of how a Wilde-forde should behave. We were to be the perfect family, as though it could make up for his scandal."

"Oh, I know," John said. "I saw how she treated your brother. Edward spent his entire youth trying to live up to her expectations."

"Well, whenever I didn't meet her lofty standards, she would punish me. Not with a rod," she said when John's body tensed. "Not as she did with Ned and Will, although I'd have preferred that. Instead, she would stop talking to me. She would stop listening to me. She would pretend I didn't exist. If I did not behave like the perfect lady, if I was not cherished by all, she completely withdrew her affection."

"That's awful," John said. "I am sorry." He shifted closer to her until his leg pressed against hers. The touch of him, their first actual contact that wasn't gloved hand on sleeve, was less thrilling than it was oddly comforting. It spurred her to tell him the worst of it, the part she'd never even told her brothers for fear of them realizing how very disappointing she must have been to deserve it.

"If I failed too badly, Mother would forbid the household staff from talking to me, even my nanny. They wouldn't look at me; they wouldn't speak to me; they wouldn't come when I called. I know, now, the impossible situation they were in. They had their own families to think of and any servant who showed me even a little kindness during those times disappeared the next day. But that sense of loneliness was ghastly."

Ghastly was an understatement. It had been soul-crushing, and she had done everything in her power to avoid it, whether that meant acquiescing to her mother's ridiculous demands, helping anyone who asked so that she would always have an invitation and somewhere to be, or asking her maid to share a bed until she fell asleep.

"That's not right," he said. "She was such a *b*— cow." He reached over and took Charlotte's hand, untwining it from the skirts that she'd clenched into knots without even realizing. "The thought of you hurt and alone makes my chest ache. You are too good, too kind, to be treated that way."

He raised her hand and pressed a kiss to it, his thumb brushing against her fingers as he drew back. *That* touch was more than comforting. It made the hairs on the back of her neck stand and her heart skip a beat before working double time. For a moment, she forgot how to breathe. She swayed toward him, inhaling the clean sweet scent of citrus, her head spinning.

For the barest second, his grip on her hand strengthened, as though he, too, had experienced something unexpected, and then he pulled away.

"No." She raised a hand to his cheek, and he stopped still. His lips were so perfect, so pink, so soft. She stroked them, and he inhaled swiftly. Even through the silk of her gloves, she could feel his warmth. Unsure of what she'd see, she looked up, meeting his gaze. His green eyes swam with the desire she knew he could see in hers. He didn't soften, though. He sat as rigid and as beautiful as marble.

She leaned forward and the breath that proved he was living mingled with hers. Slowly, tentatively, she raised her lips to his and kissed him. It was sweet and soft and every-thing a first kiss should be. Her other hand lifted by its own accord, finding rest on his jacket, through which she could feel the erratic *thump-th-thump* of his heartbeat.

She pulled away, head still spinning, but it was his turn to murmur "no." He took her face in his hands, his fingers sinking into the back of her hair. *He* kissed *her* and it was not a light embrace. There was an urgency to the press of his lips, and his fingers tightened in her curls. His tongue stroked her lips and, tentatively, she opened them, gasping as his tongue immediately sought hers out, exploring it in a way that left her unsure what was happening.

"Charlotte." He pulled away at her hesitation, and she felt the loss deep within her.

"No." She wrapped her hand around his neck and pulled him toward her, perhaps not sure what she was doing but certain that she wanted to keep doing it. Her lips met his. It was her turn to explore, her tongue reaching forward. His groan sent goose bumps skittering across her skin.

He scooped her up into his lap where the strength of his desire was plain and heat swirled in her belly, sending a tingle down her spine and lower. His fingers grazed across her back, leaving trails of desire across her.

He nudged her head backward, his lips trailing across her neck, finding a place beneath her jaw that made her throb. His hot breath on her ear made her shiver.

"John," she whispered, her fingers digging into his shoulder. "Please." She did not know what she was begging for; she simply knew that this was just the barest hint of what she could feel.

Her plea had the opposite effect to what she intended. He pulled back, and her desperate "no" went unanswered. Mortified, she shuffled off his lap.

He grasped her hands before she could get up and away. "I cannot do this," he said. "I promised...We simply cannot."

Her eyes were hot with tears. "Because you're going back to America?"

"Yes."

"And if you weren't?"

John looked agonized. "There is no point dwelling on what might be, no matter how pleasant the dream."

*Chapter 12* ────────────────

Despite the drizzle of rain, John walked the four London blocks from the Mottram residence to his home, his collar turned up to ward against the cold stream of water that tried to make its way down his neck. That, and the splash of mud that would take him an hour to clean from his shoes, was a bitter reminder that his moment with Charlotte in the warm and heavenly scented orangery was an aberration. A misstep that could not be replicated.

Charlotte was the quintessential lady of the beau monde. She wanted, and deserved, to marry a quintessential lord who could provide her with everything that meant—a thriving home, not one that was barely staffed and mostly closed, and a husband who could match her vivaciousness in every way, not a grump who would avoid every one of her favorite activities if given half the chance.

Wilde had forbidden John from pursuing his sister for

many excellent reasons. If he was a man of honor, he would keep his distance, whether he wanted to or not.

As he turned his key in the front door, he could hear the scrabble of claws on marble, and as he opened it, Newton was there, tail wagging, with a big deerhound grin. He dropped his head, the brisk wag of his tail slowing, as though he could sense that something was amiss. He stood on his hind legs, his paws on John's shoulders, and nudged John's face, rubbing against him as though he were trying to pat his master.

"All right, all right." John nudged Newton off of him and dropped to his haunches to give the dog a thorough rub behind the ears, turning his head away as Newton licked him with his giant tongue.

"Thanks, puppy," he said, wiping his cheek with the back of his glove. "It's good to see you too."

Part of him wanted to go to bed to catch up on the sleep he'd missed over the past week, but he knew that the moment he closed his eyes, she would appear and any sleep he got would be infiltrated by dreams of her.

The rest of him knew that if he could get at least one of the inventions in his head to work in reality, he might avoid marrying Luella for her money. He could go back to America.

*Or you could marry because you want to.*

John pushed that thought aside. He would not betray his best friend like that. Without Wilde's approval, he could never conceive of marrying Charlotte. That didn't mean thoughts of her weren't plaguing him.

Never before had he met a person with such a large heart. If someone was hurt, she wanted to soothe them. If someone had a problem, she wanted to fix it. She didn't just express sympathy and move on with her day; she took action. She used her privilege for those who had none.

She was exceptional. When she'd kissed him tonight, his heart and his body had come to the same conclusion—they wanted her. They wanted her in his life, in his bed, in his space. Always. Marriage to her could be a beautiful thing.

Only his head kept him from making a mistake that would ruin them both. Logically, he knew he and Charlotte were too different for a marriage to work.

In a foul mood, he withdrew the promissory notes they had won that night and stuffed them into the top drawer of his desk. Reliving that blasted kiss had made cards far more difficult than it should have been. Lucky for them, Lord Chalders and Lady Fierst had been novice players—plenty of money in the pot, but no strategy between them.

Even through the heavy tension between him and Charlotte, they had communicated well enough to take every trick that mattered. One hundred pounds down. Only thousands more to go.

John picked up the coil of wire and long bar magnet that sat on his desk. Michael Faraday had recently published a paper demonstrating how electrical energy—the same energy that traveled through lightning bolts—could be generated with just these two small objects. At a much lower level, of course, but still it was a discovery that promised endless possibilities.

Something in John knew that this electricity generator was exactly what was needed to make his telegraph work. If he could send electrical signals down a wire, all he would then need to do would be to devise a way for them to be interpreted. Of all of John's ideas, this was the one most likely to bring in enough blunt to solve his problems. The question was—could he do it in time?

John took the coil of wire and magnet and exited through the glass doors into his backyard. Days ago, he had dragged an old chaise longue from a seldom-used drawing room out onto the terrace. Mosely had thought him mad, but when John looked out into the depths of the garden— the copse of trees, the massive vines covering the back wall, the rambling rose garden—he almost felt like he was home. It was the closest he was going to get to wilderness here in London.

As he sat, he turned the wire over and over in his hands, letting his brain tumble over all the fragmented pieces of information in it.

He lost track of time. It must have been hours he sat out there. Newton had fallen asleep next to him. The hound's gentle snore matched the relaxed *whoosh* of John's breath.

Light appeared, interrupting the darkness. His eyes were drawn to it. To her. Charlotte was at a window on one of the upper floors of Wildeforde House, her hands reaching behind her neck as she fiddled with the clasp of her necklace.

She turned her head to talk to someone, gave them a smile, turned around, and put her hands to her collarbone as her maid joined the tableau, unclasping the necklace.

The gentle intimacy of Charlotte's movements tugged at his chest. She was so open and trusting. When he'd pulled away from their kiss that evening, her eyes had filled with tears and embarrassment.

He couldn't let this—whatever it was—continue. They

would never suit, despite how the warmth in his gut said otherwise. Allowing her any closer than she'd already finagled was going to hurt them both in the end when he left for America, or when she realized how incompatible they were and she left him for a proper lord.

That would break him in a way he'd steadfastly avoided since childhood.

John was still twenty yards from Wildeforde House when he saw Charlotte on the corner of the street waving down a hack. The furtiveness of her expression, her unusually plain attire, and the way she tipped her head away from people, letting her bonnet shield her face, set alarm bells ringing within him.

The hack had barely stopped moving before she had the door open and she disappeared inside. With a soft thwack of the reins, the horse took off, giving John a split-second decision: respect Charlotte's clear desire to be alone or follow, because she was not as good at scheming as she thought and she was clearly up to something nefarious.

"Blast." Charlotte was a highly intelligent woman who thought she could handle any situation. She had no maid with her and had dressed too plainly to be visiting a friend. He could think of a hundred different places she might go where she really shouldn't.

John waved down a passing cab. "Follow them."

The two cabs drove for almost an hour. The farther they traveled from Mayfair, the larger the pit that formed in his stomach. By the time they pulled to a stop in a rundown street, the road pitted with holes and the buildings one on top of the other with barely any light squeezing between them and no greenery to be seen, his dread had coalesced into anger. She was putting herself in danger traveling alone to such a place.

Ahead of him, Charlotte exited the cab and was immediately swamped by children, all with their hands outstretched. Charlotte dug into her reticule. When John reached her, she was pressing wrapped peppermints into their hands. She was so absorbed in her cheerful teasing she didn't notice him approach.

"Do you always carry a sweet stall in your pelisse?"

Charlotte gasped, her hand flying to her chest. The children scattered. "John. What are you doing here?"

"I could ask the same. Without your brother or a footman or even a maid, Charlotte."

"It's really none of your business."

He snorted. That was laughable. "Given how doggedly you involve yourself in my business, that's not an argument I'll accept. What are you doing here?"

She pressed her lips together and picked up the large basket that sat at her feet.

"Charlotte..."

She shook her head, steadfastly refusing to talk. That must be killing her. The Charlotte he knew *never* refused to talk. What the devil was going on, then? If she was here for a legitimate reason, she would say so.

He snatched off the cloth that covered the basket, not

sure what he expected to see but certainly not expecting a posy of dried herbs. "Sage?"

"You burn it and it clears all the negativity from your surroundings," she snapped.

"I—" She had never struck him as the superstitious type. He picked up the next item. "And the fern?"

"Lady Hastings was reading the most interesting book. There's a Chinese practice called feng shui. It can create positive energies."

He sighed. He knew what feng shui was—a pleasant concept with no grounding in science at all. "And this?" He held up a candle.

A muscle ticked along Charlotte's jaw. "I spoke with an apothecary yesterday, who swore that burning fir tree oil would lift the spirits."

John restrained an eye roll. This was the hocus pocus he expected from the ignorant, not an educated woman like Charlotte. "What is all of this supposed to achieve?" Perhaps it was a misguided effort to improve the welfare of an orphanage or such.

Charlotte flicked her gaze over her shoulder to a building across the road. As she did, the skin around her eyes tightened. When she looked back at John, her eyes were full of tears.

He reached for her free hand, entwining their fingers. "Charlotte, what is it?"

She swallowed, her throat bobbing. "Will has returned."

Her brother? "Isn't he fighting in Burma? Does Edward know?"

"No," she said loudly, and her fingers tightened on his. "And he cannot know. You must not tell him. Not yet, anyhow. Not until I can find a way to…" She closed her eyes and shook her head, and the way her usually straight shoulders slumped made her look decades older than she was.

"Charlotte." He pulled her close, wrapping an arm around her and resting his chin in her curls. Whatever it was, he would help her with it. She would not have to face it alone. "Are you in trouble?"

She tipped her face upward, her expression the picture of resignation. "You'd better come inside."

As they entered William's apartment, John was hit with the stench of unwashed bodies, human waste, and vomit. It was not unlike parts of his trip from Boston back to England, when the wind was up and seasickness was high.

William was sitting in the corner of the room with his head lolled, his back against the wall, a blanket draped over him. At the other end of the room was a small palette. A young boy with red hair lay on it curled.

The boy sat up when the door clicked shut, rubbed at his eyes, and then jumped to his feet, giving a surprisingly snappy bow for somebody who was asleep ten seconds prior. He looked no more than fifteen years, yet he had the bearing of a military man.

"Good morning, m'lady."

"Good morning, Private James. This is Lord Harrow." Charlotte reached into her basket and removed the herbs, plant, and candles, placing them on a table. Then came packages of wrapped cloth that he hadn't investigated. She handed them to the private, who clutched them eagerly and murmured his thanks. The boy unwrapped them, revealing blocks of cheese, cooked sausages, bread, and four pigeon pies.

Apparently, John wasn't the only person Charlotte was feeding from the Wildeforde kitchens. He wondered if her brother had noticed the increase in his food bill.

The boy got to laying the table while Charlotte crossed to William, who was still lying in the corner. "Brother, it's time to eat."

Will's eyes fluttered open. The look he gave his sister was full of contempt, and John wanted to smack the expression from him. Charlotte didn't deserve that attitude from anyone.

She and the private dragged William upright and half carried him to a chair by the table. His breeches were split from hip to knee, revealing a wide bandage that spanned his entire upper leg.

"Perhaps today we can go for a carriage ride, my darling," she said as she crossed the room. "I could ask Swinton to bring the landau so that you can get some fresh air. I'm sure that would help you feel better." She pushed open the room's only window.

William didn't respond. He didn't acknowledge John's presence. He just pushed around the food on his plate without eating it.

It had been a long time since John had seen Wilde's younger brother—close to a decade. Back then, William had been tall and full, a strapping lad who liked to eat, box, and mess about. Now he was gaunt. There were hollows beneath his cheekbones and the clothing he wore hung off him. He had the pallor of a man who'd experienced too much drink and too much pain.

Around him, Charlotte was placing candles on various pieces of furniture. Will didn't react to any of it. He sat unresponsive in the chair, no doubt an effect of the half-empty bottle of laudanum on the shelf. Physicians were quick to prescribe the stuff, but John had seen how it could ravage a person, and he wondered how bad William's injuries were and whether he still needed the pain relief. In John's experience, it was better to endure some discomfort than to fall into the grip of opiates.

Charlotte continued to prattle on in a one-sided conversation about the lords and ladies of the *ton*. John tensed as she spoke of the Mottram ball, even though he knew she would not tell her brother about their kiss.

Having placed all of her candles, Charlotte took two posies of dried herbs, held them to a candle until they were alight, and then smothered them until the flames no longer leapt and the posies simply smoldered, leaving a trail of smoke as she walked around the room.

That caught Will's attention. "What are you doing?"

She didn't answer, she just kept muttering a phrase in broken Latin over and over.

"What are you doing?" he demanded with more force.

The red-headed private spoke up. "I think she's warding off your demons, Captain. I've seen my grandmother do it."

"Don't!" Will lunged for Charlotte.

John had never moved so fast in his life. He intercepted William before the boy could reach his sister, tackling him to the ground.

Charlotte gasped. William struggled for a moment, grunting in pain, but quickly gave up, his body going limp beneath John's. The boy sobbed. "I deserve my demons. Don't take them, please. Don't take them from me. I deserve to be haunted."

Charlotte's hand flew to her mouth, her expression horrified, as though William's words were more than a blow. They cut her deeply, and her small gasp nicked at John's own heart.

Satisfied that the shaking lad beneath him posed no danger to her, John eased off him. "It's all right, lad. We aren't taking anything from you." He pushed to his feet. With Private James's help, he guided William back to the chair. The younger Stirling brother slumped over the table, his back heaving.

Charlotte rushed to him, stroking his hair. "Hush, brother. All will be well."

John doubted it. He'd seen this before. War did awful things to people. It could destroy the mind just as easily as it could destroy the body. Except, unlike missing limbs, scars to the mind were impossible to see and just as impossible to heal.

For all of her love and commitment, Charlotte would not be enough to fix her brother the way she fixed everything else. The boy needed help that she couldn't provide, no matter how much she loved him. No candles, no burning herbs could help someone overcome this level of trauma.

John stood and went to each candle, snuffing them out. He was by the door when the young private joined him.

"The captain is not a bad person," the boy said, his good arm carrying Charlotte's basket. "Whatever he says, he doesn't deserve this."

"No one does." John knelt to snuff the candles on either side of the entrance and then placed each in the basket Private James held out.

"The captain saved my life; he saved many lives. The

ones he took, he did by necessity. Anything else that happened, well, that wasn't intentional. He would never have done it if he'd known what they would do with it."

"What do you mean?" John asked. "What did he do?"

The boy shook his head. "'Tis not for me to share, m'lord. But his intentions were good. He would never have done it otherwise."

# Chapter 13 ─────────

As they crawled into the hack, Charlotte tried hard to keep the tears back. It appeared every time she visited, William's body had healed a little more and his mind had deteriorated.

She couldn't look at John, instead she kept her eyes trained on the scenery they were passing. The clouds that had been threatening to open all day gave way, sending large, fat raindrops rolling down the carriage windows, turning her view of the world watery.

"He needs help, Charlotte."

"I know that. Do you think I haven't been trying? Do you think I haven't been doing everything within my power? There are very few resources for returning soldiers. No one knows what to do with them, so they don't even try, and nothing I do seems to work. He's not improving at all."

John sighed, running his hands through his hair, leaving

locks of it standing out at jarring angles. "You can't fix everything, Charlotte, as much as you might wish to. Some things are beyond you. Men like your brother need more money and expertise than you have."

"I am his sister. I am a highly capable woman who has solved many problems. I should be able to fix this."

"Wilde has more resources than half the country combined. He should know about this. He may be able to do more than you can."

He said it kindly, but it still felt like censure, mostly because that same thought raised its head every time she despaired. "I *can't*. Will won't allow it. He's so angry."

John was going to argue, going to make a very valid point that she'd not be able to defend against. Going to say that perhaps it was time to think about what Will needed rather than what he wanted. But what he really needed was her, and if she betrayed him now...

"I could have all the money in the world and there still wouldn't be help for him. Chelsea hospital has been at capacity for over a decade, filled with soldiers of Waterloo with long-term injuries who still cannot be discharged."

John reached across the carriage and put a reassuring hand on her knee. "There are other options, Charlotte. There are hospitals that deal specifically with illness of the mind."

Charlotte's blood turned ice cold and she pulled away from him. "Are you suggesting my brother go to *Bedlam*?" Rarely was she moved to violence, but at this moment the temptation was strong. The rumors that swirled about England's mental asylums were horrifying. The things that they purportedly did to patients beggared belief.

"I will never, ever allow that," she said. "Which means,

I'm it. I'm all he has. So you can either help or you can leave."

And she would be forced to solve this on her own again.

John switched sides, coming to sit beside her. He put an arm around her shoulder and tugged her close until she was resting against him, inhaling his sweet scent of bergamot and charcoal. Her heartbeat slowed and the tension that had her coiled tight since Will's outburst began to dissipate.

"I'll help, Charlotte." He murmured softly. "You're not in this on your own."

⁓

As usual, she was mobbed for sweets the moment she stepped out of the carriage. One child looked up at Charlotte, drawing her lips back in a wide, awkward smile.

"Oh, Mary. You've lost a tooth! When did that happen?"

"Yesterday," the girl said, popping a candy in her mouth.

"Well, that is very exciting. You simply must have an extra sweet for such an accomplishment." She pulled another wrapped lolly from her reticule and handed it over. Grubby hands snatched it.

Charlotte tousled the young girl's hair, bid the children farewell, and crossed the street to William's boardinghouse. As she climbed to the second floor, she greeted his landlady, handing over a small packet that held next week's rent. It had wiped out her savings, but at least she hadn't had to sell any of her things. Yet. She would need to convince him to come home soon, though, or else she'd be making friends with a pawnbroker.

Unusually, the door was locked when she tried to open

it. She pulled out the spare key the landlady had given her and let herself in.

The stench in the room was worse than outside. William had given up bathing. His chamber pot was full, and this morning there was the distinct aroma of vomit in the air, tinged with the acrid smell of smoke. Private James was nowhere to be found.

Charlotte crossed to the window and pulled back the curtain, letting in what light she could, given the window opened up directly onto another building.

From the opposite corner, William whined in protest, throwing an arm over his face. The sight of him, huddled in the corner in yesterday's clothes with a blanket haphazardly drawn over his chest, caused a now-familiar wrench of her heart.

"Did you fall out of bed or could you not get in it?" she asked as she made her way to him. As she passed the bed, she saw the source of the vomit smell. It covered the pillows and mattress on one side.

Charlotte sat on her haunches in front of him. "Brother?" She put a hand under his chin, raising it so Will's gaze met hers. His eyes were unfocused. Beside him was an empty bottle of whiskey. But this wasn't a *drunk* unfocused gaze— she'd seen him in his cups so often when they were younger that she knew what drunk Will looked like. She glanced up at the table in the room and at the almost-empty bottle of laudanum sitting next to a completely empty bottle of whiskey and sighed.

"The doctor told you not to mix the laudanum with alcohol, darling. It's not good for you." She didn't know where he'd gotten the whiskey from. Thomas had been under strict instructions not to buy William any drink, no matter how much he begged. But clearly, with the private gone, Will had gathered himself together enough to leave the room in search of it. Perhaps that was a good thing. At least he'd attempted walking with the cane she'd brought him yesterday.

"Come on, let's get you up." She was still struggling to lift William's deadweight when Thomas entered. He immediately joined her, wrapping his arms around Will's chest to drag him into an upright position. He looked at Will's slack countenance and then to Charlotte, his eyes wide with worry and regret.

"I'm sorry, m'lady. I had to sleep. The landlady said I could take the empty bed next door if I did some work for her."

"It's all right, Thomas. Let's just get him to the chair." They lugged him to the table. With deft fingers, Charlotte undid the fall of his breeches. The bandages needed to be changed daily and William had refused a nurse, so here she was. While Thomas held him upright, she tugged down her brother's breeches—now far looser on him than they should be—and disposed of the knot around his thigh quickly. The outer bandage came off easily. The bandage that lay directly on the wound required more care.

Will hissed as she peeled it off, and he reached for the laudanum. Thomas knocked it out of Will's grasp with an elbow.

"Bastard," Will muttered.

Neither them reacted to his insult. He'd said the word so often in the past week, it no longer shocked her.

The bullets—at least that was what Charlotte assumed

they'd been—had lodged into William's side, his abdomen, and his upper thigh. Shrapnel had left deep cuts across his right arm. All but his leg wound were almost healed. The battlefield surgeon had done well to save Will's life—one generally did their best for the brother of a duke—but the scars were red and jagged. He would never be his former self again. But Will's thigh no longer festered, and beneath the stitches Charlotte could see new skin forming.

Charlotte reached up to the table and grasped the bottle of silver nitrate and a pair of tweezers. Carefully, she placed small flecks into the wound that strained against the stitches that held the skin close. Then she took a dressing that had been soaking in linseed oil and lime water and covered the wound before wrapping a fresh, dry bandage over it.

"It's looking much better, don't you think?" she asked Will. He didn't respond, but she didn't let that sway her. "I think soon you'll be ready to go outside. Not for a walk; your leg is not yet healed enough, but Swinton could bring the phaeton tomorrow."

She gathered the spent bandages as she spoke. "Fresh air will do you wonders. We don't need to go to Hyde Park, but I'm sure there's someplace by the river that isn't frequented by people we know. The weather is dull and grey, but the rain seems to be holding off."

As she was about to drop the bandages in Will's trash can, her eye caught the source of the acrid smoke that hung in the room. The bin was a burnt-out mess; the sides were covered with soot, and a charred lump sat at the bottom. But the fire hadn't consumed everything. A short length of gold braid had escaped the flames.

*His uniform.*

Charlotte's throat constricted and the tears she was usually so good at holding back sprang to her eyes. *What happened to him?* William had refused to answer questions about his time in Burma. The few times she'd broached the topic, he'd gone white and his face had contorted in pain. Thomas had told her the bare bones of the event that caused Will's injuries, but he'd been frustratingly tight-lipped about everything else.

She dropped the bandages into the receptacle and handed it to Thomas, who'd stripped the bed of its soaked sheets and made short work of clearing the room of all other rubbish. He nodded to her as he left to take the laundry outside.

"Is there anything else you need?" she asked her brother as she took the chair opposite him, reaching over to put a hand on his knee.

He looked up at her. "Money," he slurred.

A wave of disappointment crashed through her. She'd wanted him to ask to come home. Or to ask that she seek out a friend of his. Or a bath. Or a decent meal. Anything that suggested he was returning to life.

She nodded and reached into her reticule, retrieving the necklace Edward had given her last year for her birthday. "Here. Ask Thomas to sell this. It should fetch enough for the two of you to buy what you need."

She put it on the table and he immediately reached for it, gripping tight around the stones with desperate fingers.

She tried not to let that desperation affect her. "Well, let me tell you all about last night."

She was only five minutes into sharing all the gossip she had when there was a knock at the door. Perhaps Thomas had been locked out. Perhaps he was giving the two siblings some privacy. That thoughtfulness aligned with what she knew of him.

Charlotte crossed to the door, initially swinging it wide and then stopping dead at the sight of the people on the other side. Her heart skittered and she would have slammed the door shut if one of the three men before her hadn't put a hand across the doorframe and a foot over the threshold.

She had never seen someone so enormous in her entire life, and her brothers were big men—both well over six feet tall and toned from years of fencing. She didn't get the impression these men used rapiers to settle a disagreement. The big one sported a large bruise across his right eye and cheekbone. The bridge of his nose was split and the hand that prevented her from closing the door had grazed knuckles.

Beside him was a shorter man, thin and reedy, with his hair slicked back in a style that mimicked men of the *ton* but fell short due to the grease. Behind him was a third man, and Charlotte felt a touch calmer at the sight of him. He was the other young soldier who had been in the room the night William had arrived. Private Gray.

She smiled at him, but he didn't return it, so she turned her attention back to the two men in front, not letting her expression dim despite how nervous they made her. "Can I help you?" she asked.

Without a word, the greasy man put a hand on the door and pushed it open, forcing her to take a step back to maintain the distance between them. "I asked if I could help you," she repeated, refusing to retreat any farther, no matter how much she wanted to back away.

"We hear that Billy-boy is back in town. We want a word with him."

She flicked her gaze over their shoulders, hoping to see Thomas. "There is no Billy here. I'm afraid you've got the wrong room." She went to close the door, but instead of leaving, the greasy one pushed past her. Her heart, which already beat as though she'd been dancing for an hour, quickened.

The one she'd seen before—William's army friend—followed the greasy one in. He refused to meet her eye and fidgeted with a button on his ill-fitting coat.

The big one stepped into the center of the doorframe, arms crossed, filling it and essentially blocking any escape route.

Will's apartment, which had already felt cramped, now felt like there was not enough air inside it for everyone.

The greasy one crossed to where Will was slumped back in his chair, face pale, eyes closed, shirt still open.

"Leave him alone." Charlotte lunged forward, but the soldier grabbed her by both arms. She struggled, but his hands dug tight into her flesh.

"Billy-boy." The small greasy one grabbed Will's face in his hands, but Will didn't react.

Charlotte tried to wrest herself free and failed.

"Billy-boy, we've come to collect." He slapped Will across the face. Her brother's eyes fluttered open, but his expression remained slack and there was no sign he knew what was happening.

"Oh, shit," the man said, letting go of Will and letting him slump to the table.

Charlotte sank an elbow into the ribs of the boy who

held her and broke free, rushing to her brother's side. She checked to see if the impact of his head against the table had caused any cut. After assessing that he was well—or at least no less well than he'd been when the men arrived— she turned back to them.

She stood, arms akimbo, ready to give them the dressing down they deserved. She was done being a lady. She was sister to the Duke of Wildeforde, niece to the Duke of Camden, and cousin to the king. They had no idea who they were dealing with. "What do you want?"

"Billy-boy owes us some money."

"My brother has been serving in the military for the past four years. He doesn't owe you anything. Now leave."

They made no move to go. Instead, the greasy one took a step toward her. "That's incorrect, my pretty one. He owed us back then and a lot of interest can accrue in four years. His debt is five thousand pounds, and he has a month to pay it before these wounds of his are the least of his worries."

Charlotte's jaw dropped open. That was an immense sum of money. It was more than her pin money was in an entire year. Where was she possibly going to get such an amount?

"He doesn't have five thousand pounds."

The man stepped forward, leaned past her, and grabbed the necklace that was still clasped in Will's hand. He held it in front of her face. "Do you think we don't know who you are? His brother is a duke. A duke could pay that amount five times over and not even blink."

*Drat.* "William and His Grace are estranged. There is no money coming from there."

He sneered at her. "Well then, you'd better find some

other way of getting us the blunt or your brother is going to pay the cost." He pulled out a card from his inside coat pocket and flicked it onto the table.

She snatched it, letting the corners of the thick card dig into her thumb and finger. It was strangely high quality for the man she was dealing with. It had a name and address. "You're Mr. Brunel?"

The giant in the doorway chuckled. The greasy man shook his head. "No. That'll be my boss, and that address is where the money can be delivered."

Above the address on the card was a club's name—The Lucky Honeypot. "Is this a gambling den?" she asked. Drat William and his consistently poor judgment.

"That's where he lost the money. That's where he'll pay it back. Or where you'll pay it back. Feel free to join us any time if you think you have better luck than your brother." He placed a small token on the table in front of her and then turned on his heel and left the room, whistling.

The former soldier looked at William, his expression filled with regret. As it should be. The two had served together. How dare he betray her brother in such a way?

As the door closed behind them, Charlotte sank into the empty chair, knees shaking. How the hell was she going to get William out of this mess?

*Chapter 14* ——————————

By the time the hack dropped Charlotte off down the street from her house, fear had given way to the Wildeforde family's bullheadedness. Those men had meant serious business and if she didn't find some way of paying them the money that Will owed, he was going to be hurt or even worse.

She needed help from someone with a better idea of what she was dealing with than she had. A life of tea and ball-rooms and charity work had not acquainted her with such men, nor with threats so blatantly physical. She was used to negotiating other types of threats—gossip and rumors and threats to reputation and matrimony—not to having one's legs broken, which was an obvious possibility if she didn't somehow resolve this.

Her first instinct was to turn to Edward. He'd dealt with every one of Will's scrapes since the youngest Stirling brother had been in knee breeches—at least, every scrape Charlotte hadn't fixed before her eldest brother found out about it. There was nothing Ed couldn't handle. Hell, he'd rescued Fiona from jail twice.

But she also knew that if she turned to her brother, William would never forgive her; and she knew that there had to be at least one person in his life whom he could trust.

If she went to Fiona, Fiona would tell Edward, pure and simple. A wife didn't keep these kinds of secrets from her husband. Neither Josie nor Henrietta seemed like appropriate sources of help either, although they'd likely love the intrigue.

The only person she could think of was John. He was the most intelligent man in England. Even more intelligent than Edward. Surely living over in the wilds of America, he'd had some kind of exposure to such rough types.

He would help. She just knew it. He'd held her and told her that she wasn't alone in this, and he was a man of his word.

It was early evening. The streets were awash with *ton* on its way to this dinner party or that performance. She could not risk walking to John's front door, so she walked up the stairs to Wildeforde House, handed Simmons her coat, and walked right through the corridors to the outside. She crossed the garden until she reached the vine-covered wall and the secret door that she knew existed. She'd seen Edward and John use it hundreds of times as children.

She had to push away the ivy that had grown over the wood until she could find the large brass knocker. It was not locked, thankfully. With a grunt, she twisted it until she heard the latch open. She tugged on the handle, but it didn't budge. She pulled harder, her frustration growing as years of dirt and rust refused to yield. With one foot lifted and placed on the wall next to the door and both hands wrapped around the metal, she pulled backward with all of her might.

The door moved—slowly, slowly—until it gave out and she found herself on her arse in the dust.

"Drat." She stood and brushed off as much of the dirt and grass stains as she could, aware that her gloves—marred by tiny holes from the thorns, rust from the knocker, and dirt—had been thoroughly ruined.

Taking a deep breath, she channeled her frustration into purpose and crossed under the mishmash of brambles, through the door in the stone wall, and into John's yard. She was halfway across the garden when she heard the barking. Newton was sprinting toward her. He skidded to a stop at her feet and sat, tail wagging.

"Hello, puppy," she said, leaning over to scratch behind his ears. She looked up and saw John standing in the doorway that led to his study, clearly confused by her intrusion. They had formed some relationship over this past week—though not a friendship according to him—but whatever that relationship was, it did not include casual breaking and entering.

She skirted around the chaise longue that, for some reason she could not imagine, had been dragged outside. "I need help." There was no point prevaricating or wasting time on pleasantries.

He stepped aside immediately, gesturing to the door. She swallowed and entered, perching delicately at the edge of the armchair, too anxious to sit comfortably.

"What do you need?" John asked as he took a seat opposite her. "Tell me and it's yours."

Charlotte sighed, relieved that he'd gone straight to the point. Grateful that, so far, there were no conditions for his assistance.

"I need five thousand pounds."

John rubbed his jaw, then removed his spectacles and scrubbed his hand over his face and through his hair. "Charlotte, you know that I have no money to give. It simply isn't there."

Charlotte raised her hand. "No. No, I know that. I don't need your money. I need your help so that I can get my own money."

He raised an eyebrow.

The idea had come to her on the carriage ride home, as she turned that dratted calling card over and over in her hands.

*If you think you have better luck than your brother.*

Charlotte didn't need luck. Everything she needed was in this room.

"Our winnings are not building quickly enough. The *ton* like to gamble and they have money but the stakes are low because no one is going to play too deep with the grande dames watching over them, ready to gossip at the slightest hint of impropriety."

"I'm listening," he said.

He always listened. No matter how unusable her ideas were, he always listened. "There is a place that people go to when they want to gamble. It's called The Lucky Honeypot." She placed the gambling chip with the bee in the center on the table in front of him. "I know it sounds crazy, but if we're going to earn enough to get both of us out of trouble, then we need to find a deeper game."

"You're not suggesting—"

She cut him off. "I can get us an initial sum of five hundred pounds. We'll go fifty-fifty in all profits. You can pay off your debt and go back to Boston as planned." Her voice cracked a little at that last.

He shook his head. "I cannot let you do this for me. I'll marry Lady Luella before I put you in danger by taking you there."

She shook her head. "I'm not doing it for you." She quickly outlined the events of that afternoon.

John's eyebrows rose, and a muscle ticked along his jaw. He took off his spectacles and wiped them with the handkerchief he kept in his waistcoat pocket. "Five thousand pounds? And you're determined not to go to Edward for help with this? William is his brother. He has a right to know."

"Edward is why William was on a battlefield to begin with. He has the right to nothing where his brother is concerned. I won't betray Will in that manner. This is my only alternative."

John ran his hand through his hair again, leaving the strands sticking up at odd angles. "I can't do it, Charlotte. This place you're talking about is not somewhere a young lady should be. The people who frequent it are dangerous and those that own it are even more so."

Tears burned at the back of Charlotte's eyes. She had been so sure that he would help her. After all, hadn't she moved heaven and earth to help him? "I'm well aware of the danger, thank you. That fact was made clear to me today when those ruffians threatened my brother's life."

"Then you understand why you cannot go there." He sounded as exasperated as she felt.

"I understand you do not know what it means to be family if you think I won't risk my life to save Will's."

He flinched at her words and the anger in them. "There is another, safer option available to you. Wilde can pay Will's debts. I'm not putting your life at risk because your brother holds a grudge."

Frustration roughhoused through her veins like a drunken carriage driver. She stood when she could no longer sit still. "So you won't help me, after all? I'm in this alone?"

"Charlotte." He shook his head, rubbing at the spot between his brows.

Clearly, he thought her foolish. "Thank you for your time, my lord. I'll see myself out."

*Chapter 15* —————————

As John watched Charlotte walk out the double glass doors into the darkness of the garden, guilt swirled through him. Charlotte had so willingly, so enthusiastically, volunteered herself to help him and had continued to do so, even when his disdain for everything she enjoyed crept into his words. She'd been selfless and generous, two qualities often missing in members of the *haute ton*.

The first time she'd asked for anything in return, he'd said no.

In among the guilt he felt was something else—jealousy. There was clearly nothing Charlotte wouldn't do for her brothers, even risk her own safety to get William out of a hole he'd dug himself.

She'd said that he didn't know what it meant to have family, not guessing at how deeply her words would cut, because they were true. He'd never experienced family in the same way she had. Walter had barely tolerated him. He wouldn't go a foot out of his way for John if he could help it. Their parents had been the same. There was literally nothing they *would* have done for John.

The closest John had to family was Wilde and Fiona, Asterly and Amelia, and Oliver. They were the family he had chosen and the people he would do anything for.

Charlotte could never understand it, but his kinship with Wilde was *why* he could not help her. As a youth, Edward had offered him a home away from John's own family. He and Asterly had stood side by side with John as they were pelted with excrement-covered sponges by their peers, who had decided that John's stutter, Wilde's scandalous father, and Asterly's common-born ancestry were reasons enough to make their lives hell.

If it hadn't been for the two of them, John would have never made it through school. John would not betray that friendship by taking Wilde's little sister to a gambling den. That was not how one repaid such loyalty. He'd already crossed the line by kissing her. He would not cross it again. The thoughts that kiss had left him with—wanting another one, another dozen, another lifetime of them—were betrayal enough. He would not add to them.

He picked up the gambling chip Charlotte had left on the table, contemplating her idea as he turned the disc over and over in his fingers. It wasn't a terrible thought. The right game, played with his memory, could clear much of his debts. A couple of right games, and he'd be free. He could even help Charlotte with William's debt without risking her safety at all.

He'd have to be careful, though. Getting caught counting

cards was a sure way to get one's legs broken. He'd need to lose almost as often as he won so as not to attract attention. If he alternated gaming venues, visiting a different club each night, then he'd attract even less notice. All he needed was the blunt for the first game.

        ⌐

John walked down Bond Street doing his best to avoid the looks he was receiving from the many young women for whom a day out shopping necessitated multiple footmen trailing behind with armfuls of packages. A month ago he would have gone unnoticed, but now there were plenty who recognized him, and those who didn't were quickly caught up to speed by their companions.

    The assessing looks he was given made him feel like a lamb at the market, or in a lion's den. He smiled politely, doffed his hat over and over, and yet refused to stop and be forced into conversation.

    He wasn't here to shop or socialize. Thanks to Charlotte's insistence on bringing leftovers to his house every day, his food bill for the week was considerably less than expected. It wasn't much of a saving, but if combined with the money he'd put aside to make small repayments on his debts, it might be just enough to get started with the gaming hustle.

    So he was here to tell his creditors—hardworking business owners—that their next payment would be delayed.

    None of it sat well with him—reneging on his promise to make payments today, counting cards to win against those who didn't have his memory, using Charlotte's idea but cutting her out of the process. It wasn't who he wanted to be, but the thought of marrying Luella, already untenable, had soured further since spending time with Charlotte.

For the first time, the thought of spending his life with someone—having someone there when he woke up, sharing a bed with him at night, having them in his space—filled him with a sense of contentment, rather than dread. Keeping company with Charlotte didn't feel like an activity that was getting in the way of his thoughts.

He passed a tea shop where finely dressed women sat at the windows sipping on drinks and gossiping about all who walked by. The street was humming, but when he went to visit Walter's favorite tailor, the door was shut and the windows had been boarded up. The sign that hung from the wooden boards read CLOSED.

Unease threaded through him. It made no sense that the tailor would be shut on such a busy day. John ducked into the milliner next door.

"Where is Mr. Crabnaught?"

The milliner shook his head. "A right awful business, that. The watch came yesterday morning to drag him to debtors' prison. I knew it was bad, but I didn't realize it was that bad."

The blood drained from John's face. The tailor was in debtors' prison because Walter had run up debts and John hadn't paid them. "The tailor's family?"

The milliner was a big man with a grizzled beard and a thick, corded neck. He looked more like a boxer than a man who worked with fabric, but despite his gruff appearance, tears welled as he spoke. "They took the wife and those two

sweet little girls too. There was no one else they could stay
with, and she couldn't afford the rent on her own. Curse
every lord who thinks he's above paying his bills."

*John* was a man who hadn't paid his bill. He'd yet to
work out a solution to his brother's mess and now a good,
hardworking man and his family were paying the price.

"Thank you for your time," he said, though his throat
strained to say the words.

News of the tailor's incarceration had reached all the
vendors on Bond Street. His intention had been to ask them
each for a week's grace before paying his next installment
and to use that money to bankroll a high stakes game, but
he couldn't bring himself to do it now.

He gave them what cash he had and worthless promises
that he would square away his debts soon. In the past, the
vendors had responded well to John's assurances, but as he
went door-to-door this morning splitting those paltry food
savings among a dozen creditors, John's reception was less
than cordial. Hell, it bordered on ice cold. Every time he
spoke to a vendor he wondered: *Is this the next person to go
to jail for my brother's offenses?*

True, Walter's debts—though sizable—weren't large
enough to be the sole cause of Mr. Crabnaught's incarceration. The tailor likely had many other debtors. But that
fact couldn't deflect the weight of what John now knew he
needed to do.

After making the rounds of tailors and bookmakers and
gun shops, he sat at his desk, reached into the top drawer,
and pulled out that blasted betrothal contract. He would
give himself a week to come up with the money he needed.
He would even involve Charlotte if he must, despite his

instincts to the contrary. But if his debts weren't clear in seven days, he would have Luella's father seek a special license and would be married to her immediately after.

A week was longer than he wanted to see a family in prison. But prison, as awful as it was, was better than the streets, which was where they would be until he could make good, however he had to do it.

Charlotte's heart rate skittered as the wheels of the hackney she'd hired bounced over an uneven gravel road. As far as Edward knew, she was going to the Haversham ball. As far as Fiona knew, she was attending the Lester musicale. She'd told Simmons she was heading to Vauxhall with Henrietta and her husband.

If they discovered she wasn't at one event, they would assume she was at another and that communication lines had simply been crossed.

She turned the calling card over and over in her hands. She'd worried at it so much that the corners had curled and her nails had left notches along the edges. She wished John were there to calm her nerves. She was used to walking into any situation with confidence, but this was something different, and his company would have been soothing. His experience would have been useful because, in all honesty, she had no idea what she was doing. The world she was stepping into was so far from the ballrooms of Mayfair.

She'd visited Madame Bernier that morning, a modiste whose dresses could be found on opera singers and rich widows—never on a respectable young woman. Charlotte had paid a duke's ransom to have another client's almost-finished dress nipped and tucked to fit her instead, with another two dresses on the way—all three deep jewel colors with low necklines and skirts that clung to her body.

She didn't know what to expect from the club she was about to visit, but she thought it was highly unlikely that women present, if there were any women present, would wear prim, white dresses and decolletage-covering fichus.

The cab pulled to a stop. She took a deep, fortifying breath, tied a domino mask to her face, and pushed open the carriage door.

The area was surprisingly full of life. There was a tavern on the corner with flaring lights and blaring music and men leaning against the outside walls, laughing, joking, and smoking cigars. Men and women of all ages and nationalities walked past her, paying her little attention, so engrossed were they in their own conversation. A young boy, tall and lanky but still a child, slowed his run just long enough to doff a cap so worn that patches of it caught the lamplight like a puddle on pavement. He gave a cheeky wink as he passed.

No one looked embarrassed to be here. She had expected a gambling den to be dark and hidden, somewhere men went in secret. That was clearly not the case. There was a big sign above the door. Light blazed from the windows, and the doors were wide open, inviting passersby to enter.

She swallowed and tightened her grip around her reticule, the weight of the gold inside heightening her nerves. She had taken her most elaborate necklace, along with a few pieces no one would notice missing, to a pawnbroker, who had looked at her askance when she entered his premises and then promised to hold them for twenty-four hours before they were put for sale.

If she had the luck she needed, she'd be able to retrieve them tomorrow before anyone noticed they were missing. That is, assuming that she could still win at cards without John's help. She had sent him a letter via her maid, telling him where she'd gone. Perhaps he would change his mind once he realized she was going to do this with or without his help.

She tugged on the edge of her elbow-length gloves, smoothing out the wrinkles. She brushed down the bodice of her oversized coat. Looking left to make sure she wasn't about to be run down by a carriage, she crossed the street, her mouth going dry.

The man at the door in garish livery gave her a speculative look as she approached. She reached up to make sure that her mask was still firmly in place. It might make her stand out in the crowd, but that was preferable to being recognized. If her brother had lost a fortune here, there was every chance other men of the *ton* would be inside.

"Welcome to The Lucky Honeypot, my lady."

Could he tell that she was titled, or did he say that to all women?

"I'm here to play," she said, faking both confidence and an American accent. Better those inside think her a wealthy American heiress than a woman of the English aristocracy.

The butler inclined his head and stood aside so she could enter. Charlotte gasped at the sight in front of her. It was every bit as opulent as a ballroom or a London theater. The chandeliers hanging from the ceiling were ablaze with hundreds of candles. Plush oriental carpets, the kind one saw in a duke's receiving room, helped to section off different parts of the room where men sat around tables playing games that were both familiar—whist and loo— and unknown to her, games with dice and wheels and spinning balls.

"Excuse me, ma'am." A gentleman entering after her brushed past. Charlotte's cheeks flushed as she realized she was still standing at the entrance, blocking the path.

She stepped to the side where a footman was waiting to take her coat. She held it closed fast at the throat. As it was, it covered her from neck to toe, the only way she'd been able to leave Wildeforde House in a dress that would give her brother and her butler an apoplexy if they saw it. The moment she removed it, she would reveal more to these strangers than she ever had before. It was tempting to leave, to turn around and flee from a situation that was so far beyond anything she'd ever experienced. But then her gaze fell on the former soldier, Private Gray, who had been William's friend and was now watching the room with an eagle eye.

If she didn't do this, William could be hurt. That was all the impetus needed for her to remove her coat and hand it to the footman, trying to appear unaffected by the appreciative gazes of the men in the room. The deep red dress with a neckline that only just covered her nipples had felt scandalous in the shop that afternoon. Now it felt positively on fire.

A woman, even more scantily dressed, wearing fabric so sheer her form showed through it, came to Charlotte with a tray of drinks. Charlotte accepted one, took a large sip, and had to swallow her cough, the taste of spirits making her eyes water.

A hand at her chest as the liquid burned her throat, she studied the surrounding tables. There were small ones by the window where couples played whist, but she had no partner to play with. The only other game that looked familiar was a game of chance that William had taught her years ago. She had never actually won a hand of that, though. All she could do was hope that she had better luck tonight.

Curse John for not coming with her.

# Chapter 16 ——————

John's heart did not stop its frenetic racing until he'd crossed the threshold of the gaming hell and saw Charlotte, laughing as though nothing were amiss, at a table with a drink in hand, safe. *Safe-ish.*

He took the first full breath he'd managed since he'd arrived home from walking Newton to see her note sitting in the salver on the hall table. In barely legible hand, clearly written in a hurry, it said: *The Lucky Honeypot tonight.*

The bloody menace. Yet here she was. A mask covered half her face, but the rest of it was all smiles. Her midnight hair cascaded over one shoulder—a looser style than he'd seen on her before. Her dress started his heartbeat racing once more. The neckline was cut low, and the edging of lace made no genuine attempt to hide the swell of her breasts or the deep valley between them. His cock stiffened. This image would plague him for the rest of his days.

She leaned forward, giving the man across the table her full attention—and more. John saw the man's momentary distraction, the way he shook his head before dragging his eyes to Charlotte's face to answer whatever question she'd asked.

John's gut roiled—anger, fear, and jealousy all forming a wicked compound. Still, he had to give her credit. She was playing the game hard with whatever advantages she had.

He gave the footman his coat and stalked over to the card table where a sizable pot sat in front of her.

She glanced up at him briefly, but there was not a trace of recognition in her eyes. She gave him a polite nod and turned her attention back to the chips in front of her. After a thoughtful pause, she pushed a recklessly large pile forward.

The gentleman on her left looked at her bet, sighed, and pushed his own stack toward the dealer. As each man took his turn, a fortune was put on the line.

The dealer cut the deck and flipped the top card over. A ten of hearts. Charlotte flipped her own card over, revealing a jack of spades, and clapped her hands together. Around her, two men chuckled and took their winnings. A larger number grumbled as the dealer raked in their losing chips. Why they'd gambled so heavily on such average hands, John couldn't comprehend.

Finally, after accepting her winnings, Charlotte turned her attention back to John. "Are you going to play, sir, or are you just here for the entertainment?" She gestured toward the dancing women at the front of the room.

The Bostonian affect she gave to her voice was deplorable. No one who'd spent any time in America would believe it. Thankfully, no one around the table showed any kind of suspicion.

"I'm here to play," he said.

Her smiled widened further. "Well then, you must sit by me. I know not the reason, but Lady Luck has blessed me tonight. I've yet to lose. Perhaps some of that fortune will rub off on you."

Her words made his hackles rise. No one was that lucky. A footman hurried over with a chair and the men on Charlotte's right muttered as they shifted to the side so that John could sit.

"Do you have a name, sir?" Charlotte drawled.

"Lord Harrow at your service. But you may call me John."

"Mrs. Brown." She proffered up her hand for him to kiss.

"Mrs. Brown, truly?" he asked before putting her fingers to his lips, luxuriating in the warmth of her skin beneath the silk of her gloves, keeping them there for longer than would have been proper in any other environment.

Her cheeks reddened, but she made no move to pull away. From this close distance, he could see the flutter of her pulse at her throat, and he fought the urge to press his lips there too.

Eventually, a loud cough from beside him broke the moment. He turned and raised an eyebrow at the interfering young man.

"Lord Harrow, may I present Lord Brockford?" She gestured to the whippersnapper at his side. "And these are Lords Hailson, Berridge, and Colton, and Mr. Drevelin."

Each of them nodded in John's direction, but none looked pleased to see him.

"Harrow," Lord Berridge said. "I knew your brother. A

fine chap and a good friend. He always knew how to show people a good time. My condolences for your loss."

John forced a smile to his face. Accepting sympathy for a loss he barely felt was discomfiting. When condolences were served with such heaping praise for his brother, they sat sour in his gut.

The dealer shuffled the cards, his fingers deft. He cut and cut again, so quickly his hands were a blur. It was too quick for John to see proof of shenanigans, but Charlotte could hardly win every hand in a game of chance designed to favor the house without something underhanded at its root.

Cards slid in everyone's direction. John tilted the corner of his just far enough to see what it was: the ace of spades. John's suspicions grew. It was a common strategy, fixing the cards so that a person new to the game won early. It encouraged more reckless wagering and deeper losses later in the night.

Charlotte shifted her wager forward, an amount so high John's mouth went dry. If they were going to work together in this, they needed a mutual understanding of acceptable risk versus reward. Whether or not she knew it, her success was entirely in the hands of the house.

Thankfully, they both won, and then John pushed back his chair. "This game is so frightfully dull, even when you win. Who wants to play whist?"

The dealer frowned. "You've only just started, my lord. It's poor form to cut and run."

John shook his head. "Don't worry, chap. The house has plenty of time to get me elsewhere." Not that he would give them the opportunity. The only games he'd play tonight were the ones he could win with mathematics.

"Mrs. Brown, care to be my partner?"

She fluttered her eyelashes. "That's very forward of you, my lord. We've only just met." Her eyes sparkled. Clearly, she was loving every minute of the deception.

"And yet the devil on my shoulder is telling me you're the angel I need tonight." Two could play at this charade.

She leaned forward, giving him a view of her that made his cock twitch. She put a hand on his and he had to remind himself to breathe. "Well, I can hardly disappoint the devil now, can I?" she said breathlessly. Completely unaware of the wreck her flirtation was making of him, she hailed the footman stationed by their table so he could carry her winnings.

The dealer's countenance deflated, but he put on a false smile that almost disappeared behind his mustache and said teasingly, "You are on such a hot streak, Mrs. Brown. Are you sure that Lady Luck will follow you to another table?"

Charlotte gave the dealer the kind of smile that felled men. "Thank you so much for your company, Mr. Smith. Perhaps I will find my way back to you again."

The dealer's ears turned red and instead of returning to the game at hand, he watched her retreat, a somewhat lovelorn expression on his face.

The other men at the table gave John filthy looks. "That was hardly sporting, Harrow," Lord Berridge said. "You've stolen our entertainment."

His words made John seethe. Charlotte was so much more than a man's entertainment. She was kind and intelligent and loyal. She'd been playing every man at the table including the dealer and not one had picked up on it. She was bold and strategic and possessed of a confidence he could only dream of having.

She was a blessing, and John felt an urge to drag the man from his chair by his lapels and make him grovel at her feet. But all that would do would ensure eyes were on them all night, and he and Charlotte needed to play beneath people's notice as much as possible.

Instead, John pointed to Berridge's dwindling pot. "If you don't turn your attention to your cards, Berridge, you risk being the entertainment for the rest of us."

Berridge's face turned red, and he blustered. Before he could find his words, though, John strolled after Charlotte, trying to match her carefree demeanor as she approached two men lounging by the whist tables, each with a brandy in hand.

John recognized one from the ball he'd attended the other night—Lord Salter. John's heart rate surged. How terrifyingly audacious of her to sit across from a man who knew her face well. Surely, her charade would be uncovered now.

But Salter gestured to one of the empty seats and she lounged, filling the armchair like a silk nightgown thrown over it before lovemaking. It was sensual and self-assured and completely at odds with the bright, proper young woman that the lords knew. It was enough to fool them, apparently.

Heat pooled in his stomach. He didn't know how much of this woman in front of him was an act and how much of it was a part of Charlotte that was reveling in this opportunity to be free of the constraints of a proper young lady.

He took the empty seat opposite her, let Lord Salter introduce him to his playing mate, and then settled in, trying hard to rein in his senses so that his mind could do its job.

Salter dealt the cards. John looked at his hand—it was reasonable. Definitely something that could be worked with. He looked over at Charlotte, who gave him the briefest, most wicked of smiles.

These lords were about to be trounced.

⁓

"That was amazing." Charlotte didn't have the patience to wait for John to take his seat in the carriage. They had been the perfect pair, even more so than when they played in a drawing room. It was as though he could read her mind. Not only had he been so attuned to her that he knew exactly what her hand was and what the next play should be, he ran with her story, never once giving any sign that she wasn't Mrs. Brown or that they'd never met. Never had she felt so *matched*. Of course they won. How could they not?

And lord, she loved winning. She loved winning more than she loved lemon ices and a ballroom crush. She loved it more than Almack's, or rather, she loved Almack's because it was a playing field on which to win. Every person in attendance kept score of who danced with whom, who danced the most, who received the most admiring nods from the patronesses.

If the patronesses had been in The Lucky Honeypot that evening, they would have applauded once they'd overcome their seizure, because she and John had beat everyone in the most elegant manner.

"Amazing? That was incredibly foolish," he replied, but

the censure in his tone was unconvincing, distracted. His eyes were alight; the heat of his gaze burned into her.

"But it worked." They had won two thousand pounds. *Two thousand pounds.* Only a handful more nights and she could pay back William's debt. Only a month or so of this and they could pull John's estate out of trouble. If they sold some more of her jewelry, salvation could be even sooner.

"It worked." His expression didn't change. He continued to look at her as though she were a doe and he were a wolf. As though she was something he wanted very, very badly. She hadn't missed the way his eyes had dropped to her cleavage throughout the night, or the way his gaze had lingered on her lips, the way it was doing now.

Lord, it was hot in the carriage. She pulled her coat away from her body, hoping the night air would cool her. Instead, the sudden draft caused her heightened senses to leap into life.

He shifted in his seat, his legs wide, and her heart beat faster. If she was to sit forward on the edge of her seat, those long legs would envelop her. She'd be surrounded by taught, lean muscle. Heat pooled between her thighs as it had from the moment he'd walked through the doors, hair tousled, cravat hastily tied, eyes wild.

Now that heat pulsated, her body calling for him. She swallowed hard and wondered if he could sense how she was feeling. He seemed to know everything else about her. Her desire was so strong, she couldn't imagine how it could not be written across her face, just like it was written across his.

"I knew you'd come for me." Her voice was barely a

whisper, so difficult was it to speak through the tightening of her throat.

He dragged in a ragged breath. "Charlotte."

The sound of her name on his lips, half prayer and half plea, emboldened her. She didn't care what happened after. She'd waited years to feel like this. Her friends had hinted at what happened between a man and a woman when they were alone. She was done with the hints. She was done with not knowing what everyone else did. To hell with what was proper. A Wildeforde might not kiss a man in a private carriage, but she would, because she was more than simply a Wildeforde. She was Lady Charlotte Stirling and her lungs felt like they were about to bubble out of her chest.

She shifted forward to the edge of her seat and rested a hand on his thigh. His muscles tensed beneath her touch. Tentatively, she ran her hand upward, and he groaned.

His fingers reached for hers, enclosing them, halting their forward momentum. "Charlotte, we can't." His throat bobbed.

"Says who?" If he didn't want her, then she would not press him.

"Your brother."

Bloody Edward. She leaned toward John, caught his chin in her hand, and made sure he was looking at her directly. "I am my own woman who makes her own choices. Has tonight not proved that?"

He closed his eyes as though he couldn't look at her. As though he didn't trust what he'd do if he did. "I made a promise."

"He had no right to ask it of you."

John removed his glasses and scrubbed his hands over his face.

"Do you want me?" she asked, fingers gripping into his thighs. "Because I want you badly. I burn for you. Every inch of my skin feels alive in a way it has never been. It begs to have your hands on it. I watched you from across the table tonight and had to stop myself from reaching for you. I want your lips on mine, so the only question that remains is whether you want me too." She held her breath as she waited for his response.

"Yes, blast it."

*Chapter 17* ————————————

There were many reasons having Charlotte was a bad, bad idea. Her brother was against the match. John and Charlotte wanted very different things in life. And what little he could offer her—a home, a title, a position—was lessened by his inability to do any of it as well as a proper lord should.

But his body wouldn't listen to the logic, no matter how strongly John demanded that it should. Reason had become second fiddle to this biological need to be with her.

He reached across the void between them, hooked one arm around her waist and another across her shoulders, and dragged her into his lap.

She yelped in surprise, and he stilled, relaxing only when she took his face in both hands and mashed her lips to his in an eager, if unpracticed, kiss.

"Charlotte," he murmured when she pulled back for breath.

"Mmm?" Her eyes were wide and fixated on his lips.

He was about to tell her they shouldn't, that it was his mistake for instigating it. But then she caught a lock of his hair and tucked it behind his ear. The graze of her fingertip sent shivers down his spine. She placed a hand against his chest and immediately his heart *th-thump*ed erratically. She smiled as she noticed, biting her lower lip and casting her eyes downward.

His gaze followed...right to her neckline, where her breasts pulled tight against silk. His cock throbbed. He held on to his control by fingernails only.

She looked up shyly, eyelashes fluttering.

*Blast it.* She was playing him as skillfully as she played the men around the gaming table. She might be unpracticed in the physical art of lovemaking, but she was a master flirt who was leading him around by his cock.

"Just a kiss," he whispered, more to himself than to her. He skimmed his hand up her spine, taking delight in the way she shivered, and pulled her head toward his. He kissed her, softly, gently, pulling back for a moment and then pressing forward, letting her lips chase his. She was not the only one skilled in the art of the tease.

When she relaxed against him, he sank his fingers into her hair, pressing her closer to him. He opened his mouth, let his tongue run along the edge of her lips.

She started in surprise, and he paused until she relaxed once more. She opened up, just a fraction. It was all he needed. His tongue thrust forward; she responded in kind, and his cock strained against his breeches. She tasted so good—like honeysuckle on a warm afternoon.

She shifted, trying to get closer to him, completely

unaware of how the friction of her movements sent sharp bursts of pleasure through him.

"Oh God, Charlotte." He pulled away before he completely lost control. Her chest heaved, her collarbone rose and fell just inches from his lips. He bent forward, dragging his tongue along the edge of her dress. Her fingers dug into his shoulders and her head fell back.

"Please," she whispered, though he doubted she knew what she was begging for.

With one hand on her back, supporting her, he brought the other forward, cupped his hand around her breast and squeezed. She gasped.

He ran his thumb across the silk and felt her nipple harden beneath his touch. If he hadn't already been stiff, that slight movement would have done it. He leaned forward, his lips grazing across her skin, his tongue along her neckline, catching under the edge of the lace. She gasped again, and he squeezed her breast.

"More," she whispered.

He was happy to oblige. He hooked his fingers into the silk, tugging down until her breasts sprang free. He kneaded them in his hands, relishing how she moaned until he could no longer resist, and he leaned forward, capturing her nipple in his mouth, suckling gently, grazing his teeth across them.

Her breath hitched. Her chest stopped its expanding and contracting. He pulled away to see her eyes closed, her mouth gaping.

"Charlotte, breathe."

Her eyes flew open, her gaze locked on his, and she nodded, dragging in a breath. "I never knew," she whispered. "Is it always like this?"

*This* was not even the best of it, but he could already categorically say that no, it was not always like this. Never had he been with a woman whose moans wrapped around his heart and pulled the way Charlotte's moans did. Never had the feel of a woman's skin beneath his lips caused his insides to shiver. Never had such a relatively chaste encounter made him want, desperately, to take a woman and never let go.

John hooked an arm under her legs and transferred her to the opposite bench.

Her face fell. "We're not stopping?"

They should. He should. "Not if you don't want to."

"I don't." She shook her head vigorously.

"What do you want, Charlotte?" he asked, knowing her answer could mean the ending and beginning of so many things. Knowing that what happened next could fundamentally change his life.

"I want everything."

There were many reasons everything was a bad, bad idea, and for those, he would not have her the way he wanted. But for this unexplainable pull between them, he would give her what he could.

So he dropped to his knees on the carriage floor.

John was as early as he could be without raising stares. He'd paced in his rooms for a good half hour, checking his pocket watch every few minutes, until the hands showed fifteen minutes before the time stated on the invitation.

Now he was here, just him and his hostess in her drawing room making light conversation, waiting for Charlotte.

"Is it normally as wet as this in April?" he asked. "I don't remember it being so, but then I've spent the past four years abroad."

Lady Braddon shook her head. "The weather is quite uncommon. My gardener is delighted, but I've heard the grooms are grumbling."

"That I can quite understand. I love my horse, but I must confess that the odor of wet hair is one that I could do without."

"Do you ride often?" she asked. "My husband is hosting a hunt in September. You're welcome to join us."

A week ago, John had had every intention of being on a ship back to Boston by then. Now he wasn't sure that would be the case, and he wasn't at all sorry. A few days at his host's country estate might even be welcome, assuming that Charlotte was with him. "I'll have to check my diary, but that sounds delightful."

Lady Braddon beamed. "And how are you finding London after such a long absence?"

Over his hostess's shoulder, he saw Charlotte enter the room and his heart thudded. Saying good-bye to her the night before had been near impossible when all he'd wanted to do was take her upstairs.

His dreams had been vivid, lustful, and when he'd woken, it was the memory of the taste of her that urged him to satisfy himself, but no true satisfaction came. And it wouldn't, not until he could have her for more than a few minutes in the back of a carriage.

By the flush of her cheeks as her gaze locked with his and

the way she bit her bottom lip in a maddeningly innocent manner, her mind was likewise distracted.

"London is becoming more lovely by the day," he murmured to his hostess. "Excuse me."

They met in the middle of the practically empty drawing room. Lady Braddon held back, but he could feel her curious gaze on him. He didn't care. He raised Charlotte's hand to his lips and let the kiss linger, sensing a heating of the air between them.

"My lady," he said, emphasis on the *my*.

"Lord Harrow." A red flush crept up her neck and her usual chattiness seemed to have vanished.

"I trust you're well."

"I am." She looked over her shoulder and then down to her hands. She twisted the string of her reticule.

Her discomfort was slightly amusing. Lady Charlotte, who could talk her way through any situation, suddenly unable to exchange more than two words at a time.

The windows shook as a gust of wind drove a sheet of rain into them. "Marvelous weather we're having, don't you think?" he said dryly.

That earned him a raised eyebrow. "Are you mocking me?"

"Perhaps."

She leaned toward him and whispered, not that there was anyone within hearing distance. "I can't help not knowing what to say to you. What do two people normally converse about after they've . . . you know."

He did know. And he wanted to know repeatedly. His whisper matched hers. "If both parties enjoyed it, then conversation resumes much the way it had previously. Until it happens again."

Charlotte blinked. "Again?" The note of hope in her tone almost undid him.

"Assuming both parties did, in fact, enjoy it."

She nodded hurriedly. "Yes. I...enjoyed it." She paused, biting her lip once more, and swallowed. "Did you?"

It took every ounce of restraint he had not to drag her against him, wrap a hand around her arse, and show her just how much he enjoyed it, and how ready he was to enjoy it again.

But the drawing room was filling. Already there were curious glances sent in their direction. He took a step back so that there was a respectable distance between them. "Every second, Lady Charlotte," he said as mildly as though he were talking about the storm outside. "Shall we?" He offered her his arm and escorted her to where the other guests were deep in conversation.

Dinner was a surprisingly pleasant affair. As usual, Charlotte spent most of the meal gossiping and flirting and keeping the conversation bubbling along. She would draw him into a discourse about everything from the current political sentiment in the Americas to whether guinea fowl or pheasant were the tastiest game.

He didn't hate it. Talking was easier with her around, and he realized that he almost never stumbled over his words in her presence. There was something about her that relaxed him. It was like talking to Asterly or Amelia. He was so comfortable that the words came out easily.

While she chatted, he had a semi-vigorous conversation with Lady Hornsworth about the state of the nation, which primarily comprised the octogenarian pining for the days of her youth coupled with the occasional mention of Walter—"May he rest in peace. Awful business. He was so young and so charming. He made me feel like a girl again."

"He had that impact on people," John said, trying to keep the frustration from his voice—to ill effect given Lady Hornsworth patted his hand comfortingly. "I'm sure you have your own qualities, my boy. You're more handsome than he was, to start with."

John raised his brows, a little shocked at the grande dame's flirting. "Why, Lady Hornsworth, however could I repay such a compliment?"

She arched a brow. "Well, dear, you could start with the twenty quid the previous Viscount Harrow borrowed not long before his demise."

John sighed. "I'll see to it."

Despite the grande dame's antiquated political views, the two of them got on rather swimmingly for the rest of the event. She was an amusing conversationalist. They shared a dislike of the new fashions so many young lords had adopted. They had similar opinions about King George's spending and the increasing taxes that came with it, and she was well informed about the best farming practices. It turned out they were practically neighbors, separated only by the village that bordered each estate.

After almost an hour of deep discussion, interrupted only when called into the wider conversation of the group, he realized he quite liked Lady Hornsworth.

"Servants talk, you know," the older woman said. "And that talk has reached my London household."

"Oh yes?" John's chest tightened. Not a single person had commented on his financial position. Walter had done a sterling job of hiding it. But if anyone was going to discover the truth, it would be a neighbor.

"Your farms have been terribly neglected for years. It was pleasing to hear that you put that to rights so quickly. I was very fond of the previous viscount, but I am relieved to see a man with a genuine sense of duty step into the role."

There were no words to describe how happy her comment made him. After a lifetime of paling in comparison to his brother, hearing that, in this, he was his brother's equal if not more, made his stomach feel fuzzy and he couldn't stop smiling.

No sooner had the women entered the drawing room than Josefine and Henrietta took Charlotte by each arm and towed her to the corner of the room.

"Well?" Josie asked.

"Well, what?" She wasn't normally so defensive about her friends' questions, but Charlotte herself didn't quite know what was going on and had no idea what to tell them.

"What is happening between you and Lord Harrow?" Hen asked. "The two of you haven't taken your eyes off each other all night. It made me quite heated, I must say." Hen snapped open her fan and waved it dramatically.

"Nothing is happening." But even to Charlotte, her words sounded unconvincing. Her friends didn't believe it either. Their suspicious stares kept her pinned.

"Fine. We kissed. That was all." It certainly hadn't been all. But truly, how did one explain the things that John had done to her the night before? It was not the girls' usual titillating tidbits, nor even their most scandalous gossip. It was ... Well ...

She looked at her friends, both happily married. Did they know such things happened? Had they kept it a secret from her? Was this behavior commonplace?

She bent her head close and whispered, "Have your husbands ever, well, kissed you anywhere other than your lips? Farther down. There."

Her friends exchanged glances. "Occasionally," Josie said.

"Regularly," Hen added. "But certainly not before we were married. What have you been up to, Lottie?"

Charlotte's cheeks heated.

Josie snorted. "I think we know very well what she's been up to. But 'when' is the question. What opportunity has Lord Harrow had to kiss you down there?"

Charlotte couldn't answer. If she told her friends about the gaming rooms, she would have to tell them about William.

Luckily, Hen was less interested in the logistics. "Did you enjoy it?"

"Oh *yes*." Enjoyment was an understatement. Now that she knew such activities existed, she wanted to enjoy them again, and again, and again.

Josie frowned. "So, wait, does this mean that he's broken things off with Lady Luella?"

*Ugh.* Charlotte had gone the entire day without her nemesis appearing once in her thoughts. The gambling had gone so well the night before, Luella no longer felt necessary. Charlotte and John could continue in this fashion as long as it took to raise the money they needed.

"Not yet, but he will. He no longer requires her dowry and is free to follow his heart."

The girls exchanged another glance. "And his heart *is* leading in your direction, isn't it? Because, Lottie, you know, men are quite capable of kissing down there and *more* without it engaging their heart in the slightest. They're very different creatures."

Her friend's words might be cautionary, but they didn't make a dent in the wall of hope she had built.

She and John were a perfect pair. Where she was weak, he was strong. What he lacked, she had in abundance. She didn't know what the depths of his feelings were, but she knew they weren't nothing, and her own feelings were growing with each day.

At that moment, the men entered the drawing room. Her eyes went straight to him, her heart thumping wildly and erratically at the way he searched her out, at the flash of relief and satisfaction on his face when he found her, at the way heat pooled between her legs as he caught her gaze.

A hot flush crept up her neck and she spun back to face her friends.

"Charlotte," Hen hissed. "Could you be any more obvious?"

"I can't help blushing."

"You can help looking at him like he's your next meal."

"I am not," she muttered. The hairs on the back of her neck stood, and the red flush she'd felt earlier sprinted across the rest of her body. "Lord Harrow," she said, knowing he was there before she even turned around.

He stood just a touch too close to be proper. Not close enough to court scandal, but close enough for her to feel the pull between them. Close enough for her body to tighten as her sex shivered at the memory of the cliff he'd brought her to the night before.

Charlotte had never swooned in her life, but if they didn't get close to fresh air immediately, she might well.

"Shall we take a turn about the room?" he asked.

⁓

That Charlotte was the most beautiful woman he'd ever met was not new information. It had been apparent from the moment she had walked into Wilde's study with her hair in braids and her bare toes poking out from beneath her nightgown. His cock had gone hard then and had been in a semi-permanent state of arousal ever since.

That she was loyal and kind had been equally obvious from the moment she'd showed up, determined to extricate him from the debacle his brother had placed him in, at whatever cost.

That she had a dry wit and a propensity for trouble he had discovered last night, his own self coming alive unexpectedly with the excitement.

Tonight's new information, startling at that, was just how she teased the fun out of *him*. She'd even convinced him to play ridiculous parlor games that he should have hated but that were made enjoyable by her laughter, the interesting conversations she sparked, the lively and engaging small talk that was witty and humorous and yet not at the expense of others—a form of small talk he'd never previously experienced.

He found himself sitting close to her because his body

simply couldn't sit away, as though they were opposite poles of a magnetic field. Ultimately, he found himself becoming a little infatuated with this intelligent, headstrong, sweet woman.

When Lady Braddon gestured for the string quartet to play, John didn't hesitate before asking Charlotte to dance. He was vaguely aware of the looks exchanged by other members of the party. The obvious affection he and Charlotte had for each other had clearly been noticed, but while that should've been enough for him to keep his distance—for him to keep his promise to Wilde—it wasn't.

"You seem to be having rather a good time," Charlotte said as John slipped a hand around her waist and started moving them in slow circles around the room. "I'm almost loath to suggest we move on to the more important portion of tonight's activities."

The plan was to leave Lady Braddon's soiree separately. John would circle the block in a hackney cab with Charlotte's change of clothing folded neatly in the satchel he'd given to their host's butler.

But as much as they needed to return to The Lucky Honeypot, he wasn't quite ready to let her out of his arms.

"I think we have time for a dance. The night is still young. Men will lose money at the tables until dawn." He was tempted to draw her closer, but they were attracting enough attention as it was.

Yet still, she inched toward him anyway, and his temperature rose. "For someone who hates dancing as much as you, you're awfully good at it," she said.

It pleased him that she was pleased. He added a flourish to their next turn, delighting in her widening smile. "My mother insisted I learn back before she realized I was a lost cause," he said as they came together once again.

Charlotte *tut-tutt*ed. "You're the most intelligent man in London. You're a partner in a business that has not only made a fortune but also improved the safety of rail travel for everyone. You've been lauded in the business sections of the newspapers too many times to count over the past decade. You're hardly a lost cause, John."

She was so determined to see the best in people. It was a trait he didn't share and could barely understand, but he appreciated in her, regardless. "I was a lost cause to my parents. I was not as witty or charming or good-looking as my older brother, and for much of my childhood, they thought me stupid. I could barely talk and when I did, the syllables tripped over themselves so badly that I was unintelligible."

Charlotte stroked her thumb over his hand, a tiny movement that kept him here in the present rather than allowing his mind to wander too deep through his memories.

"My father knew I was defective from the beginning. He didn't waste any time or affection on me. My mother hoped I would grow up to be 'normal.' She insisted I learn every part of what it was to be a gentleman, but that I must do it better than everyone else to compensate for my failings.

"So I learnt to dance, to ride, to shoot. I can fence well enough. I can even best your brother in a boxing match, although he weighs more than I. But it was never enough. I was still broken in her mind. When I stuttered, she would burst into tears as though I was causing her physical pain."

"Which is why you so rarely speak," Charlotte whispered. "I thought it was because you didn't like people."

"I don't like people, but mostly because people seem to share my parents' opinion of my worth."

"That's not true, John." For a brief second, she raised the back of her hand to his cheek, and he leaned into it, inhaling the scent of roses and summer at her wrist. Then she dropped her hand quickly, glancing around them to see who had noticed such an intimate gesture.

"You are not defective," she whispered. "Your speech hurts no one. Truthfully, I don't even notice your stutter. I suppose it must be there if you say it is; I simply don't hear it. There's nothing about you that needs fixing."

That gave John pause. He'd spent years learning to overcome the tangle of his tongue. These days, it was only an issue that rose in times of great pressure. He'd stuttered more in the past month since he'd returned to the bosom of society than he had in the past decade.

But not with her. She was a point of safety in the turbulence.

"I stutter less when I'm comfortable. When I'm surrounded by people I trust." Which was her, apparently.

She grinned, her joy reaching all the way to the crinkles of her eyes. "My Lord Harrow, should I take it to mean that I have made it onto your impossibly small list of friends?"

# Chapter 18

Their second night at The Lucky Honeypot was proving even more profitable than their first. They'd entered separately and practically ignored each other for the first few hours to quench any suspicion that they were working as a team. John had won a fortune playing vingt-et-un while Charlotte had had mixed results at whist depending on her partner.

She'd done quite well playing with the Earl of Withington, however, and her pot was at least twice the size that it had been when she walked in.

She was relieved, though, when John strolled over just as the last trick was played.

"Mrs. Brown, how lovely to see you again."

She arched a brow. "If it was truly that lovely to see me again, you would have come over earlier rather than cooling your heels at another table for two hours."

John put a hand to his heart in mock chagrin. "Had I realized my presence had been missed, I would have attended to you earlier."

Charlotte sniffed. "I'm not at all sure that I accept your apology." Her accent wavered on that last word, but the men she was seated with didn't seem to notice. They were too busy grinning at her censure.

"Then play with me and let me make it up to you."

The earl was no longer grinning. "I say, Harrow. Wait your turn. Mrs. Brown and I are playing at the moment."

Charlotte *tsk tsk*ed. "Come now, my lord. I can't let you monopolize me all night. But do promise we'll play again tomorrow."

Withington scowled as he stood. "As you wish." He took her hand and kissed it for far longer than he would have had they been in a ballroom and had she been Lady Charlotte rather than Mrs. Brown. She felt nothing. The earl was an objectively attractive man but the touch of his lips to her fingers barely registered on her senses.

They registered with John, though. Beside her, he stiffened. Good. She liked a touch of jealousy, even though it was terribly misplaced.

He took the seat Lord Withington had just vacated and sent her a smoldering look. "So, who's dealing?"

John and Charlotte were crushing their opponents. Every time they played the last trick, and she was sure that Lord Berridge was going to cut his losses and leave, he doubled down, insisting on another game. The thrill of winning subsided, and she began to feel nauseated at his desperation. Was this how William had gotten so far into debt? Could he not tell when it was time to walk away?

"I think you're done," John said to Berridge after Charlotte played the final card and raked in their winnings. Thank goodness. She wasn't sure she could bear too much more.

"No." Berridge shook his head and reached into his breast pocket to withdraw a packet of papers. "This is worth more than enough to keep the game going." He threw it into the middle of the table.

"What is it?" she asked. She and John needed ready money, not a promissory note.

Berridge smirked. "Love letters from an earl's daughter."

"Oh." That knocked her backward in her chair, her hands gripping its arms to steady her against the shock. Across from her, John's hands flinched, as though he intended to reach for her and thought better of it.

Berridge was a right cad. The wagering of intimate letters was not something that had even crossed her mind. Did men truly do that? Any sympathy she may have been feeling for the viscount dissipated.

John shook his head. "I don't trade in gossip. We play for real blunt or not at all." He picked up the papers from the middle of the table and tossed them into Berridge's lap.

The viscount's face twisted in desperation. He untied the string that held the letters together and unfolded the top one, waving it in John's direction. "She admits to giving me her virginity, in writing."

The shock of his words felt like a slap to the face. Instinctively, she recoiled. The *cur*. It was dishonorable enough to take a girl's innocence and then not marry her. But to take her letters and share them was more than dishonorable. It was vile. It made her want to reach across the table and scratch out the viscount's eyes. It made her want to destroy him the way that poor girl must have been destroyed by his actions.

"It's a deal," she said firmly. "State their worth."

John whipped his head toward her, eyes wide in surprise. Berridge relaxed. "Five thousand pounds. Her father has already paid that twice over to keep them from the newspapers."

She swallowed. A game with stakes that high would risk everything she and John had won that night, and essentially for nothing. The letters were worthless to her. She surely wouldn't sell them—not even to save her brother.

It was a foolish, foolish risk.

"Accepted," she said, with less confidence, before signaling to a nearby footman. Lord, she needed a drink to settle her nerves.

The game was played with more intensity than it had been previously. Word spread throughout the gaming hell and they quickly developed an audience, a ring forming around the table and chairs.

The scrutiny caused her to buckle under pressure. At first they were minor mistakes—missing John's unspoken signals, putting down the wrong card—but they quickly accumulated. Add to that Berridge's unbelievable good luck, and it became apparent that everything she and John had worked for that night would be for naught.

They were losing. Hell, the writing was on the wall. They'd already lost.

She tried to keep the panic from her face, tried to appear

as unflappable as John did, but she could feel the beads of perspiration forming across her brow. When she reached for her fan, it wasn't to flirt or to send John a hint as to the quality of her hand. It was because it was hot, too hot, in here.

The more dire her predicament, the more smarmy Berridge's expression became. He and his partner took another trick. There were still a few hands left, but the job was done. She would see the game out—a Wildeforde didn't quit—but in her head she was tallying up all the ways she had lost.

"I say," came a voice from the crowd. "I saw that."

She looked up to where the Earl of Grantham was scowling.

"As did I." A plainly dressed man at her shoulder had both arms crossed.

"I don't understand," she said, only remembering her accent at the last second. "You saw what?"

To her left, Berridge stiffened.

"The bounder is floating the cards," Grantham said.

*The bastard.* It was only the shock of it that kept her from shrieking like a fisherwoman.

The viscount stood, finger pointed in Grantham's direction. "Sir, I should call you out. This is a preposterous allegation."

Two guards—the giant man who'd visited William's apartment and another of equal size—stepped forward. They both looked at the plainly dressed man at Charlotte's shoulder who had spoken. He gave them a sharp nod, and they took Berridge by each arm.

"Do you know who I am?" He tried to shake free of their

grasp. The men's grips tightened, and the viscount winced. "Unhand me at once."

The guards ignored him, and he was dragged, unceremoniously, from the room. Charlotte watched after him with her jaw open, not quite believing what had just happened. The crowd around them buzzed, with much of the audience shaking its head in condemnation.

Charlotte looked at John, who was doing his best to look unaffected, though she could see the tension in him. She turned to the man next to her. "So... what happens to the pot?" There were five thousand pounds in there, along with the viscount's letters.

"It gets split between you and your partner," the man said to her.

She would have sagged with relief if she weren't strung so tight. "Well," she said. "I'm feeling generous tonight, Lord Harrow. You may take the money." She grabbed the letters from the table and stuffed them into her reticule. "If you'll excuse me, gentlemen. The mood has been tarnished. I'm going to call it a night. Good night, Lord Harrow. It was good to see you again."

Completely muddled, she accepted the arm of the nearest gentleman and allowed him to escort her outside, only then to remember that she and John had a plan for their exit and she had just ruined it.

"Around the block, if you will," she said to the hackney driver. Thankfully, by the time they were once again in front of The Lucky Honeypot, she could see John walking up the street, his eyes peeled on the road. As the carriage pulled up beside him, she rapped on the ceiling and it came to a stop.

John peered inside the window, sighed, and climbed in, taking the seat next to her.

"I'm sorry," she said, turning toward him. "I was all befuddled and took the cab without thinking."

He pressed a kiss to her forehead. "Are you well? As long as you're well, then it is of no consequence."

He wrapped his arm around her, and she sank into him, taking comfort from his warmth and the scent of bergamot that enveloped her. "What a night," she said. "I would prefer not to run that close to losing again."

His cheek rested against her hair and his arm tightened around her, pulling her close to him so they were shoulder to shoulder, thigh to thigh, with nothing between them. "I should have seen his deceit earlier. Thank God Grantham spotted it. Now we have the money and the letters, though I don't know what we'll do with them."

Now that the threat had gone, her heart was slowing, and feeling was returning, her curiosity abounded. She straightened and dug her hand into her reticule to retrieve the packet. She tugged open the string that bound them and took the first letter.

The handwriting was perfectly formed, small and even with the occasional flourish. Charlotte turned straight to the farewell and her stomach dropped.

> *My love always,*
> *Lady Luella Tarlington*

## Chapter 19 ────────────

Charlotte, you can't." John's tone was stern, but she waved him away. Deep down, she knew she should put the letters back immediately and never open them again, but she simply wasn't that good a person.

The first letter was sweet. It was a letter she might have written to John, were they not in such constant contact.

Luella—sharp, venomous viper of the *ton*—had been besotted. The way she had openly expressed her devotion to Lord Berridge and her plans for their marriage was difficult to read, given Charlotte knew those hopes had been dashed.

The second letter was heart-wrenching. It was full of confusion—why had he not responded to her previous letter? Why had he not come to see her father, as he promised he would?

Charlotte couldn't bring herself to read the third letter.

The whole situation made her sick. How could men be so awful? And to share it with his friends? To finally visit Luella's father, not to propose, but to blackmail?

"I have no words. This is disgraceful."

John shifted away, arms crossed. "Charlotte, whatever your feelings for that woman, you cannot use those letters against her."

*Pardon?* She also shifted, putting enough distance between them that she could pin him down with a Wildeforde glare. "How could you think I would? I may not like her. In fact, to say that I loathe her wouldn't be an overstatement. But I would never use a woman's misstep against her."

He frowned. "So you won't share them? Or reveal their contents?"

Charlotte counted to five in her head before answering. "It is an insult that you think I would. Especially given what we did last night. I am certainly not a hypocrite. And while I'd love to best that woman once and for all, if I'm going to win, I want to win fairly."

John removed his glasses and rubbed a hand over his eyes. "So do you plan on returning them to her?"

"*Me?* God, no. Can you imagine how she'd react if she knew her greatest rival had seen these? She'd never feel safe again. I may hold a grudge, but I'm not cruel. You do it. Tell her you came across them somewhere. That way, she has the security of knowing they're out of that bastard's hands and never needs to know that I saw them."

John looked at her, head cocked. "You risked everything tonight for those letters. Selling them to help your brother never crossed your mind?"

She could understand his confusion. She'd told him that

there was nothing she wouldn't do to help William. What she'd meant was there was nothing she wouldn't sacrifice, but she certainly would not cause such harm. Not even to Luella. "I can't."

The look he gave her in response was heavy with thought. He tapped his fingertips on his lips before finally speaking. "You are something I do not understand."

He was in love with Charlotte.

He didn't know when it had happened or if she felt the same. All he knew was that she was the kindest, most generous, most loyal and loving person he knew. She was a sunbeam, so pure and warm and good that it could break through the darkest cloud.

For her, he would change the course of his existence. He would stay in England rather than returning to his quiet shack in the wilderness, because *with* her, all the things he feared and loathed about society seemed like lesser burdens. With her by his side, he could be the lord he must become. Together, they could ensure their estates, their people, thrived.

The sky had taken on a green hue a scant hour ago. With the promise of a lightning storm on the horizon, tonight was the perfect time to propose. He just had to settle other matters first, which was why he was now standing in Lady Luella's drawing room, staring out the window and watching the clouds roll in. Marrying her was no longer an option. Even if he and Charlotte lost every cent they had at the tables tonight, he would not marry another.

Besides, Luella deserved better than to be left hanging on a string, waiting to be needed or not. After Berridge's treatment of her, she deserved to find someone who would treat her well, who would love her in a way that John never would.

"Lord Harrow." John turned to see Luella in the doorway. Her face was pinched, her lips thinned, and her eyes narrowed. She remained motionless as he bowed.

"You're here to cry off," she said, stalking across the room and taking a seat on the chaise longue. She settled her skirts into perfect waves. John had seen Charlotte do the same thing. It was a delaying tactic, a moment to compose herself without revealing what she was thinking. The two women shared more commonalities than either would care to admit.

He kept his place by the window, hesitant to be within arm's reach of her for the conversation that had to follow. "I can't, in good conscience, marry you," he said.

She pinned him down with her stare. "I can't see how, in good conscience, you *couldn't* marry me. There is a contract. You have a responsibility. A true gentleman keeps his commitments."

The barb cut deep, and he worked to remind himself that this was not his commitment. Walter had made the bloody pact, and he'd failed to keep it the way that he'd failed all his other duties.

"Lady Luella, surely you would prefer to marry a man who *wants* to marry you."

"Lord Harrow, as my father so eloquently put it, I am spoiled goods, a fact that is not a secret amongst the men of London. No man of wealth and good breeding wants to marry me. At least, none did until Walter. He could see past my...indiscretion. He truly loved..." She pulled a handkerchief from her sleeve and dabbed at her eyes.

Despite the way she was trying to corner him, he felt sympathy for her. She'd loved his brother, however little Walter deserved it, and she would never have the life with him that she'd planned. "My condolences for your loss," John murmured.

"You are nothing compared to him," she spat. "Nothing."

The words echoed the insults his parents had thrown at him his entire childhood. They hurt less now, though. His brother might have been charming, but he had not been perfect. He had not even been good. Whether the rest of society saw that was no longer relevant.

"I am trying my best to do right by everyone."

"Except me."

Including her, though she couldn't see it. They would be wretched together. By not marrying her, she would be free to find someone who was more compatible—another Walter. "I am sorry that I've disappointed you."

"It's her, isn't it?" Luella said. "The perfect Lady Charlotte? If you were going to refuse me, you would have done so immediately. Something, someone, has changed your mind."

He couldn't deny it. If it weren't for Charlotte, he likely would have married Luella to repair the estates and free Walter's tailor from debtor's prison. His happiness, what he understood of it at the time, would have been a price he was willing to pay.

But happiness had taken on a new meaning in the

past week. It was no longer something he could bear to part with.

Luella took his silence as confirmation. "You'll regret it. She always has a cause she's pushing. You're just another one of her projects."

Her accusation struck true, leaving him anxious. He could only hope that she was wrong, that Charlotte felt more for him than she did for the dozens of other causes she championed. He hoped her feelings for him were as all-consuming as his feelings for her were.

"I regret the pain my family has caused you, my lady." He reached into his breast pocket and withdrew the packet of letters Charlotte had recovered the night before. "I only hope that these can soothe the hurt." He crossed the room and handed them to her.

She was still staring at them, hand at her throat, when he left.

⌒

Thunder cracked so hard the glass rattled. Torrents of rain beat down on the window. Charlotte hated this kind of weather. Parties were cancelled, Vauxhall was closed, and nobody walked through Hyde Park chatting. Storms had always meant time spent inside alone.

She stood at her bedroom window, her arms hugged around herself, and stared out across the garden toward Harrow House. When she'd gone over that morning with a tray of eggs, sausages, and bacon, Mosely had told her that John was out. At noon. He was usually not even risen at that hour, hence the breakfast.

Disappointed, she had left the tray with Mosely. She'd meant to spend the afternoon with William, but since the doctor had refused to provide more laudanum, her brother had been extra crotchety and had eventually asked her to leave. The rain had started not long after.

She'd toyed with the idea of going to visit Henrietta, but it was always a risk taking horses out into a storm such as this. Besides, it felt selfish to ask Swinton to drive in this weather simply because she was bored.

It was Grace's afternoon off; Edward was in parliament, and when she'd passed Fiona's laboratory, her sister had been so preoccupied with her latest gadget that she hadn't even heard Charlotte enter.

"Drat." A bolt of lightning broke through the grey clouds and she jumped. Thunder followed quickly after. The storm was getting close.

The door leading from John's study into his garden opened. She only saw his face for a brief second before the umbrella hid it, but that second was all she needed for her nerves to break out into excited fluttering. He crossed his garden quickly, making straight for the door in the wall.

Charlotte paused only long enough to change her slippers for boots before she rushed down the stairs, caring not for the looks the staff gave her. By the time she reached the door that led into the yard, John was beneath her bedroom window, stone in hand.

"John," she called, but her voice was drowned out by the sound of raindrops landing heavy on the ground. "Drat," she muttered, watching him lob the stone. She hadn't thought to bring her own umbrella, or a coat, or even a bonnet to protect her hair. With a wince, she took off into the rain and was drenched within seconds. The coiffure Grace had spent an hour on that morning melted in the wet. Her sodden skirts caught around her legs.

"John!" By the time he heard her, she was only feet from him, wiping the hair from her eyes. "What on earth are you doing?"

He closed the distance between them, holding the umbrella above her with one hand, cupping her cheek with the other, leaning down to press a quick kiss to her lips, giving no heed to the fact that it was afternoon and anyone looking out the window could see them.

"It's a thunderstorm," he said with an absurd smile.

"I know. And we're out in it." His eccentricities were charming most of the time. But she preferred them dry, not sopping wet.

He took her hand to guide her across the garden. "I have something to show you."

It was then that she noticed the strap of a satchel that crossed his body. "Now? Here?" she asked as she tripped after him. Truly, most normal men would have come calling through the front door and shown whatever it was to her in the comfort of a drawing room.

Once they'd crossed through the gate, he handed her the umbrella and then reached into the satchel, pulling out a bright red kite.

A kite. In this weather.

Perhaps he hadn't slept again. Perhaps he was experiencing some kind of delirium brought on by hours spent awake. Certainly, she had barely slept last night. She'd hoped they would repeat the kissing and more as they left The Lucky Honeypot, but the discovery of Lady Luella's letters had stolen all romance from what remained of the evening. Charlotte had gone to bed deeply unsatisfied.

"You don't think that perhaps this is not the time?" She gestured to the sky and then flinched when lightning flared. The storm was almost on top of them. Only a fool was out in this weather.

"There is no better time. Here." He pushed a ball of cotton twine into her hands and then let it unravel as he ran the kite away.

This was worthy of Bedlam, but he was too far from her to hear it. As he jogged to create lift under the kite, she jogged after him. In the past, Edward and William had gotten the kite flying and had given it to her once it was in the skies. She'd never been forced to work for it before. Thank goodness she'd swapped her slippers for boots, though her toes squelched and the wet leather rubbed.

It didn't take long for a gust to take hold of the red fabric. The string snapped and tugged and was more difficult to control than she could have expected. *Drat. I should have put on gloves.*

John strode over, anticipation writ clear across his face. The kite, then, was not the entirety of his plans because no one got this excited about a kite in the rain.

As he got closer, he frowned as though he was only just realizing how drenched she was, almost as if he hadn't noticed the downpour himself despite his hair being plastered to his neck and his cravat hanging heavy.

He shrugged off his coat and put it over her shoulders, the warmth of him enveloping her. Even with the telltale tang of a thunderstorm surrounding her, she could still smell the heady scent of him.

Then he came behind her, circled her in his arms, and put his hands on hers to keep the kite from pulling out of her grasp.

His closeness made her blood thrum. She shivered, not from the cold or the wet, but from the awareness of him.

"Just a moment," he murmured into her ear. He slipped his hand into the pocket of the coat she was now wearing. Through the heavy wool, he brushed against her thigh. The shivers moved inward, resonating through her.

He withdrew one of the foil-covered glass jars that she'd seen in his study days ago.

"What are we doing with that?"

"We're capturing electricity. Bottling it up. The air is rife with it. Did you see that?" He pointed to a spot in the sky where lightning had just forked. "That's electricity in its rawest form."

"Are you mad?" She released the kite string, but his hands caught it. She may not be a scientist, but she had seen firsthand the blackened stump in the garden where lightning had struck a tree during a particularly wild storm in her childhood.

"No, not mad. We won't bottle lightning. But there is electricity in the air. Do you see it?" He pointed to the fibers of the cotton string, which were lifting into the air, not unlike the hairs on the back of her arm lifted when she saw him.

Tentatively, she grazed her palm across the cotton, a tingle skipped across her skin, again not unlike the sensation of his hand on hers. Her fingertip got too close to the cotton, and it zapped her sharply, painfully, the irony of which was not lost on her. The more she leaned into the frisson that was between her and John, the more likely she was to be painfully shocked when he left.

She pulled her finger away and pivoted in his arms until she was chest to chest with him.

"Is this what's between us, then? This feeling that makes my heart go off kilter and my body come alive? Is it electricity?"

He inhaled sharply, fleeting expressions of hope, then relief crossing his face before settling into something far more primal. "No. There is no scientific explanation for this feeling. There is no reason or logic or laws of nature that explain it."

He felt it too then. She swallowed. "And is there anything to be done about it?" Because one way or another, it had to be resolved. She couldn't continue in this state forever, with her nerves so heightened that the barest breeze sent shivers through her, with her head so giddy it was as though she'd been dancing too fast for too long and was on the verge of fainting... or of falling more deeply in love.

John let the glass jar drop to the ground with a clunk, taking the fluttering kite down with it.

"Only this." He captured her face in his hands and drew his lips to hers. The heat of him quenched her shivering and ignited a fire within her.

She wrapped her hands into the sodden folds of his shirt and pulled him closer. She opened her lips and touched her tongue to his, seeking out the depths of him. She knew what she was doing this time. It was her turn to explore, her tongue flicking against his.

He groaned, wrapped a hand around her buttocks, and pulled her against him. Through the layers of fabric between them—his breeches, her dress, both sodden—she could feel the hard press of his cock. Her sex stirred and her hips pressed into him, wanting to get closer.

He groaned. "Charlotte." His words sounded like a prayer.

She didn't want talking. She wanted to continue tasting him, but he pulled away. "No," she whispered, wrapping one hand in his hair.

He put a gentle hand on her shoulder, putting distance between them. Rivulets of water ran down his hairline. His fine shirt had turned transparent with the wet and clung to his chest.

"Let's not stop," she said, trying to step toward him, her hands gripping his forearms, but he held her fast, a frustrating twelve inches from him.

He drew in a ragged breath. "Charlotte, make me the happiest man alive."

# Chapter 20

...Make me the happiest man alive..."

Still reeling from the kiss, she took a heartbeat to register what he was saying.

"I can't imagine a life without you."

*Wait. What?*

"Do me the honor of becoming—"

"Stop."

He stilled. Beneath her hands, his arms stiffened.

"Are you proposing?"

He swallowed, clearly nervous. "That was the plan."

Everything in her went loose and giddy. She had to work to hold back a bubble of highly inappropriate laughter. She pressed her lips together, trying desperately to keep from launching into a response before he'd even had the chance to ask. Her cheeks hurt already. She stepped backward, trying her best to repair the sodden mess of her hair, brushing down rain-soaked skirts as best she could.

*Drat.* She gave up and clasped her hands in front of her primly and looked back at him. "You may continue."

"May I?" he said dryly—the only thing about them that was. He dropped to his knee and picked up the glass jar. "I do not have a ring but I had hoped to give you this"— he held up the jar—"to show you I will one day give you the world." He looked at the empty jar and frowned. "It was supposed to be the essence of the universe, captured for you. We didn't quite get to that bit."

"Shhh. You're spoiling it."

He chuckled and tossed the jar over his shoulder, before taking her hands in his. "Lady Charlotte Stirling, will you do me the honor of becoming my wife?"

She took a long, deep breath. She'd heard those words many times—thirty-three to be exact—yet it was as though they'd never once been spoken. "Yes," she said. "Yes, I will be your wife."

The smile on John's face was wide and boyish, and as he stood, he wrapped one arm below her arse and lifted her against him, his other arm snaking behind her back to keep her secure.

The cold had disappeared. The rain dripping down her face and from the sodden ends of her hair was a mere annoyance. All that mattered was John. She took his face in her hands and kissed him again.

She was to be his wife. They would be happy together forever.

When she was finally forced to break off the kiss so she could breathe, John trailed his tongue down her neck and along her collarbone, sending a different kind of shiver across her, the kind that dipped beneath the skin, resonated through her heart, her stomach, her womanhood.

"We should get out of the rain," he murmured, his lips rasping against her throat.

"What rain?" She raked her fingers through his hair.

He looked up at her. "Where do I take you?"

She knew what he meant. They would go back through the garden wall and to her home, full of her family and servants, if she wanted. Or they could go inside Harrow House, where this kissing, and everything that came after kissing, could continue.

"Take me to your rooms," she whispered.

His eyes flared, and his fingers tightened, pressing into her backside. "As you wish." Without releasing his grip, he carried her inside.

His bedroom was not what she was expecting. Given the chaos of his study, she'd anticipated something similar. Instead, it was bare. There was a dresser with a simple wash basin and mirror. A lone chair stood beside it. The only hint that this was John's room was the notebook and pencil on the small table by his bed.

His bed. The moment he'd kicked the door shut, he crossed to it and set her down on its edge. Her feet barely grazed the floor. Her body protested at the sudden absence of him, even if he'd only gone as far as the fireplace, where he carefully stacked logs and tossed on some additional kindling. In seconds, the small flame burst to life with a sharp *pop*. A crack of lightning lit the room. A boom of thunder followed.

He turned toward her, both hands pulling through his

hair, slicking it back. The fire behind him turned his honey-brown tresses gold. His breeches clung to his legs, dipping and curving around his muscular thighs and calves. The skin at the top of his throat, before it disappeared into folds of fabric, glistened. Raindrops still clung to his eyelashes.

She might not have his perfect memory, but this image would remain in her mind forever.

His breath was heavy; she could hear it, and she could see the swelling of his chest. His nipples peaked beneath the translucent fabric of his shirt. Her fingers itched to touch him there, to feel them beneath her fingertips, to spread her hands across the warmth of his body and feel the beat of his heart.

He wanted her. It was evident in the way his muscles coiled tight and the bulge of his cock below his waistband. Still, he paused, as though waiting for a sign from her, some signal that she knew what would happen if he came closer. That she wanted it.

What she wanted was to be kissed again, down there. She would have let him do that even before he'd proposed to her. Now they were betrothed, that kind of kissing was almost respectable. Not *quite*. But no one had to know other than her friends who already knew.

John could kiss her down there again and soon they'd be married and that would make it all proper.

Still, he waited.

Charlotte stood, wiped her hands on her skirts nervously, and then took a step toward him, taking pleasure in his quick inhalation of breath.

She reached into the pocket of her gown for the

handkerchief she kept there. It had been protected from the worst of the rain.

"Here," she said, looking for an excuse to touch him. She reached up and dabbed the water that still hung at his temples, ran the handkerchief along the hard, sharp planes of his cheekbones, let her hand trace his hairline, transferring her touch to his neck, to the folds of his cravat, to the edge of his collar, to the plain silver stick pin.

"You're soaked," she whispered.

John swallowed hard. She could feel the movement underneath her fingers. "We are both drenched."

She took a fortifying breath. "We should remove this clothing, then, don't you think? We don't want to become bedridden." Her cheeks flushed. She did very much want them to become bedridden. "I mean sick. We don't want to come down with a fever."

John smiled. "Agreed." He ran his palm down her side and along her waist, before settling it on her hip. His fingers depressed her derriere.

Charlotte slid the stick pin from the cravat and slipped it into her pocket. She tugged at the knot. It didn't come apart as easily as she expected. The dampness of the fabric made it difficult to undo. She bit her lip and tugged harder, her eyes trained on the white cloth in front of her until John's hands came over hers, warm and strong.

She flicked her gaze upward. He was looking at her with an amused smile. He raised her hands to his lips, gave them a quick kiss, and then dropped them to turn his attention to his cravat. The way he yanked at it betrayed his urgency.

The heat she felt rising had nothing to do with the increased flames behind them.

At last, the knot came free. He held her gaze as he unwound the cravat and slid it off. Only when it hit the floor with a soft thwack did she realize she wasn't breathing.

She exhaled, watching his delicate fingers make quick work of the lace of his collar. He grabbed the hem of his shirt and pulled it over his head in a hurried movement, revealing all of him.

Well, not *all* of him. But certainly enough. Certainly more than she'd seen before.

He was beautiful. He had the body of a ballet dancer, lean and graceful and both undulating and hard at once. There was a shadow at the hollow of his throat—a darkness she wanted to sink into. The firelight caught the flared wings of his collarbone, and she couldn't help but reach a hand up to trace them. He tensed, and she could see the regular thrum of his heartbeat at his throat quicken, jolting her own heartbeat into an erratic thump.

Tentatively, she brushed her fingers downward, over the bone and to his chest, where light brown hair rasped beneath her fingertips. As she trailed through it, mesmerized by the feel of him, his nipples tightened, the way hers did when she had particularly untoward thoughts.

"God, Charlotte." The words were almost a plea. His chest tensed, the interlocking muscles at his waist flexed. By his side, his fists clenched, but he seemed determined to let her direct what happened next.

She stepped closer to him, until his skin was only inches from her lips, until she could feel the heat that radiated from him. She reached a hand up again, this time to his back, her palm coming to rest on hard muscle above his shoulder blade. Her other hand rested on his waist, on the rope of muscle that fit into her hand perfectly, that started above his hip and traveled down well below the waistband of his breeches.

He was magnificent. Half naked, he was a god.

Not wanting to be outdone, Charlotte undid the buttons of her pelisse, trying to ignore the shaking of her fingers. When it was free, she shrugged it off, and it landed in a literal puddle on the floor.

Her dress would be a different matter. Her fingers rested on the lace at her neckline.

John ran the back of his finger across her cheek, down her jaw, and then tipped her face so it tilted toward him. As he captured her mouth in a kiss, his hands stole around her back to deftly undo her buttons, one by one, from the neckline through to the small of her back.

"Goodness, you're an expert at that."

"No valet," he whispered. "I'm an expert at knots, buckles, and buttons."

With its fastenings undone, the dress hung loose. With a nervous breath, she let it fall to the floor.

John's hands fisted by his side for a brief second before he raised them, allowing his palms to skim over her stays and then her skin.

Goose bumps skittered across her. His touch was so, so light, yet it still felt as though he'd marked her permanently, the way a sculptor carved out stone, forever leaving a mark that could not be erased.

His fingers skimmed lower until they reached her drawers. His hands felt hot through the fine cotton. He didn't untie the laces, though. Instead, he turned his hands to his breeches, undoing the fall and unlacing the waistband. As he leaned over to peel the breeches from his skin, he caught her gaze.

It was a cheeky, scandalous look that divested her of her nerves. It promised fun and more of the naughty kissing she'd been looking forward to. As he stood, she turned so that he could undo the laces on her stays. When they were loose enough to shimmy out of, she pulled them over her head and then turned around, throwing her arms around his neck and kissing him with all the enthusiasm she could muster.

When he lifted her, her legs instinctively wrapped around his waist. When he laid her down on the bed, he put his weight into his arms.

"Are we going to do more of the thing?" she whispered.

"If you wish."

He didn't make her wait. Instead, he trailed a line of kisses down her stomach that left her insides on fire. He hooked his fingers around her drawers and slowly drew them from her. She should be embarrassed to be naked in front of a man. Instead, she felt eager anticipation.

He nipped at the inside of her thigh with his teeth, and a bolt of electricity shot through her like lightning through the sky outside. He parted her curls and turned his attention to the center of her.

She held her breath and waited.

It was every bit as thrilling as it had been in the carriage. As his tongue found the nub that made pleasure course through her, her hands gripped the sheets, twisting.

"John," she breathed. He didn't pause. She didn't want him to. Instead, he continued his rhythmic ministrations until she was gasping. Her vision blurred and she grabbed the padded headboard above her. "I can't—" *Speak. Think. Breathe.*

His fingers gripped her thighs and the pressure of his tongue increased.

"Oh God."

It felt like a cliff he was pushing her toward. He changed his tempo, quickened just a little, and the precipice was upon her. Every muscle in her body stiffened, her feet flexed, and she held on to the headboard like it was the only thing keeping her in reality as she cried out.

"Oh." She dragged in a breath. "Oh." Her heart slowed. "Oh." The ringing in her ears subsided.

John stretched alongside her and brushed a lock of hair from her face. His body leaned against hers and she could feel the hard press of his cock against her thigh.

She turned to face him. "That isn't all, is it?" she asked when the room stopped spinning.

He grinned. "No. The rest can wait." But he shifted uncomfortably.

"I don't want to wait." She'd waited for years. She'd waited a lifetime.

"Charlotte."

She caught his cheek in her hand, her thumb tracing the hard bone. "I don't want to wait. Show me."

⁓

He had proposed. She had accepted. While a gentleman did not cross the line and sleep with a young, unmarried lady, surely the line was blurred in such an instance? It was only a matter of days before she was his wife, weeks at most if her brother insisted on reading the banns.

Wilde would call him out if he knew his friend was even considering taking Charlotte's innocence now.

The decision was taken from his hands, quite literally, when Charlotte's soft fingers wrapped around his cock shyly, unpracticed, but still heightening his urgency in a way he'd never experienced.

He groaned and called her name.

Emboldened by his obvious pleasure, her grip on him strengthened. She rubbed her hand up and down, the friction against his shaft causing his cock to throb. Her touch felt so good. If she kept this up, he was going to spill himself prematurely.

"Charlotte, wait." He covered her body with his, shifting his weight to his elbows to keep from crushing her.

Her body, naked against his, caused pressure to build inside him like a steam engine ready to explode at her touch.

Unable to reach his cock, she put one hand on his chest and he felt his heart *th-thump* in response. Her other hand wrapped in his hair and she pulled him into an urgent kiss. God, she tasted of summer and honeysuckle—the English garden he hadn't realized he'd missed during his time in America.

She shifted beneath him until her knees cradled him, her legs spread open.

This was the watershed. This was the point of no return. Not the proposal. Not anything that led up to this moment. Once he had her, she would be his forever and he would be hers. There would be no one else. Ever.

"Charlotte, are you sure?" She was beautiful, intelligent, kind, and capable of having any man she wanted. That she would choose him still felt unlikely.

"I'm sure," she whispered, cupping her hand to his face and stroking his cheek. "I want you, John. I want this."

He moved, settling more comfortably between her legs, his cock poised at her entrance. He saw her swallow and bite the inside of her lip. His anxiety matched hers. He didn't know how to make this perfect for her—he knew the first time could be painful—but he'd do whatever he could for her so that she would remember this moment with satisfaction.

"I love you," he said. "I love you in a way that I didn't know was possible. I love your kindness. I love your confidence. I love the joy you give to the world. And I will love you for all time."

She beamed, her cheeks flushing red and her eyes crinkling. "I love you too."

Her words, unusually succinct, made his heart swell, and his soul—which had always sought solitude—dusted off a space next to it for her.

He leaned down to capture her lips with his, and as he did, he slowly entered her.

Good God, she was so hot. She was so wet. Her fingertips dug into his shoulders, and beneath him she stiffened a fraction.

He paused, but she shook her head and brushed a lock of hair from his forehead. "No. Keep going. It's all right."

He inched himself forward, slowly, until he was fully seated inside her. He waited there, allowing her to become accustomed to him. Once her breathing had resumed, he withdrew and then smoothly seated himself again.

Her mouth dropped open. "Oh," she breathed.

Slowly, he repeated himself. His exit sent pleasure ricocheting off every nerve in his body. His entrance setting those same nerves on fire until his very core was aflame.

Again and again he thrust, until the nervousness in her expression vanished, until her eyes closed and her hands twisted in the sheets, until her breathing matched his rhythm and his name escaped her lips—half exclamation, half plea.

Her hips pushed against his, as though both their bodies were determined to fuse together. As her back arched, he slipped his arms beneath her, one hand grasping at her shoulder, the other tightening across her waist. He buried his head in her neck, nipping and sucking at her skin, his teeth dragging across it harder as her fingernails dug into his shoulder.

Never before had intercourse felt like this. Previous experiences had sated a natural physical urge. Lovemaking with Charlotte was more than physical; it spoke to his heart and mind, and the deeper awareness in him. He could never have enough of her to sate those three things.

She wrapped her legs around his waist, pulling him even closer as though she, too, could not get close enough. The movement wrecked him. It tore through every intention he had of making this last as long as it could while they both enjoyed it.

He was so deep within her, the tip of his cock thrummed as pleasure waves coursed through it. His climax was stirring. One last thrust took him to the edge. Before he fell right over it, he withdrew, hand reaching for her drawers, which had tangled in the sheets. He spilled himself into them with a groan.

He was spent, and collapsed onto the mattress. Half lying across her, his face planted into the pillow next to her, there was not a hope of him moving. His muscles lay lifeless except for the rapid-fire flinching he could not control as aftershocks of his climax shot through him.

He should be tending to Charlotte. He'd just taken her innocence. Instead, it was she who was stroking his hair in a show of tenderness so foreign to him that it took a moment to identify that slow caress as the cause of his tightening heart.

He wanted her touch until the end of days.

*Chapter 21* —————————

Charlotte woke, feeling more rested than she had in years. According to the clock in the corner of John's room, it was almost midday. She'd slept the entire morning. She hadn't done that in as long as she could remember; her mornings were too full of meetings with the housekeeper, breakfast with Fi and Edward to discuss plans for the day, hastening to this board meeting or checking in on that event before the traditional society house calls began.

Lying on her side in John's big, four-poster bed, reveling in the way his thumb brushed over her stomach in slow, easy curves with nothing on her mind other than the way his chest pressed against her back and his arms encircled her, she felt a previously unexperienced peace.

Cocooned in his warmth and his scent, she could hear the rhythmic beating of his heart and the slow sigh of his breath in her hair.

"Are you sleeping?" she whispered.

"No," he murmured back. "But I could fall asleep with you in my arms every night."

She smiled and snuggled deeper into him. "Don't be silly. You'll be working. You don't go to sleep until after I've woken."

He squeezed his arms tighter around her. "The promise of you will bring me to bed. The chance to hold you like this is too good to pass up."

She burrowed farther into him. There could be no moment more perfect than this. "Well, I will do my best not to wake you when I rise. I'll breakfast downstairs and then pay calls. You can sleep as late as you need."

He took a lock of her hair and twisted it in his fingers. "Will you come with me when I travel to our country estates? I must oversee them properly, but I know you hate to leave London."

She turned over, so that she was on her back, looking up at him. "Of course, I will. It's my job to help you manage them. Once William is well, and as long as we're in London while parliament is sitting so that I can continue to support Edward, there's no reason I can't be in the country. And perhaps there's something I can do to help you with your inventions."

John caressed her face, giving her a gentle smile. "I'll take any excuse to have your company, but your help is not necessary."

He didn't intend for his words to sting; she knew he didn't. But they hurt nonetheless. "You don't want my help?"

He pursed his lips, as though trying to think of the

best way to phrase his objection to her assistance. "I don't require it as a condition of my love."

She frowned, tucking the cover tight beneath her armpits. "Is this because of what Luella said? That I'm only helpful because I want people to like me? Because that's not at all true." Or at least, it was only a little bit true. It certainly wasn't her primary motivation.

He raised an eyebrow. "What do you have planned for today?"

*Drat.* She could see where he was going with this, but she couldn't back down.

"I have a meeting to discuss supplies for the orphanage, then I have to set the menu for Edward's dinner with the French diplomat next Tuesday, and then I'm going to Miss Portsmith's for afternoon tea to help her with her small talk. She'll never land a husband repeating the same three sentences over and over." She refused to be anything but proud of her work today.

"Do you *want* to do all of those things?" John asked.

Generally, yes. That was how she loved to spend her days, even if it got exhausting. Even if sometimes she would rather just sit with Grace and while away the day speaking of nothing important. Today was different. "I'd rather spend the day with you," she admitted.

"Then send your apologies. Reschedule. We'll hide away from the world today."

A Wildeforde kept her commitments. A Wildeforde devoted her time to helping others. But could she—Charlotte Stirling, soon-to-be Lady Harrow—take a moment to be selfish?

"All right," she whispered. "That sounds divine."

If John had had a choice, it would have been to avoid Wilde until Charlotte was ready to announce their engagement. Despite spending the past couple of days practically living together, with Charlotte sneaking to his house through the garden wall, she was hesitant to tell her family about their betrothal. Her reasoning was that if they waited until they'd successfully pulled John's estates out of debt, then Edward would have no reason to oppose the match.

John didn't share Charlotte's optimism. Wilde's opposition had been about more than money. Her brother didn't think John was a suitable candidate for a husband. But then, he also thought John would return to America. Maybe once he saw that John would stay in London so that Charlotte could keep her life of ballrooms and house calls and charity work, he'd be more inclined to give his blessing. Maybe.

Yet, John couldn't help but feel that he'd betrayed his closest friends. Wilde and Fiona were family, and that should have been reason enough for him to keep his distance from Charlotte when they asked, but it hadn't been.

The only way he could assuage his guilt was by reminding himself that they were to marry, and he would dedicate his life to making her happy, even if that meant remaining in England. Even if it meant occasionally going to these god-awful balls, although he hoped she'd be willing to attend most with her friends and only require John's presence at one or two a month.

But the knowledge that he would make her a good husband would not protect him from Wilde's wrath in the short-term, and if the way Edward was bearing down on him this minute was any indication, the short-term started here. Now. In the middle of a London ball that John hadn't expected his friend to attend.

"Barnesworth. Dammit, *Harrow*. It's been days since Fiona and I saw you." He smiled, but the smile didn't quite meet his eyes. They'd been friends long enough for John to recognize Wilde's displeasure.

"The estates are in a mountain of t-trouble. Moving it is busy work." Damn himself for stuttering. Wilde would know his anxiety immediately.

"Does this busy work involve my sister? I know she's feeding your household from our kitchens. Four pigeon pies? I imagine your butler has never been better fed in his life."

A wash of embarrassment crept over John. Charlotte had come around most mornings with a basket of food that included breakfasts and dinners. Mosely would walk on water for her at this point. But the pigeon pies? They had gone to William and the lad who nursed him.

Not that Charlotte had shared that fact with her eldest brother, which meant John had no choice but to lie. "The pie was good. Your cook is an artist. But I wasn't aware that Charlotte hadn't told you that she was sending food. I'll ask her to stop."

Wilde rolled his eyes. "I don't mind spotting you a meal. I offered you the blunt needed to run your household, remember? What I mind is hearing reports of how my sister and the Viscount Harrow have been seen together over and over. That they're practically attached at the hip. There are rumors circulating and I don't like the content of them."

John and Charlotte should have come clean immediately. The moment she'd accepted his proposal, they should have returned to Wildeforde House and announced it. If she were standing next to him, he'd give her a nudge and confess to Wilde now. Instead, John could only deliver a half-truth.

"Charlotte is helping me win the blunt needed to save the estates. We come to a ball, we dance a little, and then we win as many hands of whist as we can without raising suspicion."

Wilde's mouth fell open—the very picture of stunned horror. Once he'd collected himself, he responded quietly, but that didn't stop the fury from seeping out of his voice. "How could you? After all my family has done for you. What if your scheme was discovered? How could you risk her reputation?"

An uneasiness roiled in John's gut. "We are very careful."

Wilde's hands fisted at his sides, and for the first time in their friendship, John wondered if they were about to come to blows. "You cannot be careful enough with her. I want your word that you'll do the gentlemanly thing and tell her to stay away."

John would not do that. He loved her; she loved him, and they were going to have a wonderful life together, whether her brother approved or not. "Perhaps you should give your sister credit for knowing her own mind. She's a grown woman. Surely she can decide what she does with her time?"

Wilde didn't like that. His lips thinned and he rubbed the spot between his brows. "Be reasonable. My sister is young and impressionable and a romantic. She's going to believe the best of a situation until it bites her."

"I will not bite her." He would do everything in his power to see her happy.

Wilde shook his head. "I wish I could believe that."

---

"That does not look like a pleasant conversation." Henrietta nodded in John's direction. Edward was storming away, his face as dark as the thunderstorms that had been rolling for days.

Charlotte shivered in a good way. She'd always hated thunderstorms. Now they would always send a tingle of excitement and longing through her.

"The duke is coming our way," Josie added. "Goodness, I've never seen your brother so determined."

Whatever Edward's argument with John had been, she was about to hear of it.

"Sister," he said, holding out a hand. "Dance."

Charlotte rolled her eyes at her friends. Edward had been better at limiting his demands since he married Fiona. His wife had tempered his temper somewhat, and she'd certainly taught him that no, the entire world did not give way before him. But there were certain topics that continued to bring out the autocrat.

John was clearly one of them.

"Brother, what are you doing?" she asked when they were on the dance floor and out of earshot of the rest of the assembly.

"I am looking out for my sister."

*Mmmhmm.* "That's what your argument with John was about? The entire room saw you. You're causing unnecessary gossip and I'd prefer you didn't." When she and John finally announced their engagement, she didn't want rumors that her family was not one-hundred-percent approving of the match.

Edward grimaced, turning away from the rest of the room so only she could see his discontentment. "If Harrow hadn't been avoiding me, I could have had that conversation in private."

She resisted the temptation to step on his foot. "And what conversation is that, exactly?" She already knew the answer; she just wanted him to say it out loud so that he could hear what a dictator he was becoming.

"This gambling nonsense that you have running with John, I want you to end it. I know I promised you I would not interfere in your personal life—"

"Then don't." On the dance floor, she couldn't punctuate the statement with the finger pointing she wanted, so she settled for a mulish, stubborn glare. "You sought no one's permission to bring Fiona into our home, despite the danger it posed to our reputation. You asked no one's permission to marry a commoner."

"Charlotte…" There was a warning tone in his voice. Fiona was another topic of conversation that brought out the worst in him.

"When the two of you messed it all up and caused perhaps the greatest scandal London had seen in decades, I supported you and did everything in my power to see you happy." She hadn't cared that her sister wasn't a proper lady of the *ton*. She'd loved Fi and had been happy to continue managing the Wildeforde household so that Fiona could continue her work as a chemist.

Edward, it seemed, remembered this at least. "I know, Char, and I am more appreciative than you could realize. I simply want the same happiness for you. I don't think John is it."

John was very much her happiness, and it frustrated her to no end that her brother couldn't see it. "Why? What reason do you have for thinking that he and I aren't well suited?"

Edward sighed. He changed the course of their twirling so that she could see all the ballroom before her. "You used to be the center of these balls, flitting between one person and another, dancing every dance. It was the thing you enjoyed the most. Now you hang around the edges."

Charlotte rolled her eyes. "I am not 'hanging around the edges.' I still dance plenty—with every person I want to, including all the men whose influence you're seeking."

His face remained grim. "You used to dance with everyone."

A shade of guilt twinged in her gut. It hadn't felt good to say no tonight. There had been more than one startled face, and no matter how softly she'd delivered the rejection, she still felt awful disappointing people.

But at the same time, she felt freed by it. The men to whom she'd said no were those who consistently stepped on her toes without an apology, or whose conversation was demeaning, or who were a touch too free with their hands. She'd never enjoyed dancing with them but had, out of a misplaced sense of obligation. Because she'd wanted to be liked. Because she couldn't say no.

Luella had been right, drat it. But John had also been

right. It was perfectly fine for Charlotte to prioritize her own wants.

"Lord Harrow has helped me see that I don't need to give other people every moment of my time and energy in order to have some worth. Is that not a good thing?"

Edward shook his head. "John loathes this world, Char. Of course he thinks it doesn't deserve your time and attention. I worry that in your effort to win his affection, you'll let him distance you from what you love—from the people you love—and that you'll end up alone and miserable."

Charlotte squeezed his fingers. Ned's fears were unfounded. John had made peace with staying in England. They'd spent the past few days planning a future together, one split between London and their country estates. John would never be comfortable in the social whirl, but the image they'd painted together of their future was one that met both their needs—a happy compromise.

"I shall not leave you, brother. And John will not ask it of me. You'll see."

Dancing with Lady Hastings and Lady Pembroke was almost as uncomfortable as arguing with Wilde. In stark contrast to the duke, both women made it very clear they approved a match between John and their friend, and that they expected a proposal imminently. Their hints were not remotely subtle. His assurances that yes, he *did* think Charlotte the most beautiful, most elegant, most amusing woman in the room were not sufficient for either of them. Neither would let up, yet he would not spoil Charlotte's opportunity to tell her friends the news herself.

His only recourse was to escape to the card room earlier than planned. It was full to the brim. One table was crammed with younger bucks who seemed hell-bent on getting as drunk as possible as early as possible. The other table was more reserved—no doubt because at its head, flanked by footmen in elaborate livery, sat the king.

John was about to turn and leave when the sovereign caught his eye, raised an eyebrow, and whispered to a man who stood at his shoulder. The man studied John for a moment and whispered back. The king crooked his finger in John's direction.

No one ignored a royal summons.

Footmen raced to find an extra chair. The other men at the table scowled and shuffled their seats to make room. Taking a deep breath, John crossed to the table and bowed deeply. "Your Majesty."

"Viscount Harrow. Sit."

John inclined his head and took the empty seat, throwing a banknote into the pot and accepting a stack of chips from Lord Haddington. He murmured his acknowledgments to the other men at the table, and they nodded in return.

Many of them he knew only by sight; Charlotte had been giving him a who's who at each gathering they attended. One though, Dickey Trembly, Lord Rhinehurst, had been John's peer at school. They'd shared a dormitory, and if John had realized Dickey was at the table, he would have left the room, the king's presence be damned.

Rhinehurst had been the most awful of John's tormentors. From the moment John had stumbled over his words on arrival until the day he left Oxford, Dickey had made his life a living nightmare. It hadn't stopped at verbal insults. Dickey had been quite a talented artist. The caricatures he had drawn and posted around various dorm rooms had emboldened others to partake in the teasing.

*It's been twenty years. People change. You changed. No one will misbehave in the presence of their sovereign.*

John raised his glass in Rhinehurst's direction, an olive branch of sorts, though it turned his stomach. The cruel smirk he received in return set his heart thudding.

Oblivious to the undercurrent, the grey and stately Lord Haddington continued the conversation John had interrupted. "If we can get them both to agree, we have a good chance at passing the resolution before the session ends."

Another gentleman shook his head as he picked up the deck of cards and began to deal. "Passed or not, the resolution will have no impact if we don't have the Americans on our side, and their lawmakers are less in love with the British aristocracy than the wealthy cits we see in London."

The king sniffed. "What are your thoughts, Harrow? You've spent time in the Americas recently. What do they truly think of your sovereign?"

Rhinehurst smirked at the difficult position John found himself in. "Yes, Harrow. You've spent more time in the Americas than the rest of us c-c-combined."

All heads turned in John's direction. He tried not to let Rhinehurst's mockery affect him, but his jaw shut tight, and his tongue locked behind his teeth.

The king regarded him with heavy expectation. *Hell.* John picked up the cards that had been dealt and studied them, taking it as a moment to gather his thoughts and work his jaw so that he could respond. He would give the truth, even if it displeased the most powerful man in Europe. "They believe the new world and the old world should remain separate hemispheres, Your Majesty."

The words came out slowly, too slowly. He likely sounded like a simpleton. But at least they came out clearly. He took a deep breath, trying to relax his body. He could do this.

The king's lips pursed. "That is…disappointing."

Haddington grunted. "But not unexpected. How will they react to this proposition?"

John rolled his shoulders, trying to shift the enormous weight that threatened to suffocate him. "Any European country that attempts to gain influence in the Americas, north or south, will be strongly op-p-posed."

Rhinehurst snorted at his misstep.

*Damn.* One stutter always led to another. It was a blasted loop that, once started, was almost impossible to break free of. He could go days without tripping over his words, but the moment he felt under pressure, his old self came back.

The king's expression darkened, and John prepared himself for the royal's wrath. The rest of the table stilled, no cards or tokens moving as the congregation waited for the king's response.

Eventually, the king looked at his hand and threw in an absurd number of tokens. "I appreciate your honesty, Harrow, though your comments displease me. I cannot lay the fault of that sentiment at your door."

John let out a long breath. The rest of the table loosened and the game resumed. Haddington dropped his cards on the table. "I fold," he muttered. He signaled to a nearby footman, who offered a tray of cigars. "You know," he said, looking at John. "I've yet to see you at the Lords."

John twisted his brandy glass. "Managing my brother's affairs has consumed much of my t-time." The truth was, he didn't feel worthy of his spot at Westminster. Walter was always supposed to be the one with the power. He was the one born to it. John was a poor substitute with a head for science, not politics.

The king raised an eyebrow. "I would have thought it was your steam engines that were keeping you from your duties."

"Your Majesty?"

"I had my men investigate you after your brother's death, Lord Harrow. I know about your career in trade and your engines. They are not an excuse to shirk your duties to the crown, regardless of how impressive your achievements have been."

The king was right. He had accepted the responsibilities of the title. The Lords came with it. "I'll be sure to at-tend the next session."

"B-b-brilliant," Rhinehurst said. "Another id-d-diot in parliament."

# Chapter 22 —————

Charlotte was well into a quadrille when she spotted John stalking across the room toward the exit. Something was wrong. His expression was grim and his hands were fisted by his side.

"Lady Charlotte?"

She returned her attention to her dance partner, but as they turned, her gaze once more sought John. He acknowledged no one as he passed them, causing eyebrows to rise in his wake.

She dipped beneath the arms of another couple, almost stumbling over their feet due to her lack of attention.

"Is something the matter?" her partner asked, displeased and following the direction of her gaze with an annoyed look.

"My lord, forgive me," she said with an apologetic wince. "I must go." It was inexcusable to leave one's partner in the middle of the dance floor. This would be gossip on everyone's lips all evening and a Wildeforde did not court gossip. But John was clearly upset, and supporting him was a higher priority than perfect behavior.

She hurried after him, weaving in and out around the guests. She ignored the footman in the hallway who offered to fetch her coat and gloves and dashed out into the night. The coolness of the night air was a welcome change from the stuffy heat of the ballroom. John was retreating down the drive.

"John!" she called as she ran across the gravel. "John!"

He turned around. She could barely see him in the dark, but at least he was waiting for her.

"What is it?" she asked as she reached him, out of breath.

"I can't do this," he said.

"Can't do what?"

He tugged at the ends of his hair, ruining his perfectly smoothed coiffure. "I can't be this person who you need. I do not belong here, Charlotte. I am not one of you."

It didn't make any sense. He'd been having a good time, hadn't he? He'd been deep in conversation with Hen and Josie as they danced. Half the party was quite taken with him. "But you were doing so well. You were fitting in perfectly."

"I was *not*. I danced because you wanted me to dance, and I made inane conversation because to not do so would be rude. But I don't fit in here."

She didn't believe it. Wouldn't believe it. For goodness' sake, he'd spent the past few days reassuring her that he would be happy living this life. "What happened? Something must have set off this...realization of yours given you were perfectly fine two hours ago."

John took off his glasses and rubbed his hands over his face. "I ran into Dickey Trembly, Lord Rhinehurst. The encounter was...unpleasant. It was an hour of snide comments and outright mockery."

*Drat.* "Dickey is unpleasant. He's a small-minded, cruel, and petty little man. Even his title isn't enough to see him invited into many homes. I'd pay no attention to what he says."

John shook his head, stepping backward to put more distance between him and Charlotte. "Dickey only says out loud what other people are thinking. That I'm a stuttering idiot who's a poor replacement for my perfect brother." His voice cracked at the mention of Walter.

Charlotte shook her head, taking a step toward him to put a hand on his arm. It killed her to see him in so much anguish. "No, that's not true. Most people are kind and generous and they care not for any trivial hiccups you make speaking. I doubt people even notice."

Once again, he moved away from her touch. "You do not know what you're talking about." It was the first time she had ever heard him yell, and she could feel the blood drain from her face. "You are a young, naïve little girl who has experienced nothing of the world. You do not know what evil humans are truly capable of."

It was her turn to step back as his words barreled into her. So he truly did think that she was some unworldly, unintelligent creature who knew nothing. It had been what she'd feared, but over the past week she'd put that fear aside.

She couldn't help the tears that sprang to her eyes or the way her lip quivered, or how a giant pit formed in her gut. "I may not have your experience in the world," she managed to say despite the tightening of her throat. "But to suggest that I don't understand people when I fill my life with them is supremely arrogant. I may be younger than you. I may not have traveled or started a business, but at least I don't hide away. I fill my week with more people than you speak to in a year, so your implication that I know nothing of mankind is ludicrous. I know more than you ever will, and as somebody who truly understands people, I can tell you that your presumptions are false. Your conclusions are wrong. It is *you* who knows nothing, Lord Harrow."

His expression flattened. It was as though he put up shutters to keep the storm of her words out. He took another two steps backward and bowed. "Very well then, my lady. I bid you good night."

Charlotte stared at his retreating back, hurt morphing into frustration. How could he walk away from her in the middle of an argument? How could retreating resolve anything? Her brothers certainly had their flaws, but at least they always stayed to fight with her.

"John!" He stopped, but it took longer than she'd like for him to turn to face her. "We had a plan. Are we still going there?"

Argument or not, they had a job to do tonight.

⌒

Whist had lost its luster after the game with Lord Berridge. Charlotte couldn't bring herself to get excited and that feeling seemed to permeate through the room. After much discussion, the house agreed to move the whist tables together to form one large one. There was a game that had recently arrived in London from Mississippi. Poker was played individually—John could not help her with it. Win or lose, it would be on her.

The dealer walked the table through the rules, answering questions and providing tips for wagering. Others stood back, watching, waiting for their chance to try this new game for themselves.

John sat across the table from her. He'd been rather silent on the carriage ride over, handing Charlotte the spare dress from his satchel and keeping his eyes averted until it was time to do up the buttons that held it together.

She'd tried to start a conversation a few times, but clearly the events at tonight's ball—*the dratted Dickey Rhinehurst*— had put John in a mood that was not easily broken. Men.

She and John would have a conversation about how they should fight. Walking away from her in the middle of one was not an option she would tolerate. But that conversation was for another day, when the pressure of bankruptcy and Edward's imminent wrath at their engagement was no longer weighing on them.

The practice round was almost over. They were about to dive into the game in earnest. John's face was as grim as she'd seen it. Charlotte put a hand to her mouth, her thumbnail pressing against her lips. *Are you well?*

John blinked twice. *Yes.*

Everyone took back their chips, stacked them neatly, and prepared to play. The novelty of the game lent a fresh air to the atmosphere. While there were a handful of serious players, the majority were showing each other their hands, asking for advice, and laughing even as they lost.

To almost all who surrounded her, poker was fun. She

struggled to find the same levity. She wanted this charade to be over. She wanted William safe and home. She wanted John to be relieved of this burden that weighed so heavily on him.

They had planned to take things slowly, to let the wins trickle in over time and in low numbers until they'd built up to what they needed while remaining more or less unnoticed. But that strategy was going to take weeks.

She was done with this. She didn't want to wait weeks. Tonight, she would take more risks for better rewards.

She didn't count on it all going wrong.

One lost hand quickly turned into another, and then another. It was as though all the things that she had learned about the people she was playing with no longer applied in this new game.

All the tells that she'd noted each night—the way Patrick rubbed his nose when he was about to lose, the way Fitzroy's eyes widened when he was dealt a decent set of cards, the silly little whistle Brockford made when he was about to take a game-ending trick—these things that had been true for the past week were suddenly not true.

John kept indicating that it was time to leave. His expression was grim, and he kept shaking his head at the end of every round when it was time to join again or get out.

But she didn't want to get out. If she left the game now, it would be at a loss and she couldn't accept that, not with so much on the line. It would come good; she knew it. So, despite John's disapproval, she tossed chips into the pot and gestured for another hand.

The cards were very, very bad. She would either need to fold immediately or bluff like her life depended on it. Or William's.

Lord Brockford sensed her bluff. Called it. Her pile of chips shrank again.

Desperation gripped her. And anger. What a hellish, hellish night. Everything was slipping away from her: William's freedom, John's freedom, the chance of the two of them building a life together. She wasn't proud of what she was about to do. It wasn't the behavior of a Wildeforde. It wasn't who she was, but neither was she the type to go down without a fight.

Her next hand was strong—two aces and a jack was a hand she could work with. She increased her bet, and then while everyone's eyes were on the player next to her, she used her fingernail to create a single tiny nick in the top left corner of both ace cards and another nick on the top right for the jack.

Will had shown her a series of ways to cheat at cards. She'd demanded he reveal his secrets after he'd thrashed her repeatedly. It would take time to mark enough of the cards to be useful, so Charlotte became more conservative, playing with smaller amounts that could help keep her in the game longer. Then, once she had a fair sense of who had what hand, she could bet big when she knew she could triumph.

Nothing was going to get in the way of her winning.

◡

Damn the woman. It had taken John the better part of a half hour to realize what Charlotte was up to. The marks she was making were subtle. But subtle or not, a skillful player was going to pick them up. The only reason it had slipped the notice of the men at the table was because they were so enthralled with this new game that they weren't taking it seriously. But these were some of the most experienced card sharks in London, and she was playing as though she were in a Mayfair parlor with debutantes and grande dames.

But every time he indicated they should take their winnings and go, she stubbornly refused to meet his gaze. To keep the attention off of her, John used his memory to win more games than he'd like, casting aside his strategy of remaining beneath notice.

"I say," Lord Hailson said as John raked in another round of winnings. "You're having the Devil's own luck."

John shrugged. "Less luck and more six weeks of non-stop playing on the sea crossing back home."

Hailson grunted. "Don't take us down too hard, chap. We're all only just getting the hang of this."

"Except Mrs. Brown. She's won almost as much as you have."

Charlotte ducked her head and fluttered her eyelashes. "I must have been a very good girl at some point for fortune to favor me so tonight." She leaned forward, elbow on the table, hand cupping her chin, breasts threatening to spill from her neckline.

The men's attention was suddenly focused elsewhere, their eyes practically glazing over, and that damning thread of conversation was effectively snipped.

"Perhaps it's time to call it a night then, Mrs. Brown," John said. "Luck is a fickle mistress. I'd hate for her to turn on you."

Charlotte pouted and John couldn't tell how much of it was an act. He smiled tightly, not allowing a measure of his annoyance to show. She'd amassed a small fortune—more than they'd won all other nights combined, as had he. They needed to leave before any of the other players questioned his skills and her luck.

"One more hand," she implored.

"You've more courage than I have," John responded. "I shan't tempt fate any longer." He downed the rest of his drink and gave his chips to a nearby footman. "Good night, my lords. Mrs. Brown." He bowed. His heart rate quickened as he walked away from the table, trusting that she would follow whether or not she wanted to. Surely she would.

He had an ill feeling in his gut. Charlotte had been reckless. Her cheating had been subtle and her outrageous flirting had blinded the other players to it. But Charlotte had forgotten that there were more people in the gaming hell than just the players she sat with.

Other than the dealer, who had given no signal that aught was amiss, at least ten employees had their eyes roving across the room. It was their job to know everything that was going on. Charlotte may have fooled the players of the game, but she may not have fooled all those who ran it.

Which was why he was loath to leave her alone, even for a few minutes. Instead of walking farther up the street and waiting for her there, John stayed outside the building, leaning against the wall by the window where he could see what was happening inside.

Clearly unhappy, Charlotte finished her glass of brandy and left it on the edge of the table. She exchanged her chips for cash, flicking through the stack and then tucking it into her reticule, leaving aside a handful of notes, which she distributed among the serving girls as she left. Charlotte's generous tipping was one reason she was so well attended to by the staff.

The majordomo helped her with her coat, and she walked out of the building without incident. As she stepped into a pool of lamplight and raised her hand to hail a nearing hackney, John released the breath that had gone stale as he'd watched her leave.

She didn't notice him until he was climbing into the hack beside her. She gasped, hand to her throat, and exhaled heavily when she realized it was him, giving him a gentle thwack on the arm. "John, you terrified me."

The soft laugh she gave as she took off her mask loosened all the buckles that had tightened within him the moment he'd first seen her marking the cards. She was safe. He took her face in both hands and kissed her fiercely. "You terrified *me*," he said as the carriage jolted into motion. "What were you thinking?"

A crease formed between Charlotte's brows. "I was thinking that I didn't want to be doing this every night for the next month. I was thinking that we both have problems we need resolved immediately. And it worked."

She reached into her reticule and pulled out a fistful of money and then another fistful. "John, it's done. It's over. Between the money we have in your safe, this money here, and my dowry, we have enough to repay all of your debts, and William's. It's over." She sagged against the wall of the carriage, a relieved smile on her face.

John looked at the wads of notes in her hands. It was their freedom, of sorts. Not the freedom he'd gone into the scheme fighting for. He wouldn't be returning to America.

Instead, he had a different freedom. His estates would soon be set to rights, he would employ trustworthy stewards to execute the bulk of the management so that he could focus his efforts on his work with the firm, and he would wake up every day next to the woman of his dreams.

It wasn't what he'd originally planned, but his original plans seemed cold and lifeless now. Charlotte had changed everything.

She was looking at him, her bottom lip caught between her teeth, her hands curled tightly around the money as she waited for a response.

"It's over." He leaned across the seat, one hand grazing over the jeweled pins in her hair as he pressed his lips against hers, the other hand wrapping around her waist. Even through the layers of petticoats, dress, and coat, he could feel the spark that existed between them. "I'm sorry about earlier," he whispered. "Dickey has always known what levers to push to get a reaction from me."

Charlotte shifted until she was sitting on his lap, her coat open, her breasts pressed against his jacket, her fingers in his hair. "I'm sorry I scared you," she said kissing his cheek, his jaw, his lips. "Let's forget about it."

The scent of her overwhelmed him. As her arse moved against his cock, he considered taking her then and there. "Charlotte, you are exquisite." He nuzzled her neck, licking and nipping at her soft skin until her moan threatened to undo him. She arched her back and his attention turned to her breasts, barely contained by the low neckline of her dress. He brought a hand up to massage them, kneading them firmly, a thrill going through him at the way she gasped.

He nudged at the lace of her neckline and when her breast

sprang free, he took it in his mouth, sucking at it, grazing her nipple with his teeth, feeling his cock throb in response. He reached between them, unbuttoning his breeches.

"John." Her fingers pulled hard at his hair, the pain adding to the intensity of his feelings.

The carriage jolted to a halt. Charlotte's eyes, still dazed, slowly focused, and a crease formed between her brows. "Surely we aren't home already?"

It took a moment for her words to sink through the fog of desire. Then all breath left him. His stomach pulled itself into tight knots. Instinct told him what this was—what was about to happen. He put a finger to his lips.

Charlotte's confused expression didn't alter, but she seemed to understand that something was amiss as she shifted off of his lap and quickly rearranged her clothing, pulling her neckline back to where it should be.

He leaned across her to the window on the carriage wall opposite the door and pulled aside the curtain just far enough to see that they were nowhere near Mayfair. By the look of the surrounding buildings, the lack of streetlamps, and the unpaved road, they were in a seedier part of the city.

John's mind ran through every scenario he could think of, searching for a way to keep Charlotte from harm, but without knowing how many men were currently circling the carriage, there was no guarantee that it was possible.

He buttoned the fall of his breeches. "Stay in the corner," he whispered.

She nodded, her face pale. As she shifted to the backward-facing bench, she too drew back the curtain. What she saw made her gasp, her eyes going wide and her fingers flying to her mouth.

He rested a hand on her knee and squeezed it, trying to give her confidence that he didn't feel, and then he faced the door, putting himself between Charlotte and the men outside.

The door opened, as he knew it would. Brunel's giant right-hand man filled the doorframe as he put a hand on either side and leaned toward them. "Let's have a wee chat about tonight's events, shall we?" he asked.

John heard Charlotte's breath *whoosh* out as she realized that her actions at the tables had not gone unnoticed as she had thought. She put a hand on his shoulder and tried to move around him, but he refused to budge.

"John had nothing to do with it," she said.

"Hush, love." He would not have her make herself any more a target than she already was.

"But—" She tried to push around him, but he flung out an arm so that she could not pass. He turned, locking eyes with her. "Wait inside. Do not say a word. There's nothing you can do."

Her face turned grey as she heard the truth in his words.

John edged toward the carriage door, knowing full well what was about to happen. It wouldn't be the first time that he had been beaten. He had survived it before; he would survive this one, so long as the attack was only on him. He didn't know that he'd survive it if they went for Charlotte also.

The brute decided John wasn't moving fast enough and grabbed him by the arm, yanking him out of the carriage. He had a wicked gleam in his eyes, as if it was nights like this that he lived for. John looked past him and locked eyes with a younger lad, who looked as though he might be sick at any moment. He clearly didn't have the stomach for this. Maybe he could keep Charlotte from harm.

"Don't let her leave the carriage," he muttered to the boy. "Please. Do what you must to me, but please spare her."

The lad didn't acknowledge John at all, but he took a spot in front of the carriage door.

Then the beating began.

# Chapter 23

At the first sickening punch to John's ribs, Charlotte launched herself forward. Private Gray caught her with a hand to her chest and shoved her backward. Her head thwacked hard against the carriage wall, and she tumbled to the floor, banging the edge of the seat on the way down.

Her vision swam as she struggled to her knees and crawled toward John. She had to reach him. She had to help. This was all her fault.

She wrapped a hand around the doorframe to lever herself upright. The turncoat slammed the door shut. It was only by a hair's breadth that it missed her fingers as she snatched them back. She pushed on the door, but it wouldn't budge. She yanked open the curtains.

And sobbed.

John was on the ground, curled into a ball, his arms

over his head as the men around him took turns laying in the boot.

She screamed, an unholy, bloody sound that was too primal to be language. She pounded on the door with her fists and pushed at the handle, but Private Gray wouldn't allow it to open.

The attack felt as though it went on for hours, but it was likely no more than a few minutes before the mob stepped back. John lay there in the middle, unmoving. All breath escaped her.

*John!*

The door swung open, and she leapt out of it, collapsing to her knees in the mud beside him. He was a bloody mess, with a gash in his hairline, blood running from his nose, and bruises already blossoming across his hands. She stroked his hair, and he moaned. A wave of relief swept through her. *He's alive.*

"I'm sorry," she whispered. "I'm so, so sorry." If she hadn't cheated, this would never have happened. If she hadn't insisted they wager their way out of debt, this would never have happened.

Brunel's thug crouched down so that he was face-to-face with Charlotte and gave her a cruel, gap-toothed smile. He nudged John's shoulder. "Lord Harrow, can you hear me?"

John's eyes fluttered open.

"We'll be taking this." The cur held up Charlotte's reticule, which had all their winnings. "You still owe Brunel five thousand pounds. Now he wants it in a week."

"I almost killed you." Charlotte had muttered the words over and over on the journey home, but it wasn't until Mosely had gone downstairs to send for a doctor that Charlotte looked John in the eyes as she said it.

"It wasn't your fault," he responded, wincing as his jaw protested the movement.

He'd known from the start how dangerous their game had been. Charlotte was naïve and optimistic, and that she had even thought to attempt cheating in a gaming hell meant that John hadn't done a sufficient job preparing her for what they were going to do.

He'd seen enough of this part of society to know that a beating had always been a possibility. Hell, they were lucky it hadn't been worse.

"Of course it's my fault. If I hadn't cheated, you wouldn't be here."

He tried to raise a hand so he could wipe away the damp tear tracks on her cheeks, but the movement felt like a knife to the ribs, so he satisfied himself with taking hold of her hand, which sat on the bedcovers next to him, and squeezing it.

"You may have cheated, but I'd been counting cards all week. That's probably *why* Brunel's men were watching the table so closely. I am every bit as much to blame as you."

By agreeing to her madcap scheme, he'd put her in an immense amount of danger. Wilde was right not to trust John with his sister. John had been a selfish fool to let the events of tonight happen.

Her grip tightened on his. "I will make this right. Whatever I must do to fix this, I will."

"No." John spoke as loudly as he could with his broken

ribs. "You are not to go anywhere near them again. Do you understand? And you're not to leave the house without an escort—a footman who knows his way around a weapon."

She cocked her head. "Because our footmen are all highly proficient with knives."

Her teasing sarcasm did nothing to lessen his panic. She was headstrong, stubborn, and possessed of the belief that she could solve anything. Her positivity had brightened up his life, but it was also what was going to get her hurt if she took on the gambling den proprietor and his men on her own.

"I mean it, Charlotte. You are not to approach them in any manner."

There was a rap at the bedroom door. Mosely stuck his head in. "The doctor is here to see you, my lord."

Charlotte gently tucked the blanket around John's chest. "What would you like me to do?"

John looked at this woman who'd set her own life upside down in order to help the people she cared about. Who'd risked everything for him and for her brother and who would continue to do so if she had half the opportunity.

"Just stay with me."

~

Charlotte crept home with the dawn. The sawbones had assured her that John would be fine—his kidneys were bruised, his ribs and nose were broken, and the gash on his head had needed stitches, but he seemed to have escaped a concussion or any other serious injury. He would be in pain, but he would live.

She lay next to him, waiting until his breathing was soft and even with sleep before she snuck out through the garden. She was exhausted, and all she wanted was to change out of this too-tight, too-low-cut, too-bright dress that had seemed so much fun at first and now just seemed like a bad talisman.

With any luck, none of the servants would realize that she hadn't entered through the front door since leaving for the ball the night before.

Luck was no longer on her side.

"Where have you been?"

She whirled to face Edward, wrapping her arms around herself to ensure the coat she was wearing did not gape and give the game away.

"It was a crush," she said. "Everyone who was anyone was there. Even the king. I'm only just getting home."

"You were not there when I sent for you." Beneath the anger in his voice was something else, something she rarely heard from him. Fear. His hair looked as though he'd been running his hands through it all night. Every inch of him was taut.

She took a step forward, placing a hand on his arm. "Brother, relax. I'm fine. I hopped from party to party tonight. I'm sorry that I didn't tell you that was my plan."

Her words had no calming impact on him. If anything, he was more angry. "William is home," Edward said. "But you knew that already."

Charlotte's stomach dropped. The look of wrath on Ned's face was not a look that he'd ever directed at her.

No, the only time she'd ever seen him this furious, the only time he'd looked so betrayed, had been the night Fiona was arrested—the night Edward had banished William from the house and enlisted him in the army.

He turned on his heel and stalked away.

"Ned, wait. I can explain," she pleaded as she hurried after him, but the only way she could explain her actions was by telling him that William had expressly forbidden her from sharing his secret. But even though the younger of her brothers had caught her off guard by revealing his presence to Edward, she still wasn't ready to break faith with him. "What did Will tell you?"

Once inside his study, Edward went straight to his desk, where a bottle of brandy already stood open. *Not a good sign.*

"He didn't tell me anything. I was at White's. Fiona was alone in her laboratory." The bleakness of his brother's gaze sent shivers coursing through her.

"What happened?" Will had been so angry at his brother, but it had never occurred to Charlotte that he might confront Edward before she had a chance to bring him to reason. "Ned, what happened?"

Edward threw down the brandy in one shot. "He knocked her over. Thank God two footmen heard his yelling and came running."

Charlotte's knees weakened, and she sank onto the arm of the chaise longue. "Is she well? Is he well?"

Ned slammed his glass onto his desk. "Neither of them is well. Goddamn it, Char. How could you enable this?"

Her fear quickly turned to anger, and she rose to her feet. "How could *I* enable this? *You* are the one who did this. You sent him off to war. I have been the one tending to his wounds. I have been the one fighting to keep him from killing himself with drink. I have been the one trying to chase the nightmares from his mind. You have no idea what I've been doing to save him. It has all been on my shoulders."

"Then you should have come to me," Edward bellowed, stepping toward her. "The moment he returned, you should've come to me. He is my brother. I had the right to know."

Unwilling to give her brother any ground, she planted herself in front of him, hands fisted at her hips. He might be taller than she was, but she made up for it in pure fury. "You had the right to *nothing* until he was willing to see you and have only yourself to blame."

Edward shook out his hands, as though he could fling all his fear and frustration away. "Will is beyond your ability to help."

Her throat tightened because she knew his words to be true. "I will never give up trying." She couldn't, even if it took every ounce of energy in her.

His tone shifted then. Anger became despair. "I don't know if there's anything we can do." His face twisted with guilt and grief, then he buried his head in his hands.

It had been in a moment of anger and fear that Ned had forced William into the army. He'd done his best to reverse the commission, but a contract was a contract and the general had been intractable. William had sent back all of Ned's letters unopened.

As furious as Charlotte was with her eldest brother, she could not bear to see him in so much pain. Tentatively, she reached out for his fingers and entwined them with hers, squeezing them gently.

"*I* did this," he whispered. "I did this." They were words she'd shot at him intending to hurt, but hearing them made her insides twist with regret.

"You did not put the bullet in him, brother. You did not make him fall down drunk in a dirty alleyway where his wound got infected. You did not put the laudanum in his hands or the drink in his mouth. You played a role in this, but it is not your fault."

Edward sank to his knees and sobbed. There was a soft *whoosh* as the door opened. Charlotte looked up. Fiona watched with tears in her eyes, her wrist bandaged.

"Will did nae mean to push me over. He fell at my feet and grabbed my legs and I tumbled. 'Tis just a sprain."

"His yelling?" Charlotte asked.

"He was pleading with me," Fi said in a broken voice. "He kept asking how I live with it. How he could live with it."

They were words Charlotte had heard Will mutter several times this past week.

A tear spilled and tracked down Fi's cheek. "Charlotte, what did he *do*?"

# Chapter 24 ————————

The doctor had come past and given William a strong sedative, along with instructions to feed him bland food and plain water for the next week. They were told to expect vomiting and shaking and a fight from him, which was why the footmen had bound his hands.

It broke Charlotte's heart to see him like this, but at the same time, there was a sense of relief. He was getting the help he needed. The help she couldn't provide.

"Charlie?" His voice was hoarse, and she crossed to his side immediately.

"Brother, I thought you were asleep."

He swallowed hard and shook his head. "Can't sleep. Too much screaming."

There was no screaming in Wildeforde House, which meant it was in Will's head.

*Breathe. Just breathe.*

She took a washcloth from the table beside his bed and wiped his brow, trying to ignore the ropes around his wrists that prevented him from doing it himself.

"Can I get you anything?"

"A drink?"

She picked up the glass of water and held it to his lips, but he knocked it away, the liquid splashing over her skirts.

"A proper drink, Charlie."

She should have expected that. She squared her shoulders, readying for a clash. "I cannot, Will. You know the doctor has given strict orders. No laudanum and no alcohol."

The look he gave her was a hateful, hateful expression that resembled nothing of the sweet, mischievous brother she knew. It filled her with anguish.

"You won't help me?"

She could understand his shock. Ever since they were children, he'd been able to rely on her to hide his scrapes or distract their mother or to shield him from the dowager's wrath. On the occasions when Charlotte couldn't, she would sneak in to see him afterward and give him the food and comfort their mother wouldn't. She'd spent her entire life solving William's problems.

"No, Will. I cannot help you."

He snarled, as if the withdrawal of alcohol and opiates was making him barely human. "Since when have you obeyed orders?" he asked. "You meddle in everything. Be on my side for once, Charlie."

The words were a knife to her chest. When she inhaled, the wound cut deeper. "I am always on your side, my darling. Which is why I cannot help you with this."

She flinched as he turned from her and spat, "Then get out."

⁓

Charlotte had been unable to sneak away until after dinner. Every time she reached the door out into the garden, a servant found her. Edward had calmed down and needed a full account of William's story. William had called for her. When Fiona mentioned she was visiting John, Charlotte sighed with relief that someone was with him—at least until Fiona returned with a scowl on her face.

It was only when both brothers had retired for the evening, Edward to his rooms and Will finally falling asleep, that she could escape to check on her other patient.

Then she took the back stairs outside, only seen by one maid, who was sure to keep Charlotte's secret. By now, she knew the path to the door in the wall by heart. She didn't need a light to guide her. Her feet took her straight to the double glass doors of his study.

Mosely, too, didn't say a word when he saw her in the corridors. She gently opened the door to John's room. A lamp was on by the bed, and John was sitting upright, his eyes closed. Newton was lying on the floor. He raised his head at her entrance, yawned wide, and then settled back down on his paws.

Charlotte crept forward, gave the dog a scratch behind the ears, and then slid as quietly as she could into John's bed.

He started, eyes flying open, mouth pressing tight at the movement, then relaxed as he saw her.

"What a day," she said. He put an arm around her and she

snuggled into his shoulder, inhaling that now-familiar scent of bergamot and graphite. "Does this hurt?"

"No," he muttered, dropping a kiss on the top of her head. "How was your day?"

She sighed as though she could breathe out all the conflict the day had brought. "William came home. It was *bad*. I cannot even begin to describe it. He and Ned are fighting; Ned and I are fighting; Will isn't speaking to me. Edward has him tied up in his old bedroom while the liquor makes its way out of his system."

She'd held on to her composure all day, but now, in John's arms, the tears fell. "I failed him."

He kissed her hair and stroked her arm. "You did not fail him."

She sobbed into John's shirt, her breath mingling with the scent of him. His arms wrapped around her created a hidden refuge she did not want to leave. "I did not fix him. He's as broken now as he was when he first returned."

John's long, gentle strokes continued, each touch slowing her breath and calming her thumping heart. "He was never your problem to fix, love. You can give him all the love you can. Edward can keep him tied to a bed in the short-term, but neither of you is responsible for solving William's issues."

Logically, she knew it was true. Will's damage ran too deep. Restoring him to his usual self was beyond her capabilities. Her heart said differently. "He has been able to count on me his entire life. How do I abandon him now?" She looked up at John, genuinely searching for an answer.

He wiped her cheeks with a bandaged thumb, the tears soaking into the fabric. "You're allowing him to stand on his own two feet. That isn't abandoning him. It's helping him to grow into the man he needs to be. You can't coddle him forever."

"I don't know how to deny him." How could she possibly keep from saying yes? She'd declined to chair three different committees in the past week, much to the surprise of those who asked, but there was a difference between carving out some space in the day for herself and allowing her brother to suffer when she could step in.

"You say no. And then you bite your tongue before you can say yes. And then you walk away before you can change your mind." John made it sound so easy. He was so used to having thick barriers up that he couldn't understand what it meant to have boundaries so blurred and porous.

"We cannot simply walk away. Brunel will not disappear just because Will has moved back home. Ned still doesn't know about the threat. I fear I must tell him but that it will sever what fragile bond remains between Will and me."

Because William's returning had solved very little. True, he would get better care now than he had been getting, but his debt remained and John's predicament hadn't altered at all. The greatest challenges they had faced were still there—a wild and dangerous squall about to break.

John's fingers tightened on her arm. "You don't need to worry about that now. Not Will's debt. Not mine. It is all resolved." His words came out half-strangled, raising the hairs on Charlotte's arms.

She pulled away, shifting so that she could face him. "What do you mean, it's all resolved? In a day when we've been trying for a fortnight?"

John shuffled farther up so he could look at her directly.

Pain flashed across his face as he did. He took her hands in his. "I've sold my shares in the firm. Fiona agreed to it this afternoon. They'll be distributed amongst her, Asterly, and Amelia. The money from the sale can settle your brother's debts and mine with no more gambling."

She pulled her hands from his, recoiling from the news the way she would from a hot stove. "No, you cannot do that. The firm is your life."

He reached out and caught her fingers. "You are my life. You and the family we'll create. But in order to see that life come to pass, I must pay off my debts and set the estates to rights."

That explained Fiona's foul look this afternoon and why she'd hidden in her laboratory rather than joining the family for dinner. Fi understood as well as Charlotte what John was sacrificing.

She shook her head. "This isn't right. You cannot give up your life's work. We will find another way to come up with the money."

John shifted and winced. "What way, Charlotte? An heiress's dowry? I will not marry another, and we've exhausted all other options."

He was right, of course. If there had been another way, they would have found it. They would have taken it rather than risking all in a gaming hell.

"We can adapt. We can beg Ned to give us my dowry no matter how hard he opposes the match. I can sell what I own to settle the rest." She didn't need dozens of ball gowns or jewelry that was only worn at state functions.

John sighed. "I'm not selling my shares only for us, love. I'm doing it for all the people who rely on the estates. It's for all the small business owners who are struggling to keep their heads above water because of the debt I owe them."

"The debt Walter owes them," she muttered.

"The debt I now owe them. I inherited the title; I inherited the duty."

He'd clearly made his mind up. He was correct; selling his company would enable them to start their life together free of encumbrances. Edward would be far more willing to approve of the match knowing that she'd have a home that was fully staffed. "You won't come to regret it? You won't come to regret me if you make this sacrifice?"

He leaned forward, grunting quietly, and gave her a quick kiss. "No, love. I'd make it a dozen times over if it meant having you as my wife."

"Dratted Walter. It's a good thing he's dead or he would experience just how much you don't want to wrong a Wildeforde."

His mouth quirked a little. "Lucky for him, he is dead. But this is the right move. It's the only way forward for us. Solicitors are arriving in the morning to draw up contracts. The sale should be final and all debts satisfied by the end of the week."

As much as she hated this course of action, she could not help feeling relieved. She wanted this entire mess done with. She wanted the banns read, the wedding over, and for her and John to start their life together.

But first they had to tell Ned.

"When do you think we should announce it?" she asked.

"When the debts are settled. When your brother can see for himself that I can give you a life that makes you happy."

# Chapter 25 ——————

A week later as they pulled up in front of The Lucky Honeypot, Charlotte wasn't wearing a mask—it was best Brunel remember exactly who he was dealing with: Viscount Harrow and Lady Charlotte Stirling, beloved sister of the Duke of Wildeforde and favorite cousin to the king himself.

"I wish you hadn't come," John said again, taking Charlotte's hand as she alighted from the carriage.

They'd had this argument over and over. John obviously hadn't realized a Wildeforde never conceded a battle if they didn't have to. "I wish *you* hadn't come. You're clearly in more danger than I am. You've barely healed since our last encounter with them."

John still moved stiffly. His bruises had almost fully healed, but she could see him wince when he took a deep breath, and his hand would go to his lower back any time he'd been on his feet for too long. "I'm still not comfortable with you in their reach," he said.

Charlotte sighed and patted his shoulder. "I know, but as I've said, Brunel expects me to deliver on William's debts. The last thing we need is for you to hand over the blunt and have him say that I haven't kept to my end of the deal."

John didn't offer a response because she knew he didn't have a good one. They'd already ascertained that the gambling den proprietor could not be trusted, and Charlotte would not leave any possibility that the money they handed over wouldn't get them out of Brunel's grip.

She gave his hand a squeeze as they crossed the road. The door, usually wide open with light spilling out, was firmly closed. They knocked and waited, her heart thumping just a little harder.

It was Private Gray who opened the door. "You're cutting it fine, aren't you, my lady?"

John had pulled every string he could to get the funds released quickly. The contracts, signed by his business partners in Abingdale, had arrived that morning by a courier who had ridden through two nights in a row.

Edward's man of business and the men at the bank had balked at the prospect of delivering the funds to John the same day, but there were benefits to being a viscount and one of those was the ability to insist on unreasonable measures.

"Hello to you too, Private Gray," Charlotte said. "Is your master in?" She breezed past him, showing no signs of her disquiet.

The casino during the day was a stark difference from the casino at night. In daylight, the furnishings looked tacky, the carpet marred with stains, and the artwork not quite as mesmerizing.

The room had taken her breath away that first night. Now, there was nothing magical about it, particularly not with the ruffians, who normally faded into the shadows, taking pride of place at a table in the center of the room, staring at them.

At its head sat a man in clothes as fine as any lord's. He had an air of confidence about him, and every person sitting there seemed to defer to him. Brunel, then. He put down his drink and clapped one of his men on the shoulder before approaching Charlotte and John. But despite the way he bore down on them, she couldn't keep her eyes from flicking toward his men. Their faces were fixed into her memory.

The one at the far end had been the first to hit John. The one to his left had landed the blow across the back of John's legs that had caused him to keel over. To the left of him was the man whose boot had connected with John's ribs.

She would not cry. She would not flinch despite the blow those memories landed. She tightened her grip on John's hand. Looking up, she could see a muscle tic along the edge of his clenched jaw.

No doubt his flashbacks to that night were worse than hers.

"Have you got my money?" Brunel picked at his teeth with a silver quill.

She reached into her reticule and drew out a weighty packet. "Here." She slapped it into his outstretched hand.

Brunel hefted it and then tossed it to one of the serving girls who was standing nearby. "Count it," he said.

*The cur.* "It's all there. I'm a woman of my word."

He cocked his head, giving her a disbelieving look.

"Given your willingness to play loose with the rules, my lady, you'll forgive me for not trusting you."

She stiffened, shame flooding her. Drat it, she hated to be in the wrong.

The serving girl came back and nodded.

"So we're done then." It was not a question. She was done deferring to the man.

He grinned. "Come now, m'lady. Is that any way to talk to a man who's shown such grace? I haven't even asked for retribution. I don't like it when people don't play an honest game. If anyone is going to be dishonest, it will be me."

"We paid your retribution," she snapped. "You almost killed him with it."

John placed a hand on her elbow and drew her back until she was behind him. Letting him do so grated, but she understood why he did it, and she would concede this moment for his sake.

Brunel scowled at John, clearly affronted. "We do not lay hands on women. Not even cheating, sharp-tongued harpies."

Charlotte started forward, but John's hand across her hips prevented her from giving Brunel the response he deserved.

John remained infuriatingly cool. "Then you won't mind that we leave," John said.

Brunel looked past John to her. "You're always welcome back, you know. The gentlemen pay little attention to the cards when you're at the table. You could fold when I say fold, distract when I tell you to distract. We could have ourselves a partnership. Make a tidy sum."

Her skin shivered at the thought of being in partnership

with this man. "Never," she spat. "Our debts are paid. I look forward to never seeing you again."

⁓

John had gone first to the bank, where he paid the tailor's debts—the full outstanding amount and not just what he owed, so that the family could be released from debtors' prison. Then he made his way to Bond Street, to the bootmakers and milliners and gunsmiths. Without fail, each thanked him profusely, surprised that he'd come good at all. How horrific that that was their expectation.

He could have had someone else deliver banknotes to the rest of his creditors. There was no legal reason to do it himself, just the desire to show people that while they may not have been able to rely on the previous Lord Harrow, they could rely on him.

By the time John reached the home of Lady Hornsworth—the last creditor on his list—the uncomfortable limp with which he'd started the day had deepened into an excruciating jab of pain every time he placed his weight on his left leg. The boot he'd taken to his kidney had left a deep purple bruise and a reminder of the night every time he pissed or took a step.

The old dame noticed his wince and immediately called for tea, shooing him into an armchair. She barely registered the banknote he handed to her, tucking it between a cushion and the side of the chaise longue.

"Yes, yes, very well. I take it this is why we haven't seen you about this past week?" She waved her cane in his direction. "What did you do to yourself?"

"I came off a horse, my lady. Deuced embarrassing." It was Charlotte's lie, and a good one at that.

"Oh, that is unfortunate. I hope you got right back on it. Can't drag that out or it becomes dreadfully difficult to try again. Sugar?"

John nodded, and she added a large spoonful before stirring and handing it to him.

"I'm sure I'll be riding again in no time," he said, accepting the cup.

"Good. That's good," she said, settling back in her seat. "After all, you can hardly host a hunt without getting on a horse."

"A hunt?" His teacup rattled in the saucer.

A flicker of confusion crossed her face. "In August. It is quite the tradition for your family to kick off the hunting season."

Damn. It had been a tradition, one John had chosen not to think about. His father had never allowed him to attend. The past viscount had been too embarrassed by his son's deficiencies to allow John's presence. Walter had always attended as the golden child. John shouldn't have been surprised that his brother had continued on with the tradition.

"I'd quite forgotten about it. I had not planned anything."

Lady Hornsworth smiled over the lip of her teacup. "Well, when you marry Lady Charlotte, I'm sure she'll take it in hand."

"Pardon?" Their engagement was not common knowledge. They'd still not even told her family. They'd planned to do so tomorrow night at dinner, once John had settled all his affairs.

Lady Hornsworth *tsk*ed. "There is no need to pretend

around me. It's quite clear what the two of you feel for each other. One just needs to see the way you look at her. Why haven't you announced it?"

His mouth opened and closed for a moment before he could respond. "We are just waiting for the right time."

"The right time is *now*, boy. Some of us despaired of ever seeing that girl in an appropriate position. She turned down many excellent matches, but while I rarely approve of such choosiness, it seems her dawdling has come up trumps. She'll have a title, wealth, and love. Just as a sweetheart like her should. Lucky girl."

It was he who was lucky. Charlotte had chosen him. "I hope I can make her happy."

"She's about to take her place as one of the *ton*'s greatest ladies. Let her host her own balls and preside over your hunts, and she'll never be happier."

It was with that conversation in mind that John spent the carriage ride back to the house whistling as he considered what would once have been unthinkable—the guest list for their engagement ball. Now that the estate accounts were flush, he could open Harrow House. Fully staffed, fully refurbished. If they got started tomorrow, then perhaps Charlotte could host events before the season ended. As long as there was somewhere quiet for him to go every few hours, it could work.

She was attending a soiree at Cossington's residence tonight. They were to meet there. He would ask her then if she wanted the Harrow Hunt to continue this year. They would be married by August, after all.

Climbing the stairs to his front door hurt more than walking down the drive. He winced with each footfall.

Mosely opened the door as he reached it, his face white.

"Never mind it," John said. "It simply needs ice and rest." He handed the butler his hat and shucked his coat.

"It's not that, my...oh lord." He made a face, looking for all the world as though he'd just swallowed rancid castor oil.

"What is it, man?" John leaned against the wall to give his leg some relief. "Just come out with it." They'd squared their debts with Brunel. Surely he hadn't the gall to approach John's home.

"I...Uh..." The butler shook his head, open-mouthed.

"Mosely."

"Your brother has returned."

# Chapter 26 ——————

Walter has returned?" John's stomach dropped, kicking off a ringing in his ears. Thank God for the support of the wall or he might have fallen.

"It seems his death was not as reported, my lord. I mean Mr. Barnesworth."

*Bloody hell. Fuck. Jesus Christ.* John had had his suspicions—the emptied bank accounts, the last-minute betrothal, the missing clothes in Walter's wardrobe. But he'd become so entangled with Charlotte and their quest to save the estates that his brother had slipped his mind.

"Where is he?"

"In your study. I mean his—I mean *the* study."

Damn. There was nothing for it. He would need to face his brother and find out what the fuck was going on.

The butler looked genuinely fearful. John couldn't blame him. Walter had driven the estates into the ground, failing to pay his staff or provide proper accommodations for them. It was only natural Mosely be concerned about what Walter's reappearance would mean.

John clapped a hand on his shoulder. "It's fine. It will be well. Though, I would appreciate your discretion. If you could speak with Mrs. Blackheath and Mrs. Scott and ask they keep this information to themselves, just until I can work out what the bloody hell is going on."

The butler nodded, and John strode down the corridor, ignoring the sharp pain in his leg. He pushed open the door to his—*the*—study. Walter had shoved John's papers and books from the table in front of the armchair and had his feet resting on top of the lacquered wood. He had a decanter of whiskey next to him, one that Fiona had given to John "so that you can stop drinking pig swill."

"This is a good drop," Walter said. "Better than I got anywhere on the continent."

"I thought you were d-d-dead." Fuck. He crossed to the chair opposite Walter but couldn't bring himself to sit.

"What have you done to my study?" Walter gestured to the devices that John had been working on that now lay scattered on the floor. "You've left silly little trinkets all over the place. It looks like a child's playground."

John worked his jaw, trying to loosen the muscles that had his entire mouth clenched. "I thought you were d-dead," he repeated, still waiting for a Goddamned explanation.

Walter waved his hand. "That was a misunderstanding."

"A misunderstanding? The corpse was dressed in your clothing. Wearing your ring." John tugged at the Harrow family ring until it slid off his finger and tossed it at his brother, who caught it and turned it over in his fingers a few times before putting it on. "Do you expect me to believe it was just a misunderstanding?"

His brother had played him. Whatever narrative Walter had concocted to explain the events would be just that— a story plausible enough that society would accept it and gripping enough to make them forget that when Walter had "died" he'd owed them money.

Walter shook his head as though it were a great shame, but the bastard couldn't hide his smirk. "It was a terrible accident. The last thing I remember is hitting my head as I fell overboard. When I woke up, it was on the shores of France."

"Right. And you stayed in France because?"

Walter shrugged. "I lost my memory. I did not know who I was until two days ago, when I slipped and hit my head again. I rushed home, obviously. I have responsibilities here that I must tend to."

John wanted to cast up his accounts. "Then you've returned to London to take my place as viscount?"

A nasty look flashed across Walter's usually charming face. "It was never actually *your* place, though, was it? Not if I was still alive. You were merely an interloper."

Frustration coursed through John. No, it hadn't been his place. He'd never wanted the position, but he'd turned his life upside down in order to do the job that was needed, and now his brother came swanning back home to take it all from him.

"You can have it," John spat. "Take the title and the responsibility and the d-d-d—" Nausea whirled through his belly.

The estates were no longer bankrupt. The sale of the firm had wiped out the debt completely. There was no money from the sale left—every penny had been poured into an estate that John no longer owned. He held a hand to his mouth to keep from vomiting.

Walter hadn't almost died. He'd left London because he'd had creditors breathing down his neck. If his brother reclaimed the title and everything that went with it, John would be penniless. *He* would be the one who couldn't pay a household's wages. Hell, he didn't have the money to put a roof over his head, let alone purchase a home grand enough for Charlotte to entertain her friends in.

Once Walter reclaimed his position, John would be left with nothing.

"How are you going to explain it?" John asked, hating how his voice came out so strangled. "Do you understand how ridiculous your story sounds? No unconscious person floats to France. Unconscious people drown."

Walter's expression turned mean. "They will be so glad to see me home, they'll believe every word. They adore me. I am the proper lord."

It turned John's stomach, but it was true. London would be in alt to have the favored son home.

"Please, give me some time," John begged. "I need to settle my affairs. There are things I must do, conversations I must have, before your return is revealed." He needed to talk to Charlotte, to warn her. To tell her that the life they'd planned together was no longer an option.

"Well, I am certain that if Lord Chester wishes not to be the subject of so much conversation, he should stop sneaking off with a different married woman at every gathering," Charlotte said, taking a sip of raffia and feeling truly happy for the first time in weeks. John's debts were settled; William was mending, cranky but blessedly sober; and tomorrow she and John would announce their engagement. Life was good. It was everything she'd dreamed of.

"Or at least he must be more circumspect about it," Henrietta added. "It's as though he doesn't even try to keep his affairs secret."

The girls watched as Lady Dunford exited the ballroom through the doors Lord Chester had used just moments before.

"I can't truly blame her," Josie said. "Could you imagine marriage to Lord Dunford?" She shuddered. Lord Dunford was nearly eighty and had a tendency to make what he thought were amusing double entendres that were, in reality, unamusing lewd comments.

Hen smiled. "There is one man to whom marriage might be rather pleasant, if only *someone* would snap him up." She inclined her head toward the ballroom entrance.

Charlotte followed her gaze. The sight of John framed by the doorway made her insides fuzzy. "Excuse me," she said to her friends, not waiting for a response. She could feel their amused stares on her as she left.

She wove her way through the crowd until she was standing before him. She itched to take his hand or to rise on her toes and kiss him. Tomorrow, they would tell Edward. After that, they could announce their engagement publicly.

Until then, she would have to be satisfied with a smile and a slight brush of the hand.

He didn't return her smile though, and on closer inspection, his face was pinched, his body tense.

"John, what is the matter? What has happened?"

"We must speak privately," John said. "Now." His tone set alarm bells ringing.

"Very well," she said, tucking her hand into the crook of his elbow. "Come outside."

She led him through the foyer and out the front door, waving off the butler as he offered to retrieve her coat. "Are you well?" she asked, turning to face him when they reached the front landing.

"Walter has returned."

"*What?* Your brother is dead. His body was recovered from the Thames." It had been the talk of London. There had even been a sketch of it in the papers, though she'd avoided looking at it.

John tugged at his hair, an anguished expression on his face. "He lied, Charlotte. He faked his death and disappeared just long enough for me to drag the estates out of trouble, and now he's returned. He probably had someone at the bank waiting to notify him the minute the accounts were replenished."

A horrified bubble of laughter escaped her and she slapped a hand to her mouth. This was absurd. It beggared belief. "But he drowned," she said. "You are the viscount."

John shuffled his feet, toying with the lone pebble that had somehow made it to the polished landing. "But I'm not, though. I never was." He kicked the pebble back to the drive.

Charlotte shook her head, pulling away from him. That dastardly fiend. "No. No, this is not right. He can't be allowed to get away with this." What could they do? There had to be something they could do.

"He can't get away with what? Taking his rightful place? Faking his death was a bastard act, but we'll never be able to prove that it was intentional. And he's not doing anything wrong by returning. He'll have to answer some awkward questions, but my brother is nothing if not charming. Whatever story he weaves, people will accept."

Charlotte paced the landing, mumbling to herself as she sifted through this new information, trying to understand the implications. Her fingers worried at the lace of her neckline. "What of the estate?"

"It belongs to him. It always has."

Drat. She spun to face him. "But, John, what of the *money*? The title is neither here nor there but the money, that was all yours. That was your life's work. He has no claim to it."

John swallowed hard, his throat bobbing. "The money is gone, Charlotte. The debts are all paid. What little was left is in a bank account that belongs to Walter. I have nothing. Not even a roof to put over our heads."

"I…" She couldn't form words. She didn't even know what to say. She *always* had something to say.

John ran his hand through his hair.

"Good God." She sank down onto the steps, pressing her fingers to her lips. John sat next to her, hip to hip, and dropped his head in his hands.

There had to be a way out of this. There had to be a fix. "My dowry," she blurted.

John laughed darkly. "Your brother didn't approve of our

union even when I had a title and the firm. He'll hardly approve of it now that I have nothing."

That was true. Ned had his own notions of what would make Charlotte happy, as ridiculous as those were. "We'll go back to the gaming rooms." Perhaps they could eke out a living that way, as much as she hated the idea. As much as it terrified her. But even if they managed to live that life without another beating, how long could she pretend to be Mrs. Brown without her ruse being discovered?

John turned to her, took her hands in his. "Come with me back to America. I still have my cottage there. It's not a London town house, but it's something. I can find a job in Boston. It won't be the life you're used to, but at least we will be together."

She blanched. Surely he didn't realize what he was asking? "Leave London? My family? My friends?" The very idea set her heart racing. Spending time in the country was one thing; it was only for a few weeks at a time and usually with one friend or another. Moving to America was something else entirely. To be separated from her loved ones by an entire ocean?

She would know no one. She'd *have* no one other than John, and while she loved him with her whole body, she'd be a fool to think that he could be everything for her. She loved him, but she needed other people in a way that he couldn't understand.

"I can't."

His grip on her hands tightened. "You can. I know it's not what we discussed and naturally you'd be apprehensive, but you could come with me." His expression was so earnest, so hopeful. He truly thought it was a good idea.

She pulled her hands away. "But I don't want to." It hurt her to say it, but she would be miserable alone.

His face twisted, as though she'd stuck a knife in him. His eyes shone with tears. "I can't stay in England, Charlotte. There is no life for me here. I gave that up. I *sold* it to save an estate that isn't even mine."

"I'm sorry," she whispered. "I'm so, so sorry. I love you, but I can't leave."

He swallowed, nodding along as though the truth of her words was wending its way through his mind. As though this moment was finding its place in the vault of his memories and cementing itself there.

"Very well." He stood and then offered his hand to her, helping her stand. She gripped his fingers as hard as she could. He was slipping away from her. What they had, this morning so tangible, now felt as amorphous as a foggy breath on a winter morning.

"John." Her voice cracked, and her throat closed up completely.

He twisted his hand out of her grip. "I love you, and I'll wait a week before I leave, just in case you change your mind."

She wouldn't change her mind, though. She couldn't bear the thought of the life he proposed. He seemed to sense that, because he stepped back and bowed coldly. Already something between them had broken.

Then she watched him walk down the drive and out of her life.

*Chapter 27* ———————————

John walked home. The fire in his lower back was a welcome relief to this pain in his chest, the cut of rejection he hadn't allowed himself to feel since he was a child. He'd spent decades building thick walls around his heart precisely to avoid this kind of situation, yet within weeks Charlotte had blasted holes right through it. Agony seeped in through that damage, twisting his insides until it hurt to breathe.

He tried to turn his mind to other things. He rummaged through the archives in his brain for something, anything, to distract himself from her. But his mind had been corrupted. Every image he reached for became Charlotte. Charlotte smiling. Charlotte laughing. Charlotte leaning over to whisper in a friend's ear. Charlotte naked beneath him. Charlotte studying her cards. Charlotte scratching Newton behind the ears.

All his life he'd been cursed to remember everything he saw—every page, every person, every street scene. But now there was nothing but her. The image that came to mind most often was of her lips as she said the words "I don't want to" over and over until they became the beat his feet marched to as he stalked home.

She was right, though. She did not belong in his house in the wilderness. She wasn't wrong to choose her life here in London. He was wrong for asking her to do otherwise, when clearly he would never be enough for her.

The weight of that awareness settled on him, making each movement sluggish as though he were walking through water.

He was grateful for the night, and he kept away from the flare of lamplights. She had been his light, one that had burned brighter than physics allowed for. Now there would be only darkness.

Logically, he knew that their relationship was over. He had nothing to offer her here in London and she did not belong in Boston. But something in his traitorous heart kept sparking.

Perhaps she would change her mind.

Perhaps she would choose him.

Perhaps she would come.

And so he would do as he said he would. He'd wait a week before he left England for good.

"You're home early," Edward said as Charlotte came through the front door. She didn't bother to hand her coat to

Simmons, instead she swept right past the butler and up the stairs that her brother and Fiona were descending.

"I don't want to talk to you." She dashed the back of her hand across her cheeks, the silk of her gloves absorbing the tears.

"Char, what is it?" Fiona asked, trying to grab Charlotte's hand as she pushed past them.

Charlotte tugged her hand out of the way. "It's nothing." After all, what was she going to tell them? She and John had never announced their engagement. They had been waiting until the perfect moment, until they could tell Edward with no care for what his response would be. If she admitted it to them now, all it would do was confirm her brother's belief that she and John were incredibly unsuited.

Edward would never use the words "I told you so," but they would still hang in the air, unsaid. Because Edward *had* known better. He'd warned her against John years ago. He had known that, when it came down to it, she and John were too different as people, they wanted too different things.

Any illusion she had otherwise was the stupidness of her heart.

"Char."

Charlotte stilled at the sternness in his tone. This was the voice he used when he would brook no dissent. The duke's voice that was so rarely directed toward her. "Tell me what the matter is. Is it William? Is it John? Did something happen at the gathering tonight?"

She whirled to face him. Duke or not, her business was not his. "I said I don't want to talk about it."

He cocked his head in confusion, his brows furrowed.

"You always want to talk. Even when you're furious with me. Especially when you're furious."

She threw her hands up. "Fine. You were right. John and I are entirely unsuited. Does that make you happy?"

The slump of his shoulders as he sighed suggested that no, he was not happy. "Char..."

She held up a hand. Whatever he was going to say, she didn't want to hear.

"Just leave me alone. I want to be alone."

*Chapter 28* ─────────

With a half dozen empty trunks at his feet, John surveyed the chaos in front of him. It might not seem like it to most people, but John's chaos always had a system. He could put his hands on anything within seconds.

In the day since Walter had returned, the chaos was exactly that. John's brother had cleared spaces by sweeping John's work into large, crushed, and tangled mounds.

Perhaps it was fitting. Walter had done the same thing to John's life—leaving it broken and abandoned.

With Newton sitting by the desk keeping a watchful eye, John began packing, starting with the journals and papers and half ideas that, had they been full ideas, might have saved him. He would ship all of it back to America. Perhaps after six weeks at sea, he might bear looking at it. For now, he just wanted it all out of his sight. It was simply a reminder of how completely he'd failed Charlotte.

"Leaving so soon?" Walter asked as he swaggered into the room. Newton immediately growled, and Walter walked in a wide arc around him. "You don't have to, you know. You're welcome to stay for another week."

Another week. How generous.

"I've booked a room at an inn," John said. "I have no role in this household, or in London, now that you're back. You are the viscount, remember? I am a nobody."

Walter took a seat, propping his feet on the table in front of him, and poured himself a glass of whiskey from the decanter Mosely had refilled and left by the chair.

"It's two in the afternoon," John said.

Walter raised his glass in salute. "There's never a wrong time to start."

Hackles rising, John gritted his teeth. Walter had learned nothing from the disaster he'd created. He was the same spoiled, selfish, irresponsible man he'd always been, a fact that did not bode well for those who relied on him.

"Maybe if you'd put less thought into what can deliver you a moment's pleasure and more thought into what the Lord Harrow should attend to, you would never have gotten into such a hole."

Walter frowned. "Do not think to reprimand me. You are merely a second son, and a poor excuse for one at that. Society barely knows who you are, or wants to, for that matter. It has no interest in you."

"Just as I have no interest in it," John replied, but the words were a lie. There were pockets of the *ton* that he'd become, dare he say it, fond of. Walter was right, of course. The moment word got out about his miraculous survival, John would be dropped like a hot brick. The only reason people had given him any consideration over the past weeks was because he was the new viscount.

"Well, I'm glad we're all agreed that my return is best for everyone."

John dropped the books he was holding into a trunk with a heavy thud. Walter's return had cost John the love of his life. He had to clench his fists to stop from strangling his brother.

"How did you do it?" Walter asked. "I thought for sure the only way out was Lady Luella's dowry."

So that had been his brother's plan—Walter had expected John to marry in order to save the estates. That was why he had returned now. He'd assumed that John had secured Luella's dowry.

"I sacrificed for the good of others," John snapped. A bigger sacrifice than Walter could ever imagine. "I suggest you try it."

Walter snorted. "No need for that. My man of business says the estates are repaired. Neither of us will have to marry that damn harpy."

Something inside John snapped. Their entire lives Walter had teased and bullied and tormented John, and John had accepted it, because he had thought he'd been a broken, stuttering outcast who'd perhaps deserved it.

But over the past few months, he'd realized that although he might not be as charming or well-liked as his brother, that he might not have Walter's looks or way with words or popularity, John was a good landlord and a good master. He'd taken care of his responsibilities.

He wasn't the defective thing his father had said he was. He wasn't inferior to his brother. He'd been a better lord than Walter ever had been. A better person. And he'd be damned if he allowed his brother to continue to treat Luella so unjustly.

He stalked across the room to where his brother sat, standing over him, forcing Walter to look up.

"You made promises to that 'damn harpy.' You convinced her it was a love match, and she grieved you when you *passed*. You will not throw her over now."

"Now see here." Walter tried to force John backward by standing but sat back down again when Newton growled. "You do not make demands of me. The girl sullied herself years ago. I saw the proof of it. I may have overlooked that when I needed her money, but I won't saddle myself with another man's leftovers if it's not needed."

John's hands clenched. Lady Luella certainly had her flaws. She was cruel and arrogant and John had done everything he could to avoid being joined with her. But knowing how poorly she'd been treated by men, was it any wonder that she was abrasive?

Walter had simply been the next in line to win and break her heart for sport. John didn't believe for a moment that Walter hadn't pressed her for the same affections for which he now damned her.

John loomed over his brother, jabbing a finger in Walter's direction. Behind them, Newton sensed his master's anger and growled. "You will marry Luella," John said. "Or you will experience what it is to be ostracized. Somehow you hid the extent of what you owed from all of society but if you do not honor your commitment to her, not only will I tell the entire world that the Viscount Harrow does not pay his debts, I will tell them how you faked your death in order to run from them."

Walter's face reddened. "You wouldn't. How would that serve you?" But there was an undercurrent of unease behind his bluster.

"Try me."

⌒

Charlotte couldn't bring herself to go down for breakfast. Nor could she go down for luncheon. She turned Grace away and remained in her nightclothes. When Henrietta and Josie showed up on the Wildeforde doorstep, she asked Simmons to tell them she wasn't at home.

They left a note that she didn't bother to read, and when Edward knocked on her door, she didn't bother to answer. Instead, she sat at her window, looking out over Harrow House, and desperately wished that John would come toward the glass door of his study so that she could see him.

He didn't. There was the occasional flash of a person, or a dog. Clearly, activity was happening within John's study. But at no point did he come to the threshold where she could see him.

And she desperately wanted to see him.

What had started as a childish tendre based on nothing but his floppy hair and graceful movements had developed into something stronger and all-consuming.

John was kind and intelligent and he loved her for who she was, not what she could do for him. He'd helped her see that it was all right to put herself first. He hadn't considered her selfish; he'd encouraged it.

He respected her as a person. He'd never forced his wishes on her. Not even at the end. Not even when he'd asked her to go with him to America.

She'd put herself first when she turned him down, and in response, he'd been kind. He'd respected her decision.

Goddamn, she wished he hadn't.

Shame flooded her. She hadn't even considered his proposal. She hadn't even tried. He'd suggested she leave her home and her friends for a life with him and she'd rejected the idea without thought.

If she truly loved him, wouldn't she at least have thought?

There was a blur of movement. The doors opened and Newton barreled out into the yard, John on his heels, tossing a ball in the air. As he caught it, he looked up.

She froze as his gaze locked with hers. Her chest tightened as he gave her a small, sad smile. Her heart shattered as he turned away, throwing the ball to a corner of the garden so that he wasn't facing her.

If she loved him, wouldn't she at least try?

A life with John in his tiny cottage in the wilderness would mean no servants, no house calls, no conversation with family or friends beyond letters and the six-week delay between them.

He said he'd wait a week before he left for America. She had six days left to work out if a life with him there was something she could survive.

～

Five days later, Charlotte was going out of her dratted mind. After the second day, Edward and Fiona had given up trying to convince her to come out of her room and had left her alone, just as she'd asked.

But a week of silence was taking its toll. She was now conversing regularly with her bed, her hairbrush, and her plant by the window, which, to be fair, was better conversation than many men of the *ton* could manage.

Charlotte couldn't read a book without providing extended verbal commentary to the thin air and she desperately, desperately needed to know what was going on in the world outside her bedroom.

"I know what you're thinking," she said to the ficus. "The newspaper is right on the other side of that door. But I shan't. London gossip will take months to reach me in Boston; I must learn to live without it."

Grace had been leaving the day's papers on a tray with breakfast. Each morning Charlotte's hand hovered over it, tempted to leave the toast and snatch *The Times*, but each morning she'd resisted, leaving her physically nourished but starved of enjoyment.

For the umpteenth time, she picked up a book, read the first paragraph, and then put it down. Books had distracted her somewhat in those first few days. She'd made her way through three full novels, but the novelty had worn off. Books were a poor substitute for people.

Her eyes tracked back outside to John's garden. She hadn't seen him again since that first day, nor had Newton been running about. Perhaps John had moved to different lodgings. After all, living with the old Lord Harrow would be awful.

Worry gnawed at her. What if John hadn't waited for her? What if he'd given up and left for America already?

She had refused him, after all. Perhaps he was done with her.

"He hasn't written," she said accusingly. The ficus didn't answer. "His were the only letters that Grace was told to let through and there have been none."

He would wait. Surely he would wait. "But what is he waiting *for*? I still cannot give him an answer." This self-imposed isolation was supposed to make it clear—either she loved him enough to forgo society, or she didn't.

Nothing was clear. It couldn't be muddier, in fact. The lack of society was driving her mad, but her love for him had not changed.

*Tap, tap, tap.* Charlotte's heart leapt at the prospect of an upcoming conversation, no matter how mundane it might be. Then she quenched that excitement. She did not need to be excited by conversation with her lady's maid. If she went to live with John in America, there would be no lady's maid and the entire purpose of this exercise was to prove to herself that she was capable of living such a life.

"Thank you, Grace, but I have no need of you at the moment." She was going to spend the day as she had every other day this week—in her nightclothes.

"It is not Grace." William's deep voice came from the other side of the door.

She rushed to it, pressing her palms against the wood as though she could feel his hands on hers. She missed human touch almost as much as she missed conversation.

"Will? Are you well?" The last time they'd spoken, he'd been suffering such intense headaches he'd sent her away as soon as she'd gone to see him.

The doorknob rattled, but she had locked it after bringing in her breakfast. "Charlie?" His voice was clear, steady, without the slur of drink or the fogginess of laudanum. It was as close to the sound of his old voice, his prebattle voice, as she'd heard.

She rested her head against the door. She wanted so badly to see him. They'd parted on such awful terms, and she hated it. She wanted to wrap him in her arms the way she'd done since they were children.

"I can't come out." The words almost died in her throat.

A pause. "Then, can I come in?"

She sighed. "No."

"Can we talk through the door?"

It pushed the boundaries of the rules she'd made for herself—more than pushed them. It almost entirely erased them—but starved of conversation, she couldn't say no. She slid down the door until her arse thwacked on the carpet. A second thump a moment later indicated that Will had done the same.

"Are you well?" she asked. "How is your leg?"

"Improving. Wilde gave Private James access to the household accounts, and the lad has purchased half a dozen different walking canes. I might need to keep the limp so as not to disappoint the boy."

He would do it too. Will might be completely irresponsible, but he was softhearted and gave to others even when he shouldn't. "And are you *well*, Will? Are you still having nightmares?"

There was a long pause before William answered. When he did, his voice sounded tight. "If I am, then there are fewer people to complain about it. There's no one else in the guest wing, and the walls have rather more insulation than the boardinghouse did."

It wasn't the answer she wanted. "Are you still drinking?"

There was a sharp rap on the door, wood against wood, one of his new canes, perhaps. "Would you believe not one person in this house will bring me a brandy? After all these years of being the servants' favorite Stirling brother." -

He might joke about it, but she knew in her heart that Will would not get any better until he stopped using alcohol to mask whatever caused him such pain. But she'd also finally realized that there was little she could actually do about it. She could not help him if he would not help himself. She certainly couldn't help him from America.

"What are you doing in there? Fi says you haven't left your room in a week."

She hesitated before answering. Truthfully, her entire plan sounded batty. Certainly, the longer it went on, the crazier she felt. "John has asked me to go with him to America. I'm trying to see what it would be like to not have people around all the time."

"And how's it working out for you?" From his tone of voice, she could tell that he knew the answer already.

She couldn't hold back a small sob. "It's miserable. *I'm* miserable. I'm trying my damnedest to make friends with the birds that sit on my windowsill, but they care nothing for me. I'm crying all the time. I don't think that I can do it. I don't think that I could leave you or Edward or Fi. I don't think that I can go live on the very edge of society and not in the middle of it. I don't think that I can marry him." She hugged her knees in close and sobbed. It had all seemed so perfect and then gone so horribly wrong.

"Charlie, please open the door."

Opening the door would make it final. Opening the door would be admitting that it was over in a way that saying the words didn't.

"You're sitting alone on the floor in tears. Is this not the proof you need that this will not work?"

# Chapter 29 ————————

"She isn't coming, Newton. I think we must resign ourselves to that fact." John stood on the pier and watched as the ship's crew loaded his trunks. They would set sail at first light, and the captain wanted to be ready tonight.

Newton looked up at him and whined.

"It's all right, boy." At least, that was what he was trying to tell himself. It was all right that Charlotte didn't want to marry him. A life together might have made sense when he was Viscount Harrow and he could work productively for something here in England and she could be the grand lady of the *ton* as she had always dreamed.

But there was nothing for him to work toward now. Not once he'd sold the firm and lost the title. He could ask Fiona and Asterly for a position. They'd hire him in an instant, but he couldn't bring himself to work as an employee at the place he'd built. Even if he could ignore his wounded pride, no working man's salary could fund an aristocratic lifestyle.

John slung the single bag not yet stowed away over his shoulder. "Come on, Newton. Let's go get something to eat."

The public house where he'd been staying had clean rooms and good food. As he entered, his stomach growled. He stopped first at the front desk. "Have there been any letters?" He'd given Mosely the address of where he was staying. If Charlotte had sent word, Mosely would see it forwarded.

"No, sir."

John tried not to let the disappointment show. "And have there been any visitors?" He hoped Charlotte wouldn't come down to the docks in person, but there was every chance she'd ignore the danger. She had prior form in that arena.

The clerk nodded. "Yes, sir. He is waiting for you in the dining rooms."

*He.* Not Charlotte, then. John nodded his thanks. He could take Newton back up to his room, but on the off chance Walter had come to say good-bye, he wanted his dog with him. Walter hated Newton and petty as it was, John wanted to watch his brother shrink back in the deerhound's presence.

It wasn't Walter, though. Wildeforde sat at a table in the corner, nursing a large beer glass. The duke rarely drank beer unless he was trying to blend in or make someone else comfortable.

John sighed. He'd been cowardly to think he could avoid this confrontation. He and Charlotte had ended their gambling scheme, but John had still broken Charlotte's heart. He deserved Wilde's wrath.

He took a seat opposite his friend and signaled to a passing serving girl for a drink and a bone from the kitchen for Newton.

"Were you truly going to leave without saying good-bye?" Wilde asked.

A kernel of guilt lodged beneath John's ribs. "I wasn't sure you'd want to see me. I assume Charlotte told you everything."

"About your engagement? Or about William's debt and the scheme you were running to pay it off? She told me about the former and my man discovered the latter."

John dropped his head into his hands. "I never meant for any of this to happen. It was an idea that started moving and just kept picking up speed. I could barely catch it, let alone stop it."

Edward chuckled, taking another swig. "That sounds like Charlotte. You might be one of the most brilliant physicists in the world, but she is still a bigger force than you can reckon with."

Wilde was right. She was the very definition of momentum. "Is she well?" he asked, apprehensive of the answer.

Edward shook his head. "Today was the first time she has left her room in almost a week. She looked like hell when she did. Her heart is broken." His hand tightened around his glass.

The news made John ill. He'd hoped that somehow it had only been his heart that had been crushed. "I love her. I know you thought we were too different and that we would never suit, but truthfully, she was everything I needed. She showed me I was wrong, that mankind is better than I assumed, that society was worth being a part of. When I get to Boston, I'll remember that."

Edward twisted his glass. "You're still determined to go to America?"

There was nothing left for him here. "I'll lease a house in the city, at least close to it, and I'll attempt to have more people in my life. To trust a few more people." He would not allow the time he spent with Charlotte to be wasted. He would be a man she could be proud of, even if she never knew it.

Wilde leaned forward, hands clasped, very duke-like, as though he were negotiating a bill in parliament. "Is there any way I can convince you not to go?"

The mere suggestion of his staying rattled John's determination. He didn't *want* to leave. He *had* to leave. "I can't stay. We can't be together, and I certainly cannot be in England without her."

Edward sighed and leaned back in his chair. He rubbed between his brows, looking years older than he was. "I was wrong," he said finally. "I thought she would be miserable. But Charlotte was happy while the two of you were spending time together. She used to flit from thing to thing, from person to person, and nothing was ever enough for her. She was always looking for more, something no single person could give. Whatever that something was, I think she found it in you."

John closed his eyes, wishing for all the world that Wilde would take those words back. "I don't want to hear that. I want to hear that I'm replaceable. That while she's sad now, someone else is going to come along and she's going to forget me. I want to hear that she's going to find happiness here in London with someone who can give her what I can't."

That was all he wanted—her happiness. The thought of her with someone else caused actual physical pain, but that pain was preferable to her misery.

Edward shook his head. "I don't see that happening. She's had four years out in society to find that person. I hardly believe I'm saying this, but I think she was waiting for you. And I don't think she'll ever *not* be waiting for you."

Nausea bubbled up his throat. He tugged loose the ribbon that tied his hair back. "I have nothing, not a cent to my name. I can get work, but does she truly want to be married to a man in trade? Where would we live? Where would she receive her friends?"

Edward sighed. "You can live with us. There's plenty of room. Nothing would have to change."

Wilde would suggest that. He didn't understand that Charlotte had grown as much as John had during their relationship. "No. It's time Charlotte stop hiding too. Being your hostess has been safe for her. She could focus her energies on you and William and fool herself into thinking she's living her own life. But she needs to move on."

Wilde grunted, obviously displeased with John's assessment.

"The problem is not just where we'd live," John added. "She needs someone who can provide for her better than I can." He hadn't meant to yell, but his frustration was boiling over. Nearby tables turned their heads and he lowered his voice. "Surely you want that for her?"

Wilde's fingers *tap, tap, tapp*ed on the table as he

considered John's words. Eventually, he stopped. "I don't think you've got the right of it. Charlotte needs her family and needs her friends and yes, I think she needs London society. But that doesn't equate to her needing riches. She's never been a girl to only wear a dress once. And while I'm not sure she could ever do without a cook, since none of us can boil water, she could do without a butler or a footman."

Wilde made it sound so simple, and it was infuriating, but it also gave him hope. "Would society accept her like that? Can you see the Duchess of Camden coming to a tiny two-bedroom apartment to pay a call?" Society might not be as cruel as John once thought, but it was certainly stratified and only a fool thought differently.

"Her dowry will absorb the worst of it. You won't have the riches she's used to, but you won't be paupers. You'll have a home. And you underestimate the strength of Charlotte's relationships. She is beloved. She won't be turned away from anywhere regardless of how small a life she lives. Society would rather see her happy than rich."

"You truly think so?" It seemed beyond comprehension to John. He could rely on a handful of people—literally six—to look beyond his flaws and accept him. To think that all of society could look past a lack of money and title, the two things they valued most, beggared belief.

But Wilde knew these people. He'd spent his life among them. If he thought Charlotte could be happy here in London in reduced circumstances, then perhaps there was a chance.

And if there was even the slightest chance that he could be happy with the love of his life, he would take it.

# Chapter 30 ⸻

Have you ever seen such a crush?" Miss Ashby said, leaning close to Charlotte to be heard over the orchestra and the gossip and the sound of shoes tapping on the chalked marble floor.

"This is always the most popular ball of the season," Charlotte explained. "Lord Ashworth stocks the gaming room with many foreign delicacies. It's one of the few nights that the men dictate where the fun is to be had."

Attending had seemed like a good idea that afternoon. Now that she'd fully resolved to remain in London, going to what was usually her favorite ball had seemed a surefire way to break out of her doldrums.

Instead, she was surrounded by two hundred of her closest friends and felt totally alone.

"We do so appreciate your finagling us an invitation," Miss Portsmith said.

"It's nothing," Charlotte replied. Helping the American girls had given her a reason to get out of her bedclothes. "I'm glad for the opportunity to help."

Miss Ashby stood on her toes to better review the crowd. "Is Lord Harrow coming tonight? That is, the previous Lord Harrow? Lord John Harrow? He's been missing for weeks now."

Charlotte tried for a smile, but suspected the result was more contorted than that. Every conversation she'd had that evening had found its way to John. It felt like death by a thousand paper cuts. "Mr. Barnesworth is returning to his commitments in Boston."

Both girls crumpled. "What a shame," Miss Ashby said. "He was so lovely."

*So lovely. Such a nice young man. So kind. A good lad.* Every person she'd spoken with had had nothing but praise for him.

"You must be sad to see him go. The two of you seemed so close." That was the other comment she'd heard over and over, always accompanied by a speculative stare or, as in this case, a pitiful one.

"I shall miss him, as all others do. Excuse me." She truly didn't need to be discussing John tonight. Not when her heart felt so raw. Not with his departure imminent. He would leave on the morning's tide, and it was unlikely he'd return. She had seen the last she was ever going to see of him.

She looked up at the ceiling and fanned herself to keep the tears from falling. Thank goodness it was such a crush. Anyone looking in her direction would simply think the heat had gotten to her.

"I need a minute," she muttered. She wove through the

crowd, trying her best to avoid her friends who were all dying to know where she'd been the past week.

The retiring room was almost empty. Only a pair of servants were in the corner, whispering. Charlotte stood in front of the mirror, trying to give life to her curls, which looked as flat as she felt.

She should be elated. This was her favorite place to be, her favorite thing to do. She should be buzzing with energy. Yet, all she wanted to do was go home and go to bed. She looked over at the grandfather clock. Midnight. She only had to fake it for a few more hours.

The door opened, and she shifted her gaze. *Luella.*

She couldn't deal with her rival right now. Charlotte had never felt so weak, so vulnerable. It would take the barest insult to bring her undone.

She brushed down her skirts and turned, hastening to the door. "Excuse me," she murmured to Luella as she passed.

Luella caught her arm, bringing her to a halt before she was even to the door. "A moment, Lady Charlotte."

Charlotte plastered on a brittle smile, conscious of how easy it would be to crack, and then faced the woman who loved to make her life difficult. "What can I do for you?"

Luella let go of Charlotte's arm, looked pointedly at the servants who were eyeing them with interest, and gestured to the window in the opposite corner.

Charlotte sighed. "Very well." Once they'd reached privacy, she crossed her arms and waited for an explanation.

"I hate that I have to go to you for this," Luella said.

"Good. What is it?"

Luella huffed and stared out the window as though she were reconsidering the entire conversation.

"What do you know of Lord Harrow's return? The *real* Lord Harrow, that is."

Of course this was what Luella wanted to talk of. Anything else would have been too easy. "He returned a week ago. It was unexpected."

Luella narrowed her eyes. "You know more than that, given your relationship with the false Lord Harrow. Tell me what you know."

Charlotte bristled at the nerve of this woman to make such demands and with such condescension. "I know it was interestingly timed. There had been financial issues with the estate. He was away just long enough for Mr. Barnesworth to resolve them without marrying you." She knew in her heart that it had been Walter's plan—to wait for John to marry Luella and save the estates, and then come back and enjoy the spoils. Wretched, wretched man.

Luella flinched at Charlotte's words. "So you don't believe his story that he was suffering from amnesia?" There was a thread of nervousness in her tone, something Charlotte had never heard in her rival before.

She sighed. "Like I said, it was interestingly timed. But you should be glad. After all, you will be the one who benefits from it. I hear congratulations are in order." She couldn't help the snarky, jealous sneer in her voice. Luella would be Lady Harrow. She would live in the house John saved, spending John's money, and all the trials and challenges Charlotte and John had faced would be meaningless.

Luella plastered on a smile that looked suspiciously false. "Yes. It is a love match, you know. He says that the first memory that returned was of me. That it was the thought of me that saved him and brought him back to England." Luella said it with her usual superciliousness, but, for the first time, Charlotte thought she heard something beneath the condescension—a nervousness. A vulnerability.

*The letters.* Luella had given her heart and her virginity to a man, and he'd not only betrayed her, he'd used it to blackmail her father. She'd had her heart broken, and her trust destroyed. She'd been made a laughingstock among men and she probably knew it. Now she loved Walter, and he was lying to her.

Luella was an awful, cruel, arrogant witch whom Charlotte couldn't stand—not for a minute—but now Charlotte felt something other than disdain. There was pity mixed in there.

"I don't like you," Charlotte blurted out.

Luella sneered. "I don't like you either."

That was fair. Preferable even. But it wasn't Charlotte's point. "As loath as I am to become involved in your affairs, I feel you should know that Lord Harrow is not an honorable man. He's an irresponsible wastrel who is not being honest with you. Even you can do better than that."

Luella's face twisted first with outrage, then with frustration, and then a look even Charlotte didn't have words for.

"How certain are you he's lying to me?"

"Very."

Luella turned back to the window, her hands gripping on to the frame. "Well then, won't our family holidays be interesting? The four of us under one roof, barely a shred of fondness between us."

Charlotte came to stand next to her. The outside garden had been lit with dozens of lamps.

"John and Walter aren't the type for family holidays, so we would never have been subject to that, thank goodness. But the point is moot. John is returning to America." As she said the words, her fingers pressed into the wood of the window frame as though the pressure could somehow keep the hurt at bay.

"He's returning without you?" Luella was the first person to say out loud what Charlotte knew everyone was thinking but too polite to say.

"Yes. He has a cabin outside of Boston."

"Surely you're not so foolish." Charlotte had been on the receiving end of many different looks from Luella, but none so contemptuous.

"What do you know of being a fool?"

Luella swallowed, her lips pursing. As she faced Charlotte, her hands fisted. "I know what it is to love someone, and if there were the slightest chance that love was *truly* returned, then there is nothing in the world that I wouldn't do to keep it." Her voice wavered as she spoke, and Charlotte wondered if she was thinking of Walter's betrayal or of Lord Berridge's.

"It isn't that simple. He wants me to leave England. I can't do that." She'd tried. She'd failed.

"Why not?"

Was Luella serious? "Leave my family? My friends? I would be so wretchedly lonely. I cannot bear the thought." She would have John, but she knew herself well enough to understand that he simply would not be enough for her, no matter how much she loved him.

Luella rolled her eyes. "You're an idiot. Everybody *loves* you. You make friends more easily than most men make fools of themselves. It's the thing I detest the most about you."

"Pardon?"

"Go to Boston and you'll have more friends in a night than most people make in a lifetime."

"I..." Luella made it sound so simple, but it couldn't be, could it? She'd spent all week trying to find an answer to this deplorable situation. The solution couldn't be as simple as just going.

"Only a coward gives up on love because they're afraid life may not be perfect." Luella's expression was full of contempt, and Charlotte hated the thought of being bested in this argument.

"Only a coward marries a man like Walter because she's worried she'll never find another." It was the truth. Luella needed to hear it.

Luella narrowed her eyes. "You are so bloody infuriating."

"Ditto."

"Ditto."

Before either girl could wrap her hands around the other's throat, Luella stalked back to the mirror, primped her perfect coiffure, and then left without a backward glance.

Charlotte watched her leave. A chasm opened up in front of her, bottomless and swirling with a fog of uncertainty.

She'd been so sure of her decision not to go to America with John. As much as it had broken her heart, she'd been certain. But Luella's words caused cracks in that certainty, and within those cracks, hope grew.

Perhaps her archnemesis was right, as loath as she was to admit it. Perhaps she had let her fear of being alone dictate her choices. Perhaps a life in Boston could work.

She wasn't sure of it, but if she was no longer sure that staying in England was the right choice, then she couldn't let John leave.

She turned to the attendants. "Fetch my coat."

~⌒~

The hackney cab from the docks to Mayfair had taken too damned long. No matter how many times John urged the driver to move faster, they still traveled at a leisurely trot rather than the full canter he wanted.

His first stop had been Wildeforde House on the off chance that Charlotte was home. She hadn't been, so he ran around the block to his old residence in case she'd left any messages that Mosely had forgotten to pass on. There were none.

With only a few hours before sunrise, before his boat to America set sail, he now had to hunt through London to find her.

John sifted through the pile of invitations that had accumulated on his brother's mantelpiece, shocked that he'd been sent any invitations at all. It seemed society hadn't thrown him over just yet. He grabbed every invitation for that night and would visit every one of these gatherings until he found her.

At Pomertin House, he thrust his invitation into the butler's hand and got four steps into the foyer before stopping. He turned back. "Did Lady Charlotte Stirling come through here tonight?" There was no point searching through the crowd if she wasn't there.

"No, sir."

John groaned. It would have been too easy for her to be at the first place he looked, but at least he hadn't wasted precious minutes searching the ballroom.

He sifted through the invitations. Lady Erstford's musicale was closest. He didn't bother with a hackney. By the time he hailed one and it navigated the traffic, he could have walked there. Instead, he ran.

Again, John handed his invitation to the butler and asked after Charlotte. Again, he turned and raced back down the drive, heading toward the next gathering, which was two doors down.

By the time John reached Ashworth House, three gatherings later, his heart was racing, his back ached, and he stood on the landing with his hands on his knees, struggling to draw breath.

"Have you"—heave—"seen"—heave—"Lady Charlotte?"

The butler nodded. "Yes, I have seen her ladyship this evening."

"Bloody brilliant." John slapped the rest of his invitations into the man's hands and then, ignoring the pain, he ran inside, through the foyer and down a brightly lit corridor until he stood upon the landing that led into the ballroom.

Blast, the ballroom was packed. Never in his life had John seen so many people in such tight quarters. The heat of all those bodies in a space with so little ventilation hit him like a wall. It carried with it the cloying scent of overdone perfume. The combination of that with his racing heartbeat and the tightening of his chest caused a wave of dizziness. He gripped the doorframe to steady himself.

A footman who had trailed after him handed his invitation to the underbutler. "Mr. Barnesworth," the man announced.

Those closest to the door turned in his direction with eyebrows raised. "It's the old viscount," one of them said, nudging her friend, who then whispered to the person next to her.

Of course, they were intrigued. This was the first time he had been seen in public since Walter's dramatic return. No doubt he'd be the prime subject of gossip in the morning papers.

He nodded politely to the people gawking and continued to scan the crowd, still trying to normalize his breathing. Still failing.

There were so many people, so many feathered headdresses. It was a kaleidoscope of faces and color. He couldn't make out Charlotte anywhere.

His vision blurred and he tightened his grip on the doorway. *Hell with it.*

"Charlotte," he called in as loud a voice as he could manage. "I've been a d-damn idiot. I should never have made you choose between me and London. I thought you needed more than p-plain old Mr. Barnesworth could give you. I thought you belonged with a proper lord. But I was a fool to even think of giving you up, and if you'll have me, if you'll marry me, I swear I will never make you choose again."

The room had gone quiet as his declaration traveled across it. The loud tone he could hear was not the orchestra but ringing in his ears.

The heat and smell of the room were almost overpowering.

Every time he inhaled, he only managed a half breath. "Charlotte?"

How long would it take her to cross the room? He looked out, but every person swayed or floated. She would come for him. She loved him. He was so sure of that. Their love for each other had never been the issue.

"Love—" She would be here in just a second. He held on to that thought as his knees buckled and it all went black.

*Chapter 31* ————————

It was the foul odor of smelling salts that brought John to consciousness. His eyes flew open, and he made the grave mistake of inhaling. *Blurgh.* He retched and retched again. When his eyes focused, it wasn't Charlotte who leaned over him, face filling his vision.

"Lady Luella? What's happening?" She was not the person he wanted to see right now. Charlotte. Where was Charlotte?

"You *swooned*, Mr. Barnesworth." The crowd around them tittered.

Damn. He remembered now. The room had been hot, and he'd been out of breath from running. The perfume had been cloying. Even now, as the scent of smelling salts dissipated, the sweetness of the air made him gag.

"Where is she?" he asked Luella, propping himself up

on his elbows. If Charlotte had been in the room, she would be there.

"Good God, you're both idiots," Luella replied. "Lady Charlotte left an hour ago."

He sat upright, the room spinning as he did so. "Where did she go?" Could he possibly track her down before his ship sailed?

"She went after you."

He sighed. Damn. Charlotte had gone to the docks.

~

"Well, brother, what do we do now?" Charlotte asked as they stood on the wharf and looked out at the many, many ships in port. They all looked exactly the same to her, except for the flags that flew, and searching each of them for John would take more time than they had.

"We ask questions." William rubbed his hands together. That was one thing the war hadn't changed about him—he loved to be involved in mischief, and Charlotte racing to the docks to declare her love was exactly that.

She'd toyed with the idea of coming alone, but she knew John would be upset if she did. It was late and dark, and she was unfamiliar with the area, so she'd snuck back into Wildeforde House and begged Will to join her. Seeing men stumble and sway as they walked the wooden boardwalk was enough to assure her she'd made the right decision.

"What was the name of the ship?"

"The *Lutetiana*."

"And it leaves at first light? Damn, Charlie. Could you not have come to your realization a few days ago?"

A few days ago, she'd been in self-imposed isolation, determined to fix the wrong problem. She'd been trying to see if she could change who she was rather than trying to make who she was fit new circumstances.

"I needed help to settle on the right decision. It came from the most unlikely of sources—you have no idea." It weighed on her that she now owed Luella a debt. Even the recovery of Luella's letters wouldn't satisfy it, especially given Luella did not know of Charlotte's involvement. At least in Boston, she wouldn't have to face her nemesis again to say thank you. She shuddered at the horror of that prospect.

A group of men were stumbling down the wharf, singing a sea shanty, something about a sunny linguist that made her ears go hot. She swallowed before approaching them, waving her hand nervously.

They stopped, except for the man at the rear, whose voice continued the tune until he walked into the back of another.

"Excuse me, sirs. Do you know where the *Lutetiana* is stationed?"

The leery expressions directed her way made her thankful for Will's presence. He was six feet and two inches of muscle at her back.

"It's not anywhere at this end," a grizzle-haired man said. "You might try further down."

"Thanks, friend." William put a hand on Charlotte's shoulder and steered her away. "I think you're daft," he said as he tucked her arm into his and they strolled down the wharf, sticking as close as possible to the lamplight. "What are you going to do in Boston?"

"I'm going to do what I do here, hopefully. There's bound to be some charities to work with—that will keep my days busy. John is going to have colleagues, so we'll have them over. It won't be to the scale of Edward's political dinners, but I can still be a hostess even if I've only one cook and no footman to help me."

Will leaned toward her, nudging her shoulder with his. "I'm going to miss you, Charlie. I don't know what I'm going to do without you."

Charlotte tightened her grip on his arm and swallowed hard. Leaving Will and Ned would be the most difficult thing she'd ever done. All of her life, she had loved her brothers above all else. She had put her brothers above all else. After all, they were all each other had.

Except now Ed had Fiona, and she had John. Everything had changed and Will... Well, he would find someone too. He just needed to forgive himself first for whatever it was that haunted him.

"You'll survive just fine without me," she said. "You survived a real-life battlefield. You can certainly live without a meddling little sister."

Will shook his head, chagrin crossing his face. "I shouldn't have said that. That was undeserved. You do not meddle."

Charlotte arched a brow.

"You do meddle, but with good intention."

"Thank you, brother. And do not fret. It won't take long for John and me to be settled and then you can come to stay as long as you like."

He dropped a kiss on the top of her head. Another group of men approached. Will disentangled his arm from hers and went to speak with them. One man pointed farther down the dock.

"It's that ship there," Will said when he rejoined her.

"Right." Charlotte strode in that direction, only slowing when she realized William couldn't keep up. It was once they'd reached the pier that they realized there was no gangplank leading onto the ship. Only a handful of lights shone through the windows belowdecks, and the deck itself was empty.

William leaned over to study the breadth of water between them and the boat, holding his hand to his nose.

"Tell me, Charlie, do you love him enough to swim through that?"

The lamplight caught on the slimy film that covered the water. She held back a sudden heave of her stomach. "If I must," she said weakly. "But I'd prefer to get their attention without taking a dip, if possible."

William squatted and picked up a pebble, hefting it in his hand a few times before tossing it to her.

"You're not suggesting I'm capable of hitting the boat with this?"

He grinned. "Surely, your love is powerful enough to give you the strength you need."

She scowled, but then turned toward the water to lob the stone anyway. It didn't make it even a third of the way across.

Will cocked his head. "Are you sure you love him?"

She had been praying for Will's improvement for weeks. She simply wished his teasing hadn't been the first part of his personality to return.

"You are a fiend. My love is very strong, thank you."

She reached down and examined the pebbles at her feet. Selecting one with a nice flat surface, she crouched, drew her arm back, and spun it across the river. It almost, *almost*, hit the ship.

True to form, Will saw her near success as a challenge and picked up his own stone and skimmed it. He hit the side of the boat, the stone making a quiet *tap*.

Charlotte's heart thrummed, and she stood on tiptoes to scan for any sign of movement. There was nothing. Will's efforts had gone unnoticed. She huffed, picked up another stone, and spun it. It reached farther this time; she saw a splash of water against the hull. She couldn't help giving her brother a smug look.

Will's next stone followed with a soft clunk of pebble against wood. Again, no one belowdecks noticed.

"Drat," she said. "Maybe it is time to swim." A rope ladder hung down the side of the ship. She eyed the river with apprehension.

"Or we wait here until the sunrise and we catch somebody's attention then. It's only a few hours away." He slid down the lamppost and brushed the dirt from the ground next to him as best he could so that Charlotte could sit.

She did, folding her skirts and leaning her head against his shoulder. "I am going to miss you, brother. I love you and Ned so, so much, but I can't spend the rest of my life being your sister first, and me second."

"I know." He entwined his fingers with hers and squeezed gently. Together they sat and watched the play of light on the lapping waves.

"Excuse me, miss. *Miss?*"

As Charlotte woke, the buzzing ballroom of her dream morphed into an unfamiliar hustle and bustle. Raising one hand to ward off the brightness, she cracked an eye open. There was a silhouette against the blue sky. A man's figure looking down on her. Next to her, a body shifted.

"Damn you, Private. It's too bloody early to be awake." William's blurred tone set everything rushing back to her: her race to find John. Their inability to make contact with his ship.

Putting a hand on Will's shoulder, she shook him awake. "Brother."

"Charlie?"

Leaving him to wake up and realize where he was on his own, she sat upright, adjusted her sleeves, smoothed her skirts, and tried to seem for all the world as though she were expecting to wake up on a London dock surrounded by strangers.

"My apologies, Mr...."

"Captain," he said sternly, reaching out a hand for her to grab hold of. "Captain Ainsley. Do you need one of my men to escort you to an inn where you can sleep off the aftereffects of your evening?"

A hot flush of embarrassment crawled over her. "No, thank you." Around them, the dock was alive with activity. Men were carting trunks and crates down the pier, looking at her rather than where they were going, curious expressions on their faces. Thank goodness the ship was still loading.

"My apologies, Captain. This must seem rather unexpected. But I need to speak with one of your passengers before you set sail."

"Well, you could have saved yourself an uncomfortable night's sleep. We don't leave for another day."

Relief washed over her, all her muscles loosening, but only for the briefest second. "John—Mr. Barnesworth—said that you were leaving at dawn on the twelfth. It is the twelfth, is it not?"

She looked over the captain's shoulder and her heart sank. There along the front of the bow was the ship's name: the *Sydney Jack*. It had been too dark to see the ship properly last night. She hadn't seen the words painted on it. Her gaze whipped to the river where several ships were already only a speck in the distance.

She grasped the captain's hands. "The *Lutetiana*. Where is it docked?"

The captain extricated his fingers from hers, looking at her as though she had three heads. "It was docked about a hundred yards downriver." The captain pointed to an empty pier. "But it departed an hour ago."

The blood drained from Charlotte's face as her heart sank. She stumbled backward. Only a steadying hand from the captain stopped her from tumbling off the pier and into the Thames.

She had come for John, and he didn't know it. He'd left for America thinking that she'd chosen London and her life here instead of the life they could have built together.

The captain's expression had shifted from patronizing to concerned. "Are you all right, miss? Can I have my men fetch you a glass of water?"

She shook her head, swallowing hard to hold back the tears. They could fall later, when she was alone.

Will took her elbow in his hand, a quiet reminder of his presence. She leaned against him, resisting the urge to turn into his chest and sob.

"It's all right, Charlie," he murmured. "He's not dead. He's just on a ship. You could write to him now and for all we know, your letter will arrive before he does."

She nodded, her throat tight and painful. John had left an address in Boston that she could write to. She knew where he was going.

*She knew where he was going.*

"I don't need to write," she said, her throat straining at the words. "I need to bathe." The stench of the Thames had seeped into her skin and her clothes overnight. "Then I need to pack my things. I'm going to America."

# Chapter 32

"Y er determined then?" Fi asked from where she sat cross-legged on Charlotte's bed, one knee resting on her husband's thigh. Edward was rubbing the spot between his eyes, as though the whole situation was giving him a migraine.

Charlotte faced them both, hands on hips, full of the Wildeforde determination that generally cleared the path before her but, when faced with another Wildeforde, only guaranteed a fight.

"I cannot be dissuaded," she said. "John and I may have challenges ahead of us, but I love him. He loves me. Together, we will make it work."

"I don't like it." Edward's tone was grim.

"I don't care, brother. I'm a grown woman who is perfectly capable of making her own decisions on the matter." She turned her attention to Grace, who had entered from the dressing room with an armful of clothing and was setting it down on the dressing table since William was currently slouched in the armchair.

Charlotte rifled through the dresses, selecting only the most practical. "I don't need any of the rest. John and I will live a much quieter life than I led here in London. I don't imagine I'll be attending a ball every evening."

Grace *tsk*ed. "You should take as many of these as we can fit in the trunks. You never know when you might need them."

Charlotte fingered the amethyst buttons on the sleeve of the dress she'd worn when she was "officially" presented to the king. It had been the matching shoe clips that she first gave away to pay William's rent. "You're correct. I can always sell them if John and I get short of money." The dresses she could remake into something more suitable for an engineer's wife. She'd become rather good at sewing and, lord knew, she'd have plenty of time on her hands.

Edward stood, running a hand through his hair, his lips pressed tight. "You will not get so short on money that you are moved to sell your clothing. I forbid it."

Charlotte rolled her eyes. "It seems like a difficult thing for you to forbid. But there is no need to worry. I have every faith that John's telegraph is going to work out. In two years' time, we may be richer than you all."

Fiona nodded. "That's possibly true. The telegraph is a brilliant idea. If he can make it work, and I'm sure he can, it will be installed in every home, eventually."

Charlotte smiled at her sister, glad to have her support. "See? All will be well. But until then, I will need to economize and Grace is right. I should bring everything I can with me." She picked up the pair of slippers that Grace had placed on the floor at her feet. "I'm sure this will fetch a pretty penny."

Edward shook his head. "No Wildeforde is going to resort to hawking their belongings in order to put food on the table. You have your dowry and I will continue your allowance until John is better positioned to support you properly."

There was part of her that wanted to reject his offer. She was ready to throw her lot in with John and whatever that entailed, even if it meant downsizing. But the more rational part of her prevailed. "Thank you, brother. It is much appreciated." She swallowed the lump that had formed in her throat. It was also as close to an acceptance of her plans as he'd given so far.

"But at least reconsider traveling to America by yourself," Edward continued. "Especially given John does not know you are coming. Surely, you could send word and wait for his response."

Ned was afraid. She could see it in the way his hand tapped at his side as he spoke and the lack of color in his face. He'd spent his entire life trying to ensure that his family was safe and well cared for. Even his decision to enlist Will into the army had been because he'd thought it would help his brother mature. She was about to fly in the face of all of that with her reckless actions.

"I know what John's response will be, brother. He begged me to come with him a week ago, but I was too much of a coward then. I am not a coward now and I will prove it by trusting his feelings for me. Besides, if I can find a ship that will sail today, then I might very well catch him at the first port. We can travel together and start our new life in Boston at the same time."

Edward rolled his shoulders. "Even if you catch him, you cannot travel unmarried."

"The ship's captain can marry us."

"And until then? Grace, are you certain that you cannot go with her?"

Grace looked at Charlotte with wide eyes. They'd had this conversation when Charlotte had first arrived home.

"No, Ned. Do not ask that of her again. She and Swinton have their own lives here." Grace's expression turned grateful. Charlotte stepped closer and clenched her friend's hand. "I have nothing but appreciation for the years you've spent as my dearest companion." Her voiced choked a little and both girls teared up.

Grace returned the squeeze before briskly leaving to collect more clothes. As she walked into the dressing room, Charlotte saw her swipe her eyes.

"Ye could hire a companion," Fi said. "I'm sure there are plenty of spinsters or widows who would enjoy the adventure."

Edward shook his head. "Who are ready to leave today? We can't possibly authenticate references in time, and I'm not putting her on a ship without somebody who has been thoroughly vetted." He turned to Charlotte. "Char, be reasonable. There is no harm in waiting until John has arrived and settled in and, at the very least, knows that you're arriving."

The frustration of the past week boiled over. "I don't want him to go a single day longer than necessary thinking that I didn't come for him. If I leave today, I may very well catch him by the end of the week." The sooner she and John were back together, the better for them both.

"I'll go with her." It was the first time William had spoken since Edward had entered Charlotte's bedroom. He refused to meet his brother's hard glare. He had apologized to Charlotte for their fight but he'd refused to speak with Edward.

There was nothing she could do about her brothers' relationship now.

"I'm not sure I'm ready to be back in England, anyway," Will continued. "Besides, I've four years of pestering my little sister to catch up on. Can't let her enter married life without a long reminder of what she is leaving behind."

"Will..." Edward rubbed between his eyes. Charlotte knew what he was thinking. William was a mess. It had only been weeks since his episode. True, he'd kept to his word and hadn't touched a drink since then, but neither she nor Edward had any illusions that their brother was healed.

Will seemed to sense it, because he stood and looked at Edward. He flinched under his brother's gaze, but he fisted his hands by his side and didn't turn away. "I have done many things that I'm not proud of and, frankly, you don't know the worst of them. But I have never, ever, let Charlotte come to harm, and I never would. I value her life and happiness more than my own."

"More than a drink?" Edward's tone carried with it all the disbelief she knew he felt. Charlotte went to William's side, taking his hand and standing by him, hip to hip.

"I will not consume a drop until I have seen her married. I swear it."

Charlotte looked to her eldest brother for his approval. She was going to go to Boston, regardless, but she'd much rather do it with his blessing and Will at her side.

Edward looked to her. "You are to send word at every port and write weekly once you arrive." His words were stern, but his voice was thick and there was a sheen to his eyes that wrenched Charlotte's heart.

She threw her arms around him and kissed him on his cheek, hoping he could not feel the wetness of her eyelashes against his skin.

He tightened the embrace, and her tears fell in earnest.

"I will write *daily*, and you must write me in return. I love you, brother. I shall miss you fiercely."

"I love you too, Char." His fingers dug hard into her shoulders, and she could feel the hitch to his breath.

"Ye're going to make us all cry." Fiona stood and rubbed her husband's back. "If this is yer last day with us, I must speak with Mrs. Phillips about luncheon. I'll see what wonder the kitchen can whip up in six hours."

Charlotte pulled away from Edward, wiping at her eyes. "I can do that. I'll go down in a moment."

"Nae." Fiona shook her head. "It's aboot time I managed this household. I appreciate these years that ye've taken on that burden, though. Ye've given me time to acclimate to my role, which I needed. But yer work is done. Ye need to spend the day saying good-bye to yer friends. There are so many people for ye to see."

Charlotte embraced her tightly. "You are the best of sisters," she murmured. "I can only leave because he has you."

Neither of them pulled away until there was an uncomfortable cough from the door. Charlotte looked over Fi's shoulder. Simmons stood in the doorway, cheeks flushing, clearly uncomfortable interrupting such a moment.

"Lady Hastings and Lady Pembroke are waiting in the drawing room for you, Lady Charlotte."

Charlotte brushed down her skirts and accepted the hand-kerchief that Grace held out. "Thank you, Simmons. I'll be down shortly."

 

"Where did you go last night?" Josie asked the moment Charlotte entered the room. "One moment you were talking with the American girls and the next you were gone."

Charlotte took a deep breath. It had been heartbreakingly difficult to tell her brothers that she was leaving, but at least the chaos of trunks and packing had distracted her—both from her own feelings and her brothers'.

There was nothing to distract her now. "We should sit," she said, gesturing to the chaise longue and wondering how she would break the news. Mrs. Phillips entered with a tea set. Charlotte busied herself with pouring, putting off the moment as long as she could.

"Did Lord Harrow find you? Lord John Harrow, not the other one," Henrietta asked.

The pot wobbled in her hand. "What do you mean 'Did Lord Harrow find me?' It was I who went looking for him. I was too late." She would not dwell on it. She'd set her course of action.

Her friends exchanged a glance. "Charlotte, Lord John—Mr. Barnesworth, whatever he's called now—came to the Ashworth ball last night in search of you. Did you not know?"

She put down the pot before she could spill boiled water all over herself. John had come looking for her?

Had he been planning to ask her to leave with him again?

Did he want to say one final good-bye?

"What did he say?" she asked once she'd found her voice again.

"It was quite the scene," Josie said. "He kept calling out your name and then he collapsed, right at the entrance to the ballroom, in full view of everyone."

Charlotte's heart thumped. "He collapsed? Was he all right? Is he alive?"

Hen shrugged and nodded. "He seemed fine afterward, a little woozy, but he stumbled out muttering something about you and the docks. Whatever was he talking about?"

John had gone to the docks looking for her. But if that was the case, why hadn't he found her? Had he gotten on his ship? Had he left for America, or had he stayed in England?

If he had stayed, where was he?

"He didn't find me," she said weakly, feeling light-headed.

Henrietta took over the tea service. "Well, did he get on the ship?" she asked as she poured a cup and passed it to Josie.

"I don't know," Charlotte replied.

"What did he want to say to you?"

"I don't know."

"What are you going to do?"

Charlotte threw her hands up in the air. "I don't *know*. William is booking me passage to Boston right now. We have most of the household packing up my things so that I can leave for America this evening."

Her friends looked stunned. That was perhaps not the best way to break the news of her departure to them, but she was too befuddled to think straight. "Where is John?" she asked, standing because she was too agitated to sit.

"We don't know," they said in unison.

Charlotte walked to the window, staring down the drive, trying to will John into appearing.

She heard the clink of a saucer being set down and then spoke. "It's possible after what happened to Lord Walter Harrow last night, John decided not to leave at all."

Charlotte turned to face them. "Wait. *What* happened to Lord Harrow last night?"

The grins that spread over their faces were borderline terrifying.

"It was amazing," Josie said.

"It was spectacular."

"I have never quite seen anything like it in my life."

Charlotte was about to lose her dratted mind. "*What happened to Lord Harrow last night?*"

"Luella." It was one word said in unison that dropped like a heavy tome.

"I know we hate her," Hen said. "I know she really is the most awful person, but the way she eviscerated Lord Harrow so ferociously was beautiful to watch. He can never show his face in society again. Did you know that he was in so much debt?"

A laugh escaped Charlotte. Her hand went to her stomach. Luella had done it.

Charlotte had told Luella of Walter's deception for no other reason than her grudging respect for her nemesis and her unwillingness to see any woman married to such a man.

That Luella had taken that information and wreaked revenge for both girls was an unexpected boon. Charlotte allowed herself a small smile. "I had no idea."

"No one did," Hen said. "He owed money to everyone, even the king."

"But that's not the worst of it," said Josie. "Apparently, he faked his own death to avoid having to repay it and he waited until Lord John Harrow, or whatever we're calling him, had settled all his debts before returning to England."

It sounded absolutely mad. If she hadn't lived through it, she would have been highly skeptical.

"But Luella had no proof of it," she murmured, more to herself than to her friends. After all, Charlotte hadn't given Luella proof.

Josie snorted. "It seems that while Lord Walter Harrow can lie to all of society without pause, he's unable to lie convincingly to the king. He—" Josie put a hand to her lips to repress the fit of giggles that had overcome her.

Henrietta picked up where her friend left off. "He wet his pants and when he tried to deny that he'd concocted such an elaborate falsehood, he spoke so fast his words barely made sense. Then the king asked him what officers of the crown would find if they were asked to investigate." She dropped her shaking head into her hand.

Josie, finally recovered, continued. "It was at that point Lord Harrow started crying."

Charlotte wished she'd seen it. She'd never enjoyed the suffering of others, but, for Walter, she would make an exception. He'd hurt John, and his actions had almost separated them. Almost. Now he'd gotten what he deserved.

"You're right," she said. "He'll never be able to show

his face in society again. He'll be forced to retire to the country." *Good riddance.*

Josie shook her head. "He may not be able to. It's said that the king demanded the prime minister be roused from his bed and that palace guards attend him at once. He was furious."

Charlotte wouldn't swap places with Walter for anything. She had a good relationship with her royal cousin—as close as one could have with a man so much older than she was—but she'd learned early on not to cross him. "What did John think of this?" He wouldn't be sad that Walter had received his comeuppance, but neither would he be pleased. He'd be wondering what Walter would do in response, what impact it would have on the estates.

Both of her friends shrugged. "John may not even know about it," Josie said. "He'd left to chase after you before Luella began her attack, and unless you were there, the first you'd hear about it would be during morning calls today."

So John might have gotten on the ship with no knowledge of the trouble his brother was in with the crown and thinking that Charlotte had chosen not to be with him.

Or, news might have spread faster than Josie expected. He might have heard of his brother's predicament and he might have heard that Charlotte was looking for him. But if that was the case, why hadn't he called on her? It was almost eleven.

*"Where the devil is John?"*

# Chapter 33 ──────────

John was sitting in a small, richly appointed chamber in the palace. Every now and then, his head would loll to the side as he succumbed to sleep, only for him to spring back awake as the smell of the docks, which had infused his clothing hit his nose.

He'd spent the night sitting on the pier out the front of the *Lutetiana*, his back against a tall wooden post crusted by salt and grime, waiting for Charlotte.

If she had truly gone to find him, that was where she would go. But she had never arrived.

By dawn, the smell of the Thames had seeped into the clothes he wore. The ship's captain had been impatient. He'd refused to delay their departure without recompense, even by five minutes. So all of John's clothing and possessions, except for what he currently wore, were on the ship heading to Boston.

That hadn't mattered. All that had mattered was getting to Charlotte, but as the hack trundled through Mayfair, John had made the stupid, stupid decision to stop by Walter's home and have his brother give him a fresh change of clothing. Surely Walter owed him that much, at least. If John was going to fall at Charlotte's feet, he'd prefer to do it smelling fresh.

The house had been abandoned. There was no sign of John's butler, housekeeper, or cook. Walter's dressing room had been in shambles, as though hastily rifled through and semi-packed.

The king's guards had shown up before John had had a moment to change. No matter how many times John insisted he was no longer the Viscount Harrow, the guards refused to listen. Apparently, they were to take any and all Viscounts Harrow to appear before the king. That had been hours ago, and while he'd been given food and tea, the attendants who waited on him refused to give him pen and paper.

"Please," he said again. "Let me send word to my betrothed. Let me tell her where I am." The last thing he wanted was Charlotte thinking that he had boarded the ship without her. He didn't want her believing for a moment that he had chosen his life in America over a life—any life—with her here.

After several more hours, John was escorted from his chamber to the throne room, where the king sat unamused, flanked by equally grim-faced attendants.

"Your Majesty," he said as he bowed, trying to keep the frustration from his tone. Whatever Walter had done now, it was once again impacting John.

"Mr. Barnesworth," the king said. "I can smell you from here."

John was a good twenty feet in front of the throne, but he was unsurprised. The attendants on either side of His Royal Majesty snickered, but John didn't have the energy to care. "My apologies, Your Majesty. My clothes are crossing the ocean as we speak."

The king looked across at one of the aides standing at the edge of the room. "Find Mr. Barnesworth some clothes that don't smell like arse."

John gave his thanks and then waited to find out what the king wanted of him, too tired and too keen to see Charlotte to truly care.

"Your brother is proving quite the issue. My officers say that he has once again disappeared from England to escape the consequences of his actions."

Damn. "I apologize for whatever my brother has done this time. He is...irresponsible."

"He is a liar and a fraud and he deliberately preyed on my good nature, with no intention of returning the money he owed me. Faking one's death for financial benefit is against the law."

"Oh, *that*." It served his brother right that his schemes had come undone so quickly.

"Were you aware of your brother's deception?" The king traced the beveled edge of the throne's arm with his fingertip as his gaze bored into John's. His tone might be calm, but the violence in his stare made John swallow.

"Not until his return, Your Majesty. I would not have taken p-part in such actions."

There was silence as the king's finger went around and

around the edge of the throne. John's eyes found his boots, and they remained there as the monarch weighed John's response.

There was a muted clap as the king smacked his hand on his thigh. "Very well. There will be consequences for your brother. I have already spoken with the prime minister. There will be a motion to strip Lord Harrow of his titles put forward in tomorrow's session. I do not enjoy being fleeced, Mr. Barnesworth, and I think you'll find the rest of the House of Lords agrees. They will be quick to pass such a motion, I think."

A breath of relief escaped John. The estates reverting to the crown would give the people who worked and lived on them a modicum more security than they had with Walter as their lord. "Your decision is wise, Your Majesty."

The king's eyes narrowed. "I do not need your approval, Mr. Barnesworth."

John nodded hurriedly. "Of course not. I spoke out of turn." Perhaps that would be all and the king would allow him to leave, finally. John waited to be dismissed, heart sinking as the king motioned to one of his pages, whispered in his ear, and then turned his attention back to John. It wasn't over then.

"Is it true that you sold off your business to pay your brother's debts?"

"It is." And despite how ghastly it had all turned out, if John was faced with the same situation, he would make the same choice. He'd sold the firm to extricate Charlotte from Brunel's clutches. Her safety would be worth it ten times over.

"I like you, Mr. Barnesworth. I have always liked

innovative people. I like the creative energy they bring to a room. I like their ideas. I am a great patron, you know." He sat back in the throne, his displeasure and judgment replaced with an air of curiosity.

"I am aware of Your Majesty's generosity." For what else could one say?

"I have made my decision. Your contributions to society have not gone unnoticed. Your new steam engines have been a boon to the country's economy and to the safety of its citizens. Your inventive spirit promises great things and your work has been a true service to me and my people."

"I... Thank you..."

The king sniffed. "I am bestowing upon you an earldom in reward for your service. I will transfer your brother's estates to your care and protection as soon as the legalities of stripping him of his titles are done. I trust this is agreeable?"

Agreeable? Only a month ago, becoming the Viscount Harrow had felt like the worst thing that could happen to him. A title had been the last thing he'd wanted. He'd railed at the thought of returning to England, resented the responsibilities, and been terrified of what they'd meant—a life in England, among the society he'd hated. Just a month ago, he'd have thanked the king but politely declined.

But as an earl with estates and his fortune returned, he could give Charlotte the life they had planned for. And truth be told, he didn't hate the idea of living among the *ton*. He knew he could be a good lord and he could make his way in society just fine. His heart didn't leap in breathless anticipation at the thought, but neither did it shy away.

"It would be a great honor, Your Majesty. One that I would

not take lightly." He would give his new role all the care it required. Tomorrow. Today, he was busy. "But if you'll excuse me, I really, truly need to go see my betrothed."

The king nodded, and a small smile played across his face. "Am I to assume you mean my cousin?"

"Yes, Your Majesty."

"Good. That pleases me. She has been unwed for far too long. Tell Lady Charlotte I expect to see her for dinner next Tuesday."

⁓

Charlotte stood with her hands on the iron railing, feeling the sharp cold sting of the metal through her kid gloves. The ship rocked ever so slightly beneath her fingers, and she tightened her grip. Lord, she hoped the nausea was just her nerves about leaving and not seasickness. Six weeks of this as they crossed the Atlantic would be unbearable.

"Any regrets, Charlie?" Will asked as they watched the captain finish his final inspection of the ship and signal to the boys waiting at the end of the gangplank, who picked up the ropes that held the walkway secure.

"No regrets," she said. There had been a moment of hesitation following her friends' news about Walter and his ruination, but as the day went on she felt more and more secure in her decision. After all, if John hadn't been on a ship to America that morning, he would have come to see her.

"Can I take this for you, miss?" A cabin boy gestured to the small satchel at her feet. All of her other possessions had been stowed.

"Thank you. I will be down shortly." As much as she needed a moment to sit and collect her thoughts, she didn't want to be belowdecks when the ship set sail. She wanted to witness the shore disappear into the distance. It was such a significant occasion, it would be anticlimactic to miss it.

With a rasp the wooden gangplank slid from the ship's deck and hit the pier with a loud clang. There was a rattle as the heavy chain of the anchor was raised. Charlotte could feel a change in the way the ship rocked the moment it was no longer securely fastened.

"There's no turning back now, sister."

She gave a small smile. "This is the right choice."

The captain blew a whistle and in unison the crew dipped their oars into the water. At the first stroke, the ship inched backward. At the second stroke, the ship drew away from the wharf. By the fifth, the ship had glided into a turn, positioned to sail down the Thames.

There was a sharp *snap* as one of the sails dropped open. Charlotte almost lost her balance when the ship lurched, and she had to grab Will to stop him from falling as his cane slipped out from under him. Once they'd steadied, she dropped to her haunches and picked it up. It was one of the ebony canes Private James had purchased. She wondered how the boy was doing in his new position as assistant groundsman.

As she stood, she had a direct view of the pier they'd just pulled away from, and the horse that was riding up it, and the rider who was swinging off, then running a hand through his hair.

"Oh my God."

"Is that Barnesworth?"

"Oh my God," she repeated.

William whistled, a low sound that ended with a nervous chuckle.

On the pier, John was untying the rope that held a small tugboat fast. A young lad approached, waving his arms. John reached into his pocket and shoved something in the boy's hands.

"Oh my God."

As the ship continued its journey down the river, the scene onshore got harder to see. John was climbing into the boat, then he had an oar in each hand. The boy gave a hard push, sending the small tug toward the ship.

"He's not going to make it."

Will was right. There was no way John could match the speed of the ship, no matter how hard he rowed.

Charlotte whirled around, casting her eyes across the deck until they rested on the ship's captain. She hiked her dress and ran toward him, only slipping a little.

"Captain," she called. "Captain."

He turned around, his displeasure rolling off of him. "I am somewhat busy, my lady."

"We must go back," she said.

If he'd been displeased initially, he was outraged now. "Absolutely not."

She had to make him understand. "I thought my betrothed had left for America, but he has not. He's back there." She pointed in John's direction. "We must go back."

The captain sighed. "My lady, we are already late. If we were to return now, we would miss the tide, and I cannot be delayed by an entire day because of one young lady's affairs of the heart." The condescension with which he spoke had echoes of Luella.

Will arrived then, and he put a hand on her shoulder in support. "We will give you twenty pounds to turn this ship around."

The captain scowled. "It is no easy feat to turn a ship around, particularly in the middle of a river. Now I ask you to please go belowdecks. We are working."

"Fifty pounds," Charlotte blurted.

The captain remained silent.

"Need I remind you who I am?" she snapped, squaring her shoulders, fists on her hips. At this, the men around them, who were watching avidly, exchanged expectant glances.

William raised his hands as though trying to ward off a physical altercation between her and the infuriating captain. "You do not need to turn around. Just pause a moment, while her betrothed catches up."

"Pause?"

"Lower the sail. Drop the anchor. Whatever you do to stop a ship from continuing its forward path. She'll give you a hundred pounds. Surely that's worth your time. You can buy the crew several casks of brandy at the next port to make up for their troubles."

The captain looked at his men, who were nodding to each other. "Fine. A hundred pounds and she"—he jabbed a finger in her face—"leaves the ship."

"Done," Will said before she could respond to the captain's rudeness. With a hand on her back, he guided her toward the railing.

"I cannot believe we're paying that man such a fortune,"

she muttered. "How hard could it possibly be to turn around?"

"Sister, this is not the time to quarrel."

Will was right. Now that the anchor had been dropped and the sail furled, the small tugboat was gaining ground. It took only a few minutes before it was close enough that she could see John's face. His cheeks were puffed, no doubt from the exertion of rowing, but his expression was shadowed with relief.

Beside her, one of the deckhands threw a rope ladder over the railing. "Are we to climb down *that*?" It shifted as the ship did, and looked suspiciously flimsy.

Will handed over the small satchel she'd brought on board. A deckhand must have fetched it for her. "No, *we* are not disembarking. Someone must chaperone your things to Boston and back."

"You're not coming with—" There was a hard *thunk* as something hit the side of the ship. She looked overboard to see John, shielding his eyes as he looked up at her. All of the yelling and the chaos melted away and she took a full breath for the first time that day. He'd come for her. She'd come for him. Whatever happened next, they could face together.

She turned back to William. "Will you be all right?" His leg had not fully healed, nor had his mind. He was sober, but could he stay that way surrounded by sailors?

"I'll be fine, Charlie. An adventure will be good for me."

She rummaged through her satchel until she found her reticule, stuffed with more cash than she'd ever carried at one time. "You're going to need this. Please don't spend it on booze."

He winked at her, and then took her bag and dropped it overboard into John's arms. He offered her his hand.

With a thudding heart, she took it. Her slippers weren't made for climbing rope ladders. The wind whipped her hair across her eyes. *Drat. Dash. Darn it. Don't let me die now. Not when I finally have all I want.*

She swung a leg over the side of the ship, gripping on to the railing with every ounce of strength she had. As she put her weight on the ladder, it swung to the side slightly and she yelped.

William's hand, which was fisted in the back of her dress, yanked upward. "It's all right. You've got this. Next foot."

Each rung gave a little as she stepped down. The rope was uncomfortable to hold. So focused was she on not slipping that it wasn't until John's hands were on her hips and he was guiding her into the wildly rocking boat that she remembered to breathe.

"John." She turned the moment her feet hit the wood and she threw her arms around him, burying her head in his neck. Above them, the crew whistled wildly and she could hear Will protesting.

John sank one hand into her hair; the other arm caught her around her waist and pulled her close. "Love," he murmured. "Oh, love." He loosened his grip on her and she stepped back, throwing her arms out as her shift in bearing threw the boat off-kilter.

He sat and helped her to a spot on the bench by his side.

She took his face into her hands and kissed him deeply, ignoring the catcalling from the ship. She reveled in the urgency of his lips against hers and the feel of his day-old whiskers beneath her fingers. "Where have you been?" she asked when she could finally bring herself to pull away.

"You will not believe my day," he said. He brushed aside a flopping lock of hair and caught her gaze in his. His green eyes, though pinched with exhaustion, were full of love and humor and acceptance. His lips, soft and full, were smiling at the sight of her. His hands, his long and slender fingers, settled on her thigh, drawing her close. They were exactly as they should be—together, with barely an inch between them, let alone an ocean.

"John," she whispered. "Last night, you should know that I—"

He put a finger to her lips. "Charlotte, wait. I need to apologize first. I should never have—"

"No," she interrupted, pulling back. "No, I must apologize first." She brushed down her skirts and tucked a loose curl behind her ear before launching into the speech she'd rehearsed. "John, I love you. I love you with every ounce of my being, but you know that already. Love was never our problem, was it?"

John's lips quirked. "No, love was never the issue."

She nodded, glad for the confirmation. "The issue was that I was terribly, terribly afraid. I have a happy and comfortable life here in England and there's nothing that has really challenged it. When I said no to you, I was acting out of cowardice. I had no confidence in my abilities to succeed elsewhere. I'm terrified of being alone and I let that fear force me to make a decision that I shouldn't have.

"Because I won't be alone, will I? I will have you by my side and, in that case, I know I can establish myself somewhere else. I know we could go to Boston together and I would find new people. I would make new friends, and you would be my family.

"So I changed my mind. Yes, John. Yes, I'll come with you to Boston." She paused and looked up. "Just not on this particular ship because I do not think the captain cares for me."

Now that the words were out of her, she could study his reaction. If anything, he looked disappointed, which was not at all the reception she was going for. She put a hand to his chest, felt the unsteady *thump...th-thump...thump* of his heartbeat. "John, what is the matter?" She thought he'd be thrilled. Instead, he looked devastated.

"I should never have made you choose," he said through a strangled throat. "It wasn't fair. And though to hear you say such words makes my heart leap, the reality is you don't need to come with me to Boston."

She furrowed her brow, confused. "You don't *want* me to come with you?"

He took her shoulders in both hands. "I want you with me always. But you don't need to come to Boston for that. We will have a life here in London."

Charlotte furrowed her brow. "But would you be happy? With all the people?"

He smiled and shrugged his shoulders, a resigned but not unhappy movement. "I don't mind all the people," he said. "Not when you're one of them." He tipped up her chin with his finger and captured her mouth with his.

It was a kiss to get lost in. A kiss that promised a future of more kissing, kissing everywhere. It promised quiet nights spent together and noisy ones spent with friends. It promised a happiness she didn't know was possible.

A horn blasted. She looked up to see the deckhands scurrying off. Only two people remained watching. The captain, whose foul mood seemed completely unaffected by her and John's joyful reunion, and Will, who winked before sauntering off.

John pushed an oar against the side of the ship and their little boat glided away from it. "Give me one," she said, holding her hand out.

"You do not have to row."

She shook her hand at him. "Just give it to me. You do not have to do all the work on your own. I'm sure we can keep in time with each other."

He handed it over and she settled herself, rolling her shoulders.

He leaned over and pressed a kiss to her lips, sending shivers through her. "You really will not believe my day."

# Chapter 34

*January 1828*

Charlotte?" John's voice echoed down the hallway and through the open bedroom door. Daphne, the kitchen maid at their Hampshire estate, shot Charlotte a panicked look.

"It's perfectly fine, Daphne. You're not doing anything wrong."

The maid obviously didn't agree, her hands squeezing creases into her apron. "Mr. Bellswap would have a fit if he discovered I was in your bedroom, my lady."

Charlotte sniffed. "Bellswap is a snob, and his lordship won't tattle on us." Their country butler had been overcome with joy when the estates passed from Walter's hands into John's. He'd quickly replaced the silver, restocked the wine cellar, and increased the number of staff, and now, almost three years later, the house was running in a manner he deemed proper for an earl and his countess. Except when said earl and countess were not entirely proper themselves.

John entered the bedroom and Daphne curtseyed, keeping her gaze trained on her shoes as she scurried out of the room.

"Good afternoon," John called after her. He was uncomfortable with the staff's deference but they continued to pay it to him, no doubt in fear of Bellswap's displeasure. With a sigh, he turned to his wife, then his gaze traveled to her desk. "Again, Charlotte?" He gestured toward the telegraph that Charlotte was sitting in front of, and to the lists that sat next to it, neatly written in their cook's prim hand.

"Lady Hornsworth did not answer, once again. She refuses to use it. So I asked Daphne to bring me the cook's grocery orders."

John ran a hand through his hair. They had proved his technology worked. They'd installed a telegraph at the Hornsworth estate as well as every store in the village, with the wires crisscrossing the county a full twenty feet above the ground.

The signals operated as they should. Charlotte could press a button on her end and a sound could be heard at the other. The challenge was that it took so long to convey a message. Charlotte had become a quick telegraphist—the fastest in the house—but speedy fingers did not entirely solve the problem.

Lady Hornsworth might have agreed to have it installed, but she'd yet to have a single conversation through it given it was "tiresome" and "unnecessarily lengthy" and "inferior to a house call."

To add salt to the wound, Charlotte suspected that the only reason the butcher and baker and greengrocer continued to accept orders through the telegraph was because none of them wanted to disappoint the enthusiastic Countess of Clayfield. Once she and John left for London, Daphne would no doubt recommence placing orders by written note.

"But I think there is a solution," Charlotte said.

John dropped a kiss on the top of her head and then crossed to the bed, where he started to unlace his boots. "You always think there's a solution. That is one of the reasons I love you. Let's hear it."

Charlotte shifted the chair around so that she faced him. "I've been exchanging letters with your friend Samuel Morse since he came to visit, and I do really think we've hit on something."

"That's excellent. How is he?" One by one, John's wide network of scientific peers across the globe had found their way to England, specifically to John and Charlotte's home, eager to accept the invitation to come and stay with the newly titled Earl and Countess of Clayfield.

It had become a truth universally acknowledged that Lady Clayfield's drawing room was the epicenter of scientific innovation. Invitations to her dinner parties had become London's most highly sought-after item.

While John's interactions with his houseguests were still focused on the work they were doing, Charlotte formed relationships with them based on their lives, drawing the network closer than it ever had been. Over time, Charlotte had developed the understanding of science that she'd feared she was incapable of. Not only could she understand the conversations at her soirees, she contributed a unique perspective to them.

"I told Mr. Morse that we needed a new alphabet, which sounded like a ridiculous notion when the thought first came to me, but he's taken the idea and simply run with it. It's really quite remarkable."

John raised his eyebrows as he unbuttoned his waistcoat and shucked it. "Morse has invented a new alphabet? As in, an entirely new language?"

As usual, Charlotte's attention wandered as her husband undressed. Thank goodness it took no effort at all to keep talking, despite the somewhat lurid direction her thoughts were traveling in. "It's not quite a new language," she said as John pulled his shirt over his head. "It's more like a code. I really do think it's exactly what you need in order to make the telegraph more palatable to impatient people."

"Show me," John said, coming to take a seat next to her. He smelled so good. His skin radiated warmth, and she found herself less interested in explaining this potential solution than she was in not talking at all.

With Morse's most recent letter next to her as a reference, she quickly tapped out a series of long and short tones.

"What did that say?"

She ducked her head and looked up at him through her eyelashes. "You look good without a shirt."

John raised an eyebrow. "I'm certain that when Morse imagined the news of his code spreading, he did not anticipate it being used for such flirtations."

Charlotte walked her fingers up his chest, until they reached the base of his neck, where they twirled in the curl of hair that was usually hidden by his cravat. "I'm certain that mankind has been flirting since language first developed. Perhaps facilitating love stories will be your telegraph's legacy."

He tucked an arm around her hips and yanked her against him, his fingers pressing into her thigh. He bent down and kissed her before pulling away just a fraction to say, "I'm fine with that. As long as their love stories turn out as well as ours did."

She raised a hand to his cheek, thumb brushing against his smooth, sharp cheekbone. "Perhaps with a little less loss of property." William had escorted her things back to England without issue; he'd been unable to locate John's belongings.

"I could hide away with you forever," John murmured, reaching for the buttons of her dress and flicking them open one at a time. As the fabric loosened, he turned his attention to her neck, his tongue trailing across her collarbone.

Charlotte shivered. At this moment, with John half naked and the bed right there, she had to agree. Hiding away was divine. She dropped her head back, her hands going behind her to keep from falling.

John tugged her fichu from her neckline, tossing it to the floor, and crossed her décolletage with lines of light, hot kisses. Her shivers intensified, internalized, until the core of her was rioting.

"Let's go to bed," she whispered.

"As you wish." John scooped her into his arms, and her hands twined around his neck. His emerald eyes sparked with intensity, and he bit his lip as he crossed the room—a quiet promise of all the things he was about to do with his teeth, his lips, his tongue.

An hour later—both fully sated, their muscles loose, their bodies sinking heavily into the mattress—John was tracing circles over her stomach. "I know we agreed to return to London next week, but I wonder if it's best we leave tomorrow instead. It would be nice to spend some time with the others before the demands of parliament start." He looked up from her stomach to gauge her reaction.

Charlotte couldn't help beaming. She had enjoyed her time in the country. The quiet had given her and John time together that was different from the time they spent together when in the city—deeper, more intimate. When they didn't have guests visiting, she'd used these months to return to hobbies that she'd enjoyed but had cast aside in her quest to be more useful. Her watercolors would never hang on the walls of the National Gallery but they brought her quiet joy.

That said, she was desperate to return to the hustle and bustle of city life. The season was almost upon them and she was more than ready to see her friends. She was going to be the busiest of bees this season. She had to be. Who knew what life would look like next season? It would certainly have changed.

She reached up and cupped his cheek in her hand. "I'm so glad you suggested it," she said. "Because I'm afraid we're going to have to cut our time in London short by at least a month." She tried to look disappointed—that's what he would expect—but she could feel the corners of her mouth tip up.

John's brow furrowed. "Why would we need to do that?"

Charlotte screwed up her nose. "Because by then, I will need to go into *confinement*." The word should leave a bitter taste in her mouth. She'd tried confinement just that once and it had been awful. But her joy overrode her distaste, and her delight as understanding dawned across John's face fizzed like sherbet across her tongue.

"Confinement? Charlotte, are you truly telling me…" His voice trailed off, as though the news had stunned him so completely that he'd lost his words.

"I'm telling you that I am with child, John. And you had better be with me every day that I'm sequestered away, because months without even houseguests is going to be unbearable."

John leaned down and kissed her, his palm now splayed reverently across her stomach.

"Every day," he promised. "Every moment of every day, I will be yours."

Want more of the
Rebels with a Cause series?

Don't miss Amelia and
Benedict's story in
How to Survive a Scandal.

Available Now.

# About the ——————
# Author

**Samara Parish** has been escaping into fictional worlds since she was a child. When she picked up her first historical romance book, she found a fantasy universe she never wanted to leave and the inspiration to write her own stories. She lives in Australia with her own hero and their many furbabies in a house with an obscenely large garden, despite historically being unable to keep a cactus alive.

You can follow her writing, gardening, and life adventures on social media. For a bonus epilogue that revisits all your favorite Rebels with a Cause characters, sign up for her newsletter at her website.

You can learn more at:
  SamaraParish.com
  Twitter @SamaraParish
  Facebook.com/SamaraParish
  Instagram @SamaraParish
  Pinterest @SamaraParish
  TikTok @SamaraParish

*Get swept off your feet by charming dukes,
sharp-witted ladies, and scandalous balls in
Forever's historical romances!*

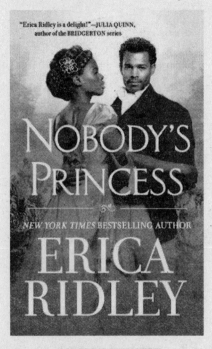

"Erica Ridley is a delight!" —JULIA QUINN,
author of the BRIDGERTON series

NOBODY'S
PRINCESS

NEW YORK TIMES BESTSELLING AUTHOR

ERICA
RIDLEY

**NOBODY'S PRINCESS**
**by Erica Ridley**

When Graham Wynchester deciphers coded messages in the scandal sheets,
he's convinced a royal is in need of rescue. But his quarry turns out to be
not a princess at all... The captivating Kunigunde de Heusch is on a mission
to become the first female royal guardswoman—*without* help from a man,
not even a devilishly handsome one. But will she have to choose between
achieving her dreams and following her heart?

*Follow @ReadForeverPub on Twitter and join the conversation using #ReadForever*

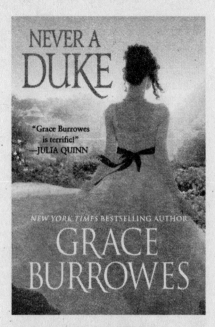

**NEVER A DUKE**
**by Grace Burrowes**

Polite society still whispers about Ned Wentworth's questionable past. Precisely because of Ned's connections in low places, Lady Rosalind Kinwood approaches him to help her find a lady's maid who has disappeared. As the investigation becomes more dangerous, Ned and Rosalind will have to risk everything—including their hearts—if they are to share the happily ever after that Mayfair's matchmakers have begrudged them both.

**Discover bonus content and more on read-forever.com**

Connect with us at
Facebook.com/ReadForeverPub

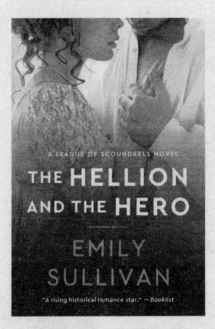

A LEAGUE OF SCOUNDRELS NOVEL

# THE HELLION AND THE HERO

## EMILY SULLIVAN

"A rising historical romance star." — *Booklist*

**THE HELLION AND THE HERO**
by Emily Sullivan

Lady Georgiana Arlington has always put family first—even marrying a man she didn't love to save her father. Now years after her husband's death, a mysterious enemy jeopardizes her livelihood. She must go to the one person she can trust: the man she left heartbroken years ago. Now a decorated naval hero, Captain Henry Harris could have his choice of women. But no other woman has Georgie's allure, nor her tenacity. Will he choose to assist her at the risk of his life and his heart?

## Find more great reads on Instagram with @ReadForeverPub

**DUKES DO IT BETTER**
**by Bethany Bennett**

Lady Emma Hardwick has been living a lie—one that allows her to keep her son and give him the loving home she'd never had. But now her journal, the one place in which she'd indulged the truth, has been stolen. Whoever possesses it holds the power to bring the life she's carefully built crumbling down. With her past threatening everything she holds dear, the only person she can trust is the dangerously handsome, tattooed navy captain with whom she dared to spend one carefree night.

**AN HEIRESS'S GUIDE TO DECEPTION AND DESIRE**
**by Manda Collins**

Miss Caroline Hardcastle's reputation once cost her a fiancé—but her notoriety now aids her work as a crime writer. When Caro's friend is kidnapped, she is shocked that the same man who broke her heart has become her ally. So how can she trust Lord Valentine Thorn? But when Caro's investigation forces them into a marriage of convenience, Val sees his opportunity to show her he's changed. Can he convince her to give their love a second chance—before death does them part?

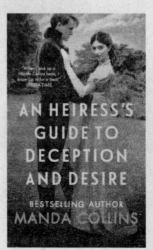